THE H

"What are you going to do?"

At first Mair did not answer, trying to stop her trembling, to quench the hot flood that swept her to damnation. She licked her lips, then touched his nose and cheek with the tip of her tongue. Mair moved next to the back of his neck, slipping her hands into his thick, curly hair. It was so springy and smooth, it reminded her of an animal's pelt. She tipped his cap, nudging it until it fell on the ground.

The light was fading rapidly and she could barely distinguish his features. His face was all black angles and planes. As he turned his head, his dark eyes glittered. With a sob of pleasure she sought the soft heat of his mouth, reveling in the taste, and the feel.

"What would you like me to do?" she whispered at last, her lips against his.

Other Leisure Books by Patricia Phillips:

THE ROSE AND THE FLAME

PATRICIA PHILLIPS

Nightingale

LEISURE BOOKS   NEW YORK CITY

A LEISURE BOOK ®

March 1991

Published by

Dorchester Publishing Co., Inc.
276 Fifth Avenue
New York, NY 10001

Printed in the United States of America.

PART ONE
WALES

Chapter One

Llandare lay below.

Mair Parry steeled herself, fighting a wave of
depression at the sight of those drab terraces and
gray slate rooves gleaming wetly after the rain.
Hundreds of identical dwellings all marching like
a troupe of soldiers to the gates of the mine. Even
from here Mair could hear the creak of the winch
as the day shift descended into the black depths of
Owen Pit Number One.

Along the narrow streets doors opened, dis-
charging shawled women into the early morning
gloom, their steel-tipped clogs ringing on the rain
darkened cobbles. Those would be the pit head
girls. Now a verse from a hymn drifted uphill as
some industrious housewife began the ritual
morning step whitening. A baby wailed. From the
distant grandeur of craggy Pentre Fawr echoed a
sheepdog's excited bark.

"Well, Mair, I'll be off," rasped Tomas the Milk.

His voice was an unexpected interruption. Mair turned to him with a smile of gratitude. "Thank you for the ride, Tomas. It'd have been a long walk."

The weatherbeaten farmer nodded and clicked to his pony. The trap lurched downhill with its load of milk churns, bound for Llandare's main street.

Mair stood, waving still, though Tomas's greasy cloth cap had long since disappeared in the misty morning gloom. She could have ridden with him into town, yet she preferred to walk. She needed time to prepare for Llandare, the place where she was born.

Her bags were heavy, but Mair was young and strong. Hefting the old valises containing all her worldly goods, and balancing the small potted rosebush she had brought with her from Tal-y-bont, she walked slowly along the flinty track.

The damp air was heavy with the acrid bite of coal smoke. Breathing deep, Mair reacquainted herself with that distinctive smell. No scent of roses and honeysuckle here—just coal, smoke and drains.

Those two heavenly years she had spent at Tal-y-bont had not outwardly changed her. Mair's thick yellow hair was still an unruly mop of waves and curls, her smooth fair skin unblemished. Care lines had temporarily etched themselves around her dark blue eyes and traced a pattern on her broad brow. Her figure had filled out, curving voluptuously above and below her slender waist. It was inside that she had changed the most. And that kind of change made coming home to Llandare harder than ever.

She had scraped her hair into an unbecoming bun, anchoring it firmly on top of her head, decorously hiding the gold mass beneath a felt-brimmed hat. It was a magnificent Prussian blue hat, trimmed with bedraggled birds' wings and two kinked partridge feathers. The hat was Mair's badge of defiance. Llandare women wore shawls over their heads; only folks from the big house wore feather-trimmed hats. That this specific piece of finery was one of Miss Jenkins's discards mattered not at all.

A lump came into her throat as she thought about Miss Jenkins. Frown lines formed on her smooth brow; her soft, rosy mouth drew tight as a spinster's. It still hurt to think about Miss Jenkins —and what might have been.

She increased her pace. The sharp flints underfoot bruised her feet, reminding her how thin were the soles of her black buttoned boots. If only Miss Jenkins had lived, how different life could have been. Tears prickled Mair's dark blue eyes and she shook them away, fiercely annoyed by her weakness. "No use dreaming about what might have been, girl," she reminded herself with blunt Llandare logic. "Best get used to what *is*."

She had been in service with Miss Grace Jenkins of Tal-y-bont. The lonely old woman had treated her more like a companion than a servant. Enchanted by Mair's beautiful voice, Miss Jenkins had arranged for her to take singing lessons. Along with much encouragement, her employer had given Mair ample time to practice her scales at the piano in the parlor, just as if she were family. Nice, was Miss Jenkins, the way gentry ought to be, Mair thought with a wistful smile. Then, when she

9

thought about those final days, Mair's smile faded. A stroke transformed Miss Jenkins into a helpless invalid. Mair had nursed her mistress, sang to her, read to her—oh, yes, she could read. Mam had always insisted on regular attendance at the free school.

Much good all the learning had done, Mair thought glumly, setting down her bags on the coal-flecked grass beside the track. The day after Miss Jenkins died, her relations had come clamoring for the spoils. Always too busy to bother with the old lady while she was alive, they had descended like carrion after her death.

"Your services will no longer be needed," Miss Emily had told Mair, all hoity-toity. "Pack your bags and go home."

Still in shock—for events had happened so fast—Mair did as she was told. Only at the last, when they refused to pay her what was owing, did she rebel. They told her she was lucky to be getting a reference, forward hussy that she was. Reminding her of the idle life she had led at Tal-y-bont—'money for jam' Mr. Edward had called it—they claimed she had spent her wage a dozen times over whilst aping her betters. "We can't afford to keep an idle girl. Now be gone before we call the constable."

Her protests had fallen on deaf ears. Mair found herself pushed out in the rain without even a mid-day meal. Told she would not be welcome at the funeral, she had defiantly decided to go anyway. But the driving rain, her lack of money, and the need of a place to lodge for the night soon changed her mind. She headed south, back to Llandare.

A local farmer had given her a ride as far as his sheep farm atop Pentre Fawr's bleak heights. Roundly cursing Miss Jenkins's money-grabbing relations for turning Mair out, he had insisted she spend the night with him and his wife. They were good people, the Morgans. Filled with despair over her bleak future, Mair had shed a few lonely tears in their attic bedroom while she listened to rain sluicing down the pane.

Mair picked up her bags. An annoying mist clouded her vision as she headed the last fifty yards into Llandare. She'd had a bit of vengeance on Miss Emily and Mr. Edward after all. The rose she carried had been named for Miss Jenkins. When in bloom the miniature bush was a mass of fragrant pink blossom. Stealing, she supposed they would call it. Still, they had so many roses, they'd never miss this one. It had always been special to Miss Jenkins, and Mair felt closer to her just by having it.

A small churchyard, the weathered gravestones dark with moisture, lay on her left. A plain gray stone chapel stood guardian over this blighted plot where wildflowers straggled and an old yew sheltered the graves with rain-jeweled branches.

Pushing open the gate, Mair started down the cinder path. Miss Jenkins's rose would look lovely on Mam's grave. It seemed fitting that the two should meet, even if it was only in the afterlife. They were the only two people she had ever really loved.

Mam's grave was in the new section. A cluster of fresh markers now kept her company, for winters were hard in the Welsh coal valleys. A straggling clump of Marguerites gone wild were the grave's sole decoration. Running her hand across the lettered headstone, Mair read:

"Mary Parry, beloved wife of Robert, mother of Evan, Ivor and Mair, gone to her eternal rest, November 15, 1883."

They had done Mam proud. This granite marker with scrollwork and lilies bordering the script had been chiseled by one of the Italian masons from Maen Gwyn. It was at Mair's insistence that they paid extra to give Mam something special. It had seemed only right. Poor Mam. Life had given her little beauty or dignity. Not even her fine English relatives could scorn this marker, that's if they ever came to pay their respects. So far they'd never set foot in Llandare, but Mair lived in hope.

She glanced about for something to dig with. She hadn't thought about needing a trowel. A broken rain-sodden branch lay against the wall; Mair used this to scrape a hollow in the soft earth as tears filled her eyes. Her grief watered the plot as she mounded earth about the rose. It looked so forlorn in this lonely place.

"Oh, Mam," she whispered beneath the dripping yew branches, "oh, Mam, I loved you so."

For a few minutes longer Mair sobbed quietly, then regained her composure and stood, brushing earth from her serviceable navy skirt. Come summer Mam's grave would be the prettiest in the whole cemetery. Silly, really, bawling like a child. All the tears in Wales wouldn't bring Mam back— nor Miss Jenkins, either. Nor her own dream of singing before audiences, of becoming famous instead of merely poor down-at-heel Mair Parry . . .

Impatiently wiping her eyes on her sleeve, Mair turned and picked up her bags. No use feeling sorry for herself, either. Life is for the living. Now she had to get out there and live it!

The stern reminder was just what Mair needed. Straightening her shoulders, she walked away from Mam's grave. The wind blew chill, sending showers from the yew branch onto her cherished hat. She closed the wet wooden gate with deliberate finality. The past was shut out. Only the future lay ahead.

Head down, Mair walked briskly away from the chapel, unaware that a man quickened his step to catch up with her. Though her intentions were brave, her mind was filled with doubts. Aunty Bet, who had kept house for the family since Mam's death, wouldn't be pleased to see her back home. She'd have to share her small bedroom and the running of the household. Her brothers, Evan and Ivor, would scorn her attempts at refinement and scoff at her newly acquired manners. And Da. Would he register the least bit of pleasure at having her home? Mair doubted it. Da was as unloving as a block of wood.

"Let me carry those bags. They're far too heavy for you."

The man's voice, coming disembodied out of the gloom, startled her. Mair turned to find him already reaching for her valises.

"No need, I'm all right. I've already carried them down the hill."

"All the more reason for taking a rest."

Mair's face softened in reply to his infectious grin. He was young, of medium height and build.

13

Thick dark hair curled from under his cloth cap. His high bridged nose was prominent in his smooth olive-skinned face. Slightly jutting cheekbones and a square determined jaw gave the lie to his soft dark eyes. Brown they were, all gentle like the doe Mair had seen in the woods at Tal-y-bont. Yet she doubted his eyes would stay soft for long, not in Llandare. Men here were hard living, hard drinking, made old before their time. Likely he was a stranger to the valley, for there was a foreignness to his speech and appearance.

"Thank you but I'm only going as far as Maes-y-Groes."

"That's halfway across town," he said with a grin, taking her bags from unresisting hands. "Are you visiting relatives?"

"No. Coming home, worst luck."

"Been gone long, Miss . . . er . . ."

"Two years, and it's Mair Parry."

"Mair Parry, that's right. I thought I knew you. The whole town knows about little Mair who went off to serve the gentry in the wilds of . . .?"

"Tal-y-bont," she provided with a giggle. "It is in the country, but it's not nearly as wild as it gets around here."

"You probably don't remember me. I've been away myself. Nico Castelli."

Now Mair understood why she had considered his appearance foreign. He came from the small Italian colony at the edge of town. Though his English had a Welsh accent, there was another unfamiliar inflection to his speech. "Oh, aye," she said, "from down Maen Gwyn way."

"That's right," he agreed in surprise, glancing

14

sideways at her pretty face partially hidden by the hat brim. Then he laughed at his own stupidity. "I shouldn't be surprised—my name gives me away. All the Italian families live at Maen Gwyn."

"Do you work down the pit?"

"Used to. Don't tell me you haven't heard about *me*. I'm famous hereabouts. A real rabble rouser. Been driven out of town, I have, told to get packing."

The bitterness in his voice made her sorry she had asked that question. Now that he mentioned it, Mair did recall that one of the Italian's sons had tried to organize a local miners' union at Owen Pit Number One. Aunty Bet had mentioned in her letter that Mr. Owen had given him the sack. And, using his considerable influence in the district, the mine owner had forced the offender to leave Llandare in search of work. Mr. Jasper Owen's word was law; no one dared employ the outcast.

"Yes, Aunty Bet did write to me about the mine union trouble. That was the most excitement in Llandare since the Prince of Wales got lost on his way to Cardiff."

"Or the big mine disaster," he reminded, his face hardening.

"Yes, or that," she agreed, made vaguely uncomfortable. She didn't look at him, but she guessed his eyes weren't soft now. Thirty men had been killed, including two of her uncles. Though it had been six years, the locals still spoke about it as if it were only yesterday.

"I hope to God I'm proved wrong, but the way I see it the next disaster's just round the corner. No safety practices to speak of. Worn out equipment.

Nothing spent to improve working conditions—all the money goes to line the pockets of Mr. Bloody Jasper Owen and his spotty-faced son."

The passion in his voice made Mair gasp. When she first heard about the labor trouble, she'd been surprised that the tough local miners had followed a foreigner. Though this younger generation had been born here, the native Welsh still regarded the Italians as foreigners. Mair wondered no longer. To a crowd of miners who already resented the injustice of their position, Nico Castelli's fiery rhetoric would be sheer dynamite.

He grinned ruefully. "Sorry. I was about to give you a real earful there."

"Don't be. Everything you say's true. Still, what can we do about it? The Owenses have been the masters here as long as I can remember."

"But that doesn't make it right."

Mair was startled to realize they were already entering Maes-y-Groes. They seemed to have gotten there so fast. Nico Castelli stopped and put down her bags. They stood beside the solid wall at the end of the terrace, temporarily out of sight of the neighbors. Here and there as they walked along the street, Mair had seen grimy lace curtains twitched aside. Let them look. Give them something new to gossip about.

"Are you home for good, Mair Parry?"

"Probably. Miss Jenkins passed away."

"Oh, I'm sorry. You can get very attached to someone in two years."

To her surprise, he laid a comforting hand on her shoulder. Tears pricked her eyes at his kindness. Such quick sympathy was unusual and most disarming.

"What will you do now?"

Swallowing, composing herself, Mair shrugged. "Try to find another post, I s'pose. And you . . . are you back for good too?"

"No, I'm just visiting my family. I work with my uncle in London. We hire dockhands to unload the ships."

"Are you trying to organize them too?"

"Well, funny you should ask."

They laughed. Unexpectedly he gripped her arm. He stood close, looking down at her. She could see by his expression he was forming a question. Strangely, Nico Castelli's nearness made her heart flutter; her knees felt shaky too. Of all the fool things, she admonished herself silently, clearing her throat. It was going to take far more than stern reminders to pull herself out of this self-pitying slump. Yet when he smiled at her as he pushed an errant strand of yellow hair back under her hat brim, the surge of heat that rocketed through her body bore no relation to self pity. Mair was in a quandary what to call it. Shocked, she realized she had wanted to feel Nico Castelli's hands on her face. She even imagined the pleasure of his arms around her. The thought brought a flush to her cheeks.

"Will you come for a walk with me later?" he asked softly, his fingers still grazing her brow. "Spring's late this year, but it's finally come on the mountain. The birds are singing and the trees are turning green. I often walk to the top farm for eggs and butter for my mother. Will you come with me?"

Quickly, before she could talk herself out of the foolishness, Mair agreed. "I'd love to. That's a favorite walk of mine, or used to be. Pentre Fawr's all that's left of the countryside. Up there it's like another world. Clean and fresh. You can forget all about the pit, the grime . . . everything."

She could tell by his expression that he knew what 'everything' meant.

"Shall I come for you about four?"

Come for her! Mair blanched as she pictured that event. "Oh, no, I'll meet you by the chapel, how's that? We'll be part way there already."

Without hesitation he agreed. Then, taking up her bags, he asked in which house in Maes-y-Groes she lived. "So many people round here have the same name, it's easy to get them mixed up."

"That's the reason we call each other Jones the Milk and Jones the Coal . . . it works quite well."

"So I've discovered, although in London they can't believe such measures work. There are people of every nationality there."

"Someday I'm going to London."

"You'll have to visit me. I'll show you around. The docks where my uncle works stretch for miles. Huge places they are. Now, you live at number . . .?"

"Er . . . ten, but there's no need to come any further. I'm grateful for your help."

"Oh, no, I'm a man for seeing things through."

Mair swallowed uncomfortably. Now what was she to do? He had no idea how staunch chapel-going Aunty Bet regarded the Italians. *'Heathen savages worshipping graven images, lighting candles to 'em, wicked it is.'* "No, really, you mustn't bother, Mr. Castelli. I've already imposed on you enough."

"Nonsense. It's only a few more steps. Number ten, you say?"

And he was off. There was nothing for it but to brazen things out. Lord, now she'd get a double earful for her homecoming, arriving with one of *them* in tow.

He banged loudly on the dark painted door of No. 10, Maes-y-Groes. Though they waited only a minute or so on the doorstep, Mair felt as if they stood there for ages. She was vastly uncomfortable, knowing the neighbors were taking it all in.

"Yes," said Aunty Bet hesitantly, opening the door a crack. She peered shortsightedly at the stranger with the bags, her round face a study of bewilderment.

Despite herself, Mair had to smile. "Don't you know your own niece?" cried she, stepping around Nico Castelli.

Aunty Bet was momentarily speechless. Then, finding her voice, she cried, "Well, now, Mair, why are you hiding by there, trying to frighten your old Aunty?" She was laughing as she pushed the door wide to admit them, though she still looked curiously at the strange man. "Who's this then? 'Ave you come on a visit like?"

"No, Aunty, I'm back for good." Mair plunged ahead, prepared for the shock on her aunt's face. "This is Mr. Castelli. He was kind enough to carry my bags."

"Oh, aye. Well, thank you kindly, Mr. Castelli," Aunty Bet said somewhat formally.

"Good day to you, Mrs. Parry . . . Miss Parry." Nico Castelli had taken off his cap; nodding politely to them, he made his farewells. Then he was gone, striding jauntily along Maes-y-Groes, breaking into a whistle before he reached the corner.

"Well, now, girl, come you inside."

Aunty Bet grabbed Mair's shoulder and yanked her over the threshold. "What might *he* be doing carrying your bags—one of them heathens—for shame, and you knowing how I feel about them."

"He carried my bags because no Welshman offered. It's as simple as that."

"I'll thank you to keep a civil tongue in your head, my girl."

Mair dragged her bags off the step into the small living room. The dingy room looked even smaller than she remembered. Smoke-blackened floral wallpaper and dark brown curtains merely deepened the murk. The sparse furnishings were nicked and well worn. Two rooms up, two down, the front room on both floors being the larger of the two. There was absolutely nothing about number ten to distinguish it from its neighbors. Clean, but dark, shabby, crowded—Mair's stomach lurched at the prospect of resuming life in Maes-y-Groes.

"Oh, now, would you just look at that hat!" exclaimed Aunty Bet, admiring the blue feathered hat, making Mair turn around so she could get a better look at it. "Tell me what you're doing here, if it's not a visit. You surely didn't get turned off by that Miss Jenkins. Did you disgrace yourself, girl? So help me, if that's the case—"

"Nothing like that," Mair interrupted loudly. "Miss Jenkins is dead. Her relatives didn't need a maid."

Aunty Bet gasped, her face crumpling in pity.

"Oh, that poor, dear old soul. And her like an angel to you. Oh, Mair, what a pity, what a pity."

Mair swallowed. "Aye, Aunty Bet, it's a pity all right. It gets worse, so you might as well hear the rest. There's no money, either."

"Money? Oh, you mean she didn't leave you nothing. Well now, girl, you couldn't expect it, not you coming from Llandare and not being gentry."

"No, I don't mean a legacy. I mean there's no wages."

"What?"

"Mr. Edward and Miss Emily said I'd already spent them in high living, that there wasn't no more coming to me. Even said I was lucky to get a reference, for all the good that's going to do me here."

Aunty Bet sat down suddenly on the windsor chair beside the sulking hearth. "Well, now—oh, wicked that is. Wicked! And you having it coming. You've earned it. Why, you've not had a penny since well before Christmas."

"It can't be helped. I was afraid they'd call the constable if I argued too much."

"Right you are. You can't force their hand, not with them being gentry."

The two women looked at each other bleakly, that final statement seeming to hang in the air.

"What's all this bloody talk about gentry? Where's my food? Who's that you're gossiping with, Bet, instead of feeding me?"

Mair moved toward the low doorway leading to the scullery. Robert Parry stood there, blinking in the gloom, trying to identify this strange woman in the feather trimmed hat.

"It's me, Da. Mair."

"Mair? It's never you, surely. Another visit so soon?"

"She's been turned off, Robert."

"For what bloody reason?"

"None of my fault, Da," Mair reassured quickly as her father shambled toward her. He was not beyond giving her the back of his hand for the slightest transgression.

"Poor old Miss Jenkins passed away. Her relatives didn't keep Mair on. They didn't pay her no wages neither, more's the pity."

Roaring in anger, Robert Parry smote the dining table in frustration. "They can't get away with that! Wages is wages."

"They already done it, Robert. Sit down and I'll get your meal."

Aunty Bet got to her feet, brushing back a strand of gray hair that had escaped from the bun at the back of her neck. Straightening her apron, she went inside the scullery where the kettle was boiling on the hob.

"Will you have tea with us, Mair, or are you too fancy for that now?"

Mair gritted her teeth. It had begun. "I'll have tea, Aunty Bet," she said, trying not to let her irritation show. "And a slice of bread and butter, if you have it."

"Oh, we got it, girl, not exactly poverty stricken yet," her father said, taking his seat beside the hearth. He stirred the embers with the poker. "So, now what you going to do?"

"Look for another place."

"You won't find nothing like Miss Jenkins hereabouts. You could get on at the pit, I s'pose. Several

22

girls was took bad last winter, couple of empty places now—"

"For shame, Robert!" Aunty Bet silenced him with a glare as she came inside the room carrying the teapot and cups on a battered tin tray. "Our Mair could always do the sensible thing. She's had her bit of adventure—now maybe she'll settle down with a good man and raise a family."

"Not with Davy Hughes, Aunty Bet. Please, I've just got here."

"It's never too soon. Davy'll be over the moon when he knows you're back. Maybe I'll just slip over there and—"

"No! I'm sure he'll find out soon enough," Mair said through gritted teeth.

"Oh, too good for Davy Hughes now, is it?" her father challenged belligerently. "You need a good hiding to put a bit of sense in you."

"Yes, and poor Davy smitten like he is, and those poor, motherless babies needing care. Oh a wicked crime, that's what it is, Mair Parry."

Mair was tempted to jump up and run outside to escape the bombardment. But where would she go? "Please, both of you, let me do things in my own time. I never fancied Davy Hughes before and I don't fancy him now," she explained, trying to keep an even tone.

Aunty Bet looked daggers at her. Da spat in the fire, muttering about ungrateful children.

"S'pose you fancy one of them heathen foreigners more, do you?" Aunty Bet asked in a challenging voice. "Came traipsing home with one, large as life. I nearly had a turn when I saw him, smarming about, carrying her bags like some fancy porter."

"Don't you bring no bloody foreigners to this

house, girl. One of them Italians from Maen Gwyn, was it?''

"That's right. Now what did he call himself?''

"Nico Castelli.''

"Castelli. Isn't that the one who was sacked when old man Owen had all that trouble?''

"That's right, Da. He's the one.''

Aunty Bet gasped, then her mouth tightened in disapproval.

"Well, now, you would pick the worst of the bunch. Never one to do things by half measure, are you Mair Parry?''

"Now, Bet, he's all right. Evan and Ivor said—''

Eyes flashing, Aunty Bet rounded on her brother.

"Never did I think to hear you take up for one of them heathens, Robert Parry. Evan and Ivor wouldn't know the devil if he came prancing down the street, so you can't bank on their say-so. Now, no more of it. I'll not have those heathens discussed in this house. As it is, I've got some explaining to do to the neighbors. S'pose you never thought how bad it'd look, did you, coming home of a morning with him, setting tongues wagging—''

"May I go upstairs and change?'' Mair interrupted. There was only so much of this she could endure.

"Be careful of my things. I wasn't expecting you. We'll have to get that old bedstead out of the shed, Robert. What with my bad back and such, I can't be expected to share a bed.''

"Bloody hell! That's going to be a lot of trouble, Bet. Are you sure we need it?''

24

"Positive."

When Bet's mouth formed that pursed button and she held herself rigid, there was no more to be said.

"Aye, aye, all right then. I'll get it later after the rain."

"It stopped raining hours ago, Da."

Mair couldn't resist imparting this bit of information as she took her bags and headed toward the stair. She didn't look back; she had no need. Da would be wearing that aggrieved look, annoyed because now he couldn't use the weather to excuse his laziness.

Up the stairs she went, her bags bumping and banging against the wall on the narrow staircase.

"Watch that wall, you'll have it scraped bare!" Aunty Bet shouted.

Mair put down the bags on the landing, fumbling for the door handle. This small back room, already crowded, could barely accommodate the iron bedstead. Anger, disappointment and loneliness combined to fill her with frustration. She could have cheerfully pitched the bags through the small grimy window and followed after, she thought angrily. Then the picture of her landing in the cobbled yard amidst the tin bath and the washtubs, or worse still, on the roof of the ramshackle privy, dissolved her anger in a halfhearted laugh.

Careful not to crease the quilt, Mair sat on the edge of Aunty Bet's bed. "Welcome home, Mair. Everything's just as cheerful as you remembered," she whispered to herself bitterly, wanting to cry. But tears didn't come. Just an empty, aching loneliness. What had she expected? A red carpet?

She was an unwelcome burden in this tiny house. Another mouth to feed, stretching the limited wage even further. Long past marriage age and with an eager bridegroom five doors down, she supposed she couldn't blame Da and Aunty Bet for their annoyance.

The prospect of daily reminders of Davy Hughes's worthiness were an added unpleasantness to bear. She had hoped in her absence he had found himself another bride. Though only thirty, Davy Hughes already looked like most of the older miners in Llandare. Hard drinking, hard fighting, hard swearing, a real 'man's man' as Da proudly put it. Before Da's accident he and Davy Hughes had worked on the same shift. Always leering at her, Davy Hughes had his eye on her long before his wife's death. Now that he needed someone to keep house for him, to mother his runny-nosed kids, he had redoubled his loathsome attentions.

Mair thumped the flock mattress in frustration. What was left for her there? Marriage to Davy Hughes or working at the pithead—both equally hideous prospects. With a sigh, Mair lay back on the bed, her body fitting comfortably into the sagging mattress. Now, if Davy Hughes had been like Nico Castelli, there'd be no hesitation on her part. Life with him would have been pleasure, not pain. Smiling softly, she repeated his name. It had a nice sound to it. To be Mrs. Castelli instead of Mrs. Hughes was much to her liking. But she knew she couldn't marry Nico Castelli, even if he'd asked her, him being Italian and Catholic and all. But it didn't hurt to dream.

Eyes closed, Mair pictured Nico coming to take

her out, assuming Da and Aunty Bet could have accepted him. That event couldn't be just a dream, it would be a miracle! How thrilling it would be to open the door to him, to have him smile at her in that special way and maybe tell her how beautiful she was. There'd be no revulsion over a kiss from him or maybe even more than a kiss. The idea of doing *that* with Davy Hughes had always made her gag. Though Mair was still afraid of that forbidden act, the prospect of having Nico Castelli make love to her was not unpleasant. In fact, her heart quickened as she imagined his kiss. His mouth was firm and strong, his lips smooth, devoid of several day's growth of beard. And he didn't smell. Though his clothes had not been posh, not like Miss Jenkins's friends' clothes, they were clean. The absence of jagged nails permanently etched in black made his hands look like those of a gentleman. That was something Mair had noticed as soon as he took her bags.

Mair sat up, pulling off her hat. "Bloody Prince Charming, isn't he?" That's what Da would say had he been able to monitor her thoughts. And with a grin, Mair decided Nico Castelli was probably as close to Prince Charming as she would ever get.

Chapter Two

Mair was afraid Nico Castelli would not come.

She hurried toward the chapel, already prepared for disappointment. When she saw him leaning against the gray stone wall, her heart lurched, then began a thundering beat. On his back was slung a canvas knapsack to carry home the products from the farm.

"Early, aren't you?" she said, swallowing her nervousness.

"I didn't want to miss you."

Unable to keep from glancing behind her, Mair satisfied herself that for the moment the street was empty. News of her arrival had already spread through Maes-y-Groes. To assume she could have walked through town unobserved would be foolish; that no one saw whom she met was all she could hope. Her friendship with Nico Castelli was too wonderful to have it spoiled before it began.

They walked in companionable silence until they left the cinder track. As if this were a cue, he started to tell her about London. Mair was content to listen to him describe the crowds, the traffic, the noise, enjoying the pleasant lilt of his voice, not too deep, nor yet too high. But then, she thought with a satisfied smile she was unable to contain, had she expected anything less of her special Prince Charming?

"You make it all sound so exciting. If I tell you something, promise you won't laugh."

"Can I smile a little?"

She dimpled. "Maybe just a little. A month ago I was preparing to take London by storm. I dreamed of becoming a famous singer . . . you aren't smiling."

"I haven't heard anything funny yet."

"Miss Jenkins actually had me believing I could do it. She had a lot of musical friends, you see. And they went into raptures about my voice. It really turned my head. She had a friend in London who trains singers for the opera. When I was ready she was going to ask him to accept me as a pupil. Oh, I had my wardrobe planned for when I became rich. I even thought about what I'd eat at those fancy restaurants. Fool—I should've known it couldn't happen to someone from Llandare."

"Every famous singer has to come from somewhere. Llandare's as good as anywhere."

Mair smiled at his observation. "I s'pose that's right, come to think of it. All my life I've loved to sing, only Da and Aunty Bet think singing's a waste of time. Serious singing is good for leading the hymn in chapel, but that's all. If I even suggested going on the stage, Aunty Bet would have a stroke.

She thinks everyone in the theater is bound for hellfire."

"My mother's cousin has an opera company of sorts—Cousin Guido. Personally I think he's a big bag of wind, but Mama thinks he's wonderful. He visits, tells us all his big tales, then disappears again. Maybe you can sing for him sometime."

"Oh, really? Oh, I'd like that! Does he really have an opera company?"

Nico laughed. "So he says. He moved from Modena to London to form this company, though in all the time I've been in London I've never heard a word about his precious company. I think he's a fraud, but don't tell Mama. She idolizes him. Nothing's too good for Cousin Guido."

"He would know if I can really sing, if there's any hope for me to sing professionally, wouldn't he?"

"Certainly, for all the good that would do. He usually visits his lowly relations about this time of year, so maybe you'll be lucky. If we hear he's coming I'll let you know. I take it Miss Jenkins is the only person who's ever encouraged you to sing."

"Encouraged—she did that, all right. She paid for my lessons with Mr. Crossley. He's a funny little man with a twirly mustache. He always made me laugh. He said he hadn't heard a voice like mine in all his years of teaching. He even said I sang as well as Madame Patti."

"Adelina Patti—that's high praise indeed." Nico grinned at her. "I suppose Miss Jenkins gave you that hat too."

Mair preened slightly, proud of her hat. This afternoon she'd left her hair loose, the hat setting firmly atop the luxuriant mass. The Prussian blue felt made her hair seem all the brighter in contrast.

"Like it? I've never owned a hat before."

"Very elegant. I much prefer it this way, with your hair down. You look like an angel. I've never seen hair as bright as yours before. It's magnificent."

That was almost as good as saying she was beautiful. Mair's mouth curved wider and wider. Oh, he was nice, so kind and understanding. She glanced sideways at him as they walked, finding his profile sterner than she'd expected. All Italians seemed to have that certain look about them, dark eyed, olive-skinned, black haired. Many of the Welsh were dark also, but in a different way; they lacked that same Mediterranean quality. Nico Castelli reminded her of the Renaissance men grouped in adoration about the Virgin and child in those old paintings at Tal-y-bont. Mysterious, noble, exciting.

"Your family don't approve of me, do they?"

Mair gasped, taken back by his blunt question.

"Well, no. Not really," she faltered.

"They don't know you're out walking with me?"

"No." Mair was nervous, wondering if this made any difference to him. For a bit he was silent, considering his position. Then to her relief she saw him smile.

"I like to know where I stand. That our friendship's supposed to be a secret, I mean. My family wouldn't be thrilled about it either."

Mair bristled at his statement. "What's wrong with me?" she demanded hotly.

"Nothing, little Mair, you're perfectly lovely.

You're just not a good convent-reared Italian girl. It's that simple. My family have the future mapped out for me."

She relaxed and the heat subsided in her cheeks. "Mine too. They expect me to marry Davy Hughes down the street. Who'd have thought he'd still not be married? He's been waiting for me, worse luck."

"Too set on a singing career, too ambitious to settle down yet. I like that. You see, I'm ambitious too."

Mair allowed him that assumption. No point in going into how much she disliked Davy Hughes. Her intention was merely to please Nico Castelli, which she had unwittingly done.

"And what are your ambitions?"

"Oh, about as far flung as yours. Someday I'm going to make a difference for ordinary working men. I'm going to speak out in a way that makes people listen and understand their grievances. I intend to get the workers a share of this country's wealth, to try to lift them out of this grinding poverty. There's no justice for men like your father and brothers. I'm going to give them a voice to speak out against little tin gods like the Jasper Owenses of this world."

"That's a big ambition. How do you intend to do that?"

"Oh, I've already started—without much success in these parts, I must admit. But some men find what I have to say to their liking."

"In London?"

"There—and other places."

He seemed intentionally vague. Maybe he did

32

not want to reveal his plans. "You remind me of one of those itinerant preachers at the chapel. All fire and righteous indignation."

"Preaching's not what I've got in mind. Political position would have the most influence among the ruling class. Maybe someday I'll sit in Parliament."

Mair gasped at the suggestion. "You *are* ambitious."

"When we both reach the pinnacle of success, perhaps we'll remember today," he said softly, pausing at the brow of the first incline.

Behind them the land rolled downhill to the ugly smoke-blackened sprawl of Llandare and its neighboring towns and villages. Miles of coal mines merged with ironworks climbing toward Brecon Beacons, swallowing all that had been green and pleasant. In a dozen towns just like Llandare, men and women toiled away their lives like ants in a hill. Perpetually smoking chimneys formed a shroud above the close packed streets, shutting out sun and air. Up there on the mountain the land was green and the air fresh with the scent of healthy vegetation.

"If ever I do achieve my ambition, I'll never come back to Llandare," vowed Mair, her face hardening at the unlovely sight below.

"That's something I vowed when Jasper Owen threw his weight around—but I'm back. Never say never, little Mair."

They were standing very close, and the warmth of his body engulfed her as the mountain wind buffeted her skirts. Hand on her hat, she smiled up at him. "I'll always remember today for such a lot of reasons," she confided shyly. "Mostly because you're the first real friend I've ever had. I don't tell my dreams to everyone."

"Nor I."

He smiled down at her. The weight of his arm rested about her shoulders, setting her heart racing. For that heavenly moment he squeezed her in a friendly hug. His eyes weren't meltingly soft now. The impenetrable blackness beneath the brim of his cap gave Mair the shivers. Not in fear, though goosebumps were her usual reaction to that emotion. She wanted to stop life right now, to stay up here on Pentre Fawr forever with his arm around her.

"Come on, we'd best be getting to the farm. I want you back before dusk. I heard a cuckoo in the woods yesterday. That's proof spring has come. In Llandare they've forgotten that spring ever was. Up here it's different."

Along the road to Bedallt Farm the blackthorn was starred with white blossoms. In these tangled hedgerows birds twittered about their nest-building, scattering in alarm as they passed. Dandelions formed gold medallions amidst the roadside grasses. Overnight the birches and mountain ash had sprung to fresh green life.

Mair filled her lungs with the pure clean air, and if she hadn't checked herself, she would have burst into song.

"Oh, my, I almost started to sing," she disclosed in surprise.

"Wonderful. Sing all you want."

"Someday. Not yet," she whispered, suddenly turned bashful. Maybe he wouldn't think she sang as well as she thought. She couldn't bear for him to think less of her.

Later, when she entered No. 10, Maes-y-Groes, Mair had to force herself to act normal. Her smile would not be quelled, bursting forth till her face was so sunny that Aunty Bet blinked in surprise when she came inside the scullery.

"Well, girl, where've you been? Mrs. Evans said she saw you heading toward chapel several hours ago."

"I went for a walk up Pentre Fawr, like I used to," she explained, hoping Mrs. Evans knew no more than she had already revealed. "Mam's headstone looks nicer than any of the others," she added, pulling off her hat and reaching for one of the coarse ticking aprons hanging behind the scullery door.

"You been to the graveyard then. Doesn't do to grieve too long, *Cariad*," said Aunty Bet kindly. "I know you and your Mam were very close, but she's been gone four years. It's long enough to mourn."

Mair smiled, touched by Aunty Bet's unexpected concern.

"I've been gone a long time myself. Haven't been to see her lately. I brought a rosebush for her grave from Tal-y-bont. Mam would've liked that."

"You're a thoughtful girl, Mair. Always loved flowers did Mary. Thought Wales a poor place after England. She missed all those lovely flower gardens. Still, discontent's a miserable companion on life's road. That's something you'd do good to remember. Them as is satisfied with their lot are happiest of all."

Mair did not comment. She began to peel the potatoes Aunty Bet had left soaking in a tin bowl. This understanding mood was too good to be true.

If she knew Aunty Bet in a few minutes the conversation would turn to Davy Hughes.

"You done any asking about work?"

"Mrs. Evans didn't need anyone. Roberts the Grocers said when Nerys is closer to her time, they can use me for a few weeks."

"Well, you don't sound too happy about it. And when's that going to be?"

"End of June."

"Two months! What we going to do for money in the meantime?"

"I'll promise not to eat much."

Aunty Bet glanced sharply at her but said nothing. The sound of clattering pans and a vicious stoking of the fire bespoke her annoyance. Finally, unable to stay off the subject any longer, she said, "S'pose you didn't go down to Davy's?"

"No. He knows I'm here. It'd look like I was eager if I went to his house."

"Well, you should be eager. A fine man who's waited patiently for you to get all the foolishness out of your system . . . the only man who's spoken for you. That Miss Jenkins, bless her soul, didn't help none letting you think you could earn a living from singing. Utter nonsense—surely you're not still dreaming about that!"

Mair encountered Aunty Bet's sharp eyes behind the steel rimmed spectacles. Her silence spoke reams.

"Well, you'd best stop, right now, Mair Parry. You're young and strong, capable of bringing in a wage—or of making some man a good wife. Those are the only two choices you have in Llandare."

Later, after the meal was eaten, after Mair had

endured her brothers' teasing about her fancy manners and the menfolk had departed for the Miner's Arms, she was blissfully alone with her thoughts.

Mair washed the crazed white dishes, swirling the suds in the tin bowl while she relived this afternoon. Innocent it had been really, no more'n children would have done. But because of that walk up the mountain, she felt inescapably bound to Nico Castelli. Well, why not, she thought indignantly. He was her friend, the only person with whom she could discuss her dreams without fear of ridicule. Guilt at her dishonesty brought a flush to her face. She must admit it wasn't merely as a friend she pictured him. The quick embrace of friendship was not all she wanted. Mair dwelled on the idea of Nico Castelli as her lover, bound together for all eternity. Just the way the hero had always been in the lovely novels in Miss Jenkins's library.

Mair glanced down at her hands, the knuckles reddened by the hot wash water. She was no pale, fainting heroine pining away for the sight of her lover. She was made of far sterner stuff, quick-tempered, independent, determined. Yet her heart was every bit as vulnerable as the most fragile heroine's.

Glancing through the uncurtained window over the sink she saw the lighted scullerys of the row of houses backing onto Maes-y-Groes. The sight was a fresh reminder of reality. Whatever life held for her, it did not include romantic love. In these mean streets there was little room for fairytales.

Here she was, home less than twenty-four hours

and already she had become involved in a hopeless relationship. But Mair did not care. Just the memory of his voice brought a smile to her mouth and made her heart flutter. Could it be possible that she had already fallen in love with Nico Castelli? Mair already knew the answer before she asked the question.

Chapter Three

Da was snoring in the next room. Mair turned over on the creaking iron bedstead, wishing she could stay asleep and thereby escape another dreary day. She had been home just over a week, but it seemed like months. The past two days had been worse than ever because Nico had been over at Moel Fawr Ironworks where his younger brothers worked. Though he was supposedly visiting his family, Mair suspected Nico had combined business with pleasure. Recently there had been a lot of talk about labor unrest at Moel Fawr. And he was always so evasive about his union business, she could not help concluding that might have been the real purpose behind his visit to Wales. Anyway, whatever his motives, he had planned to return last night and had arranged to meet her this afternoon for their daily walk. These walks up Pentre Fawr had quickly become the brightest part of her life.

Da constantly grumbled about her being a use-less drain on their meager resources. Between them her brothers earned a reasonable wage, but it didn't go far in supporting five adults, especially when three of them spent every evening at the Miners' Arms. Aunty Bet no longer scolded the menfolk for their intemperance as she had done when she first came to keep house for them. Now she merely threatened them with the fires of hell in payment for their sins, proceeding about her daily life with a martyred air.

"Mair, you up yet?"

"Be down in a minute, Aunty Bet."

Mair jumped out of the covers, shivering as her feet touched the chill wooden floor. Taking her dress off the hook behind the door, she slipped it on. A perfunctory drag through her hair with the boar bristle brush, a quick, breath-taking douse of water from the flower trimmed bowl atop the dresser, and she was ready.

"I've already been down to the shops. There'll be no more of this lazing about once you're married, you know," reminded Aunty Bet as she hung her wool shawl behind the door.

The criticism seemed less sharp than usual. Mair took down the plates from the dresser to set the table for Da's meal. Evan and Ivor had left for the mine before sunrise, taking their meal with them to eat at the morning break.

"I didn't 'laze about' as you call it, at Tal-y-bont."

But Aunty Bet wasn't listening. "You're the luckiest girl in Llandare, you are indeed. Guess what I just heard at Evans'?"

That Davy Hughes had eloped with another

woman, was probably too good to be expected. "No idea, Aunty. Tell me and save me the suspense."

Aunty Bet's face was one vast beam as she turned from the hearth, the bubbling kettle in her hand. "Olwen Evans is going to work at her brother's fancy dress shop in Merthyr!"

Mair failed to see what connection that news had with her own good fortune. "That's nice for Olwen."

"Nice! Oh, girl, you don't have the sense you were born with. Must be the English in you. Olwen kept house for Mr. Tegwyn Williams, the chapel organist, him with the nice big house in the trees behind the chapel. He's going to need a woman to come in and do for him."

A smile dawned on Mair's face. "I see. And I've got a chance at the job?"

"Go on with you, not just a chance. You've already got it. I told Olwen you'd be thrilled to pieces. And she said she'd tell him she'd found someone who couldn't be bested with proper references and all. A nice clean, honest, refined girl, if you will . . . oh, a lovely recommendation she's going to give you. There's plenty money to spend there. You'll be able to buy the best of everything. Oh, *Cariad*, I'm that pleased for you. You aren't the kind of girl to work at the pithead. I've always sided with you against your da there. Common, dirty-minded girls, that lot, not at all like my lovely Mair."

To Mair's amazement, Aunty Bet enfolded her against her full bosom and gave her a joyful hug. The embrace was unexpected and Mair felt so vulnerable that tears filled her eyes.

"Oh, Aunty Bet, thank you," she whispered, licking her lips.

"There, there, no tears," Aunty Bet soothed, patting her shoulder. "Now, let's get your da's meal on the table. I hear him stirring."

While Mair turned the griddle cakes and mixed the porridge she reviewed the unexpected news. The more she considered the prospect, the more pleased she became. An added benefit while she lived at Mr. Williams's house would be relief from the daily reminders of Davy Hughes's undying love. Last time he brought his children to see her in hope of awakening her maternal instinct. The sight of that grubby, sniffling trio had done little to sweeten his proposal. And that is exactly what he had done—proposed! Fortunately Aunty Bet was gone visiting down the street. This allowed Mair to plead appearances, suggesting it would not look right, their being alone. Not anxious to get into her family's bad books, Davy had left.

"Where's my food?" came her father's gruff demand.

"Here he is, quick now, set the food on the table."

Giving his usual greeting, Robert Parry thumped his way inside the room, all bleary-eyed and unshaven, the lingering aroma of the Miners' Arms wafting about him. "You still here?" he grumbled, as Mair put down his plate.

"Aye, Da, the Queen hasn't asked me to be her lady-in-waiting yet, but I'm still hopeful."

"Oh, give over, Mair," laughed Aunty Bet, her face one huge beam. "Now, Robert, get ready for some good news."

Rasping his unshaven chin, the sound putting Mair's teeth on edge, Robert Parry looked from one to the other.

"She's accepted Davy?"

The two women shook their heads.

He took a swig of tea.

"How about getting on at the pit—you went down there like I said and got a job, is that it?"

"I got a job, Da, but not at the pit."

"She's going to be housekeeper for Mr. Tegwyn Williams!" cried Aunty Bet, overjoyed at being the bearer of such wonderful news.

"The choirmaster? Him as told me I was bound for hell for taking a drink?"

"Now Robert, it's a great honor. He's an employer to be proud of. It'll be a real feather in Mair's cap. Well respected, he is. There'll be no lost wages there."

"Aye, well, I s'pose that's something to be thankful for. At least you'll be working. And what's Davy going to say to this?"

"I don't have to consult him about everything I do."

"No need to get on your high horse—he's your husband to be. He has a rightful say over matters."

"He's *not* my husband to be. I keep telling you, Da, I don't want to marry Davy Hughes. Not now, not ever!"

"Mair!" they chorused in unison, shocked by her anger.

"It's nothing new. I keep telling you, but neither of you listens. The only thing left is for me to tell Davy Hughes to his face that I'm not his intended, nor have I ever been." Mair pulled off her apron as

43

she spoke. "I'll go over there now before this foolishness goes any further."

"Bet, stop the girl from making a fool of herself. Stop her doing harm that can't be undone."

Mair was already out the door. Aunty Bet called sharply after her, but Mair ignored her. She marched grimly down the street, stopping before Davy's front door five houses away. A light shone through the window and she was glad he had not yet gone to bed after his night shift. As she raised her hand to knock on the door, it opened as if by magic. Davy Hughes had seen her pass the window.

He stood on the threshold in his dingy undershirt, braces hanging loose at his sides. His black hair was damp from washing coal dust off his face and neck. Fatigue after a night's work had deepened the seams about his wide mouth and the network of lines under his dark eyes.

"Mair, love, come in. I wasn't expecting you. Mari, Bethan, see who's come to visit," he called to his little girls who came crowding behind him, peering through the gloom at their visitor. The girls' hair straggled into their eyes, and as usual their noses were streaming.

Mair went inside and sat stiffly on a ladderback chair beside the hearth. Davy smiled at her— leered would have been more apt, she thought in distaste. His naked thoughts were revealed in that first quick assessment he made of her breasts, full and high inside her high-necked bodice, and of her curving thighs beneath her navy skirt.

"Changed your mind, 'ave you?"

"No, I haven't," she said, thrusting his hand from her knee where it boldly rested. "I've come to

44

tell you I'm taking the position of housekeeper to Mr. Tegwyn Williams."

Davy's already slack jaw dropped another notch. At his elbow one of the girls wailed and Mair absently patted her tangled hair in a futile effort to pacify her.

"Housekeeper," he managed at last. "Well, now, girl, where does that leave us? Two years is long enough for any man to wait."

"I never asked you to wait. In fact, I wish you hadn't. There are plenty of other women in Llandare."

"None like you, *Cariad*," he said, his tone wheedling. "Not a one to match you."

"Listen, Davy—I'm not going to marry you."

"Aw, come on, your Aunty says you don't know your own mind. Your da told me—"

"It's *me* you're asking to marry you, not Da or Aunty Bet. No one has ever considered my feelings in the matter. You'd better find another woman to care for your children—they look as if they're in need of it."

"Exactly. And how can you, in all Christian conscience, walk away and leave us without a backward glance?"

Mair stood up and declined the mug of tea he offered her. "I must go. I just wanted to explain, to play fair with you. No, Davy," she cautioned, as his rough fingers encircled her wrist. "Let me go. Don't make things worse than they already are. You know I don't love you, I never have. All of you thought eventually I'd come round, but I'm not going to change my mind. I'm sorry it has to be this way, Davy. Goodbye. There's no point to us keeping up this pretence."

"Got a little something going with old Tegwyn Williams, have you? Fancy sharing his big house and all that furniture."

"That's got nothing to do with it. I've never even been inside his house, so I don't know what he's got."

"Like hell!"

Mair had backed to the door. She reached behind her for the knob. Angry, Davy smashed down his mug, sloshing tea all over the table. Mair already had the door handle in her grasp. She turned it, pulled open the door and stepped outside as Davy lunged for her.

Swearing, his coarse face dark with anger, Davy yelled, "Come you back here this minute, girl, we'll finish this in private."

"It's already finished," Mair cried, jumping down the steps before he could grab her. Then she began to run.

He started after her, shouting, the children wailing behind him as they clutched at his legs. Doors popped open and lace curtains twitched as she raced past. Mair's only thought was to escape. Finally slackening her pace, she found to her relief Davy had abandoned his pursuit. A slammed door further attested to her deliverance.

Mair leaned gasping against a nearby wall as tears of fright and relief rolled down her cheeks. What a fool thing to have done! Davy Hughes could have easily overpowered her, forcing her to stay. Thank the Lord he was not as quick-witted as she, or she would never have escaped from his house.

Once her racing heart had slowed and her knees stopped shaking, Mair debated whether to go home. The atmosphere would be decidedly hostile.

Better to stay away for a while and let them both get used to the idea. Had she been an accepted visitor to Maen Gwyn, she would have gone to see Nico. There were so many hours to wait until the afternoon. Then a wonderful idea sprang into her mind. Sometimes he waited for the carters' wagons to take the embroidered goods his mother worked to be sold in the city. That was where he had been the morning she met him. Maybe she would be lucky enough to meet him coming back down the hill.

A fine drizzle began as Mair labored up the flinty track. She pulled her shawl over her head, glad she had not worn her hat. The bottom road was empty. The carters must use the top road.

Further uphill she went, the track growing steeper. The otherworldliness of the mountain engulfed her. Birds twittered in the hedges; the wind sighed through the trees. With the exception of a distant shot—probably some farmer sending off a fox— the muffled silence was unbroken. It was lonely up here, but she loved the solitude. Someday she would live on a mountain, Mair determined, as she paused to catch her breath. Leaning against a stile, she gazed enraptured at the panorama of thickly hedged green fields, rolling sheep-dotted pastures, and dense woodland merging with the lowering gray sky. In the distance a rider jumped a hedge, then retraced his steps and took the jump again. On the far side of this mountain much of the land belonged to Jasper Owen. Amidst the treetops to the west she could see the chimneys of his big house, all turreted and corbelled like an ancient manor, though built less than fifty years before. Nico's father had been one of the Italian craftsmen brought over to embellish the gothic mansion. Terazzo floors, marble steps, paintings, statues, all had been created by the Italian artisans. When the job was done many of them stayed, joining the Welsh in the region's burgeoning iron and coal mines. Others, like Nico's father and uncle, still practiced their craft, largely confined these days to chiseling graveyard monuments.

A small animal darted ahead of her. Startled, Mair wondered at first if it was a fox. Then a few yards further along she discovered it was one of the short-legged, tailless cattle dogs used by local farmers and drovers.

The dog approached her warily. Crouching down, Mair held out her hand, speaking in Welsh, for that was probably the only language the dog understood. Pricking up its gold brown ears, the foxy-faced dog whined and ran ahead. It stopped, watching her intently, head cocked to one side. When she walked a few paces, the dog repeated the maneuver until it finally came whimpering to her feet. Wondering what game the animal played, she followed good-naturedly. Every few feet the dog stopped and glanced toward her, making sure she still followed.

Through damp undergrowth, over a stile, deep into a farmer's pasture it led her. Mair began to wonder at the wisdom of her blind obedience, yet usually these intelligent little dogs were not given to wild goose chases. The dog stopped before a rocky outcropping beneath a thicket of mountain ash. Its bright eyes fixed on her, the dog began to wag its stump of a tail until its entire hindquarters writhed in pleasure.

Mair stepped forward, wondering why the dog

had brought her to this spot. There, in the wet tangled grasses lay a large mixed breed dog, its brindled coat bright with blood. Mair gasped at the pitiful sight. Crouching, she tentatively put out her hand, surprised to see the big dog's tail thumping rhythmically.

"Efa," she gasped in surprise, suddenly recognizing the animal. And the big tail thumped even harder. "Oh, *Cariad bach*, what happened to you?"

Though she had been away for some time, the dog still remembered her. Efa belonged to Dan the drover who lived beyond Maen Gwyn, and she was a familiar sight in the area. The small dog must be her working companion. Thinking perhaps Efa was caught in a trap, Mair pulled off her kerchief and attempted to clean away the blood. Within minutes the fabric was saturated. Yet the dog's paws were undamaged, so the blood on Efa's muzzle came merely from licking her wounds. After a gentle examination, Mair found a number of profusely bleeding punctures on her hindquarters where jagged edges of bone protruded. Someone had peppered the dog with shot!

Efa gently clamped her jaw about Mair's arm in warning as the dog's pain increased. Mair soothed her in a crooning voice while she wondered what to do. Though Efa must have dragged herself this far, there was little chance she could get home. The drover lived on high ground beyond the town, and the dog was too heavy for Mair to carry. Her only hope lay in getting help from Beddws Farm. Everyone thereabouts knew Dan, and his cattle dogs had always been treated kindly. Who could have done such a cruel thing? The shot she heard earlier must have been the one that maimed Efa.

Yet surely no one could mistake such a large dog for a fox.

Mair rocked back on her heels. Approaching hoofbeats reminded her of the rider she had seen in the lower pasture. Perhaps he would go to the farm for help. She could hear the clopping hooves coming up the road.

Mair ran to the hedge, hoping to catch the man on the road, but by the time she got there he had already turned into the pasture. Shouting for help, she raced back, waving frantically to attract his attention. Brambles snatched at her skirt and shawl, wet branches slapped against her face.

The rider reined in atop a knoll about thirty feet away. To her dismay, Mair noticed a shotgun slung across his back. Could he be the culprit?

"What do you want, girl?" he shouted, his speech bearing clipped English accents.

Mair walked closer, her original intention abandoned. If she had the criminal before her, he was certainly going to hear about it. "There's an injured dog over there. Don't suppose you'd know anything about it?"

"Why should I?"

"She's been filled with shot. Some fool mistook her for a fox."

She could see he was young, his pale complexion spotty. Sandy hair straggled across his brow under his hat brim, partially hiding his close-set hazel eyes. Mair found his face vaguely familiar, but she could not place him until he haughtily announced:

"Have you any idea to whom you're speaking? I am Heath Owen."

Anger shot through her. "And I'm Mair Parry.

50

And around here we don't shoot dogs for nothing, Mr. Heath Owen."

"Loose dogs on my property are fair game."

"She wasn't a loose dog. These are Dan the drover's dogs. Everyone knows them. He must have sent them home alone. How could you do it?"

"How very touching," he sneered, sliding from the saddle. He swaggered toward her. "Where is this poor creature?"

Mair walked a few yards toward the dog's hiding place. Sensing danger, the little male dog began to growl at the man's approach.

Heath Owen stopped. "There's nothing wrong with that dog."

"You can't say the same for poor Efa. The least you can do is get help, or ride over to Dan's place and tell his people to come get her."

Heath Owen threw back his head and roared with laughter.

"What do you take me for, a messenger boy? My father owns everything in this town. I don't take orders from pit girls."

Mair's eyes flashed. "I'm not a pit girl. And your father doesn't own me."

"The best I can do for the bitch is put her out of her misery."

A cry of horror was ripped from Mair's throat as he unslung the shotgun and levelled it at Efa's resting place.

"No, damn you! Don't you dare!"

Mair flung herself at Heath Owen, startling him and making the shot go wild into the nearby hedge. The little male dog began a frenzied barking and Efa started whining in fear.

"Get off me, you fool," he yelled, trying to shake

Mair off his arm. "Do you want your own backside full of lead?"

Suddenly caught off balance and unable to save himself, Heath Owen sprawled backwards in the grass. His face turned crimson with injured pride.

Moving quickly, somewhat surprised by her own boldness, Mair seized the fallen shotgun. Racing downhill, she flung it into the pond at the bottom of the pasture. A satisfying splash rewarded her efforts.

Now he was yelling and cursing in rage. A few minutes later he was beside her, his face dark with fury.

"You fool girl! That's an expensive gun. Now it's ruined. Oh, you'll pay dearly for this, I promise you that. And all over some mongrel bitch—two mongrel bitches to be exact."

He grabbed Mair's arm, yanking her about.

"Let me go! You don't deserve a gun until you know how to use it properly."

"My father'll hear about this. You're coming with me, you're going to tell him what you've done."

"No I'm not. I'm going to get help for the dog. If not from you, then I'll get it from someone else. Even your father wouldn't have shot one of Dan's dogs."

"You're coming with me."

Cruelly he wrenched her arm, throwing her down. The gallant little male dog raced down the incline, growling, barking, trying to protect his newfound friend. Heath Owen kicked at the animal, sending him yelping away, only to return to the attack moments later. Picking up a tree branch, he finally whacked the dog hard, forcing him to retreat.

Mair was struggling to get up. Smashing her back down, Heath Owen straddled her, his feet on her skirts. Something about his expression stabbed fear through her body. The mounting flush on his spotty face suggested another, even stronger emotion.

"Well, I've got you cornered now, you scrappy little bitch. What did you say your name is?"

"Mair Parry," she repeated sullenly, trying to formulate a plan of escape.

"Well, Mair Parry, if you promise to be nice to me, I'll forget about your crime. I might even forget to tell my father about you."

"This is as nice as I'm going to be to you, Heath Owen. And it's far nicer than you deserve. Now get away and let me up."

Anger flashed in his eyes as she thumped at his legs, trying to force him off her skirts.

"Is that so? We'll soon see about that."

He dropped down onto her, his thighs grinding her into the ground. Shouting, screaming, Mair dragged her fingernails across his cheek. Aroused by her resistance, he struggled to pin her flailing arms above her head.

Aware the little dog still skulked nearby, Mair shouted to him in Welsh. Like a bolt of fury he came running, hurling himself at Heath Owen, growling, worrying, ripping the man's fine tweed jacket.

The commotion masked the approach of a second man. Mair saw the flash of another body hurtling forward, and then Heath Owen was bowled aside. Shrieking with fear and relief Mair saw it was Nico Castelli who grappled with the landowner's son. Punching, shaking, cursing, the two men rolled downhill. To her horror Mair saw Heath Owen was now on top, trying to choke his assailant. Nico finally thrust him away, getting the upper hand. He pinned Heath Owen in the marshy bottoms beside the pond.

"Do you know who I am?" Heath Owen demanded breathlessly, his voice high and squeaking.

"I know who you are right enough, Mr. bloody Heath Owen. And I'm telling you, if you ever touch this woman again, I'll kill you. Don't even try to speak to her, or you'll have me to answer to."

"You? And who are you?"

"I'm Nico Castelli. You can ask your Da who that is. He knows me well enough. Now get back to your mansion—that is, if you can still sit your horse."

Scrambling to his feet, Heath Owen backed away. Muttering and cursing beneath his breath, he stumbled uphill to where his horse patiently waited. The little dog raced after him, snapping at his heels, earning several kicks for his pains, but successfully driving the mineowner's son at a quick trot. Once in the saddle, Heath Owen tried to ride down the dog, but it was too skilled at dodging hooves for that.

"I'm warning you, Owen, if you ever try anything like this again, you'll have me to answer to."

"You'll regret this day, you Italian bastard! My father ordered you out of town. He'll not be pleased to know you're back defying his orders."

"Mighty Jasper Owen hasn't the right to order

anyone out of town. I'm a free man. I go where I please."

"Not if I have anything to do with it."

"While you're at it with that tale, don't forget to tell your da you were trying to rape one of the local women, will you?"

Muttering angrily, Heath Owen swung his mount about and sped across the pasture.

Nico knelt beside Mair who crouched sobbing, more from relief than fright. "Are you all right, Mair love? He didn't hurt you?"

"No . . . no. I'm fine," Mair assured, sniffling and dabbing her eyes. "How about you? Oh, it's a miracle, you coming when you did."

He took out his handkerchief and wiped tears and mud from her face. "I was by the crossroads when I heard all the barking and shouting. Anyone would have investigated. You were the last person I expected to find with that . . . that bastard!"

"He's more of a bastard than you think. He wounded one of the drover's dogs. He was trying to kill her. That's why we were fighting at first. Then, well, he soon forgot about that."

"What are you doing up here in the rain?" Nico asked, pulling her shawl over her wet hair.

"Coming to meet you."

"Meet me? How did you know I'd be coming along the road?"

"I didn't, just hoped, that's all. It's so long till this afternoon. I didn't want to wait to talk to you." Mair stopped, remembering the wounded dog patiently waiting beside the rocks. "Come look at Efa, tell me if she'll be all right."

Hand in hand they went up the incline, Mair panting as they reached the rocky bower. The small tailless dog raced ahead of them, well pleased by the account he had made of himself.

"That little one was worrying the daylights out of Heath Owen. Too bad he didn't take a bit of flesh along with it."

"Isn't it." Mair chuckled at the thought of fancy Heath Owen riding home with his jacket in tatters and the backside of his britches waving. "The dog came to my rescue. I'm thankful for that. There's a good boy, aren't you, *cariad*?"

Mair patted the frisky little cattle dog while Nico gently examined Efa. She licked his hand, the end of her tail fluttering weakly.

Nico shook his head. "I'm afraid she'll never use this leg again."

Mair gasped in horror, dropping down to stroke the rough brindled head stiff with blood. "It's broken then?"

"Shattered. There, now, don't cry," he soothed as big tears rolled down her cheeks. "Dogs can manage with three legs."

"But she's a drover's dog. What use will she be now?"

"She's probably old enough to welcome the rest. Come now, Mair, it can't be helped. Don't fret about it. What's done is done. We have to get her home to her people."

Over the hedge two cloth caps appeared and someone shouted. "What's going on by here?"

"Heath Owen's shot one of the drover's dogs," Nico called back. "Can you help us get her home?"

Cursing soundly at the discovery, the two farmer's sons climbed the stile and came to have a look for themselves. Efa also greeted them as friends.

One of the men ran back up the road to the nearby farm, soon returning with a pony and trap. Between them they lifted the wounded dog as gently as possible onto a blanket and carried her out of the pasture. They laid Efa in the trap as her anxious companion leaped up beside her.

"Want to ride over there with us?"

"Thanks. We'll explain everything to Dan's wife."

Clicking to the pony, the farmer's sons drove down the track. They were soon in Llandare and turning into the road behind the chapel, skirting the settlement at Maen Gwyn before heading up-hill.

The drover lived in a gray stone farmhouse perched on a craggy spur at the foot of the mountain. When the trap approached, his wife and children ran outside.

As the story unfolded there was much crying by the women and much swearing of vengeance by the men. Gently the family carried the big dog indoors, taking time to thank all concerned for their bravery in rescuing Efa.

Nico declined the farmer's sons' offer of a ride back to town, and Mair was glad. She did not want to leave him yet. Squeezing his arm gratefully, she smiled and asked him, "Where are we going now?"

"Home."

"Home . . . to your house?"

"You can't go back looking like you've been dragged through a hedgerow." He laughed and thrust the wet hair out of her eyes. "Mama will be delighted to have someone to look after. You've got a few bad scratches that need to be cleaned."

Chapter Four

Mair hunched before the blazing fire, nursing a hot mug of tea. The warmth and unexpected kindness she had been shown in Nico's home took her by surprise. In a mixture of Italian and broken English, generously spiced with laughter, his mother, father, aunt, uncle and cousins exclaimed over Mair's bravery, then all voiced their anger at Heath Owen's cowardly act.

Nico's mother, Anna, had bathed Mair's wounds and applied salve to heal the cuts and bruises; she even insisted Mair wear one of her frocks while her own dried. It was all so unexpected, Mair wanted to cry, touched by their wholehearted acceptance of her.

"They like you," Nico confided when they were alone in the small parlor made gloomy with heavy fringed green velvet curtains and dark wood furniture. The men had returned to the workshop next door, the women to the kitchen to prepare the midday meal.

"I never expected them to be so kind to a stranger. Your family are very warm and loving."

"That's the Italian way," Nico explained in surprise. "Aren't your family warm?"

Mair pictured Da—sullen, unloving, belligerent. Aunty Bet had her better moments, but even she could not have been described as warm. As for her brothers, they wouldn't have dreamed of hugging or kissing their sister.

"No," she said, gazing into the fire. Only Mam had been warm and she was dead.

"People react in different ways, that's all. Mama's making a big bowl of soup to restore your strength. And she'll be offended if you don't drink some of her medicinal wine. They think you look like an angel."

Mair smiled in pleasure. That must have been the part in Italian that she had not understood. "You're very lucky to have such a family."

Nico smiled, nodding his agreement. He leaned over to rearrange the soft cushions behind her head, critically viewing the darkening bruises on her face. A deep bramble scratch scored her cheek; a purpling graze marred her chin.

"You still haven't told me why you were so eager to see me."

She glanced away from his probing gaze. The expression in his dark eyes made her heart flutter. If only she could tell him what she felt in her heart—if only he felt the same way.

"You've been away since Tuesday. I had a lot of things to tell you."

59

"Well, why not start now, while we're waiting for dinner?"

Mair related the details of her unpleasant tangle with Davy Hughes, told him about the promised job with Mr. Williams, and so much more. Confidances seemed to flow unceasingly within the warm security of that room. While Nico listened, she noticed he drummed his fingers nervously on the chair arm. There was such hidden strength in those slender, olive-skinned hands, red and bruised after his encounter with Heath Owen. Mair pictured how it would feel to be caressed by his finely shaped hands. How warmly exciting it would be. The very thought made her shiver. His voice would be low with husky endearments.

"Now we eat. Anna's best soup," announced Aunt Renata as she carried a steaming kettle into the room. The bubbling pot was placed before the fire to keep warm as Nico's mother carried a platter filled with thickly sliced homebaked bread to sop up the soup. Out of deference to his position as eldest son, Nico was fed first, his deep earthenware bowl filled to the brim with rich thick broth in which floated vegetables and meat. Mair, as the guest, was served next. The men from the workshop took their midday meal in the back kitchen.

By early afternoon, Mair felt pleasantly warm both inside and out. Anna Castelli's homemade herbal wine had something to do with her glorious sense of well-being, though mostly it came from the friendly acceptance she had found inside these walls. Best of all, she was highly aware of the growing intimacy she shared with Nico, almost as if she were a member of his family.

When Anna Castelli heard that Mair sang as well

as Adelina Patti, she clapped her small hands in delight. Opera was her passion. With great pride she unveiled a shiny black piano hidden under yards of fringed green cloth.

"Come back when you feel better. You sing, I play for you," she promised, beaming at the pleasurable prospect.

Mair was treated to the story of wonderful Cousin Guido. Only yesterday Anna had received a letter revealing her cousin's plans to visit Llandare the following week. Mair would have to sing for him. Who knows, perhaps she might even join his opera company. It would be such a wonderful opportunity.

It was finally time to leave. Nico kissed his mother goodbye, grateful for her kindness to Mair. Anna insisted Mair use her shawl while her own dried, and that way, she archly suggested, Mair would be sure to return.

They stood on the high step, saying goodbye. Mair was sorry to be leaving. These past hours inside the Castelli home had made her feel far removed from Llandare. But once they were outside, she was again aware of the thick gray pall overhead which the sun barely penetrated.

As they walked away from the low, sprawling stone house and workshop, Nico's mother stood on the step waving goodbye, a short stout figure in a voluminous white apron.

"It's almost time for our walk, or have you had enough of the mountain for one day?"

For the wonderful chance to be with him just a little longer, Mair would have crawled up Pentre Fawr on her hands and knees. "Can we?" she asked eagerly.

"We'll go round behind the mine."

They skirted the sprawling mine buildings. The yard was mounded with great slag heaps where tip girls sifted through the cinders. Men shouted and rattling coal carts clanked along the narrow siding. Once the noise and the smoke stacks were left behind, Mair began to feel the weight lift from her heart. She greatly resented the stark intrusion of the mine into these precious hours she spent with Nico.

As they moved uphill, taking the narrow track beyond the railway line, the sun broke weakly through the haze, its pale yellow shafts lighting their faces. Now Mair noticed Nico's face was bruised also. Gently she touched the purpling area spreading over his high cheekbone, fading into a graze across his right temple under his thick curling hair.

"Sorry you had to defend me, but I'm very, very glad you were there when I needed you."

To her surprise, he caught her arm and pulled her about. They were standing beside a tumble-down stone wall that separated the upland sheep pasture from the grazing land of the bottom farm.

"I always hope to be there when you need me."

"I'm not planning to have another run-in with Heath Owen."

"I wanted to kill him for touching you," Nico confided, his voice low and shaking with emotion. "If he'd hurt you, I'd have smashed his face to a pulp."

"Lucky you didn't need to do that," she whispered, made slightly uncomfortable by his intensity, yet finding it exciting at the same time. She stood close, trying to control her erratic heartbeat. "You are my champion. You and Dan's little dog."

He didn't smile at her joke. A pulse jumped in his jaw and his mouth was set as he gazed down at her. His eyes looked black in the shadow beneath his cap brim. "Mair . . . I'll have to go back soon."

"Back? To London?"

He nodded, his fingers softly grazing her cheek.

"When?"

"I'm not sure. When they tell me."

"They?"

"Never mind," he dismissed the question quickly, his hands on her shoulders.

Mair's heart was beating so fast she could scarcely breathe. Her knees felt so weak, she marveled she could stand. "Promise you'll not forget we're special friends."

"Never. Our friendship's too precious to me."

She gazed up into the liquid blackness of his eyes. Time stood still on the mountain. In the distance sheep bleated and the wind stirred the new green foliage on the birches above their heads.

"Oh, Mair, how much I'm going to miss you," he whispered, drawing her closer.

The heated fragrance of his body acted like a powerful drug. Suspended in the magic of his nearness, she unconsciously yielded against him, so that he held her close against his body. Mair became aware of his heartbeat thudding through her clothing. His arms tightened around her, and Nico's mouth came down on hers, hot, tender, drawing forth a trembling response. His kiss sent blood surging through her veins, making her heart thud dangerously and robbing her of breath.

For a long time they stood close. Then, as if remembering what they were about, he gently set her aside. His grin was weak, his breathing shallow.

"We'll never get to the farm this way," he said, taking her hand. "Come on. You already have enough explaining to do as it is."

For the next hour Mair moved in a trance. They collected butter and cheese from the farm, then made the return journey to Llandare. To Mair's disappointment Nico did not attempt to kiss her again, nor did he allude to the heightened emotion of their friendship. In fact, he purposely kept the conversation casual. She listened, but had little idea what was said. All the time her heart was thudding to the rhythm—he loves me, he loves me. Nico had not spoken those words, but his tenderness, the veiled passion in his kiss, spoke loud and clear. Mair was content.

They had made no plans to meet the following day, Sunday, and when she asked him about it, Nico's face tightened.

"Not tomorrow. I may have to go back to Moel Fach. I won't know till this evening."

Mair mustered the courage to suggest, "Sunday it is. They won't be working then. Can I come with you?"

"No," he dismissed sharply, his hand hovering about her shoulder before he reconsidered and thrust his fist deep inside his pocket. "You'll be better off here. There could be trouble."

"At the works? Then you *were* trying to organize the men to form a union."

"Yes. I didn't tell you because it was better that you didn't know. There are many Irish employed at the mine earning such low wages that they're little more than slave labor. There's a movement afoot to better their—I've already said too much. I can't really tell you about it yet. Be patient. Only trust me, whatever you hear said, my purpose is to make a better life for them, not just to cause unrest."

Mair found his statement puzzling and a little frightening. "Are you in danger?"

"You mustn't worry. I can look after myself."

"Be careful. There's such hard feelings in these valleys. Men can't do as they please."

Smiling, he placed his finger on her lips. "I know. You mustn't worry about me. Promise. I'll see you on Monday, the same time."

Mair nodded and after a whispered goodbye, he hitched his knapsack more comfortably on his back and strode toward Maen Gwyn along the road behind the chapel.

Fear gripped Mair. Maybe it would have been better had she not known his purpose at Moel Fawr Ironworks. There'd been bloodshed there before, for the owner did not tolerate outsiders telling him how to run his works.

Chilled by both the sharp wind and the forboding she felt, Mair headed home. Mentally she braced herself for the fireworks which she knew she must face after this morning's row. Even the wonderful memory of Nico's kiss, of the promise relayed by his lips, was not sufficient to vanquish her growing apprehension. There'd be no hiding these scratches and bruises. To turn the attention to Heath Owen's cowardly act would be her best course. Nico's part in her rescue must be mentioned, for if she had not heard already, Aunty Bet would soon learn that he was involved. But she must make it all seem like a coincidence that he happened by at just the right moment.

Bracing herself for battle, Mair opened the door of No. 10 and walked inside.

Sunday was a day of blue sky and bright sun. Mair could scarely believe the sight as broad beams of sunlight streamed through her dingy bedroom window as she dressed for chapel. Today the mines were closed. There was no heavy pall of coal dust and smoke hovering over Llandare to dim the light. Surely it was an omen! Uneasily she considered Nico's probable danger at Moel Fach Ironworks. He had not said there was to be a rally, but she guessed as much. After chapel the men would march to the mine owner's house prepared to talk business. That was how it began when they tried to form a miner's union at Owen Pit number one. Much shouting, a few scuffles, black eyes and split lips, had been the extent of the damage here. She had heard the owner of Moel Fach had armed his foremen and bosses; there would be a lot more danger there than a black eye.

She put her feathered hat on top of her coiled hair, pulled on her shawl, and hurried downstairs. Aunty Bet would be seething at her delay. This day of chapel going, singing and praying was the high point of her week.

"Oh, coming this month, are you?" Aunty Bet rapped, as Mair entered the front room. "Thought maybe you was waiting for Christmas."

"Sorry, Aunty Bet. Surely we're not late yet."

"Not yet, but we will be if we don't hurry," grumbled Da, running his fingers inside the constriction of his unaccustomed collar and tie. "Bad enough going in the first place all done up like a dog's dinner, without being late and causing a stir."

Aunty Bet looked daggers at her brother, but refrained from reprimanding him.

Setting forth like a galleon under full sail, Aunty Bet led the way, splendid in her best black straw bonnet trimmed with grosgrain ribbon and her black bombazine mourning gown. Over her shoulders was draped her finest Welsh wool shawl with the black fringe. The only splash of color allowed was the dark red cushion she carried to soften the chapel's hard pews. The usual sermons delivered in fiery rhetoric by the Reverend Emrys Hughes lasted well over an hour. Aunty Bet made this concession to luxury only because she had a bad back. Those hellfire and brimstone sermons had become famous throughout the Rhondda valleys. As usual there would be a packed house and she did not intend to miss a word.

Curious heads turned as they entered the chapel and, with many apologies, squeezed into their pew. Ivor and Evan were already here, appearing strangely alien in their Sunday suits, pale faces scrubbed clean, hair slicked down with pomade. The family sat in a row, hands folded like saints, awaiting the day's moving Christian experience.

Mair ignored the turning heads, the whispers, as the congregation remarked on her bruised face, a wonderful medley of blue, black and purple this morning. After chapel everyone would know what had happened if the wagging tongues and bobbing heads had anything to do with it.

Serenely Aunty Bet ignored this palpable undercurrent inside the gray stone chapel. She'd had her say last night, as had Robert, Ivor and Evan. Mair knew where she stood now, rescue or no rescue. Whispers had come to her these past few days about Mair walking with that foreigner to Beddws Farm. It was as well she was going over to Mr. Tegwyn Williams's house this very afternoon. The care of the chapel organist and his lovely home would fill her time. Bet was a great believer in the old adage that the devil makes use of idle hands.

Reverend Hughes appeared, his shock of white hair catching a ray of sunlight shining through the oblong windows, making it gleam like silver against the chapel's somber woodwork.

Organ chords reverberated through the stone building. The congregation stood. The music the organist played was an old familiar hymn, and Mair's voice soared in joy, strong and clear above the rest. Around her the volume of singing lessened as people lowered their own voices, the better to hear her sing. That wonderful voice had been absent these two years past. It was good to have Mair Parry back amongst them again.

After several hours of enduring Brother Emrys Hughes's fiery warnings of coming damnation, of watching the shameful spectacle of accused sinners publicly repenting before the congregation, Sunday morning worship neared an end. Mair realized she was shortly to be set free. When the final hymn was over, the organ notes gradually dying away, she couldn't wait to go outside into the sunshine. Today she had been assured of one fact—her voice was still there! In the sad days following Miss Jenkins's death, she had been fearful she had lost her ability to sing. When her heart was sad, she was like a songless bird. The time of grieving was over. Today she had sung better than ever.

People crowded round Mair, sympathizing with her about her ordeal at the hands of Heath Owen. The attention was gratifying and most unexpected.

Mr. Tegwyn Williams, squat and round in his shiny black serge suit, his bald pate agleam with sweat, thrust his way through the other worshippers.

"Mair, my dear, how delighted I was to hear your lovely voice. This chapel's not been the same since you went away, indeed it hasn't. I'm happy to welcome you back to Llandare. Knowing how anxious you are to start, Olwen's already left for Merthyr. Come over after chapel and we'll get you settled."

Mair agreed to his proposal, somewhat disconcerted by Mr. Williams's open appraisal, beady eyes black as buttons behind his steel-rimmed spectacles. His fleshy lips were wet, his tongue licking them as he looked at her, reminding her of a slavering animal. Warning bells jangled in her head. Holy, respected, chapel organist though he was, Tegwyn Williams was also a man. Though she knew him only slightly, she already had him pegged as a sanctimonious hypocrite. The lustful look he had given her, thinly disguised even in this sacred place, was one with which she had grown familiar. When she was younger, men's lascivious glances had frightened her. Now she felt better prepared to take them in stride.

Fortunately Aunty Bet had already prepared her

for Mr. Williams's eagerness to have her begin her duties. That fact had been angrily hurled at her head when she returned last night. Aunty Bet was incensed to think that holy Mr. Williams had been trying to reach Mair all day while she had been gallivanting heaven knew where. Mair also learned how poor Davy Hughes was sunk in depression over the cruel way she had rejected him.

All during this tirade she had stood there, her bruised face throbbing, forced to recount the nightmare of the wounded dog and Heath Owen's conduct. When she contemplated Nico's danger, fear pierced her heart. The one bright gleam in the darkness was the memory of his kiss, of the tenderness in his brown eyes. It was the look of love, for surely he loved her as much as she loved him.

Chapter Five

Mr. Williams's house stood amidst tall beech, fir and poplars inside a low, shrubbery-screened wall. Set slightly apart from the rest of Llandare in the road behind the chapel, Brynteg was the most splendid house on this side of town. The foursquare house was of gray stone with a slate roof. A curving cinder path led to the front door painted dark green and flanked by miniature evergreens in brass tubs.

Mair had never ventured inside the grounds of Brynteg, merely glimpsing the gloomy house from the road. An Anglican vicarage in the days before Methodism grasped the coal valleys in a stranglehold, Brynteg was one of the few houses in the district with any pretensions of gentility. Mr. Williams had inherited Brynteg from his mother, who was a distant cousin to Jasper Owen.

Mr. Williams had not yet left the chapel. He had

given Mair the house key and she found it odd to be stepping inside a stranger's house. Brynteg was like a mausoleum, silent and gloomy. Mair felt as if she should tiptoe in reverence. Black and white tiles covered the long hallway. Ferns and potted plants in tall legged brass containers flanked the entranceway. Several large oil paintings depicting biblical scenes hung from the picture rail on tasseled yellow cords. Chill formality radiated through the spacious rooms, all furnished in rose-wood and mahogany polished to a mirrorlike gleam by her predecessor.

Mair decided to wait downstairs for her employer. She sat on a horsehair sofa, positioned near the parlor door so she could see when Mr. Williams arrived.

She did not have long to wait. A few minutes later he pushed open the door, puffing from the exertion of the short uphill walk. His face was suffused with pleasure when he saw her.

"Ah, there you are, like a good girl," he fussed, taking her wool shawl. "Your brothers will be by presently with your things. I've already spoken to them."

Mair was temporarily estranged from Evan and Ivor after last night's row because they had sided heavily with Da and Aunty Bet against her.

"This way, my dear."

Mair followed his portly figure as he puffed up the narrow stair to the second floor. A row of closed mahogany doors led off the gray painted hallway. Stopping before the last door, Mr. Williams threw it wide with a flourish, almost as if he expected her to squeal in delight, Mair thought, stepping inside the small room.

A narrow, high-backed bed neatly covered in a white cotton counterpane, a carved wardrobe, a dresser and a chest, and a straight-backed chair comprised the room's furnishings. A deep window overlooked the green vista of Pentre Fawr's lower grazing land.

"There now, this is far better than you're used to, I'll be bound," remarked Mr. Williams with a twinkle.

Mair bit back the reminder that she had recently been living at Tal-y-bont, saying merely, "It's certainly a lot roomier than Maes-y-Groes, Mr. Williams."

Pleased, he patted her shoulder. Going to the wardrobe he opened the door, eager to display the full length mirror inside. "See here, Mair, you can admire your pretty figure," he suggested slyly.

She smiled, making a mental note to be exceedingly careful of Mr. Tegwyn Williams. When she came inside the room she was relieved to see the door had a lock. If she didn't miss her guess, she would greatly appreciate that safety measure.

"Olwen left some half-finished dresses for you. Won't be needing them herself. I'm no miser when it comes to fuel, so you can have the fire lit whenever you want. I keep an open account at Evans the Grocers. I like a good table, Mair, but you probably guessed as much," he chuckled, patting his paunch. "Now, *cariad*, this is for you."

Warily Mair accepted the ten pound note he extracted from inside his coat. "Thank you very kindly, Mr. Williams. Is this for the household expenses?"

"No, indeed. To spend on yourself. Buy something pretty. Pretty girls like pretty things." He touched her cheek and she shrank inwardly, trying not to flinch. More briskly now he continued, "All the household bills come to me, so you won't have to be responsible for accounts. You are to keep the place tidy—Nansi Roberts comes in to light the fires and do the heavy work, and cook my meals and help me entertain my few guests. Most important, Mair, you are to sing. We'll practice every afternoon. I expect you to start singing solo every Sunday in chapel. Who knows, we might go on to sing in an *eisteddfod* one of these days, we shall have to see. Your wages will be paid to your Aunty Bet, as she requested. Now, don't look alarmed. You'll want for nothing. I promise you, Mair, you'll—"

A loud banging on the front door announced her brothers' arrival. To Mair's relief, Mr. Williams went downstairs to admit them.

Evan and Ivor came clumping up the stair, their eyes sticking out on stalks as they admired the luxurious surroundings. They gasped in awe when they saw their sister's room.

"You don't have to share with anyone?" asked Evan in surprise.

"There's only me and old Tegwyn Williams here."

"Aye, and you'd best lock your door, or you'll be sharing with him against your will," suggested Ivor with a scowl.

Mair breathed a sigh of relief. "So it's not just me. You feel the same way about him. Not near as holy as Aunty Bet thinks."

"Only got to see him watching you to know that. Might be Mrs. Williams someday, girl. Couldn't do much better than marry him, not in Llandare."

Mair pulled a face. Ivor laughed. "Just a suggestion in case you fancied him more than Davy," he added in an undertone, giving her a nudge.

Soon it was time for them to leave, and though yesterday Mair had been so angry she thought she would never want to speak to either of her brothers again, they were still her family. And they were leaving her alone with the chapel music master.

"Take care. I'll visit you often, I promise. Life shouldn't be as hard, now you've got my wages coming in. Perhaps Da won't grumble so much."

Evan laughed. "The day Da stops grumbling they'll be laying him out. Be a good girl now and look after Mr. Williams proper like, won't you."

Mair grabbed them both and kissed them. The boys flushed to the roots of their light brown hair, protesting, giving her quick affectionate pats before they bolted for the door.

Their embarrassed reaction made Mair smile. The last time she had embraced them was when she had left to work for Miss Jenkins. Their reaction had been the same then.

Later that evening, by the light of a pearly globed lamp, Mair examined the unfinished garments left in the wardrobe. Olwen was fatter than she, but the same height. The clothing would need very little alteration. She smiled in pleasure as she held the serviceable gowns against her body, admiring her reflection in the long mirror. Olwen was an expert seamstress and these unexpected gifts were most welcome.

The garments consisted of a serviceable blue serge skirt with three deep tucks above the hem, a plain cotton blouse, a gray wool skirt and coateee trimmed with black braid, and a summerweight cotton of dark blue striped in gray. Much of the work was already done. Olwen had even left a roll of calico in which she had folded scissors, threads and needles for Mair to complete the job.

Mair began work first on the serge skirt, sewing on a button and working a buttonhole. While she sewed she reviewed her first day at Brynteg. For his dinner she had given Mr. Williams a couple of rashers of gammon, fried potatoes, baked turnips and swedes, followed by a dish of stewed apples and custard. Though Mair knew the meal had been uninspired, her employer had been unusually lavish in his praise. This evening after chapel he was joining Brother Hughes at the home of mutual friends, so there was no evening meal to prepare. Because this was her first day at work, Mair had been excused attendance at evening chapel, but next week she would be expected to be there, reminded Mr. Williams with a stern face.

Pondering her life in these luxurious surroundings, she decided she would soon get used to the cleaning and cooking. It was Mr. Tegwyn Williams himself who presented a problem. His speech was far too flattering, and he was much too handy with those seemingly innocent little pats. His leer could turn her stomach. By a sheer stroke of luck, when she had asked him for the room key he was with Brother Hughes. Rather than arouse the other man's suspicions, he produced the precious key with an oily smile of apology, offering the lame excuse of having forgotten to give it to her. Without the safeguard of the locked door, Ivor's suggestion might have proved too true for comfort. Keeping her employer at arm's length would be a full-time job. Yet she could not seek support from

Aunty Bet for the problem, for her aunt considered Mr. Tegwyn Williams to be wholly beyond reproach.

Mair gazed into the fading dusk, wondering if Nico had returned, praying he was safe beside his own hearth. Tomorrow afternoon she would keep their rendezvous, though she would have to explain she could no longer meet him for their daily walk to Beddws Farm. She had been given one half day and three evenings off a week: the day she would spend at Maes-y-Groes, but the evenings she would keep for Nico.

The next morning when she went out to buy the day's provisions, Mair received a shock. The town was buzzing with news of a near riot yesterday at Moel Fach. The police had been called to put down the violence. Several arrests had been made.

With jumping heart she listened as she chose carrots and potatoes. The news she heard as she stood waiting at Jones the Meat to buy lamb chops for Mr. Williams's supper was even more grim. Talk there was that the ringleaders were to be sentenced, that influential labor leaders from Lancashire were already on their way to free their friends. No names had been mentioned, but in her despair, she was positive Nico was one of those imprisoned.

Mair hurried back to Brynteg. Mr. Williams had gone out. Unable to stand the suspense any longer, she pulled on Anna Castelli's shawl and slipped out the back door. Over the paddock she went, knowing no one would see her leaving by the back way. She hoped that when Mr. Williams returned he would think she was still out shopping.

So anxious was she for news of Nico's fate, Mair

ran part of the way to Maen Gwyn. Nervously she raised the shiny brass knocker on the front door of his home, hoping beyond hope it would be he who opened the door.

"Mair! Come in. Oh, your poor face!"

Mair was quickly enveloped in Anna Castelli's warm embrace. Nico's mother seemed so happy, surely there could be no bad news to relate. An unfamiliar male voice boomed out of the back room, speaking in rapid Italian. Anna beamed.

"You come just right time. Cousin Guido arrive today. He want to hear you sing. I knew he would."

"I brought back your shawl. Is Nico here?"

"Nico? Oh, he not back from his visit," Anna dismissed the subject quickly, pulling Mair with her, eager for her to meet the famous Cousin Guido.

Mair bit her lip. His mother did not know. In the excitement of her cousin's arrival, she must not have been out to the shops this morning. Should she tell her what she had heard, or wait until they knew the facts instead of repeating gossip?

"So. You're the golden angel. Bellisima!" thundered Guido, his arms outstretched in delight as he saw Mair. He pulled the shawl from her hair and gasping in admiration, gently took a handful of the curling mass in his huge hand.

All the while Anna was chatting excitedly in Italian, her face one huge beam. Mair stood there uncomfortably, not understanding a word they said and wondering whether she should go or stay.

Cousin Guido was splendidly dressed in a dark brown suit with narrow pinstripes and a large pink carnation in the wide lapel. Yellow spats covered his gleaming brown shoes. A bowler hat and heavy wool overcoat with an astrakhan collar lay across the chair. Several valises stood in the hallway.

While he spoke Cousin Guido waved an unlit cigar, a wide gold ring glinting on his stubby fingers. This big, expensively dressed stranger looked every inch the impressario. Mair was both nervous and impressed.

"I have only a few days. You sing for me now," he commanded, waving her toward the piano. "What pieces did you bring?"

"I . . . nothing. I haven't any music," she faltered uncomfortably.

"No music!" he thundered, his heavy brows meeting over his dark eyes. "How you intend to audition?"

"Not to worry. I play for her."

Anna Castelli patted Mair's arm, nudging her toward the piano, unveiled now in all its glory. Feeling miserable, Mair focused on a photograph in a silver frame that hung above the piano. Cousin Guido's manner had made her unusually tearful. So much depended on her singing well, yet to have to audition today of all days, when she held the secret knowledge of Nico's probable fate locked inside. . . . She looked at the picture of Nico with several young men, possibly his brothers, and a pretty, dark-haired woman. It was terrible to have to keep silent when at this moment he could be in jail; terrible to have to sing joyously when her heart was faint with worry.

"Come on, I've not all day to wait," thundered Guido, waving his cigar. "The stage is no place for timid mice."

Bracing her shoulders, Mair swallowed and moved closer. Anna had seated herself at the piano and she nodded for Mair to begin. The only music that came to her mind was the old Welsh hymn she had sung yesterday in chapel. Eyes closed, Mair began the familiar tune, a hymn she had sung since childhood and which had always brought her comfort.

Though the tune was unfamiliar to her, Anna Castelli began to pick out the notes until she was finally accompanying Mair's strong soprano. Her clear voice soared until its beauty filled the room. When Mair was finished she gradually became aware of a sea of faces crowding the doorway, of silent figures who suddenly came to life, applauding thunderously and shouting encouragement.

Guido appeared unimpressed. "What else you sing?" he asked, crossing and uncrossing his legs, admiring his shiny new shoes. "This is the theater, not a church."

Anna began to play the first notes of 'Addio del Passata' from *La Traviata*. Mair smiled in relief. She knew that piece and she nodded agreement, finding Anna's supportive smile comforting. Taking a fresh stance where she could see trees and gray sky instead of Cousin Guido's heavy, critical face, Mair began to sing. Concentrating, she recalled Mr. Crossley's explanation of Violetta's longing as she sang the Italian phonetically, trying to phrase the aria as she had been taught.

When Mair had finished, there was silence. Her heart turned over. It had not been good enough. They did not like it. Then suddenly she noticed large tears rolling down Anna Castelli's cheeks, at odds with her rapturous smile.

"Was that good enough?" Mair asked tentatively,

glancing round at her audience. "I know some other pieces."

"Sung like an angel. Such a voice!"

Mair smiled in pleasure at Nico's father who had come inside the room, speaking in English for her benefit.

"Promising," Cousin Guido allowed, nodding his large head. "Let me hear some more, some Donizetti. Anna, a piece from *Lucia*."

"Ah, yes—she's born to sing Lucia."

Triumphantly, Anna fluttered a sheet of music.

Mair took the music from her and her face broke into a smile. Lucia's aria beside the fountain from Act One. Mr. Crossley had prepared her in this. Nodding confidently, she leaned forward and showed Anna where to begin.

Again everyone listened enthralled. When she had finished, her silvery voice echoing about the small room, the listeners clapped and shouted *bravo* so loudly that Mair blushed with pleasure. It was all so wonderful, so unexpected. Then she noticed Nico's picture afresh and her heart plummeted. She had already decided to say nothing, not wanting to spoil the mood they had created.

"Am I good enough to sing in the opera?" she asked Cousin Guido, her confidence restored.

He pursed his thick lips and considered her solemnly. "There's far more to singing in the opera than a few pretty arias."

"I understand that. But without a voice to start with there's no hope of appearing on the opera stage. Have I such a voice?"

He stared at her a moment, then his heavy face broke into a smile. "You have indeed."

Patricia Phillips

Mair gasped, clasping her hands in delight. Her eyes shone. "Oh, do you mean that! You really think I sing well enough for the opera?"

"With that voice you could sing on any opera stage in the world—after some training, of course. You're still very young and you don't know the first thing about the stage. But, yes, I think you have potential."

"Oh Mair, that's what you've waited to hear," cried Anna, clasping her in her arms and hugging her tight. "You will be famous. You have the look of destiny. Someday we'll pay much money to hear her sing, eh, Guido?"

"You could be right, Anna."

"Will you teach me how? I want to sing in the opera more than anything in the world. Can I sing in your opera company?" Mair wanted to know, sitting beside him and looking most appealing. Her delight had finally overcome her awe of this great impressario.

"She's good enough. Won't you give her a place?"

"We're a full company, Anna." He watched Mair's face fall. "Still, perhaps I can find a place for such a promising voice. I'll speak to your parents."

"Oh, no, no, you can't do that," Mair dismissed the idea in horror. That would sound the death knell on any operatic career. "Can't you teach me here?"

"Here, in a few days' time? Don't be ridiculous! I can't languish here in this dirty coal town. London's the home of the opera. London, Paris, Milan—you'll have to be more ambitious than this."

82

"Well, my family don't approve of the stage. And I haven't any money for travel. Later, when I've saved some wages, I thought, perhaps . . ."

"No, if you're not prepared to dedicate yourself to your art, you're no use to me."

Tears stung Mair's eyes. Raising her head and blinking rapidly, she said with dignity, "I'm prepared to work hard, but I can't go to London just yet. I'll need more time to arrange matters."

"Ah, you have plenty time." Guido smiled and patted her arm. "I'll be here all week."

"That's only a few days, that's not enough."

"Surely that's long enough for an ambitious young lady like yourself."

Tiring of the discussion, Guido got up and went toward the scullery in search of refreshment. Mair stood there, her hands shaking. It was all so sudden. And to have happened today, of all days! Now she had thrown away her chance of singing in the opera.

"Forgive Guido. He's so impatient," Anna said with a sympathetic smile. "Let me talk to him, see what I can do."

Mair was preparing to leave when she saw a group of men coming along the street. With a cry of delight she ran to open the door. The sight of Nico as he walked up the path made her gasp. His face was swollen, his eye blacked; one of his hands was swathed in bandages. Several of the other men were bandaged also.

"Mair, what are you doing here?" he cried in surprise, as she ran to meet him. Forgetting the others in her joy and relief, she fell into his arms. Nico gave her a quick clasp of friendship, no more.

At first Mair was annoyed and disappointed, but when she turned and met his mother's gaze, she was glad. Anna Castelli's eyes had narrowed menacingly, the welcoming smile Mair was used to seeing swiftly replaced by hostility. Mair remembered what Nico had said about his family planning his future. Anna would never sanction anything more than friendship between them. Already her sharp eyes detected something that put her on guard.

Everyone began to speak at once in Italian, clamoring for news and explanations. Anna's voice rose above the others, exclaiming in dismay over her son's wounds. The others crowded around the newcomers, until Mair could not see Nico for a sea of relatives. She felt shut out and forgotten in the excitement.

Mair backed away until she stood alone beside the road. She felt very forlorn. Just before the men went inside the house, Nico turned, looking for her. He mouthed "Meet me later," before he disappeared in the press of people.

Left alone on the deserted road, Mair felt rejected. Tears pricked her eyes as she turned about and began to walk rapidly toward Brynteg. Hot tears rolled down her cheeks and splashed on her dress. The hostility she had seen in Anna's face had wounded her to the quick. And she remembered Nico's warning that his family would not approve of their friendship.

Who was that young woman in the silver-framed picture? Nico had no sisters. Was the pretty girl who stood smiling up at him in the picture a suitably convent-reared Italian girl, already chosen to be his wife? The acknowledgment was so painful, it robbed her of breath. In all her hopes and dreams, her prayers, she had never considered such a possibility. Anna Castelli's changing expression was a warning. It was as if the door of friendship to the Castelli home had been slammed in her face.

Chapter Six

Mair had waited a long time, and finally her heart sank as she decided he was not coming. She was about to go back to Brynteg, but first played the childhood game of counting to fifty. By then, if he still had not come, she would leave.

"Nico," she gasped as she saw him sprinting along the tree-shaded road behind the chapel. Suddenly she was in his arms, careless of who might be watching. He did not chastise her, merely squeezed her against his chest before setting her aside.

"Sorry I'm late. It was hard to get away," he said, propelling her briskly along the cinder track. Instead of going along the main path, he led her toward a narrow footpath beaten along the edge of the farm pasture. Here they were sheltered by the blackthorn hedge, safe from prying eyes.

"I was so worried about you. Oh, Nico, they said the police came and arrested people. I was sure you were in jail. And you're hurt. Oh, tell me what happened."

"There were some arrests and violence. No more than we expected. I'm all right. Just a few cuts and bruises. You mustn't worry so—this won't be the first time, silly girl. We're fighting a battle of sorts. We have to expect opposition. Anyway, we've made a big dent in the management's armor. They're prepared to discuss matters with representatives of the miner's union. We did it, Mair! We finally did it!"

Her eyes shone with triumph. A grin of achievement lit his face. After fighting Heath Owen and now this second bruising, Nico reminded her of one of the contestants in the bare-knuckled fights on which the local miners betted.

"But to take such a beating—oh, Nico, it's too dangerous! Are you always going to look like you ran into a brick wall?" she asked, masking her fear with humor.

"Possibly. Don't you love me when I'm not pretty?" he asked jokingly.

Mair swallowed, taken back by his question. They had never exchanged mutual vows of love. But she did love him, more than she could have thought possible. And he knew. Or why would he have asked such a thing?

"Love . . ." she faltered weakly, "who said I loved you?"

His face tightened. "It was just an expression, that's all."

"No it wasn't."

He stopped on the path, looking down at her. His fingers bit into her upper arms so hard, she was sure they were bruised.

"Mair, don't."

"Don't what?"

"Don't make things any harder between us."

"Are they hard?"

"You know they are."

"I thought you didn't care what my Da or Aunty Bet felt about you."

"I don't."

"Well then?"

"It's Mama. She spoke to me about you. We'll have to be more careful."

Mair's deep emotion quickly flared into anger. Eyes flashing, she pulled her arm free. "How's that? Doesn't she fancy me, then? Fine enough until she thinks I've got designs on her wonderful son."

"It's not that. You just don't understand."

"Then make me understand."

Nico groaned as he gripped her shoulders, swinging her around. "I told you my family had my future planned. In Italy it's the custom to make arrangements between sons and daughters when they're only children."

A cold wave gripped her heart and spread slowly through her body. "That girl in the picture . . . is she your sweetheart?"

"Teresa Gambino's their choice for me. In Italy our families are very close. Their land adjoins, they are business partners. It's just expected."

"But you're not actually engaged to her?"

"No."

88

Mair began to smile, the chill lessening by degrees.

"Well then, tell them now that you're older you've changed your mind. Or . . . do you love her?"

He shook his head. "No, I barely know her. I've only seen her twice in the past five years. Since they went to London her family have become quite well off. Teresa's pretty, sweet, good, and—Mama's prime requisite of course—she's virginal, chaste and holy."

"I'm virginal," Mair blurted, "why won't I do?"

"Oh, Mair," he groaned, pulling her into his arms. "Sweetheart, don't. You're not Italian, you're not Catholic—those are reasons enough. This doesn't mean we can't see each other. All it means is we have to be more careful."

She buried her face in his coat, finding the tweed rough against her skin. The beat of his heart was comfortingly audible beneath the fabric. Really, she thought, all it meant was they would have to meet further along the track, they wouldn't be able to be more than the most casual of friends in front of others. Maybe it wouldn't be so hard.

"Mair," he breathed, his mouth against her hair. "You do, don't you, sweetheart?"

"Do what?"

"Love me."

She hesitated. It was foolish of a girl to tell a man she loved him before he had made the first declaration. It wasn't done. Pride should step in and speak for her.

"Yes," she whispered, weakly capitulating. "From the first time I saw you I've loved you."

"Oh, darling," he breathed, holding her so tight she had to fight for breath. "I was afraid you wouldn't say yes. Oh, Mair, I love you so much, the thought of leaving is terrible."

"Leaving?"

"Going back to London. I told you, remember?"

"Oh, aye. I remember."

They stood there saying nothing, just holding each other. It was like that other time on the mountain when time stood still. Mair closed her eyes and willed everything to stop, drinking in the smell of wet grass, the bleat of distant sheep—and the comforting thud of his heart.

His hands moved over her back, caressing, spreading warmth in a weakening flood. Finally Mair raised her head and looked up at his strong throat pulsing beneath his smooth olive skin, the heated comfort disappearing inside his collar. She laid her face against his neck, shuddering at the warm pleasure it gave her. Tentatively her tongue traced the saltiness of his skin, revelling in the taste of him, breathing deep of his distinctive, arousing scent. Her mouth moved upward of its own accord, seeking his lips.

Nico kissed her, his firm mouth hot on her own, drawing the utmost emotional response. Mair felt the earth going out from under her, felt her knees turned to liquid. In that kiss their souls fused. She had never expected such emotion from the mere touching of mouths.

Softly his lips caressed her closed eyes and he tasted the salt of tears. His heart leaped at the discovery of her deep emotion for him. Somehow they had sunk to the soft trampled grass, spring-fresh and tender as their love.

Surprised, but not afraid, Mair realized they lay side by side on the ground behind the hedge, sheltered and protected from wind and passers-by. She was wise enough to know the danger of such close proximity with him—to know and disregard. Intoxicated by his nearness, by the unaccustomed warm scent of his body, she felt incapable of action, drifting blissfully into an unknown world of sensations both sweet and alien.

"Will you always love me, little Mair?"

"Always, always," she breathed against his face, thrilling to the hard hot pressure of his muscular body against her own.

"I've never felt this way about another woman, never loved anyone like I love you."

His vow was music to her ears. The throbbing of her veins shook her body, making her feel hot, melting. A curious trembling was coursing through his body; Mair could feel the tremors beneath her hands. She trailed her fingers inside the open vee at his neck, touching his hot smooth skin, wondering at its fine texture and golden, unblemished beauty.

Nico cupped her face in his hands, covering her with tiny warm kisses. Mair was quickly aroused, finding this sensation different from the one produced by hard kisses of passion, yet equally as pleasurable. The tension in his body was conveyed by the steel hardness of his legs pressing against hers. As if from a great distance the knowledge of the source of that other hardness driving into her thighs came to her. Stark reality pierced her pleasure. All along she had understood the danger of allowing him too much liberty with her body. Yet even as this fresh reminder entered her mind, she found her own thighs straining against his, aching to feel the intimate contours of his body. Mair knew such feelings were wicked. And she did not care.

"You're so lovely, Mair." He smiled down at her, his shadowed eyes black as night. "Mair of the golden hair. It must have been lovely girls like you who inspired all those old legends."

She smiled in pleasure at his nonsense.

"And some of them must have been about men like you who'd taunt a poor girl past redemption," she countered with a breathless laugh. "Now stop. We must stop."

He smiled lazily and shook his head. "You don't really want me to stop, do you?"

"No," she admitted honestly, "but I don't always do what I want."

"I'd hoped today you'd do what I want."

A throbbing silence lay between them. Nico did not try to press his advantage, wanting her to come to him of her own accord. His hand rested lightly mere inches from her breast. The knowledge made Mair shake with anticipation.

"I'm afraid of doing that," she confided shyly, glancing away.

He moved from her, taking away the burning, tantalizing pressure. Lazily he stroked her face, forcing himself to be patient. "I don't want you to be afraid of me, Mair. You know I won't ever hurt you. You can trust me."

"I know."

"When you're ready to make love with me . . ."

"Oh, Nico, I want to now, but I can't." She pushed against his chest when, thinking she acquiesced, he eagerly moved forward. It was so hard to

92

say no to him when she was on fire from head to toe, when her stomach was tied in knots and her legs shook.

A sudden shrill whistle from beyond the hedge brought them jacknifing up. They stood shaking, adjusting their rumpled clothing, brushing back hair, setting things to rights. The sound of scuffling in the undergrowth followed by a shrill bark betrayed a passing dog and its owner on the other side of the hedge. They stood very still, hardly daring to breathe, trusting their dark clothing was not visible through the blackthorn. To their relief the steps continued along the track, the dog's excited yips growing fainter.

Silently Nico cursed the intrusion, while silently Mair blessed it. She had come so close to yielding to him. Had he persuaded just a little longer, had her willpower weakened a little more—a shudder went over her.

He laughed. "Cold?" he asked, slipping his arm protectively around her.

"A little. I'd best be getting back. Mr. Williams will be expecting his supper. I can't see you again till day after tomorrow."

"Mair," he drew her close, his arms encircling her slim body. "We might have to say goodbye then. Within the next few days my orders will come. Our work here is done for the moment."

No longer did she question these mysterious orders, nor did she really want to know what new danger he faced. She had resigned herself to accepting Nico's strange way of life. There was no denying the crusading fervor that blazed within his breast.

"Why must it always be so sudden? All right . . .

all right," she smiled when he frowned, preparing to explain. "Promise to write to me when you get to London. And promise to love me still when you're far away."

He took her chill hands, pressing them against his hot mouth. "I'll love you as long as I live, Mair Parry. And even beyond the—"

"No." Quickly she laid her fingers against his mouth, too superstitious to listen to that vow. "That's good enough for any girl."

Her smile was so sweet and full of love that he groaned.

"You're so much better than I deserve. Oh Mair, knowing you love me makes me more determined than ever to make a difference in this dirty, unfair old place. Just wait and see. You'll inspire me to great things."

She smiled and nodded, not really believing those words. But he did and that was all that mattered. They kissed again deeply, standing swaying slightly in each other's arms. The dangerous acceleration of mutual passion forced Nico to put her aside.

"Come on, dutiful housekeeper," he rasped, his voice harsh, "that old windbag will be shouting for his supper."

They walked back along the path, stepping out cautiously onto the cinder track. Fortunately, all was deserted. After a whispered goodbye, Mair hurried toward the chapel.

When she turned around she saw Nico standing watching her. He waved and she returned his wave, her heart pitching afresh at the sight of him, at the reminder of their heated passion for each other.

She had never expected to feel all hot and trembling, desperately wanting to reject all the restraints she had been taught a decent girl should observe. Maybe she wasn't a decent girl. Maybe she was wicked like those tip girls Aunty Bet was always lecturing her about.

Mair paused, her hand on Brynteg's iron gate. In all her life she had never met a man who had made her more willing to be wicked.

Was it only her imagination that Mr. Williams was looking differently at her, Mair wondered? He had lavishly praised his supper, praised her singing when they spent an hour going over the hymns for Sunday chapel. Yet, despite his apparent good mood, there seemed to be an undercurrent of tension building. As usual he managed to touch her in passing, but she had grown adept at sidestepping him. Proper old lecher, he was.

Though at first Mair had wondered if she would find the need to avoid her employer's advances a burden, it had become almost a game. She discovered she was more than a match for him. Mr. Tegwyn Williams was careful not to make his advances too obvious. Couldn't publicly advertise the fact he was a true hypocrite by supposedly taking her into his house out of the good of his heart, then trying to force himself on her, now could he?

Moonlight splashed her small room with silver. Everything looked so lovely, the silent garden a mysterious place of silver-tipped shadows. Such a fierce ache of longing for Nico spread through Mair's body she was shocked. If only she could have walked in the moonlight with him. He would hold her close and kiss her tenderly . . . heat flushed her cheeks. She had properly fixed it this afternoon. There'd not be much kissing and innocent hand-holding now. In a way she was glad, for his passion was contagious. When Nico wanted to make love to her she had felt so excited, she became a different person. Mair Parry had never experienced such deep emotions before.

If only she could have talked to someone about the frightening changes she felt when he was near. The stifling racing heart, the weakness in her legs, the unnameable longing that wracked her body with actual physical pain. There was Nico of course, but telling him how excited he made her feel would be like setting the fox to guard the hens. Could she have even confided those feelings to Mam? That was a foolish question—Mam was dead. Now all she had left to talk to was Aunty Bet, who would be scandalized to learn her niece had such thoughts, let alone had allowed a man sinful caresses out of marriage.

Mair turned over on her narrow bed, thumping about, trying to get comfortable. Not only was she worried about the deepening of her emotions for Nico, but there was Cousin Guido's tempting offer to consider. Next time she met Nico she would discuss her operatic future with him. Tonight there had not been time, everything had happened so quickly that she'd been swept off her feet. Nico would know the wisdom of accepting the proposal. Yet aware of Nico's skepticism about his mother's cousin, Mair suspected she already knew his answer. Apart from the wonderful opportunity to sing, if she went to London, she and Nico could meet. When she had become a real singer, he would be proud of her. Then she'd be able to dress to impress him, no serviceable navy serge and heavy boots, but fine silks and satins all embroidered and flounced. Her eyes shone at the thought.

When she became a famous singer and he became an influential politician, they would ride together in a carriage drawn by sleek horses. They would dine at London's fabulous restaurants and visit rich, elegant people! Mair clasped her hands in delight, thrilled by that mental image. Gradually she began to relax, sinking into the flock mattress. A smile lifted the corners of her mouth as she took a dream journey through the magical city of London with handsome Nico at her side.

Chapter Seven

Mair thought the hours till evening would never pass.
Mr. Williams had gone out to visit a dying parish-
ioner, so she had left him a cold plate for his
supper. Not having to cook a meal gave her more
time to prepare for her evening rendezvous. She
washed and brushed her hair till it shone like spun
gold. Mair would have only a few hours with Nico
at best, but maybe old John Jones would last the
night, keeping Mr. Williams too busy to notice how
late she came home.

The evening was mild, with a fresh breeze blowing from the mountain. A row of daffodils nodded
beside the driveway and a clump of frilly pink
tulips encircled the marble bird bath. Brynteg's
grounds were lovely. Mair knew how lucky she had
been to have found this job. Wouldn't it be perfect
if she could have invited Nico to the house instead
of having to meet him on the mountain? Though

Mr. Williams was out for the evening, it was a chance she dare not take.

Tonight Mair walked further along the track, far beyond the usual meeting place. Funny, just this morning Mr. Williams had asked her how she enjoyed her evening walks. That question had taken her back a bit. Still, there was no law against walking up Pentre Fawr. Very nice indeed, she had said, quickly, not letting him see how much he had surprised her with his knowledge.

Nico was waiting by the stile. At her approach he came onto the road and they ran the last few feet, meeting in a joyous embrace. He swung her off her feet, laughing in delight at being with her again.

"Oh, how long it's been since I've seen you," she gasped as he set her down on the track.

"An eternity. Mair, sweetheart, you're even lovelier than I remembered."

"No, you're just saying that," she protested as he hugged her again. The remembered scent of his body, the heat, the pleasure, all came flooding back in a weakening wave.

Slowly they walked hand in hand along the track, drinking in the peaceful beauty of the mountain. Overhead, homebound birds wheeled and called; distant cattle lowed. Closer at hand in the nearby pastures ewes answered the bleat of their new spring lambs. The roadside grass was starred blue and yellow with wildflowers and the tall blackthorn hedges frothed with white blossoms, petals falling underfoot.

Mair spoke about such ordinary things, about Mr. Williams's vigil at John Jones's cottage, about the cold supper waiting for him. Nico played the same game, discussing his father's latest masonry project and their neighbors' new baby. Anything to keep the meeting light. Soon Mair began to dread the slackening of this stream of idle conversation, anticipating the confirmation of her worst fears. Somehow she knew this would be the night of parting. Nico's face became grave, belying the lightness of his subject; his handclasp was tight; his kisses urgent.

Finally, unable to stand the suspense any longer, she blurted, "Well, out with it. When are you going back to London?"

His jaw tightened. "Tomorrow," he said, clearing his throat. "Someone's coming for me early in the morning. Oh, Mair, how I wish we had more time. Everything's happened so quickly, there wasn't enough time for us . . . not for a minute did I expect to fall in love with someone from Llandare."

"Fancied those women in London more, did you?"

"No! There's no one there like you, sweetheart."

"I don't doubt that. For a start they wouldn't be wearing these mended clothes and patched boots."

He stopped on the track and his smile was sad. "Mair, you really don't know much about London. Everyone round here thinks Londoners are rich. That's very far from true. The men I represent are casual dock laborers, lucky to get eighteen shillings a week to feed their families. They've no rights, no voice. That's what I'm fighting to change. To them you'd look like a princess, patched clothes and all."

"Really?" Mair was pleasantly surprised. That was one hurdle out of the way. She had considered her clothing to be so poor and provincial there was no way she could have worn it to travel to London.

"Anyway, love, let's not talk about London tonight. For just a little while let's forget it even exists. Let's talk about us."

"After you're gone there's not going to be any *us* to talk about."

"We can write. Surely you can receive letters. I promise to visit when I'm able. London's not that far away."

It was Mair's turn to smile sadly. As far as she was concerned, London might well have been another continent.

"Nico I talked to your mother's cousin about singing in the opera."

"He heard you sing? What did he think?"

Her eyes shone. Stopping in the middle of the track, she clasped her hands nervously as she spoke. "He thinks I'm good enough to sing opera. He says he might be able to find a place for me in his company."

"His company," Nico repeated scornfully. "And what did you say to that?"

"Well, I had to say I'd think about it. London's a long way off. I've no money to go now."

"Good. You mustn't go yet. I don't trust Cousin Guido. There's something fishy about his success, nothing I can quite put my finger on, but something that doesn't add up. Oh, he's well dressed, so he must make money somehow. But I don't think it comes from a grand opera company. I'd have heard about it by now if his tales were true."

"I knew you'd say that. This is my first big chance to sing on the stage, to be someone."

"You're already someone. You're Mair Parry and

I love you for what you are, not for some dream of what you might become. You're far better off staying here."

"Here, in Llandare? Stuck here for the rest of my life?"

"You've a job here. You said yourself you're lucky to be working at Brynteg. You don't have to live in Maes-y-Groes anymore. For the moment you couldn't do better."

"That's easy for you to say—you already live in London."

"Give me a chance to find out more about this opera company. You know, he's never once given us a return address. In fact, he's never told us where the theater is. Have you noticed how evasive he becomes when the subject's brought up? I know London's a huge city, but after all, a theater and an opera company aren't the sort of things you hide in an alley. Mair, he could be a fraud."

"I never asked him where the theater is. It didn't seem necessary. Listen, Nico, your mother played two opera arias for me. Everyone clapped and cheered—it was wonderful! Oh, this is the chance I've been waiting for. He actually believes I have talent."

"I don't want to hear any more about Cousin Guido, damn it!"

"Are you jealous because your mother thinks he's so wonderful? You are, aren't you?"

"Maybe I am," Nico dismissed angrily, then grew remorseful when he saw tears glittering in her eyes. "He's a wonderful fellow. All right? Now, enough of Cousin Guido and his offer. Oh, Mair, love, it's already dusk. You'll have to be in soon and

God knows how long it'll be before we see each other."

She blinked rapidly, still upset by his angry words. Nico's hands bit into her shoulders as he pulled her about and drew her against him. His hot mouth covered hers.

"Just tell me how much you love me. Don't waste precious time, Mair. Mair . . . I love you so."

The tension in his body made him feel hard, unyielding, his muscular frame bruising her soft limbs. Yet, at the same time, Mair found the urgency in his voice, his barely contained emotion, exciting beyond measure.

They leaned against the barred gate to the pasture, braced against the weathered wood. Nico pulled Mair against him, sliding down until she was molded against him so intimately, she could not control her own shudders of passion. His hands moved over her back, his breathing growing shallow. Mair knew she had already betrayed herself, that if she did not stop him now there would be no stopping.

"How much do you love me?" she asked, playing for time. She rocked against him, thrilling to the heated, driving force of his passion. "Enough that you won't be giving the eye to all those London girls?"

"More than enough."

"And I bet they're not virginal, chaste and holy."

"I'm sure they're not."

"What does your Mama say about them?"

"She doesn't even know about them. To her I'm still virginal, chaste and holy myself."

Mair grinned at his admission. "Ah, but I know

differently. I bet you haven't been virginal since you were . . . how old?''

"Fourteen. That's got nothing to do with it, you silly girl. Are you going to talk all night?''

"No.''

"What are you going to do?''

At first Mair did not answer, trying to stop her trembling, to quench the hot flood that swept her to damnation. She licked her lips, then touched his nose and cheek with the tip of her tongue. To her delight he shuddered at the feather-light touch. Mair moved next to the back of his neck, slipping her hands into his thick, curly hair. It was so springy and smooth, it reminded her of an animal's pelt. She tipped up his cap, nudging it until it fell on the ground.

The light was fading rapidly and she could barely distinguish his features. His face was all black angles and planes. As he turned his head, his dark eyes glittered. With a sob of pleasure she sought the soft heat of his mouth, reveling in the taste and the feel.

"What would you like me to do?'' she whispered at last, her lips against his.

He groaned by way of answer, burying his face in her scented neck. The heat of his flesh increased the fire blazing in her veins. Mair shuddered as he slid his hand over the prominence of her breast, softly fondling, tracing the erect nipple with his thumb. No man had ever touched her breasts before. She was ill prepared for the surge of heat that spread between her thighs. She could feel the burning high inside her belly, until she thought she was melting. To Mair's surprise she found he had opened her bodice and he slid his hot fingers inside the fabric. When he touched her breasts, Mair gasped aloud. Nico cupped the fullness of her breasts, hot fingers stroking the satin smooth skin while he murmured extravagant praise and endearments. Then he lowered his head and she gasped again as his tongue moved around her nipple, sending waves of delight to the very core of her body.

"Oh, Mair, I want you so. Let me love you tonight. Don't turn me down, not tonight," he whispered, his words barely audible. His mouth met hers, his tongue parting her lips, invading her mouth. Clutching him for support, Mair was barely able to stand.

"Say yes to me, Mair . . . love me, love me."

All the time his soft husky voice tempted, until Mair could no longer stand against it, until she whispered assent, tormented with longing.

"Oh, yes, yes."

"Mair, oh sweetheart," his words were almost a sob of joy as he pressed her close, showering her face with kisses.

The light was gone, but it was still not full dark. She could barely see his face, his jaw tense, his expression grim, as he unlatched the gate and swung it inwards. The creak of the gate jarred Mair back to the present, returning a little of her sanity. She grasped his arm, hesitating, knowing she should say no. Nico was so handsome, fascinatingly different from anyone she had ever known before. His face was a dark shadow, his pronounced features unyielding as granite.

Sensing her withdrawal, Nico drew Mair gently

toward him, enfolding her in his arms and kissing her tenderly.

"Don't be afraid, little Mair," he whispered huskily, "I want you to have pleasure too. Trust me, sweetheart, you're all I'll ever want or need."

The passionate throb of his voice lulled her, the heated softness of his mouth, drew her out. Mair barely noticed the deepening of his kisses, the tightening of his embrace. Gently he laid her down where the ground was mossy and soft. Mair discovered her bodice gaped open only when she felt the chill night air on her breasts. Nico lay beside her, a warm arousing presence in the soft spring darkness. His mouth sought her nipple. Tracing his tongue around that throbbing point, he aroused her until she began to strain toward him, unable to withstand the torment of passion.

When Nico finally pressed her deep into the springy ground, his weight was a joyous punishment, increasing the heavy sensation of her own limbs, fanning the fires of unfulfilled desire. She slid her hands inside his coat, fumbling with his shirt buttons. When she touched his hot chest, she shuddered in pleasure. Tangling her fingers in his crisp curling hair, touching his nipples, she was surprised when he gasped aloud at her intimate caresses.

More aroused now and unwilling to delay, Nico unfastened his clothing. He pressed her hand down. Mair gasped as she encountered the fiery brand pulsating against her fingers. Deep shudders wracked her body, but they were not out of fear, these intense shudders were of pure delight. She had always feared the mysterious change that happened to a man's body; not once had she anticipated such joy with the discovery. The furnace of her own body blazed white hot, but not as hot as the proof of his passion for her. Now, at last, she longed to take Nico deep inside her. Tonight she would finally belong to him.

Nico pushed aside her heavy skirts. His hot mouth traced a fiery passage along her inner thighs where the skin was satin smooth. Even in the dusk her flesh gleamed white; beautiful white breasts heavy and full, silky firm thighs and long, finely shaped legs. Nico shuddered again for the pleasure her body gave him and for the knowledge that she loved him and was about to give herself to him.

"Mair, you're so beautiful, even lovelier than I dreamed," he breathed passionately as he lay against her. The heat of his arousal forced against the constriction of her maidenhead. Now their mouths seared together. Her arms went around him, her legs strained against his. Mair finally opened to receive him, trying to relax, trying to maintain her ardor through this discomfort as the resistance was met—and vanquished.

Nico covered her mouth with his own, swallowed her sharp gasp of pain, lying still until she no longer resisted, stroking slowly, whispering tenderly, kissing her, until she was finally ready. Mair strained to meet him, fondling his back, his neck, running her fingers up into his hair.

The world swam into deep velvet blackness. Tears on her cheeks were swiftly transferred to his, their kisses salt-tinged. Then Nico moved, slowly, rhythmically, the heated pressure inside her beginning to recapture the joy of passion. Mair gasped as that heat accelerated, not knowing why she felt as if she was about to lose control, not understanding the sweeping change her body experienced. Fear of the unknown made her gasp, but Nico quickly swept away any reluctance, carrying her up on a tide of emotion which knew no bounds. Mair was dimly aware of his whispered endearments, of his hot mouth drinking from her own. Fire was ignited deep inside her, jangling all the nerve endings of her body. Now she was losing all identity, becoming one with him in the molten joy of passion. Then, unable to hold on any longer, that clenching, shuddering climax to all her striving overtook her. Mair cried out in delight, clinging to him, not wanting the pleasure to stop. Nothing or no one existed beyond this dark sweep of passion that carried them both to the edge of consciousness.

For a long time they lay together, still shuddering slightly, clinging to each other, seeking comfort for the shattering emotion they had shared. From now on they belonged to each other, hearts, minds and bodies fused on the white-hot altar of passion.

Chapter Eight

It was very late when Mair let herself inside Brynteg. All was in darkness. As she crept past Mr. Williams's door, she saw it stood ajar. Peering inside the room she satisfied herself that he had not come home. The moonlit bed lay smooth and undisturbed. Now he would be none the wiser that she had stayed out past her allotted time. Had it been necessary, she would have made some excuse. She could not bear to think of his reaction had he actually known what she was doing till this hour, him being such a pillar of the chapel.

Though it was long past midnight, Mair could not sleep. Her body throbbed with the glowing aftermath of Nico's lovemaking. In her saner moments she found the realization of what she had done most sobering. And she fervently prayed no unwanted pregnancy would result from her experience. Smiling, Mair pushed aside those unpleasant thoughts as she mentally relived each touch and endearment, marveling for the hundredth time at the all-consuming force of their passion. No wonder Auntie Bet had always preached loud and long against that specific sin. Let girls even suspect how lovely it could be, and there'd be no stopping them. Yet again, perhaps not everyone enjoyed lovemaking as she did. Why else would women consider it something to be suffered in silence? Must be that she was bad after all. Good girls merely did their duty to their husbands, whereas bad girls were the only ones who found pleasure in such things, according to Auntie Bet.

Mair's heart fluttered uneasily as she recalled how those lectures had always included a list of the dire consequences of a woman's fall from grace. But she mustn't keep worrying about all that. Such grim predictions spoiled the wonder of her love. If the worst did happen, Nico would take care of her. He had sworn he loved her. Hadn't he shown his love for her in every word and touch?

Sometime later a loud thumping downstairs roused her from sleep. Fear shot through her. Was it burglars? Then, as more thumping sounded, followed by the sharp rat-tat of the doorknocker, Mair laughed at her own foolishness. It would be a funny burglar who knocked to announce his presence. Must be old Mr. Williams gone out without his key. What was the time? Surely it must be close to morning.

Mair pulled her shawl around her to cover her nightgown and hurriedly slipped her feet inside her cold boots. All the while someone kept pounding on the door. Lucky there weren't any close neighbors or they'd all be out of bed by now.

At last she unfastened the front door, drawing back as Mr. Williams rushed inside, nearly pushing her over in his haste.

"Where were you, girl? Anyone'd think you were dead, the racket I had to make," he grumbled, pulling off his coat and draping it haphazardly over the hallstand.

"Sorry for being so slow, Mr. Williams. I was asleep, you see, and my room being in the back of the house, it took me a while to hear you. Besides, I'd expected you to have your key."

Sourly he regarded her, unusually careful to keep his distance. When he stumbled against the bottom stair, Mair knew why. Old holy Tegwyn Williams had been at the bottle! It was such a surprise, in fact, she wondered her mouth had not hung open at the realization. 'Never a drop of alcohol should pass the lips of a sincere chapel goer,' had been his very words, to which Da had taken such exception on the only occasion Mr. Williams had visited them in Maes-y-Groes. Now here he was coming in at—she glanced at the hall clock, bathed in moonlight—four in the morning! And tipsy to boot!

"Had a good evening, did you, Mr. Williams? And how's poor old John Jones?"

Mr. Williams leaned against the bannister as she stepped on the first tread. "He passed on, Mair, soon after midnight. God rest his soul."

"Amen," she replied automatically. She stood on a level with him now and by the light of the candle she held, she was amazed to see tears

111

glistening on his fat cheeks. An unexpected wave of pity gripped her. He must have really liked old John Jones, after all. This mustn't have been just another pious duty in attending the dying.

"Now, don't take on so, Mr. Williams," she said softly, patting his arm as she passed. "Old John Jones led a long and good life. You go on up to bed and get some rest."

He nodded assent and sniffled loudly as she moved ahead of him up the stair. Couldn't be beer, rum, or whiskey, he'd been at, she would have smelled that. Must be gin. One of Miss Jenkins's guests was very partial to his gin bottle, taking it in the belief gin would not be detected on the breath.

Mr. Williams paused before his door and asked plaintively, "Would you make me a cup of tea, Mair? There's a good girl. I'm feeling chilled. I know it's late, but I have a fancy for some tea and a couple of slices of *bara brith*."

Mair agreed with a good grace, though she would have preferred to go back to bed. In the chilly dark kitchen she brewed tea and sliced and buttered the fruit bread.

When she knocked on his door, Mr. Williams bade her come in. Mair found him slumped beside the hearth. He had thrown a match into the ready laid fire, and meagre flames licked the coals.

"You're a good girl, Mair. Come, sit down and share with me."

"Thank you, Mr. Williams, but if it's all the same to you, I'd rather go back to bed. I only brought one cup."

He smiled lopsidedly. "We can always share."

Mair smiled in reply as she backed toward the door.

112

"Better get some sleep," she advised cheerfully, "you'll likely have a bad head in the morning."

Alerted by her words, his head snapped up. "You're talking in riddles, you silly girl. Why should I have a bad head? I've never had a bad head in my life."

"Yes sir, anything you say."

Mair had barely closed the door behind her before he wrenched it open.

"Come back here. I'm not finished with you yet."

She sighed. He was going to be difficult. The drink did that to some men. Hadn't she had to put up with Da's cantankerous behavior all her life? Obediently Mair stepped back inside the room.

"You surely aren't suggesting I've been drinking."

She met his gaze. His small beady eyes looked like black currants in the glow from the purple-shaded lamp.

"Your secret's safe with me. I promise not to tell a soul. With the upset of John Jones's passing and all, I understand. Surely, I of all people, can attest to the fact you're not a drinking man."

"That's right. And don't you forget it," he cried belligerently, his heavy jowls set. "Of all the ridiculous suggestions for you to make."

Stung by the injustice of his words, she added unwisely, "On the other hand, Mr. Williams, I'm not blind. Nor is there anything wrong with my sense of smell. You forget you're talking to Robert Parry's daughter. But, as I said, I'll keep your secret."

His face blanched. Several times his mouth opened and closed as he considered trying to bluster his way out of the situation. A decidedly nasty expression settled on his face and Mair took a defensive step backwards.

"Good at keeping secrets, are you?"

"Yes, if I want to, I am."

"Keep a few of your own now and again, don't you?"

"Not sure what you're talking about, Mr. Williams, but I don't intend standing here all night playing twenty questions. Good night."

"No you don't," he bellowed, surprising her by his agility as he leaped from his chair and seized her arm. Mr. Williams banged the door closed behind him and smiling slyly, turned the key in the lock. "Now, you won't be going anywhere for a while, will you, Mair?" He put the key in his trouser pocket.

Mair gasped at his audacity, color rising in her face. "Now look here, Mr. Williams, this has gone far enough. Open the door and let me go to my room."

He waved her toward the chair on the opposite side of the hearth. "Might as well sit down and make yourself comfortable."

"The only comfortable I want to be is in my own bed. If you don't want the whole town to know about your little pats and pinches, all the sly tricks I pretend not to notice, you'd better let me out."

He smiled amiably, not in the least displeased by her angry tone. "How would you explain being in my bedroom in your nightgown? You'll have to do better than that, Mair. Sly tricks indeed—you've got a few of those up your sleeve as well, Mair Parry, indeed you do. Taking such long walks up the mountain lately. 'Nice bit of air, it is, Mr. Williams.' Do you take me for a fool? I know why

114

you're always traipsing up that track. You're meeting that Castelli fellow, the one Jasper Owen drove out of town."

Mair swallowed nervously, hoping the color had not wholly drained from her face. How did he know about that?

"What's this, Mr. Williams, tit for tat? I told you no one would learn about your lapse from me."

"That's uncommonly generous of you. Now I suppose you expect me to make the same promise, that no one shall learn of your lapse from me."

Mair regarded him stonily, not knowing what to say. If only she knew whether he were merely guessing. "Don't know what lapse you're talking about. It's not a crime to meet someone, you know."

"No, not meeting them, but you surely don't think I'm fool enough to believe that's all you do. Not with one of them . . . a girl like you."

"Just because some people have dirty minds, Mr. Williams, doesn't make it so."

"Have you ever been up in the attic, Mair?"

She shook her head.

"From the attic there's a grand view of Pentre Fawr. You can see right over the fields and hedges, past the stile. Ah, I can see you're beginning to remember."

Could he have seen them making love? Mair chilled at the thought. Then quickly she discounted the idea. He might have seen them embracing beside the stile, but he couldn't see higher up the hill into the pasture, not through the blackthorn hedge.

"All right, so maybe I don't *just* meet him. There's nothing wrong with a couple of kisses."

He snorted in derision. "If I truly believed that was all there was to it, I'd open that door and let you go to your room. We both know better, don't we?"

Mr. Williams came unsteadily toward her, his hands outstretched.

"You're drunk, Mr. Holy Tegwyn Williams, so I'll overlook this. But if you don't want everyone to know about it, you're taking some big chances," Mair hissed, holding up her arms to ward him off. "Don't touch me. Leave me alone."

"That's not what you say to your Italian lover, is it, Mair? You don't know I wasn't behind the hedge listening to all your unholy whisperings."

Gambling that it was all a bluff, she said, "Well, if you were, you wouldn't have heard much."

"All I'm asking is that you be half as nice to me as you are to that foreigner. That's not much to ask, is it?"

Mair felt a shudder of revulsion creep along her spine as his fleshy hands stole beneath her shawl. He clutched at her breasts, panting in excitement. She hit out at him angrily, knocking aside his arm.

Wrapping the shawl tight about her body, she glared at him and spat, "Don't ever do that again."

"If you persist in this attitude, you leave me only one recourse. I'll have to present your sin in chapel on Sunday."

Mair gasped in horror. She had witnessed those public confessions, the humiliation, the degredation, the vicarious pleasure taken by some of the more hypocritical members of the congregation during the detailed recounting of the sin.

"No," she croaked, "not that."

"Oh, yes. And that'll only be the beginning of

116

your punishment, unless you start being much nicer to me. After I've revealed your sin I might ask leniency for you, might keep you on in order to cleanse your soul."

"You filthy hypocrite! We both know how you'd do that. Oh, you're so smug and holy sitting there in chapel playing the organ, mouthing the scriptures while all the time your mind's eaten up with lust . . ."

"Shut up! Shut up! How dare you!"

His face went white, then purple. Seizing her shoulders, he tried to wrestle her to the bed. Mair kicked at his legs, her boots delivering some bruising blows to his shins, making him cry out in pain. They struggled as he attempted to rip her flannel nightgown from her shoulders, his greedy fingers fumbling with the front placket. Mair seized a candlestick to defend herself, striking him an ineffectual blow across the side of the head before he angrily wrenched the weapon from her.

Panting, she watched him like a cornered animal. Uneasily she wondered what she should do next. He was much stronger than she had anticipated, his sheer bulk making him a formidable opponent. She looked about desperately, seeking a weapon to use against him.

They stumbled against a chair, sending it skidding into the nightstand where the purple-shaded lamp toppled and crashed to the floor. Mr. Williams stamped on the flame that threatened to set fire to the bedclothes, shouting at her in anger for the loss of his prized lamp.

If only he had not put the key in his pocket, Mair could have used this opportunity to escape. She glanced at the windows. They were on the second floor with no tree or balcony to aid in her descent. If she jumped, she would probably break her legs, yet even that fate might be preferable to the one she would encounter inside this room.

"All right, Mr. Williams, I'm asking you one last time: give me the key. Just go to bed and sleep it off. If you don't stop now, you'll be ashamed of yourself tomorrow."

"Not on your life. I'm not drunk, just pleasantly tipsy, you little fool. You'll not fob me off that easily."

Grimfaced, he moved toward her. In panic Mair glanced about for a weapon of self-defense. The only implement she saw was the poker in the brass hearthset. Wielding the blackened brass above her head, she dared him to come another step.

Laughing in derision at her feeble attempts at defense, Mr. Williams came on, pushing aside the fallen chair, narrowing the gap between them.

With thumping heart, Mair raised the poker and aimed a blow at him. To her shock, she missed, merely knocking a vase off the bedroom mantel. The incident afforded him much amusement. She chilled as she heard his cruel laugh. And all the time he was slowly advancing toward her.

Once more Mair brandished the poker, but this time her aim was true. She felt the sickening thud as the poker connected with flesh and bone. He cried out. For a moment longer she saw his shocked face, before he fell, striking his head on the hearth.

Her legs shook so badly she could barely stand. Mair threw the poker on the carpet. Mind jangling, her only thought was to get the key while he was stunned. Crouching beside him, she pushed and shoved at his bulk until she partially rolled him over. Reaching deep inside his pocket, she felt the heat from his body and shuddered in revulsion. She found the key and ran to the door.

Her hands were shaking so much that she could barely insert the key in the lock. Finally it turned and she wrenched open the door. She glanced back to make sure he was not pursuing her, then raced back to her own room. Only when she was inside with the door locked did she feel safe. She gasped for air, trying to regain her wits. There might be a second key to this room, but so far he had never tried to use it. She prayed he would sleep off his excess and leave her in peace.

As she sat on the edge of the bed wondering what to do, she realized her legs were shaking. The very thought of his fat greedy hands groping her breasts made her retch. How clever she had felt at being able to outwit him at his seductive game. But she hadn't counted on him drinking, or on her feeling sorry enough for him to let down her guard.

Mechanically, Mair went to the wardrobe. Good job or not, she couldn't stay at Brynteg now, even if Mr. Williams asked her to stay. After tonight she seriously doubted he would want to lay eyes on her again. Tears slid down her cheeks as Mair grabbed the first dress that came to hand and pulled it over her nightgown. She would go to Nico and tell him what had happened. There was no use going home with her complaints; she'd get short shrift there. Aunty Bet would simply not believe Mr. Williams capable of such crude behavior. Ivor might stand up for her; he had already remarked on the organist's lustful glances. She might even persuade her brother to come to her defense, thus preventing

119

Mr. Williams from carrying out his threat of exposing her sins at Sunday chapel. Once people knew his accusations were in retaliation for her rejection of his advances, she might gain some sympathy. As it was, the wonder of her love for Nico would be made to appear filthy and sinful. The very idea brought nausea to her throat. Those parishioners who had been sympathetic toward her last week would turn against her. With a shuddering sob, Mair accepted probable defeat. It was unlikely her word would be accepted against that of the chapel organist. No one would believe her except Nico.

Tears trickled down her nose and, irritated, she brushed them away. As yet there had been no sound from Mr. Williams. He was too heavy to walk noiselessly along the creaking hallway.

Tiptoeing into the hallway, she paused before his open bedroom door and looked inside. She saw he still had not moved. Torn between escaping while she had the chance and investigating the damage she had inflicted, Mair chose the latter.

Crossing the red Axminster carpet, she approached his dark bulk. In the firelight she could see his eyes were closed. Was he trying to trick her? Tentatively she tugged his sleeve, ready to leap aside before he could grab her skirts. But he did not move.

Mair crouched beside Mr. Williams and turned his head aside. She saw the jagged wound that marred his left temple. As he fell, instead of hitting the brass fender, he had struck the sharp corner of the Welsh slate hearthstone. A trickle of blood oozed from the wound and congealed on his waxy face.

Mair rocked back on her heels. She began to shake in fear. Dear Lord, had she killed him? Surely not with one poker blow. Looking more closely she discovered a lump the size of a pullet egg on top of his bald head. That was where the poker must have struck him. The real damage had been done when he fell against the hearth. Dread gripped her. No one would believe she had been defending herself. She was just a servant, whereas Mr. Williams was a pillar of the community.

Horror-stricken, Mair backed away. She had not meant to kill him. Though she had not felt his pulse, she was certain he was dead. Nico must help her decide what she must do. There was no one else she could turn to for help.

Mair shivered as she hurried through the morning chill. At this early hour the streets were deserted, but they wouldn't stay that way for long. Mair cast a practiced eye at the sky. First light was already breaking. Soon the miners and the tip girls would fill the streets on their way to work.

By the time she reached Maen Gwyn, she was no longer cold. Perspiration poured down her face, for she had alternately walked and run the entire distance. So far she had seen no one she recognized—but just in case, she had shielded her face with her shawl.

A light was on in Nico's home, glowing through a chink in the heavy curtains. She knocked on the door. To her surprise, Cousin Guido stood on the threshold.

"Yes?" he said, not recognizing her at first until she threw back her shawl. "Ah, it's you . . . changed your mind, after all?"

Mair blurted, "Nico. I must see him."

Cousin Guido shook his head. "Not possible."

"Why?"

"He's been gone almost an hour. Didn't you know he was leaving today?"

Mair sagged against the doorjamb, defeated. Yes, now she remembered. Oh, why should he have left today, of all days? What was she to do now? There was no one else she could turn to. All the way over here she had wrestled with the dreadful knowledge she had killed Mr. Williams. She would be charged with murder!

Tears filled Mair's eyes as she looked pleadingly at Cousin Guido.

"You better be quick if you coming. Where are your bags? I will leave soon."

"Leave?"

"Sometime I think you have no wits. Today I go back to London. I'm busy man. Can't waste more time here. I leave on morning train."

"Oh! You think I'm coming with you."

"Aren't you?"

Mair said nothing, stunned by the realization that here was her chance to escape arrest, prison, and being branded a murderess. Cousin Guido was her savior. Tears of relief trickled down her cheeks.

"Yes! Yes, of course I'm coming. You didn't say what time."

"I tell you already. Morning train!" Guido repeated irritably, throwing up his hands in exasperation. He withdrew a watch from his pocket. "Hour and half. Silly girl, you should have brought bags with you. There's not time now. I haven't met your parents. I don't know, maybe next time. We wait."

"No! No, my parents won't mind. I'll run home and get my things. If I meet you at the station it'll save time. Don't leave without me."

He smiled and placed his huge hand on her shoulder. "When train comes, I go. No wait for nobody."

Stumbling along the uneven pavements, running till she thought she could go no further, Mair made the return journey to Brynteg. A stitch gnawed at her side; her breath was tangling in her chest; her throat burned. Oh, Nico, Nico, if only you hadn't left, she kept crying silently. Yet, it was possible that even he could not have saved her from such a grave charge as murder. In London she'd be safe. No one would expect her to go that far. By the time Mr. Williams was found, she would be miles from Llandare. Out of Wales. Lost in the sprawling city.

Still hoping against hope that Mr. Williams had recovered in her absence, Mair found him exactly as she had left him. A fresh surge of horror gripped her at the grim realization she had killed a man.

Spurred to swift action, Mair raced to her room and emptied both bureau and wardrobe. There was not much to pack, but she had better take everything she owned. What would she do for money? She had no idea of the fare to London. Cousin Guido had never suggested he would pay for her ticket. Then Mair remembered the ten pounds her employer had given her. She could have wept in relief. When Mr. Williams had tried to bribe her with the princely sum, neither of them had suspected how she would use it.

Struggling under the weight of her bags, Mair realized her journey to the station would be far slower than had been her flight back to Brynteg. The gowns Olwen had left for her had greatly increased the weight of her baggage.

After a final glance at her dead employer, Mair bolted along the hall and down the stairs. Carefully locking the front door behind her, she flung the key far into the shrubbery. Dear Lord, let her be in London long before they found him. God knows she had not meant to kill the old lecher. But God would not come forth as witness to defend her. She had no alternative but flight.

Mair went to the station by a circuitous route. A few passers-by stared at her hat, and she questioned the wisdom of wearing her pride and joy—a shawl over her head would have made her less noticeable. It was too late now for wisdom. She would have liked to say goodbye to her family, but that was out of the question. Once she reached London she would write to assure them she was safe, telling them she had left to make her fortune.

The station was deserted. Somedays the morning train did not stop in Llandare. There were only two passenger coaches, the rest being coal cars. On designated days the coal was collected from Owen pits. To her vast relief Mair saw several loaded coal cars waiting in a siding. Silently she gave thanks that today was the day.

Mair bought a ticket to Cardiff. When she changed trains there, she would get her ticket for the rest of the journey. This was an extra safeguard against discovery. She had expected far more change than the old stationmaster handed her. Uneasily she began to wonder just how long her ten pounds would last.

She had waited a few minutes in the dingy waiting room before she saw Cousin Guido's bulky figure through the smokey glass. It became apparent they were together when he gave her a booming greeting. Foolish really for her to have thought she could slip unnoticed out of Llandare.

"You're sure your parents know you're leaving?" he asked suspiciously.

"Oh, aye, they know," Mair informed him brightly, trying to smile, though the expression was forced.

"Don't want no papa chase me, threaten to beat me up."

"You're safe there. Da would never threaten that," Mair lied brightly. If only he knew. Soon not merely Da, but half the constables in Wales would be looking for her. Cousin Guido's mysterious location in London would serve her purpose well. If what Nico had told her was true, even Anna Castelli could not give his address to the police.

Glancing repeatedly over her shoulder, Mair expected to see the constable walk inside the station any minute. If only the train would come. The stationmaster kept looking at his watch. A milk cart had pulled onto the platform, and a few middle-aged women and a child waited to board the train.

A low rumbling sound came to her ears, and soon the waiting room began to vibrate as the sulphurous smell of coal smoke belched forth. The train had arrived.

Virtually sobbing with relief, Mair grabbed her bags and bolted for the platform. Cousin Guido moved slowly behind her.

"What's the hurry? They wait for us," he grumbled amiably as she pulled open a compartment door and flung herself inside. He followed and with much puffing hefted his own bags onto the luggage rack. Mair managed a smile of thanks when he placed her bags next to his. To her relief their compartment stayed empty. At Cardiff they would change trains, but by then it would not matter. Once they left Llandare, no one would know her.

Peering anxiously through the grimy windows, afraid the police would run onto the platform any minute, Mair realized she could not relax as long as they were in Llandare. At last the stationmaster blew his whistle and the great belching train picked up steam and began to pull out of the station.

With a great sigh, she gradually allowed herself to relax. Nervously Mair smoothed her navy serge skirt and loosened her tightly wrapped shawl. They were finally underway.

Cousin Guido eyed her curiously, aware of the transformation taking place before him.

"You're a little liar," he blurted suddenly. "You were terrified your papa would stop you leaving. I'm right, eh!" He laughed in glee at the shock on her face.

Finally recovering herself, Mair grinned too, albeit sheepishly. "Yes, I was afraid of being stopped. You're far too clever for me, Mr. . . . I only know you as Cousin Guido."

"My name is Signore Guido Agnelli, but you can call me Guido. Ah, yes, starry-eyed little girls who want to go on the stage aren't new to me."

"I admit I was terrified. But we're safe now, aren't we?"

"Yes, it's too late to go back now. Today you are beginning a brand new life."

A new life!

Mair rested her head against the glass, barely noticing the green trees and fields rolling past the windows. Dear Lord, let there at least be a life. She had just killed a man and here she sat, acting as if nothing had happened. How much she had always longed to be taking this journey. Excitement had always gripped her when she contemplated traveling to London, yet today she felt only fear and apprehension.

As the miles between the train and Llandare lengthened, Mair began to lose a little of her fear. She was finally embarking on her lifelong dream. The very thought made her stomach flutter. She could hardly believe that tomorrow she would awaken in London. She had taken the first step to becoming an opera singer. Destiny had marked her for this journey, she was convinced of it.

In London she would be safe. After a while they might even tire of looking for her.

Growing drowsy, lulled by the motion of the train, Mair slid down in her seat. Cousin Guido was already snoring, his vast stomach threatening to pop the gilt buttons on his brown waistcoat. His bowler had slid over his eyes, giving him a comical, tipsy appearance.

Hardly able to believe the truth, once again Mair repeated to herself she was actually on her way to London. That meant not only was she going to be on the stage, she would also be seeing Nico. She might even arrive in the city before he did, as the train probably traveled faster than road transport.

The thrill of this realization set her spirits soaring. She almost forgot the doom hanging over her head as she anticipated being with him again. At first he would be angry because she had defied him by accepting Cousin Guido's offer before he had the chance to put his seal of approval on the move. But surely, when he held her in his arms, that anger would dissolve. Once he understood the dreadful trick of fate that had driven her to undertake the journey, he would soften. Though she hated to think of it, she knew she had to tell Nico what had happened. Would he feel the same about her once he learned she was a murderess? Even thinking the word to herself made Mair's skin creep, and a chill sped down her spine. If Nico truly loved her, whatever she did would not change his feelings. And he did truly love her. Her heart understood the depth of his feelings. Nothing could alter that.

With a great sigh, she settled lower in the red upholstered seat. Untold happiness awaited her in London. She had to believe that. The alternative was too terrible to consider.

PART TWO
LONDON

Chapter Nine

Mair's first impression of London was formed by the tremendous noise made by the crowds of people thronging the huge vaulted station. She paused to gaze in awe at the glass roof supported by gigantic steel arches, looking for all the world like some gigantic cathedral! The relentless surge of humanity virtually swept her off her feet. Not much like Llandare's station, this. The tracks, waiting room and all would fit into one corner here.

"Come on, you, no time for stargazing."

Guido yanked Mair's arm, spinning her about.

Somewhat offended by his action, Mair sharply protested, but her words were drowned by the sudden deafening blast of a train whistle. A railway official in braided cap, a gold watchchain hung across his ample paunch, hurried past, announcing the impending departure of the express. The atmosphere thickened as the train puffed and belched great clouds of sulphurous smoke, waiting with seeming impatience for the last weary traveler to disembark.

"Everywhere's so big, so crowded! Give me a minute, will you? I've got to catch my breath."

"I'm hungry, tired, and we're not finish yet. We don't got a minute," Guido said irritably as he scanned the crowd for a porter. Finally flagging down a uniformed man trundling a handcart, he supervised the loading of their bags.

With little regard for her safety, Guido thrust Mair into the press of people. She found herself propelled through the thick of the crowd where she was jostled, elbowed and kicked, bumped by valises, pierced by umbrellas and birdcages. It was a relief when at last they were free of the crowded platform.

At the station entrance the porter dumped their bags onto the pavement and vanished in search of more custom.

Hardly able to believe she was actually standing in a London street, Mair eagerly looked about. Another shock awaited her, for what she saw was far from the magnificent vista of broad streets and elegant buildings she had always envisioned. A light drizzle was falling and misty darkness partially shrouded the close-packed buildings. The pavements gleamed wetly beneath wavering gaslights haloed in mist. The air was filled with the unaccustomed smells and noise of this main thoroughfare where a constant parade of horsedrawn buses, hansom cabs and pedestrians passed before them.

Guido hailed a hansom. After telling the cab driver their destination, he thrust Mair before him up the steep steps and into the conveyance.

She had never ridden in a cab before! The wonder of this experience was somewhat tarnished by the hansom's dirty interior and stale smell. The windows were too grimy to see out, so Mair cleaned a patch with her sleeve. As the hansom cab driver cracked his whip and the horsedrawn vehicle lurched forward, she peered into the darkness, eager to see more of London. Street after endless street was swallowed up in the darkness, the scene illuminated by mere pinpricks of light as the fog deepened. Close-packed buildings towered above them, seemingly reaching to the sky. A warren of narrow archways and entries branched off this main street, presumably leading to still more streets hidden behind the buildings.

They soon left behind the broad lighted thoroughfare. The part of London they entered now had not even a steady parade of gas lamps to light their way. On some corners dingy lamp standards shed small pools of light across the cobbles; the remainder of the streets were murky black. The plentiful public houses punctuating this vast wasteland remained oases of light and life, their windows making broad yellow splashes across the wet street. There were no dark forbidding mountains or farmer's fields here; this London darkness was composed of miles of brick walls stretching endlessly into the night.

The hansom suddenly lurched to a stop. Guido, who had begun to doze, jerked upright and peered through the window. Then, with a nod of satisfaction, he announced, "This is it, Mair Parry. Come on, shift yourself, journey's end."

Not journey's end, only journey's beginning, she thought, her stomach pitching in excitement. Mair unlatched the cab door and carefully negotiated the narrow steps down to the cobblestones.

This street where they had stopped seemed barely wide enough to allow the hansom to disgorge its passengers. They stood on a corner where several streets intersected, yet even this open space did not lessen the suffocating feeling of being hemmed in. The air was so thick, Mair could hardly breathe. The acrid smell of coalsmoke eddied about them in the thickening fog. She was used to that smell. What she found most offensive was the nose-wrinkling odor of foul drains, gutters long uncleaned, of rancid cooking oil and spoiled food. In fact, so diverse were the smells of this quarter that Mair was hard–pressed to identify them.

Grumbling about the rain, Guido urged Mair around the corner. He stopped before a doorway recessed in a high, windowless wall. Banging on the door, he shouted something in Italian.

Eventually the door opened and a woman holding a candlestick peered out. She wore nightclothes, her gray streaked hair hanging unbound around her shoulders. After exchanging greetings in effusive Italian, Guido and the woman hugged. When Mair stepped over the threshold, the woman flung her a questioning glance. Guido was following close behind. He hefted their bags inside the hallway, then, uttering a sigh of relief, he slammed the door on the wet night.

"This is my beloved wife, Amelia. *Cara*, meet my latest discovery—Mair Parry."

"Discovery," Amelia repeated suspiciously, holding the candle high, the better to see this stranger. Candlelight disclosed a young face beneath the dark blue hat, tired, worn, but still ravishingly beautiful. Abundant golden hair sprouted from under the dark hat brim. Amelia's sharp eyes noted Mair's trim waist and curving bosom. "What you do here?" she demanded tersely.

"I came to sing in the opera," Mair explained, taken back by the other woman's hostility. "I come from Wales. From Llandare."

Amelia's puffy face relaxed, her anger dissolving in a welcoming smile. "Ah, Wales. A little singer, that's good, very good."

"Both me and the little singer are starving. What's to eat, wife? Come, Mair, this way to the kitchen."

Mair followed them down a narrow hallway where the flickering candlelight revealed dingy floral wallpaper and bare floorboards. The Agnellis certainly lived frugally, she thought, trying to quell her uneasiness, stirred afresh by the sight of this shabby place. Was Nico right? Did Cousin Guido's opera company exist only in his imagination? Well, girl, you'll soon find out, she reminded herself grimly. She was completely at their mercy. At the time she had been grateful to Cousin Guido for her deliverance, still was, yet . . .

A picture of Tegwyn Williams lying lifeless beside his hearth flashed into her mind, sending a chill of fear through her veins. They would have found him by now. Perhaps at this very moment a warrant for her arrest was being drawn up. 'Wanted for Murder: Mair Parry, former housekeeper at Brynteg, Chapel Road, Llandare.'

"Sit down. I'll see what's left."

Mair gulped, forced back to the present. Careful, mustn't give herself away. Smiling at Amelia Agnelli, she seated herself on a bench beside the fire. The blaze in the blackleaded hearth welcomed her as no other comfort could have done. Thankfully Mair stretched her hands to the fire, thrusting her feet closer to the hearth to dry her boots. Both the hem of her skirt and her petticoats were soiled from trailing through the puddles in the cobbled street.

Amelia dished out plates of stew which she warmed in the oven. While she worked, husband and wife carried on an animated discussion in rapid Italian. There seemed to be a difference of opinion, if not a downright argument, taking place. Mair's suspicions seemed founded when Amelia angrily banged down a plate before her.

Thanking Cousin Guido's wife for the food, Mair grew increasingly uneasy in this anger-fraught atmosphere. Was her unexpected arrival the cause of their disagreement? Lucky they didn't know the real story behind her flight from Wales. Her stomach turned over at the very thought. Still, she would have to stay with them tonight at least. She didn't know anyone else in London. Except Nico! Her heart raced at the thought of their joyful reunion. He would be happy to see her, even though at first she expected he would be angry because she had disregarded his advice. His anger would soon dissolve and he would be overjoyed at her impetuous move. Should she ask for Nico's address tonight? The idea was tempting, but Mair decided against it. It was very late. It might not be convenient for her to arrive at this hour, for she was not aware of his circumstances. Nico told her he worked for his uncle, but she did not know if he lived with him also. That would cause a sensation all right, her arriving unannounced in the wee hours.

Amelia hovered at Mair's elbow, waiting for her to finish. Puzzled by Amelia's attitude, Mair nonetheless thanked her for the tasty stew as she handed back her plate.

"You go to bed now," Amelia said sharply, "so we all get some sleep before morning."

Dutifully Mair stood up. Cousin Guido waved goodbye, indicating she was to follow Amelia. In his wife's presence the bombastic side of his nature was vastly toned down.

Though Mair tried to make conversation, Amelia met her friendly overtures with nods and grunts. Up a narrow flight of stairs she followed, round a corner, up another flight of stairs, until they finally stopped outside a closed door.

"Here you stay till tomorrow."

Amelia shone the candle inside the small room crammed almost wall to wall with three empty beds. A dresser with a broken mirror hanging above it stood next to the door. Overlooking the street was a small window half covered by a sagging lace curtain.

Although not impressed by these accommodations, Mair understood beggars could not be choosers. She had little left from her ten pound note once her fare and meals had been bought.

"Thank you very much, Mrs. Agnelli. Which bed is mine?"

"By the window. The other girls will be back later."

With that Amelia left, shutting the door behind her.

Mair stood in the chill room. There was barely room to move around the beds. Her bag had not been brought up and she did not trust herself to find her way back downstairs to retrieve it; she would have to put up with unbrushed hair and a night spent in her traveling clothes.

Though she had not expected to be able to sleep, Mair dozed off almost as soon as her head hit the pillow. She was awakened later in the night by giggles and bumps and the rustle of clothing as the room's other occupants prepared for bed. She did not rouse sufficiently to speak to them and they did not disturb her.

In the morning Mair received yet another dose of reality. When she woke to the dingy light invading the tiny room, Mair was dismayed by the poverty of her surroundings. The room and the beds appeared to be clean: that was the biggest compliment she could bestow. She lifted the lace curtain and looked out over a sea of dismal smoking chimneypots. The overcast sky lay like a blanket over the rooves, where tiles were missing and soot etched a drab mosaic. A pair of scrawny cats stared unblinkingly at her from their perch beside the narrow chimney stack a few feet away, where they crouched for warmth.

Mair dropped the curtain back in place. This was definitely a poor quarter of London. She was not fool enough to think the entire city looked like this; she had heard too much about the capitol's many wonders for that. Uneasily—and this time she was unable to squash down the feeling—she admitted Nico was probably right. If Guido Agnelli ran a grand opera company, why would he live in such poverty-stricken surroundings?

Scrambling out of bed, Mair tried to open the door; it was bolted from the other side. She had intended to go in search of the privy. Now she was forced to use the battered chamber pot beneath the bed.

The others slept blissfully unaware. Covertly she looked at their faces against the dingy pillows, surprised to find both women were heavily rouged. The flounced brightly colored gowns tossed across the foot of their beds were made from cheap, gaudy fabric. They looked for all the world like streetwalkers! Not that she had much experience with that profession in Llandare, not with the chapel having such a stranglehold on the town's way of life. Yet once, when she visited Swansea, some women were pointed out to her as sinful street women. Gaudily dressed, cheeks highly rouged, they had stood apart from their more respectable sisters. They would have felt quite at home with this pair, and no mistake.

The door rattled as the bolt was drawn back and Mair reached over to open the door. A young skinny maid in a soiled hessian apron jumped, not expecting the door to open. On the floor beside the girl was a bowl and pitcher of water.

"For your wash, miss," the maid explained, sniffling and wiping her dripping nose on her sleeve.

"Thank you. What's your name?" Mair asked,

smiling in thanks as the girl handed her a towel. A clean one at that, she was glad to see.

"Pearl, miss," said the girl, quite surprised that anyone should show interest in a maid-of-all-work. "The master says you's to come down and talk to him."

Mair lathered her face with the minuscule piece of soap provided, rinsing the suds away with luke-warm water. Thinking perhaps she should wake the others while the water was still warm, she shook the nearest woman's shoulder. For her pains she received a torrent of abuse. Finally, thrusting her away, the woman burrowed beneath the covers. Well, they could sleep till the cows came home, for all she cared.

Mair let herself out into the gloomy corridor, following the buzz of sounds echoing up from the kitchen, which she later discovered was the house's common meeting room.

Mair stopped in the kitchen doorway as all heads turned to stare at the stranger. She stood there diffidently, taken back by the large group of people filling this low-ceilinged room. Several women and girls sat at the wooden tables eating bread and drinking tea. Two women clad only in their petti-coats were mending stockings before the hearth. A group of men cooked over the fire, pungent her-rings sizzling in their frying pans. At her unex-pected appearance the buzz of activity in the room ground to a halt. No one spoke until Amelia poked her head around the scullery door.

"This is Mair Parry from Wales. She's come to sing with us."

Then the laughter and chatter resumed. Mair

smiled and nodded as the others greeted her, turned unusually shy by the unexpected audience.

"Come over 'ere, love. 'Ave a slice of toast," invited a woman at the closest table, moving on the bench to make room for her. "Don't s'pose you've got anything to eat, being new and all."

Mair welcomed the friendly advance. She had not expected to provide her own food. The range of foodstuffs being consumed in this common kitchen told her this must be the custom. Someone munched a savory meat pie, while another devoured pickled whelks swimming in vinegar.

"I'm Daisy and this is Flo."

The speaker was a petite blonde with long, straggling hair. She must have been pretty once, but age and a pock-marked complexion robbed her of attractiveness. Daisy was dressed in a faded red wool dress trimmed in black braid; her dark-haired companion wore serviceable bottle-green serge that had seen better days. This woman was older and heavier, her brown eyes deeply shadowed. But she gave Mair a friendly smile and pushed a plate of thick toast toward her.

"Singer, eh? Bet me boots you's a sweet little soprano," Flo said, as she poured tea into a chipped mug and handed it to Mair. "Used to be one meself. Good too, I was, though I says so meself. Before the bronchitis got me. Terrible for bronchitis it is round 'ere. Go on, eat up, it'll be a while before you get anything else."

Gratefully Mair ate the toast, washing down the thick bread with hot tea. "Why are there so many people here? Is this a lodging house?"

"This, my love, is the *company*," explained Daisy

in heavy theatrical accents. "Signor Guido Agnelli's Grand Opera Company performing weekly at the magnificent Coliseum."

Both women spluttered with laughter, spraying tea across the table. Their hilarity over that description did little to calm Mair's fears.

"Are all these people part of the company?" she asked, glancing around, somewhat relieved to discover there really was a company.

"Most of 'em. A few wives, a few dollies. You spent last night with Janey and Pie, didn't you? Well, there's a few like them 'ere too. Sometimes they sings and sometimes they don't."

At this the two women exchanged winks. Mair grew uncomfortable, knowing she had not entirely grasped the situation but not wishing to ask for more information. Just then a flurry of greetings announced Guido's arrival. Mair stared in amazement at this stranger, trying to reconcile him with the flashily dressed Cousin Guido of her acquaintance. This morning his former air of prosperity had flown; Guido wore baggy flannel trousers, a patched check jacket, and a knitted muffler wound round his thick neck.

"Those two lazy sluts still not up," he rumbled, glancing around the room for Janey and Pie.

As if on cue, the two women in question stumbled into the kitchen, garish in their smeared makeup, hair straggling over faces still heavy with sleep.

"Cor, you try being out all night and get down here for nine," one of them muttered as she passed, shoving her way to the hearth. "'Ere, it's perishing cold in this place, shove over."

142

"Before you toast your lazy carcass, Pie, hand over what's owing for rent," Guido growled, amazing Mair with his unexpected Cockney accent.

Still grumbling, the woman reached inside her bodice and handed him some money. Guido quickly took and counted the proffered change. When the other woman gave him a ten shilling note, he smiled.

"See now, that gentleman was well worth your time, after all." His glance came to rest on Mair and he motioned to her. "This is Mair," he announced, turning her about before the rest of the company. "Depending on how fast she learns, she's going to be our star. She sings like an angel. Everyone treat her right, or you've got me to deal with."

A murmur of assent greeted his announcement. Pleased, Guido smiled and nodded. Then he motioned for Mair to follow as he headed for the door.

Mair's mouth set in a determined line. Pausing just long enough to thank Daisy and Flo for sharing their breakfast with her, she followed him outside.

"You not stay with those flossies tonight, that was only temporary, little Mair." He was actually smiling at her as he took her arm and guided her inside a small room beyond the kitchen.

Once inside the room, Mair faced him. "Now, look here, Cousin Guido," she began, trying to stay calm. "I need to know exactly what's going on here. If my eyes don't deceive me, those two women aren't exactly chapel-goers now, are they?"

He looked surprised, tried to appear innocent and failed. "All right, all right, you're not as sweet as you look," he muttered sourly.

"Sweet's not the same as simple–minded. Are they streetwalkers, or not?"

"Yes and no."

"What's that mean? They are or they aren't."

Guido pursed his thick lips, his dark eyes glowing with laughter. "This week they are, maybe next week they won't be. It all depends."

"On what?"

"On whether they come up with their rent, or booze it away at some gin palace. As I said, sometimes they are and sometimes they aren't."

"Well, at least now I know where we stand. What about the others?"

Guido shrugged. "Depends. Most of them will turn a trick if times get hard."

"I won't, however poor I get."

"Pity. You've got the looks that appeal to real gentlemen. Still, suit yourself. Besides, when I'm finished with you, Mair Parry, you'll have rent money and more. None of the others ever had your potential. You'll practice hard, so hard you won't be able to stand me or Amelia. We'll make a famous opera singer of you."

Mair was not going to be sidetracked by promises of future glory. "That's another thing. Where exactly is this opera company of yours? Where's the theater?"

Guido's eyes flashed. "That old harridan Flo's been talking. Today we're poor, we're small. Someday we sing at Covent Garden. Someday you sing there too, eh, Amelia?"

Mair turned in surprise to find Amelia standing in the doorway. This morning she was a new woman. Her gray-streaked black hair was braided in a coronet surmounting her sallow face. A serviceable navy wool gown modestly covered her soft, dumpy body.

"When you open your mouth is time enough to tell. Sometime Guido's a fool for pretty faces. Come, we see how you sound. If you no good, you stand outside to attract custom."

At Amelia's dismissal, Mair's heart sank. With each passing hour she grew more aware of the foolhardiness of her flight to London. Though Nico may not have actually known the truth, he had guessed at it very closely.

Growing impatient, Amelia motioned Mair to follow her into a large, high-ceilinged room, partially curtained off. Screens and stacks of lumber and ramshackle furniture were stacked at the far end of the room. An old battered piano stood in the corner. From beyond the curtain came the sound of hammering. Snorting in annoyance, Guido lifted the curtain and yelled to someone to be quiet.

When Mair looked beyond those frayed red velvet curtains slung on a rope, she understood at last where she was. This was the Coliseum— Guido's grand opera house! This room heaped with furniture and plywood was the stage. Never having seen a stage before, Mair had not immediately identified her surroundings. The company must live in several houses adjoining the theater. This ramshackle old theater had rows of shabby red seats sprouting stuffing; some of the seats were devoid of all padding. The entire place would not hold more than two hundred people. That street corner where the cab had stopped must have been the facade of the Coliseum, home of Agnelli's Opera Company.

Guido turned around, seeing Mair's pale face and understanding the reason behind her shock.

"What you think, you sing at Covent Garden? Little fool! Someday, not yet. Now get over there and sing. Show Amelia I'm not out of my mind."

And sing she did. Mair's eyes stung with tears, her fists clenched in anger and disappointment. She sang as she had never sung before, rendering a tragic outpouring of all her disappointment in 'Addio del Passata.' Quickly picking up those first few notes of the aria from *La Traviata*, Amelia played a tinkling accompaniment. Mair knew now she had sold herself to them in exchange for her safety. But she had come to London to sing in the opera. And, dear lord, that is exactly what she intended to do.

When the final notes echoed away, there was a stunned silence. Then a burst of applause came from behind the curtains. The theater carpenter certainly approved of her performance.

Nervously Mair searched Amelia's face for a sign, anxious to know her opinion of her voice. The Agnellis were shabby and poverty-stricken, yet instinct told Mair they would recognize talent when they heard it. Finally Amelia nodded in approval. Guido and his wife exchanged triumphant glances. Saying something in Italian, Amelia stood up and clasped Mair's hands.

"One day you be famous. One day," she repeated, as tears of relief spilled down Mair's cheeks. "But not on the strength of one aria. You already know it by heart. How come you learn Traviata?"

"I worked on that aria with a singing teacher. I know others," Mair offered eagerly, anxious to demonstrate her versatility.

"Good. And I have many more for you to learn. First you sing many scales. Then you learn to act, to move, and—most important for a singer—you learn to breathe. You have much to learn. Guido, when you want to use her?"

"Two weeks. We have the perfect Violetta, and we'll rehearse Eddy as Germont, eh? Amelia—we'll fill the house."

Amelia nodded. "From now on, Mair, you will be busy every day. Are you ready to spend every waking minute learning, working?"

"If it means I'll be able to sing for money!"

Amelia's mouth twisted in a wry smile. "We don't make much of that lately. Maybe you bring us luck." Then, to Mair's surprise, Amelia swiftly embraced her, kissing her wet cheeks.

"Thank you both. I promise to work very hard."

Chapter Ten

Mair never dreamed singing would be such hard work. The better she sang, the harder Amelia pushed her. By these standards Mr. Crossley had been vastly indulgent. Amelia stressed correct breathing. This technique was achieved by first locating Amelia's ribcage beneath layers of clothing and fat, then feeling the rhythm as she demonstrated the correct manner of phrasing a piece. Mair then had to duplicate that same feeling within her own diaphragm.

In her younger days Amelia had been a passable soprano, but she was a much better teacher. Guido also knew exactly what he wanted to hear, frequently yelling at Mair when he felt she was not trying hard enough. Several times she burst into frustrated tears when she seemed unable to please either of them. Yet though her feelings were hurt and her ego bruised, Mair understood this volatile couple was striving to make a performer out of her. In that respect the Agnellis' goal matched hers—to be able to produce the best possible sound from her voice.

After frequent prodding, Guido had reluctantly given Mair an address for Nico near the docks, at the end of Southampton Street. But he also dissuaded her from visiting him, warning her Nico lodged in a very rough neighborhood.

Mair's first letter went unanswered. She even wondered if Guido had actually posted it or simply had thrown it into the fire. Her second letter she was determined to post herself. As she sealed the envelope, her hands shook. How many days would it be before she received an answer?

Wrapping her shawl tight to ward off the morning chill, Mair slipped outside at first light. Scavengers and rag pickers slunk along in the shadow of the buildings; they carried spiked sticks to impale any salvageable material found in the heaps of refuse piled in the gutters and behind the houses. These foul smelling men and women traveled many miles daily, scavenging for anything they could sell. Rags, bones, cinders, edible scraps of bread, everything went into the greasy sacks slung over their shoulders. Though the rag pickers' appearance was frightening, Mair's new roommate, Rose, assured her they were harmless.

Rose was a slight, elfin little creature, bright as a sparrow. She was the company's seamstress and a native of this part of London. Kindly befriending Mair, she laughed about the funny Welsh way she talked, trying to change her speech to a more acceptable Cockney dialect. The attempt failed. Rose had taken Mair exploring about the neighborhood. On their walk they sampled pickled whelks and treacle toffee, drank hot elderberry elixir and bought a wooden monkey that danced when you pulled a string.

Mair had enjoyed exploring with Rose, yet she had no desire to venture far by herself. Many unsavory characters roamed the streets at all hours of the day and night. Wisely Mair did not intend to enter the maze of filth-choked courts and alleyways where thousands of poor Londoners lived. Mair shuddered at the hair-raising tales Rose told of people being knifed, robbed, or even murdered in the vile courts to the northeast leading off Cloth Fair. Of course, Rose also recounted some wonders Mair was anxious to see. The big West End theaters for one, with their bright lights, lifelike scenery and thousands of glittering, bejeweled patrons. Mair's head spun with visions of the Lyceum, Drury Lane and Covent Garden. Someday she would sing there, thrilling those titled patrons with her voice. She smiled to herself; Guido's incurable optimism must be catching.

To her horror, Mair saw a policeman moving toward her through the early morning gloom. But he passed, brushing her with his navy cape. Heart thundering as if it would explode, she leaned against a doorway, wiping sweat off her brow.

When she was out walking with Rose she had seen two policemen, and the scare made her heart race. Convinced they would arrest her on sight, Mair had feigned illness and cut their walk short. All this waiting was getting on her nerves. Every day she wondered if it would be her last day of freedom. Now she spent more time worrying about capture than agonizing over the actual murder. God forgive her, she had never meant to do it. Old Tegwyn Williams had given her little choice. In her saner moments Mair reminded herself no one knew she was in London. If only she could tell Nico; he at least would believe she had not meant to kill the old organist. Though wisely she had not revealed her secret in her letter, she had told him there was something very important she had to tell him. The thought that she could be arrested without ever seeing him again was too terrible to contemplate. She had to stop thinking about being arrested. No one round here knew the truth. Both Rose and the Agnellis assumed she had run away from Wales to go on the stage. Then, just when she had succeeded in making herself feel better, Mair wondered how many girls called Mair lived in London's east end. All the girls round here seemed to be called Daisy, Lily, or Flo.

Forcing herself to walk slowly, in case the policeman turned around and wondered why she was hurrying, Mair headed for the letterbox she had seen outside a neighborhood chophouse.

Men and women already lined the pavement waiting for the cook shop to open. Today's menu, scrawled on a card in the window, offered a bowl of oxtail soup and bread for fourpence. According to Rose, this chophouse served good meals at cheap prices; this was the reason people lined up around the corner to eat here. How poor, threadbare and hopeless these people looked.

After posting her letter, Mair hurried away. The dinginess of this neighborhood got her down. She never imagined London would be like this. Yet, according to Rose, Primrose Court and Duchess Street weren't bad. Mair had no desire to venture into any worse districts. When she had suggested going to dockland to visit Nico, Rose had rounded on her with a burst of profanity. "Get attacked in the middle of the day down there, you will," she had warned. "It's asking for it, a girl like you. 'Ave to brush em 'orf like flies. I don't want to hear no more about that little journey." Duly chastised, Mair had settled for the written word, though her heart ached for the sight of Nico. Her memory readily supplied the intoxicating taste of his warm lips, the clasp of his hand. A warm feeling flooded through her, threatening to reduce her to trembling longing. Only a few more days to wait, she consoled herself. As soon as he received her letter he would come to see her.

Smiling as she pictured their joyful reunion, Mair let herself into the theater by a side door which, on the day before a performance, was left unlocked for deliveries. This afternoon, printed handbills describing Saturday night's astounding program would be distributed in the surrounding streets. The cooking of meat pies and hard sugar candy had already begun, the mingled sweet and savory aromas greeting her when she stepped indoors. Pails of pickled whelks, barrels of ale and a basket of apples and oranges stood inside the door. They were to be sold at tomorrow's performance.

Mair had been impressed with the Agnellis' sheer ingenuity. No stone was left unturned as a source of revenue. Even the sale of sexual favors outside the stage door she had come to accept as part of the business. Though with her Llandare background, steeped as it was with constant reminders of sin, Mair could never quite condone that aspect of the profession.

Last week the Agnelli Opera Company had given their first performance since her arrival. To Mair's vast disappointment, the only operatic piece on the entire bill had been a solo by Eddy Lewis, the company tenor. The program had been more of a music hall bill. When questioned about this misrepresentation, Guido had indignantly pointed out that in this neighborhood people demanded variety for their money. Signor Santino and his performing dogs headed the bill, along with Pie and Janey, dressed in bathing suits, presenting a selection of current music hall songs whose ribald lyrics made Mair blush.

"Mair! I tell you not go out alone," Guido thundered as she passed the cubbyhole grandly referred to as the office. "Too dangerous for a woman like you."

"I only went to post a letter."

"Not to that hothead? Ah, I knew it! Best thing you do is forget him. Besides, he not answer your last letter."

Mair's head snapped up. "I posted this one myself. That way I *know* it went into the post."

Guido bristled at her accusatory tone. "So, you think I not post it! Ah, you little fool." He stopped, studying her before he casually asked, "How you feel about singing tomorrow night?"

Mair's eyes widened and her heart missed a beat. "I'm not ready," she gasped, growing faint. "Amelia says years . . . it'll take years."

"Tomorrow night," Guido repeated, fixing her with a stern gaze. "Something easy, something you sing good."

Horror-stricken, Mair sat in the only available chair. She had always intended to sing. That had been comfortingly in the future when she became a great singer. Not now. Not when she did not really know how to handle herself onstage.

"*Addio del Passata* you know already by heart."

Her mouth opened and closed; she twisted her skirt in sweating hands. "I can't."

"You can . . . *will* . . . forget the audience. Pretend it just me and Amelia like always. One more thing."

Mair stared up at him, her dark blue eyes round with dismay. "Yes," she whispered, her throat gone dry.

"Your name we change." Guido looked at her, his lips pursed. "Something exotic. Mair Parry, Mair Parry," he repeated, deep in thought. "Maria Parigi! Is perfect. You now Maria Parigi."

"All right," Mair agreed breathlessly, sitting up, trying to get used to the idea. Maria Parigi sounded glamorous indeed. What's more, the police weren't looking for a foreign singer—the accused murderess was a Welsh housekeeper. The more Mair thought about the idea, the more she liked it. Maria Parigi it was. "Isn't it too late to put that on the handbills?" she asked, remembering the string-tied bundles she had seen in the kitchen.

"Have you read one?"

Mair shook her head.

Guido smiled, his thick upper lip twitching as if he fought laughter. "Here, read it."

Mair took the yellow paper, holding it toward the dingy window where the first beams of sunlight struggled to penetrate. It was the usual music hall fare, the headliner being Stefan the Fire Eater. That should excite the unruly Coliseum audience. Then, at the bottom of the sheet, in large letters, she read:

"By special arrangement, Maria Parigi, fresh from her continental triumph, has kindly consented to sing an aria from Verdi's *La Traviata*. Prices for this limited engagement, 10 pence, including refreshment."

How could that be? He had only this minute decided on a stage name, only just now decided to put her on the bill—or had he?

Mair's head shot up and her nostrils widened as she drew in her breath. "You twister," she gasped, "you already had those printed before you even asked me."

Guido laughed at her indignation. "So all you have to do is agree. Easy."

"What if I'd refused? What if I hadn't wanted to change my name?"

"I not accept refusals," Guido dismissed, tiring of the conversation. "Come, let's go to kitchen. Time to eat."

All day, whenever Mair contemplated going onstage, her heart beat so frantically, it nearly flew into her throat. Rose eagerly assisted her with her costume, pleased by her friend's chance to shine. From the company's limited wardrobe she selected a thin white negligee with a ragged lace hem, to be covered by a heavy white silk wrapper embroidered with pink roses.

In this final act of the opera, *La Traviata*, the character Mair was to play lay on her bed reading a letter from her lover's father. All Violetta's longing for Alfredo's love was reflected in the poignant aria. Dying of consumption, the French courtesan knows her days are numbered; so little time is left to see her beloved. Mair was able to portray that emotion convincingly, for she longed for Nico with all her heart. It was quite possible her own days were numbered. They surely must come looking for her soon. Not only that, since Guido dropped the bombshell about her unexpected debut, Mair felt she needed Nico's support more than ever. He should be here to listen to her sing onstage for the first time. By the time he came to see her, she would already be a seasoned performer. But if she were a success—and she could not allow herself to doubt she would be—Nico would more readily accept the idea of her singing in London. Even Nico could not argue with success.

On the morning of the performance everyone slept late; the houserule of having to be in the kitchen before nine was suspended. A Saturday night performance was the logical choice for this shabby neighborhood. Though laboring men were often paid by the day, those with a weekly pay packet could be counted on to have full pockets on Saturday night. Sunday was often a holiday and they could sleep late the next morning.

At the end of April the London Social Season had begun and sometimes moneyed patrons strayed to the East End in search of a Saturday night lark. The Coliseum's general audience consisted of laborers, cabmen and their wives and girls, street vendors and craftsmen from the surrounding streets. It was not usual to draw a wider audience, though last week a few well-to-do men in evening dress had attended the performance.

Mair was well rehearsed in her aria. In truth, there was little demanded of her that she had not already done many times before. It was far different, however, to sing lying down. The old tapestry daybed from which she was to make her triumphant debut took some getting used to. Trying to avoid the bursting springs that were discreetly hidden beneath a blue counterpane might prove to be one of the more difficult aspects of her performance.

Far from being jealous as Mair had expected, the rest of the company treated her like an indulged child. Guido had warned them that Mair was not to be annoyed, taken advantage of, or approached for favors—this latter directed at the males of the company. In fact, she was to be treated like the Queen of the Coliseum. That is what she was called behind her back. Mair could not have blamed them had they been jealous of her privileged status. She did not even need to provide her own board. Mair, Eddy Lewis and Rose all ate from the Agnellis' own table. Like everyone else, however, she was required to pay rent. They did not hound her for money but took her on trust, which was fortunate, for so far Mair had done little more than sell oranges at last week's performance. Each member of the company had a range of jobs, singers and dancers doubling as ticket sellers, food servers, carpenters or scene painters. Even the small orchestra, comprised of violin, cello and flute, was drawn from amongst the company. Amelia was the rehearsal pianist; she also played for the performance and could provide a stirring drum roll when needed.

As Mair had expected, Guido was the front man. Dressed in his best, cigar in mouth, he looked every inch the impressario. The only time that he had worn his splendid suit and overcoat since they left Wales had been last Saturday night when he strutted about the theater lobby.

Now Mair even had an answer for his annual forays to Llandare, which at first had made no sense. When she asked Rose why the theater handbills mentioned theaters in both London and Bristol, the other girl had laughed. Apparently Guido still owned a rundown music hall in Bristol for which he collected an annual rent. From Bristol he traveled to Llandare to visit the Castellis, eager to impress them with his money and success. Mair had not known the reason behind Amelia's hostility on the night of her arrival. She later discovered too much rent money had been spent to impress and not enough had reached London. That, coupled with the unexpected appearance of a pretty young woman, aroused Amelia's anger. Though Guido appeared trustworthy, Amelia knew only a fool would trust a man implicitly. She had suspected Mair was just another pretty woman of limited talent who had cajoled her husband into giving her a chance to appear on stage.

The hours to curtain flew by. Mair could hardly believe it was already time when she heard the noisy crowd stampeding to their seats.

Flo helped her with her makeup, remarking she

was the healthiest, most beautiful consumptive she had ever seen. Mair hardly recognized the face which stared back at her from the dingy dressing room mirror. Darkened lashes and brows made her eyes appear larger, until they became huge dark blue pools in her pale face. Her lips were painted red, her long hair draped about her shoulders in a lustrous golden cloak.

Mair stood in the corridor watching the audience through a spyhole beside the stage. Steps behind her, and the scent of bay rum, announced the arrival of Eddy Lewis, company tenor and fellow privileged soul.

"A pity we're not singing a duet tonight," Eddy remarked, smiling appreciatively at Mair.

"That'll be next week," Mair said, not wanting to look at him. It was apparent Eddy fancied her; his calf-eyed gaze had already told her that much.

Eddy's large blue eyes and tightly curled blond hair gave him the appearance of a cherubic choir boy. In truth he was thirty-five. Eddy's voice was more lyric than dramatic tenor, much to the Agnellis' disappointment, for they had visions of presenting opera's famous heroic tenor roles, full of bravado and ringing High C's. Eddy's constant straining in an effort to satisfy this urge had caused him to develop a tremulo which would worsen with time. Yet, for the old Coliseum in Duchess Street, Eddy Lewis was a surperb artist. And he knew it. Until Mair came along there had been no one else to equal him. He could have been jealous of this ravishing little girl; instead he preferred to picture them singing together as the perennial hero and heroine of the Agnelli Opera Company.

To develop that partnership off stage, as well as on, was his foremost aim.

Tonight Eddy was dapper and handsome in formal dress. His swallowtail coat was shabby as were all the costumes in the company wardrobe; over the footlights the threadbare fabric would never be noticed. With the gaslight haloing his fair hair, his slight figure drawn to full height, he made a splendid appearance. He was to sing a medley of old English songs which would precede Mair's stunning debut—or at least it was hoped it would be stunning.

Eddy slid his arm about Mair's shoulder, the heat of his hand quickly penetrating the thin layers of silk clothing. Mair tensed. So far Eddy Lewis had not overstepped himself, but she soon expected him to increase his pursuit. Then she would have to actively discourage him. It was a job she did not look forward to. He, Rose, and the Agnellis, had become her new family. Eating together at a separate table, confident in the knowledge they were special, had produced a certain bond between them. She was very reluctant to destroy the friendship. Still, if Eddy pressed his unwelcome attentions on her too vigorously, it could not be helped.

Mair turned aside, sliding out from under his arm.

"We're going to rehearse *Lucia* all week. We'll be together most of the time," he reminded huskily, his fingers trailing down her neck. "Why not come for a walk with me to the park some afternoon?"

"That might be nice, Eddy. I'll have to see." Mair tried not to dismiss him too unkindly. By next week Nico would have visited her, then Eddy would understand her reluctance to respond to his advances.

The dreaded hour finally arrived. The house was half full, which was good considering tonight's price increase. Though refreshments had cleverly been included, the increased ticket price supposedly reflected the spectacular nature of the entertainment being presented. All those laughing, noisy people out for a Saturday night frolic were here again, waiting expectantly for the curtain to go up. Even the same two well-dressed men who had been there last week were sitting in the front row, indulging in paper cones of pickled whelks and mugs of warm ale along with the more plebian members of the audience. Mair wondered why they came to a theater like this. Surely they could find more suitable entertainment in those flashy West End theaters Rose had described to her. Naively, Mair thought gentlemen would not be entertained by vulgar music hall songs. Perhaps they came to hear the more classical pieces provided by the company's operatic voices. It gave her a thrill to realize she would now be numbered amongst the real singers.

Eddy sang, 'Mistress Mine,' 'The Last Rose of Summer' and 'Drink to Me Only.' To Mair's surprise his performance was very well received. Though the audience were raucous during the more popular pieces, singing along and stamping their feet in time to the music, they had been surprisingly polite during the cultural part of the bill. Whether they actually appreciated the classical voice, or merely endured it because they had come to expect such offerings at the Coliseum, Mair did not know.

The red curtain sagged on its rope, effectively shutting out the hostile world. Mair's heart thundered as she lounged elegantly on the chaise lounge, propped against pillows, her golden hair spread seductively around her. When all was ready, everyone left her, bringing momentary panic. She could see Guido and Amelia anxiously watching from the wings. She was alone onstage!

The small orchestra began the prelude to Act Four. This popular piece had been chosen to introduce Violetta's aria, though it did not actually follow in sequence in the opera. The Coliseum management routinely nipped and tucked, highlighting popular melodies, skipping over the boring segments, aware of their audience's limited concentration on all but the most catchy refrains.

Slowly the curtains opened, and for a split second Mair panicked. She couldn't do it! She couldn't sing a note! Then, in surprise, she heard a soft pure voice. The murmur of appreciation from the audience as they saw the beautiful Violetta reclining on her bed was silenced by those opening notes. Mair heard the voice and at first did not know it was she who sang. Soaring, gaining strength, the voice went on, almost as if it were a separate being. Mair could not sing the aria, the difficult Italian words escaped her. She panicked, her hands wet with sweat, the letter she held drooping from the moisture. But the Voice kept singing. The Voice knew all the Italian words, understood Violetta's pain . . .

The aria was over. There was a stunned silence,

then the motley crowd began to applaud, whistling, stamping, their enthusiasm unbridled. She had done it! For the first time in her life she had sung on stage. And she had done it well. More important than that, the audience loved her—these poor ragged men and women with their ale and pickled whelks, the mingled scent of spiced vinegar, oranges and beer, wafting to her across the footlights, were applauding wildly. Tears ran down Mair's cheeks. At that instant she loved them all. Emotion crossed the flickering footlights in a great wave, and she held out her arms to them, not understanding why, just knowing in her joy she wanted to embrace this ragged cockney audience.

The rest of the night was a daze. The other members of the company congratulated her. Both Guido and Amelia embraced her. Her friend Rose kissed her cheek, saying when she first saw Mair across the footlights she gasped because she thought she was the most beautiful thing she had ever seen. And Eddy Lewis pouted, sorry he had not thought of that compliment first.

Chapter Eleven

" 'A ravishing creature by the name of Maria Parigi thrilled audiences again and again with her soaring notes, so pure, so angelic, one would have thought her descended from heaven.' "

"Coo, go on," Rose cried, enthralled by the review Eddy was reading out of a London newspaper. "Don't 'ardly believe it's our Mair they's talking about."

"The man was swayed by your appearance. Can't say I'd go to such lengths . . ."

Mair kicked him smartly on the shin. "Read!" she commanded, hardly able to believe such praise herself.

" 'Lately the old Coliseum in Duchess Street has become a mecca for opera lovers. This rundown music hall has given birth to a scintillating young diva. The small cast also includes a competent tenor, Mr. Eddy Lewis,'" Eddy paused, bowing his fair head in acknowledgment of the round of applause his words elicited, "'the baritone and bass are also unknowns, yet they ably support this splendid young voice. The final tragic act of *La Traviata* was a vocal triumph worthy of a West End theater. How fitting, that in this Jubilee year, Londoners have the privilege of hearing a great artist at the beginning of her career. A Golden Nightingale singing for Her Majesty's Golden Jubilee!'"

Every time Mair reread the review her eyes misted with emotion. She could hardly believe so much had happened in one short month. The second time she sang the theater had been filled with friends of the two well-dressed gentlemen who usually sat in the front row. A second performance had been added on Wednesdays to accommodate their larger audience. Now they no longer needed Stefan the fire-eater, or Signor Santini's dogs to help fill the theater. In fact, last Saturday night there had been standing room only, well-dressed men and women making up the bulk of the audience. The cost of a seat had now risen to a shilling.

Guido ferociously guarded Mair's privacy, insisting Signorina Parigi never gave interviews or spoke to admirers.

Bouquets arrived for Mair at the stage door. Men besieged her with invitations hastily scrawled on their calling cards, which were usually accompanied by bunches of lilies or roses. Soon the small room she shared with Rose overflowed with perfumed bouquets. The extra flowers decorated the

Coliseum's shabby foyer, adding an unmistakable touch of class to the dingy maroon and yellow walls.

Mair still found it hard to believe that her singing had caused such a furor. So grateful was she to those two well-to-do men for telling their friends about her, she wanted to make an exception to the rule by thanking them personally. Guido would not allow it. He insisted mystery added stature to a performer.

Complete scenes from operas were now standard fare on the Coliseum program. Mair had to work harder than ever to memorize the entire musical score, complete with stage directions, instead of merely learning the showpiece arias. The theater presented *Rigoletto, Lucia* and *Traviata* in rotation, for they were all Mair had mastered.

Guido had great plans for renovating the theater. Ever more seats were to be installed, and a trunk of used costumes had been purchased from a West End theater. A lovely blue velvet gown, decorated with pearls, would soon be altered to fit Mair. This was the most expensive item in the company wardrobe, and Guido had bargained for the garment with Mair in mind. With minor adjustments it would be suitable for Gilda, Lucia and Juliet, a role he was still teaching her. There was even a new backdrop for the popular duet she sang with Eddy from Act One of *Lucia*.

Everything was wonderful. Almost. Nico had not answered her letters! The awful waiting had come to a miserable end one day a week earlier when the postman returned a small bundle of letters, the envelopes marked with a crudely pencilled message: 'Addressee not here. Stop sending.' Oh, how she had wept at the discovery, all her joy over her triumph evaporating.

Cleverly Guido had refused to allow Mair to wallow in her misery. He was constantly at her elbow, urging her on. Triumphantly he waved a newspaper that devoted two lines to an exciting young singer the writer had discovered in an East End music hall. He pointed out reporters in the audience. He constantly reminded her that her dream was on the point of coming true. No time now for tears. There was always the next performance to be rehearsed, more lessons, constant need for improvement. Numbly Mair obeyed, knowing that work would take her mind off her pain. There could be a simple explanation why he had not answered her letters; it did not have to mean he no longer cared for her. Nico could have gone on union work outside London. Though she found it odd that no one at the address knew where he had gone, not once did Mair suspect that Guido had not given her Nico's correct address.

The year, 1887, was Queen Victoria's Golden Jubilee, and Londoners planned a huge celebration. There would be a grand procession on Jubilee Day, June 21. The old queen would drive from Buckingham Palace to Westminster Abbey for a service in thanksgiving for her long reign. The streets would all be decorated with flags and bunting. Even the pubs were to be allowed to stay open until two a.m. so that all London could celebrate fifty glorious years of Victoria's reign.

Guido was putting the finishing touches to the program he had drawn up to commemorate the big event. Jubilee Day fell on Tuesday and would take the place of their added Wednesday night performance. Wisely he had included a little more music hall fare in this elaborate program, suspecting that many of their wealthier patrons would be attending far grander functions on Jubilee Day. To satisfy the few better class patrons who did attend, however, he planned to include two popular scenes from *Lucia*: the famous duet from Act One where Mair could shine, and the final death scene wherein Eddy Lewis made a spectacular suicide. It was the least he could do to appease his tenor, whose feelings were understandably hurt by all the attention Mair had received. Instead of including the more taxing Mad Scene from the same opera, Guido had been coaching Mair in the very difficult 'Rondo' from *Sonnambula*, an aria made popular by the great Adelina Patti. Everytime he thought about their recent good fortune, Guido could only rub his hands in glee. For this gala event the price would be raised to one shilling and sixpence. For that extravagant sum the audience would have their choice of refreshments and each would receive a complimentary slice of Jubilee cake. Guido had no reason to doubt that, despite the price increase, the theater would be filled. Many of their old regulars complained bitterly about the toffs taking all the seats. Even the two extra rows that had been installed, bought cheaply when the Hippodrome remodelled, had not been enough. The Coliseum was literally bursting at the seams. Maybe this time next year they could move to a better location—maybe begin, as he had always dreamed, to build a real opera company. And it was all because of that little Welsh girl.

Guido glanced toward the stage where Mair was rehearsing, the door left open so he could keep his eye on her progress. She looked even more ravishing, sang better than ever . . . but she was not happy. That was all because of that damned Nico. If only the silly girl would forget him. Should he relax his rule and allow her to meet some of their better class patrons? She would soon forget Nico Castelli then. But Mair wasn't quite ready. If she spoke too much, people would detect her Welsh accent; the mystery would evaporate. No, she would have to suffer a little longer.

Guido watched her moving gracefully toward Eddy, arms outstretched, while Amelia trilled the opening bars on the piano. His conscience pricked him when he saw how unhappy Mair looked, but now, more than ever, he had to protect his opera company. When those letters were returned from the Southampton Street address he had hoped things would be better. All he needed now was for that hot-headed Nico to fill her head with foolishness, persuading her she really wanted to be a wife instead of an opera singer. *Dio*, it made him sweat just thinking about it.

The closing notes ended. Guido went across the passage onto the stage.

"Good, is very good, Mair."

She smiled, but only with her mouth. "Thank you, Cousin Guido." She still thought of him in that manner and, as he had never objected to the familiarity, Cousin Guido he remained.

"Are you going to watch the parade on Jubilee Day?"

"May I?" Her eyes lit up.

Guido smiled, patting her shoulder. "Go early, get back in time to rest. Eddy can go with you and Rose—to keep an eye on you is all," he added, fixing Eddy with a stern look. He was not blind. Eddy was far too interested in his little nightingale, and that would never do.

It was a glorious June day; chilly in the early morning; warming steadily under the sun.

Mair was beside herself with excitement. For just a few hours she would forget about being a wanted woman, about being an opera singer, about everything—even Nico. Today she would be just another sightseer at the parade.

Rose would not hear of her wearing one of her serviceable Llandare gowns. In the theatrical hamper there was a gray silk afternoon dress, which Rose had altered to fit Mair. Big pink satin bows trimmed the bustle and slight train; deeper pink roses clustered at neck and bodice. It was splendid. Perhaps too splendid for watching the Jubilee procession, but Rose refused to let Mair talk herself out of wearing it. A hat decorated with pink cabbage roses and designed to perch forward on her upswept hair, completed the costume.

Mair looked beautiful. When she saw herself in the mirror, she kept thinking she was dressed to go onstage. The gown was intended for *Traviata*, but Rose thought it far too lovely to be kept merely for that. In the fitted dove gray silk and soft pink satin, Mair looked as delicate as Dresden porcelain.

Rose wore a frilled gown of blue striped voile, borrowed from the same hamper. On her brown curls perched a yellow straw bonnet trimmed with a bunch of cherries and blue silk streamers.

Because Guido would never have sanctioned them wearing their stage costumes outside the theater, Rose had to watch out for him, waiting until the coast was clear to slip out the side door without being spotted.

Eddy was waiting for them further down the street. He was wearing an elegant dark gray morning suit and a top hat, all borrowed from the theatre.

How grand they all were! Eddy made a very distinguished-looking gentleman and the women appeared winsomely pretty in their borrowed finery. The trio reflected in the distorted glass of a shop window suggested three opera characters escaping offstage, eager to lose themselves in the busy London streets.

They were all three glad to leave their dismal neighborhood as they headed west to the edge of the Holborn district. At the junction with City Road, they caught a horse-drawn omnibus.

It was the first time Mair had ridden on a bus, and she wanted to sit on top in the open air so she could see the sights. The further they travelled, the better the view. Under the sparkling blue sky, the London of her dreams gradually unfolded. The streets were thronged with scores of well-dressed ladies carrying parasols and escorted by gentlemen in top hats, bowlers and straw boaters. Carriages and omnibuses continued to disgorge hordes of passengers all eager to see the Jubilee procession.

Today all London was in a festive mood. The shop fronts sported red, white and blue bunting, which fluttered gaily in the breeze. Proud union jacks snapped back and forth from a multitude of flagpoles. Even the statues and the fountains were patriotically decked out in red, white and blue.

Stands had been errected at intervals along the route for the more well-to-do spectators.

The omnibus finally dropped them off at Birdcage Walk. Rose and Eddy hurried Mair along, too anxious to get a good spot from which to watch the grand procession to allow their provincial friend time to gape at the sights.

They managed to push their way to the forefront of the crowd already gathered ten deep to see the queen. Mair breathed a deep sigh of pleasure as she looked across the broad avenue. There were tall trees with young green leaves rippling in the summer breeze. Bright flowers bloomed in the park, huge bays of red and white glimpsed through the iron railings. This part of London was filled with color, life and beauty. The very idea of returning to drab, dirty Duchess Street was so depressing, Mair decided not to think about it until it was absolutely necessary.

Dozens of vendors passed before them, crying their wares, each trying to shout loud enough to drown out their competitors while hoarsely competing with the noise of the crowd. The warm sun made them thirsty, so they bought cups of lemonade. Then an Italian vendor pushing a pink handcart tempted them with mounds of frozen hokey pokey, which deliciously numbed their throats and made them shiver. Next Eddy generously treated them to Jubilee cakes; each small fruit-studded cake was decorated with white icing with a paper union jack stuck in the top. Mair licked the sticky icing from the flagstick and put it inside her silk purse as a souvenir of the day.

A stir came from the crowd, the sound escalat-

ing to a roar. Horses' hooves were heard as with a
chorus of excited shouts and squeals, the mounted
household cavalry came into view. They were
splendid soldiers wearing bright red coats and tall
helmets, mounted astride the most lovely horses
Mair had ever seen. The troupe rode past in a
jingling cavalcade, passing so swiftly she had not
enough time to take in their magnificence. She had
never seen soldiers look so tall and arrogant.
Several Regimental marching bands followed,
holding themselves stiff and strutting proudly.
Mair likened them to a parade of tin soldiers. A
long succession of dignitaries in horse-drawn carriages followed, all guests of Her Majesty. The
dozens of brilliantly colored liveries of the outriders, the sparkling trappings on the jingling horses,
all flowed past like a glittering river to dazzle her
eyes. Inside several of the carriages she could see
magnificent, turbanned Indian princes and
maharajas dripping with jewels and dressed in
brightly colored rose, emerald and gold brocade
costumes. Mair had to crouch down slightly to see
inside the closed carriage windows. Though Rose
admired the exotic spectacle, she expressed her
disappointment that the Indian rajas were not
riding elephants.

At last there was a shout of 'Here she is!' The
massed bands struck up 'God Save the Queen,' and
the jostling multitude reverently provided the
words. Slowly, majestically, Queen Victoria's open
landau came into view, pulled by six magnificent
cream stallions. Eddy whispered to Mair that these
horses came from Her Majesty's famous stable
of champions. Mair craned forward on tiptoe to

see the Queen. To her disappointment, instead
of a woman gowned in sumptuous robes and
wearing a jeweled crown, she saw a small, dumpy
old woman. Dressed in mourning as was her custom, the Queen wore a lavender bonnet shaped
like a crown and trimmed with point d'Alencon
lace and diamond ornaments that winked in the
light.

"Is that really the Queen?" she gasped incredu-
lously, her face close to Eddy as they both strained
forward.

"Not half as splendid as you, is she, my love?"
Eddy whispered warmly, slipping his hand about
her trim waist.

Mair tried to move out of his grasp but the press
of people were too confining. "Remember, Eddy,
you're just our escort," she hissed in warning, as
his fingers strayed imperceptibly higher, coming
dangerously close to that luscious dove gray silk
bodice.

"We surely don't have to be obedient all the
time," he suggested, trying to maintain his good
humor, despite Mair's aloofness.

"We're three friends out to see the parade."

"And I'm trying to get a little more friendly."

Mair felt the heat of his fingers brush the under-
side of her breast. Swiftly she stepped sideways,
crunching his toes in their smart, patent leather
shoes.

"That's too friendly for me. Wait till you're
invited."

Eddy yelped indignantly as the heel of her canvas boot ground his toes. Damn her! The little
Welsh bitch! Chastised, he removed his straying
hand.

"Better. Now watch the parade and behave yourself."

Rose giggled, squeezing Mair's elbow in sympathy. She was up to Eddy's tricks. Fancy son of a country squire he might be, but he bore just as much watching as any laboring lad, all hands and winning smiles. "There you is, Eddy, you's been told off good and proper," Rose added, much to Eddy's discomfort.

When the final carriage and outriders had passed by, the crowd began to disperse, spilling out into the street.

The glorious parade was over.

Mair had throughly enjoyed herself. She bore no hard feelings toward Eddy, giving him a big smile when he bought her a white china eggcup with a picture of the Queen painted on the side.

Atop the omnibus they all three chattered and laughed about the wondrous spectacle of the Jubilee parade. Mair strained to see the big beds of flowers in the park, pools of yellow, scarlet and white amidst the spring green lawns. This part of London was like another world. It was shocking to realize many of Duchess Street's inhabitants had never seen these lovely sights. The fare for an omnibus ride was beyond the reach of many. Short of walking the long distance, there was no other way they could have seen St. James's Park.

As the grand parks and buildings gradually faded into the distance, Mair's mood sobered. The other two still chatted and laughed, remarking on the passers-by, but she grew silent. The streets they traversed now were dirtier, the pedestrians shabbier. Minute by minute they retreated into the drab world of London's 'other half.' Strange that her most cherished ambitions had come to fruition in this dismal quarter.

Tonight would be another performance; the reminder thrilled her. Already Mair's stomach was tied in knots, the mixture of hokey pokey and lemonade not riding well in the bounce and sway of the omnibus's upper deck. The theater would be full. For many their memories of Jubilee night would include a visit to the Coliseum. Rose had prepared the blue velvet gown for tonight's performance, taking in the waist, letting out the bodice, sewing on pearls. It was sumptuous; fit for a queen. And when she wore it Mair truly felt like the queen of the Coliseum.

"What you smiling about?" Rose asked, seeing Mair's full pink mouth curving in secret humor.

"I was remembering that tonight *I'll* be queen of the Coliseum."

"Correct, my love, and I'll be your king," Eddy reminded, breathing huskily against her ear.

"Cor, Eddy, don't you never give it up?" Rose remarked sharply.

Mair didn't take offense at Eddy's renewed efforts at seduction. She smiled down at the eggcup. She had never owned an eggcup before. Whenever she looked at it she would remember Queen Victoria's Golden Jubilee.

They managed to slip safely inside the theater without getting caught, this hour being reserved for Guido's siesta. Rose giggled nervously as she returned their borrowed finery, hoping the clothing had not been missed. It seemed such a shame to put these lovely clothes away. It didn't matter that the dress hems were frayed, or the rose petals crumpled, these were the most gorgeous clothes

176

any of them had ever worn. Along with these garments she packed their holiday mood. It was back to business as usual. Tonight there was another show to give.

The June evening was warm. Dusty sunlight glanced off the windows across the court. Even though she pined for a breeze, Mair knew better than to open the window and breath in the odor of drains from Primrose Court. What wouldn't she give for a good breath of air on top of Pentre Fawr! An unexpected wave of homesickness gripped her, making her gasp for breath. Mair wondered how Aunty Bet was doing. How cross she must be with her, after having such high hopes for her 'lovely Mair.' Moisture filmed her eyes as she pictured the familiar rooms at home, cramped and nasty though they were. Compared to the accommodation in Primrose Court, No. 10 Maes-y-Groes was most desireable. Several times Mair had begun a letter home, just to let everyone know she was still alive. But always she resisted the impulse just in time. Letters bore postmarks. No point in letting the world know she was in London. Even if she didn't put a return address on the envelope, she was still revealing her hiding place. Far better to let it go.

She swallowed the lump rising in her throat. The trouble with homesickness was that it inevitably brought about that other sickness. She could hardly repeat Nico's name without feeling a flood of heartache. It had been bad enough losing her family and her country, without losing her love as well.

Mair jumped at a knock on the door, half rising

from the couch where she was resting. The evening rest was a ritual strictly adhered to ever since she had become a star. For an hour before she sang, Cousin Guido insisted she lie down to revitalize herself for the big event.

"Come in," she called, knowing it would be Cousin Guido.

"We going to do well tonight. I feel it. There's a big crowd stuffing their faces. Better get ready."

Mair smiled. "I wasn't resting very well, anyway. It's too warm in here."

Guido grunted some unintelligible remark and ambled away. Already wearing his official impressario clothing, he was eager to mingle with tonight's audience. Lately he had given several interviews to newsmen who had come to hear the Golden Nightingale, which is how the press now referred to Maria Parigi. 'Yes, she is a foreigner, no, definitely not English. Young, yes, aloof, very talented.'

Flo came to help Mair with her makeup. The other woman's unsteady gait and the vague aroma of gin hanging about her revealed that Flo had been celebrating Jubilee Day in typical style. Sometime ago Mair had abandoned the idea of trying to save Flo. She had soon learned it was not just Pie and Janey who frequently drank away their rent money; half the women in the company regularly drowned their sorrows in this palliative of choice. Still, gin or no, Flo's hand was steady as she deftly outlined Mair's large blue eyes, then handed her the necessary brushes and powder puffs for her to continue the task.

Reverberating through the old plaster walls

came the strains of an exuberant singsong as the audience took part in rollicking music hall ditties, accompanied by much clapping and foot stomping. Mair found it strange to be costumed for a classical opera role in this setting. Hopefully the audience's raucous enthusiasm would have worked itself out before the classical part of the program. Eddy would be mortified if there was any hilarity when he was agonizing over his lengthy death scene.

Finally it was time for Mair to leave the safety of the cracked plaster sanctuary with its peeling paint, flaring lights and upended orange crate tables. Fear, which usually evaporated once she sang her first note, still gripped her. Mair swallowed several times, trying to prepare herself mentally for her role as Lucia. Her lover would soon appear; they would embrace and pledge their enduring love. How wonderful if the lover she was about to meet had black hair and strong Italian features, instead of Eddy Lewis's cherubic blond countenance.

The scene was well received. The time slipped by almost without Mair's knowledge. It was an uncanny feeling to know she had been onstage, had sung her part, yet not really to remember doing so. Eddy completed his famous death scene, unfortunately not escaping without a few irreverent titters as he rolled down makeshift steps strewn with grass and leaves, the titters escalating to outright laughter as he thrashed about in his final death throes.

"Drunken louts," Eddy snarled as he finally stepped offstage.

Mair uttered vaguely sympathetic words, too

busy concentrating on the unfamiliar aria she was about to sing to spare much sympathy for the conceited Eddy.

A sea of expectant faces met her when she stepped onstage. Mair gripped her hands nervously and, at a cue from Amelia at the piano, she began the aria. When the 'Rondo' from *Sonnambula* was over she was greeted by thunderous applause. Single blossoms were thrown at her feet by the regulars in evening dress who sat in the front row. Cleverly she kissed her hand to these wealthy patrons, touched that they had forgone more elaborate entertainment just to hear her sing. Her gesture further endeared her to her gentlemen admirers.

A welcome cool breeze blew along the corridor outside the dressing room. So nervous had Mair been onstage that her garments were damp with perspiration, and the breeze was uncomfortably chilling. Like magic, Cousin Guido was there, solicitiously draping a cloak around her shoulders. He was beside himself with joy over her superb performance. Effusively praising her in a mixture of English and Italian, he told her the Duke of something or other had come specially to hear her sing. There had been two reporters in the audience again tonight. Oh, they were doing wonderfully well, and all thanks to Mair.

She smiled and squeezed his hand. Tired, drained, but immensely happy, she lay across the dressing room couch, trying to gather herself. This coming down to earth was necessary after her nervous expenditure of energy. Pray God, whenever she walked onstage, it would never fail to go well, that the audience would always be delighted by her performance. She didn't think that now, even after so short a time, she could endure their disapproval. Already she fed hungrily on their praise and admiration. It was almost like a sickness. The terrible stage fright she endured before each performance evaporated as if by magic when she went onstage and felt the flood of emotion cross the footlights. The audience's admiration made her heart soar.

Rose poked her head around the door. "Better than ever," she said with an admiring smile. "It'll be tuppence to talk to you someday, my girl."

"Thank you, Rose, love. You know I'll never charge you a penny."

Mair sat up, smoothing back her hair which stranded damply over her brow.

"Someone outside to see you."

"You know Guido will skin me if I speak to anyone."

"He's ever so nice. Says to me, 'Here, give this to Mair.'" Rose brought out from behind her back a bunch of fragrant, pastel-hued sweet peas.

Wearily Mair held out her hand. Guido was imposing an unfair restriction on her. Sooner or later she would have to speak to her public; this mystery woman act could not be kept up forever.

"Tell the gentleman thank you, for me, Rose. Mm, they're lovely."

Rose stood looking at Mair. "Think you should see this one. Young 'e is, real appealing. And he must know you."

"They all ask for me, that doesn't mean they know me," Mair dismissed, wondering where Rose had left her sense.

"But they don't never ask for Mair."

181

Mair! A thundering began in her chest. With paling cheeks Mair stared in bewilderment at Rose. "Did he call me that? No one in the audience knows that's my name. Oh, Rose, he's not a policeman, is he?"

"Lord luv us, of course not." Rose cackled. "You and them policemen . . . anyone'd think you'd done a murder, the way they scare the daylights out of you."

Mair's face blanched even whiter. "You're sure," she whispered.

"Positive. C'mon, while Guido's talking to them reporters. The fellow's standing outside the door waiting for you."

Mair pulled her wrapper about her and, chilled with apprehension, she followed Rose into the dark corridor.

Chapter Twelve

A cool breeze blew through the door opening onto the street. Laughing people could be seen milling about the pavement, some swaying drunkenly. The smell of horses wafted indoors from the hansoms waiting at curbside. Following the example of the West End theaters, Guido now ordered hansoms at eleven to take theatergoers home. Of course, Duchess Street could only accommodate a half dozen cabs at the most, but it was an added nicety in deference to their better class patrons.

Rose grasped Mair's arm when she hesitated, determined to have her meet this special admirer. Poking her head out the door, Rose glanced about. "There 'e is, under the awning."

The man stood in shadow beneath the theater awning, his dark clothing blending with the buildings; from here Mair did not recognize him. At a signal from Rose, he came toward them. The lithe manner in which he walked and moved his compact body reminded her of Nico: Mair's heart contracted at the memory. The man was dark haired, his olive complexion turned swarthy in the flickering gaslight. Could it be he? Dare she hope? No. His clothing was too well cut—dark coat, top hat—typical theater dress. Nico did not frequent theaters, nor did he wear such expensive clothing . . .

"Mair?"

"Nico?" Her voice was strangled, weak with longing. A mirage, it must be a mirage.

"Oh, Mair, love, I knew it had to be you."

She leaned against the doorjamb for support, her legs shaking.

Mindful of the milling crowd, of Rose, standing there gaping, Nico merely took Mair's hand and raised it to his lips.

"I wrote to you. You never answered. The letters came back," she whispered accusingly, the pain from his rejection not yet healed.

"I never received any letters. Mair, oh, Mair. Why are you here?"

She stiffened slightly at the disapproval in his voice.

"You know why—I'm singing."

"Look, there must be somewhere we can be alone."

Mair glanced at Rose who was standing there, mouth agape, taking everything in. At a nudge from Mair, she came to life.

"The dressing room's clear," Rose volunteered, looking Mair's admirer up and down, trying to calculate his worth. She was not going to have her friend taken in by some Dapper Dan up to no good.

In a daze Mair turned back inside the dark theater. Loud voices echoed through the walls, cockney accents, Italian. Soon Guido would be coming to the dressing room to talk to her. There was so little time.

Highly aware of Nico standing behind her, Mair entered the shabby dressing room. Rose stayed to help her take off her makeup, determined not to leave Mair vulnerable to this man's whims until she was sure he could be trusted.

"Alone, Mair? This isn't alone. Come to dinner with me, then we can talk about all this?" He waved his hand, the gesture taking in the poverty of the room.

"I can't. I've nothing to wear," Mair said lamely, her hair falling across her face in a golden curtain as she paused, brush upraised.

"Wot about that gray silk you wore this morning?" Rose hissed down her ear. She had reached a decision. The pain in Mair's face, the burning intensity in the man's dark eyes, suggested far more hinged on this meeting than met the eye. Always an incurable romantic, Rose had become their instant ally.

"Can you get it without him knowing?" Mair asked uneasily, wanting to go with Nico more than anything in the world, yet held back by fear. Did she fear learning why he had not contacted her, or was it more the terrible confession she must make that made her hesitate?

"Be 'alf a mo'." Rose disappeared, leaving them alone.

"Why did you run away?"

"I had my reasons."

"Reasons? Oh, they're plain enough. You wanted

to be an opera singer. Despite all I told you about Guido."

"You told me only what you suspected. You didn't know."

"But I was right. Or do you think this is the grand opera house?" he snapped, his dark eyes hardening. "You didn't listen to me. Have you any idea what could have happened to you—what still might?"

Rose reappeared at that moment, cutting short his angry outburst. Nico moved aside and leaned against a stack of orange crates.

"Here, be quick, change behind the screen," Rose urged, pulling Mair to her feet. "He'll be down 'ere afore long."

Galvanized into action, Mair stepped behind the wooden screen. Nervousness made her fingers clumsy as she fumbled with the fastenings of the blue velvet gown, her mind in turmoil. Not once had Nico said he had missed her, nor had he complimented her on her appearance. In fact, had she not known it was he, had her heart not reacted with that same frenzied beat, she would have thought this dark-haired man in top hat and black coat was a stranger.

Rose would not allow Mair to waver in her decision to go to dinner with her handsome admirer; pulling, pushing, unpinning, she worked feverishly. A hat not being acceptable wear for a fancy after-theater supper, Rose ripped the silk cabbage roses from the dress's matching hat and deftly wove them into Mair's upswept hair, securing them with a handful of hairpins. So swiftly did she work that Rose's upper lip beaded with sweat from her exertions. But she had Mair ready in record time.

The old black cape lying across the couch, edged in Spanish lace and fastened with jet and *passementerie* frogs, was suitable for most occasions. Rose thrust the wrap into Mair's hands.

"Go on, love, hurry up. He'll be down here in a minute."

"We'll wait. I'd like a word with Cousin Guido," Nico announced with set mouth.

"Oh, no, please, not a scene. Let's go. We can speak to him later," Mair pleaded, having no intention of carrying out that suggestion. All she wanted was to get away from here without trouble. Once she had told Nico her terrible secret, she knew his intentions would change. They couldn't afford to anger Cousin Guido.

"Yes, go on, I'll tell 'im something," Rose urged, seeing the distress in Mair's face.

Shooing them before her, somewhat surprised that they both meekly obeyed, Rose moved them out into the corridor where Guido's voice could be heard booming from the depth of the theater.

Wonder of wonders, they were finally standing outside in the cool night. Most of the theater crowd had already dispersed, but several empty hansoms were still waiting at the curb.

Nico gripped Mair's arm as he signaled to the first driver. Then, before she could change her mind, she found herself propelled inside the vehicle.

"The Coburg," Nico commanded, before stepping inside the cab and slamming the door.

When Mair glanced back at the stage door, she

saw Rose had gone. Now she was alone with him in this confined space. The realization made her nervous. Anxiously Mair clasped her sweating palms. They sat opposite, their knees virtually touching. Chills ran up and down her body at the warm exciting pressure from his legs as they rounded a corner and were pressed even closer. This was not what she had expected when they met again. Nico was supposed to sweep her in his arms while he declared his undying love; instead he was being decidedly hostile.

Nico finally spoke, unable to hold his tongue any longer.

"Well, come on, I'm waiting to hear a few of those reasons," he commanded harshly. "Don't you realize you could have been murdered or raped. Anything could have happened to you alone in London."

"I'm not alone. I'm with Cousin Guido."

"Oh, and a grand escort he's proved to be. Here you are, living in this district, pigging in with that lot. What are you thinking about, girl?" Nico demanded angrily, emotion making him lapse into more recognizable Llandare accents.

Now Mair felt a little more on home ground. "Well, I haven't been murdered, raped, or any of those other horrors. And what's more, I'm singing onstage and doing a good job of it. They write about me in the papers now, you know."

"I know, that's how I found you. The 'Golden Nightingale,' Signorina Maria Parigi. And whose bright idea was that?"

"Cousin Guido's."

"I should've known. Still up to his old tricks,

pretending you're some continental opera star to fill the theater.''

"Now listen here, there's no trickery needed these days to fill the theater. They come all the way from the fancy West End to listen to me, or didn't you know?''

"I'm well aware of that. I've spoken to some of them. Going into raptures over you, they are, gawping at you onstage in your nightgown.''

"Oh, so that's it, is it. You don't want other men seeing me in my nightgown. Oh, well, now we're at the bottom of this. I thought it was my welfare you were worried about—I should've known.'' Anger over his typical male objection shot through her body, threatening to bubble over.

"Mair, stop it!''

Nico grasped her wrists and shook her, dislodging waiting tears, which coursed down her cheeks and splashed onto the black cashmere wrap.

"You stop it then,'' she croaked, licking tears from her lips.

"I'm sorry. I didn't mean to be angry with you,'' he apologized, squeezing her hand.

"All right.'' She sniffed hard, blinking back her tears. "Apology accepted—I s'pose.''

"You suppose!''

Her mouth twitched with the glimmer of a smile. "You're forgiven only if you start being nice to me.''

It was Nico's turn to smile. He was so emotionally involved with Mair he had allowed his passion to errupt in anger.

"Sorry, girl,'' he whispered huskily, "I'll try to keep my temper.''

"That's better." She gave his hand an answering squeeze, shivering as the warm strength of his fingers closed over hers.

Afraid to destroy this truce, neither of them spoke for the rest of the journey. The cab stopped before the grand facade of the Coburg Hotel off Grosvenor Square.

Mair looked out at this broad thoroughfare brightly illuminated by gaslights. A large painted royal standard was affixed to the top of each lamp standard. The elegant facade of the hotel was decorated for the Royal Jubilee with streamers and bunting. Through its windows ablaze with light could be seen merrymakers dancing and dining in the hotel's splendid reception rooms.

"Can this be the right place?" she whispered, awed by these grand surroundings.

"This is it. Oh, I've come up in the world. You'd hardly know me now."

Nico's words struck a sad chord. He was right there. Up until thirty minutes ago she'd begun to think her memory was playing tricks on her, that this was not the man she remembered, after all.

They alighted in the mild summer darkness. Gay orchestra music echoed from inside the building. A constant stream of splendidly dressed patrons moved up and down the marble steps in front of the hotel, getting in and alighting from a string of hansoms that lined the curb.

Nico paid the cab driver and they headed for the hotel's canopied entrance atop a broad flight of steps. Huge doors stood open invitingly, beckoning them inside the marble-pillared foyer.

"How can you afford to stay here?" Mair whispered as she ascended the steps on his arm, smiling serenely at passing guests as if she did this every day.

"I've got wealthy friends," was all Nico said in answer to her question.

Realizing they were heading for the dining room, Mair caught Nico's arm. "Please, there's something I must tell you first, something that can only be said in private."

With a shrug, he obediently turned away from the dining room, going instead to the right. They moved up a broad marble staircase. Mair looked over the bannister to admire the foyer. A hotel? It was more like a palace! All the other guests were so well dressed that Mair's gray silk gown, which had once seemed so lovely, paled by comparison.

They turned several corners and crossed landings until Nico finally stopped before a cream-painted door, heavily embellished with gilded moldings.

Mair gasped in amazement as the door swung open to reveal a lofty bedroom. The gold satin draped windows and matching bedcover were fit for a queen. The carpet, floral patterned in shades of fawn and magenta, was so deeply piled that her feet sank into it as they crossed the room. Everything was so luxurious, Mair could scarcely believe her eyes.

Nico smiled at her repeated gasps of wonder as he quietly closed the door. "Now love, I don't want to hurry you, but they'll not be serving supper indefinitely. Tonight's late menu is special for Jubilee Night. Here, sit down, and now tell me this terrible secret."

Mair sat as instructed, slightly nettled by his amused tone. Oh, he'd be surprised all right when he knew what her 'terrible secret' was. There'd be no humor then, no teasing banter. His presence had not made her feel safe as she had expected. Far from it. In his current mood she felt exposed to criticism and certain condemnation.

Nico nervously drummed his fingers on the mahogany marble topped sideboard, waiting impatiently for her to begin. Mair cleared her throat and, after working up sufficient courage, she finally said:

"You wanted to know my reasons for leaving Llandare. To sing, of course, but I had intended to take your advice. It's just that something happened so suddenly, I couldn't stay. Nico, I never planned this, I want you to understand that. You of all people should know I never meant . . ." Her mouth began to tremble and Mair fought the urge to burst into tears.

Nico pitched his coat and top hat on the bed. He was trying patiently to listen to her garbled tale, but she could tell he was not making much sense of it.

Mair swallowed and began again on a new note. "You know I'm not an evil person, that I wouldn't intentionally do such a thing. Surely . . ." She stopped, a sudden thought flitting through her mind. "You've been back to Llandare since I left, haven't you?"

"How else would I have known you'd disappeared without telling a soul? I guessed you'd gone with Guido, but I didn't tell anyone. I had to be sure first."

If he'd been back to Llandare then he must know everything. And if he knew, why was he making her go through this tortuous explanation? Mair's head snapped up indignantly and her mouth tightened.

"Go on, then. Ask me if I did it."

Nico threw his hands in the air. "Did what? You'll have to explain yourself better than this?"

"Kill old Tegwyn Williams, that's what! Why are you insisting on me telling you, like you never knew about it? You should've already realized I had no choice but to leave. Strange as it may seem to you, Cousin Guido save my life."

Nico stared speechless at her, trying to fathom what on earth she was talking about. "Kill old Tegwyn Williams," he repeated, baffled. Then he gave her his handkerchief, for she was sobbing wildly.

Mair mopped her streaming eyes and blew her nose. When she finally spoke, her nose was stuffed and her speech adenoidal. "I never meant to do it. He attacked me. He wouldn't take no for an answer—drinking he'd been, at old John Jones's funeral. Oh, they'll put me in prison, you know they will—might even hang me. Oh, Nico, I've been so afraid."

He caught her hands and pulled her from the couch.

"You haven't killed anybody."

"I didn't mean to, but they won't look at it like that. He was important see, they'd never believe me."

Nico took her shoulders and shook her gently. "Stop it. Stop crying and listen to me, you silly girl. Old Tegwyn Williams isn't dead. He's hale and hearty as ever, the old hypocrite. Do you hear? *Not dead*!"

Mair's mouth opened and her eyes widened. "Not dead?"

"No, he's very much alive. Now, you're saying you tried to kill him?"

"No—not meaning to. I hit him when he wouldn't let me alone. And he fell and struck his head. I was so sure he was dead when I left!"

Hugging her to him, Nico chuckled, pressing her hot face against his coat. He stroked her hair. "Oh, hush, hush. Now it's becoming clear. I thought his story was a bit fishy from the start. You just knocked him out, that's all. He told everyone he'd fallen and struck his head—don't suppose he wanted the real story to get out. Then, as you couldn't be found and no one knew where you'd gone, there were a few ideas about the true version of the tale, him not being quite as holy as he pretends."

"I didn't kill him? You're sure he's not dead? The police aren't looking for me?"

"I'm the only one been looking for you," he whispered softly against her hair. He hugged her close. "I'm telling you once and for all, you didn't kill him. All this time you've been worrying for nothing."

Mair still cried, but her sobs became soft and relieving, spawned by deep weariness instead of anxiety. The waiting was over. No more need to fear policemen. No more wondering when they'd catch her. Even the guilt for taking a life could be laid to rest.

"Oh, Nico," she whispered brokenly, "all this time I've been so afraid of them arresting me."

"Hush, it's all right. No need to be afraid any longer. I'm here now," he comforted, stroking her hair, her neck, whispering soft endearments as she continued to sob. Finally the heaving of her shoulders lessened. Mair gazed up at him, blue eyes red-rimmed with weeping, but dry at last.

"You say you've been looking for me?"

"When you didn't answer my letters, I went back to Llandare to talk to you. That's when I found you'd gone. No one knew where—supposed to be Cardiff. Don't know where they got that idea."

Mair did, recalling the tickets she had purchased in an attempt to put people off her trail.

"What about Da and Aunty Bet?"

"Angry that you left such a good post, but sad too, because in their way they love you too. Oh, now, no more tears."

Mair was crying again at the thought of the pain she had caused her family. Now she could put things right. She would send them a letter of apology, explaining what had happened, telling them what a success her singing was.

"Come on, sweetheart, let's go downstairs to celebrate. Tonight we've both been reborn from the dead."

Laughing, crying with joy, Mair smoothed her hair and tried to rearrange the crushed roses on her gown. By degrees her heavy burden of guilt and care was lifting. She felt young and light-hearted again. How good it was not to dread tomorrow.

"Did you hear me sing tonight?" she asked him curiously.

"Yes, and you were wonderful, even better than I expected—come on, sweetheart, let's go downstairs."

"But surely my hair . . ." she faltered, looking in

a huge bevelled glass mirror beside the door. "Oh, it's sprouting everywhere," she cried in dismay.

"I promise you'll be the most beautiful woman in the dining room," Nico assured, leading her from the room. "After we've eaten we'll come back here and . . ."

Their eyes met and the burning emotion she saw reflected there made her shiver in anticipation. "Yes," she whispered in assent. And she squeezed his arm beneath the fine black serge. "That will be the perfect end to Jubilee Day."

Great palms and banks of fragrant flowers decorated the gilded and paneled dining room. The tables, topped by stiffly starched white cloths, were set with fine gold-trimmed bone china dishes and gleaming silver cutlery. Bouquets of red and white carnations surrounded by blue statice and verbena nestled inside lace doileys in the center of the tables; more elaborate flower arrangements graced the larger banquet settings.

Though they had no reservation, a place was found for them. They were directed to a table in a secluded corner behind a potted palm. The waiter privately considered this a most undesirable table for the hotel guests who usually wished their evening finery to be seen. For a romantic young couple, however, the location was ideal. Between courses, when Nico took her hand and raised it to his lips, there was no one to observe except the monstrous palm.

Dinner began with mock turtle soup, which Mair found delicious. A silver platter of soft white rolls, spread with thick yellow butter accompanied the soup. Poached salmon, garnished with sprigs of parsley, followed. They both declined the roast

beef in rich gravy, though they each took helpings
of fresh minted garden peas, braised turnips and
roast potatoes. Wine was served with the dinner.
Not wanting a muzzy head to interfere with their
long awaited reunion, they both drank sparingly. A
dessert of molded milk jelly in patriotic colors and
surrounded by a sea of brandy-poached pears
completed the meal. The platter of cheese, grapes
and biscuits, was left untouched.

Almost in a dream Mair put down her stiffly
starched serviette. As they crossed the dining
room, her knees felt weak, and it wasn't from the
wine. Decorously Mair rested her hand on Nico's
arm. Beneath his coat sleeve she could feel tremors of excitement and the knowledge that he was as
excited as she at the prospect of their lovemaking
made her heart race.

Today had been the most wonderful day of her
life. First the grand Jubilee procession, then
tonight's successful performance—yet they both
paled to insignificance before this, the most wonderful event of all.

"You never answered my letters," she accused,
suddenly remembering that major oversight. They
were ascending the broad staircase to the upper
floors.

"Where'd you send them?"

"An address in Southampton Street that Cousin
Guido gave me."

"I haven't lived there in several years."

"Oh! He mustn't have known."

"He knew. You don't think he wanted his star
attraction spirited away, do you? He probably
hoped you'd forget about me."

"No—surely not," she protested, feeling immense goodwill toward the world in general. "Anyway, I'll ask him."

Nico smiled cynically. Mair hadn't changed much, despite her stay in London. Touched by such innocent simplicity, he slid his arm around her waist and hugged her to him. The corridor was temporarily deserted and he felt safe from discovery. Mair had tilted up her face to his expectantly, longing for his kiss. Nico's mouth came down on hers, hot and arousing. She knew he was holding back his passion, waiting until they could be alone.

Arms around each other's waists, they slowly walked along the corridor to his room. When he unlocked the door they found the room partially lit by a pearl-shaded lamp the maid had left on when she came to turn down the bed.

Once the door was safely closed against the outside world, they were free to love without restraint.

"Come here," Nico invited huskily, arms outstretched.

Slowly Mair came to him, the few feet seeming like miles. At last she reached the safe haven of his arms, the sanctuary she had longed for with all her heart. She laid her head against his shoulder, breathing deep of the scent of him, so well remembered. How warm, how safe she felt, clasped in his arms. Nico's hot lips softly teased her neck, exploring the sensitive nape exposed by her upswept hair.

Tremors of excitement shot through Mair's limbs; the heated swell of passion coursed through her veins.

"This has to be the most perfect night of my life," he breathed against her ear, his hot tongue stealing about the lobe, teasing, tickling. "How much I hoped this fabulous woman they were all raving about was you."

"What if it had been some other woman? Would you have invited her to dinner instead?"

He chuckled, knowing she teased. "Perhaps, depending on how pretty she was."

Mair punched him playfully and he captured her wrists, stopping the blows.

"To think I have to listen to such talk," she cried, struggling halfheartedly to free herself. "You should be ashamed of yourself."

"Maybe I shall be—much later."

Without warning, he seized her, half carrying her toward the bed. Mair squealed in mock fright as they fell together on the smooth satin coverlet, the fabric cool against her warm skin.

Slowly, methodically, Nico pulled out her hairpins, dropping the bone pins on the bedcover. Mair's beautiful golden hair came tumbling down, falling like a cloak about her shoulders. Nico shivered at the glorious sight. His hands trembled as he smoothed the silken strands off her face, placing light, tantalizing kisses across her brow, down her nose and cheek, until his face came to rest amidst the silken cabbage roses edging her bodice.

The pressure of his hot mouth, the arousing flutter of his breath against her skin, made Mair shiver deliciously. When Nico fumbled with the fastenings of her bodice, she helped him, frustrated because he worked so slowly. Secretly she would have liked him to rip the bodice from her aching body, impatient to feel his hands, his mouth, on those secret places. Yet she was too wise to urge him to do that. This gown had to be returned undamaged to the costume hamper or poor Rose would suffer the consequence.

Gently Nico drew down the dove gray fabric, his mouth following the passage of whispering silk. The milk-white smoothness of her flesh was exposed. Fire rocketed through Mair's veins as she felt his hot, questing lips move across her breasts, coming to rest on the upthrusting pinnacle of her nipple, firmly aroused beneath his mouth. Moaning in delight, she fastened her hands in his thick black hair, sinking her fingers in the waving depth, moving down to his neck where the skin was smooth and hot.

As if by mutual agreement, they moved the resisting dove gray silk gown to a safe place on the couch. Nico stripped off his dark coat, pausing to look at her, his shirtsleeves gleaming in the soft lamplight. Mair reclined seductively on the gold satin bedcover, wearing only her drawers and petticoats. Her shapely stockinged legs in their dark canvas boots were curled lazily beneath her. Her lovely pink-tipped breasts invited his caress. Carefully he placed his own finery beside hers on the back of the couch, mindful of the expense and purpose of these tailored garments.

When Nico stood undressed, the pearly lamplight caressing his broad square shoulders and high, firm buttocks, Mair shuddered in pleasure at his beauty. He stood so still, his hard majestic profile might have been chiseled from marble. Once again she was reminded of his racial ancestors depicted in the old masters at Tal-y-Bont. The difference between them made him excitingly exotic, yet at the same time unattainable. She shrugged off that unwelcome thought as she eagerly held out her arms to him.

Nico resisted no longer. The bed dipped suddenly as he lunged for her and captured her easily, their bodies sliding over the smooth satin cover. Mair shuddered as she ran her hands over his hard shoulders and muscular back. Gently she tangled her fingers in the springy black hair on his chest, then taking his brown nipple between her lips, she teased him with her tongue until he groaned in pleasure. How smooth and firmly shaped were his lean flanks, his belly, where the black hair formed a vee. Wickedly tracing that shape with her tongue, she finally allowed herself to capture the treasure she sought. Nico gasped aloud in delight as she softly laved her tongue around his hot, swollen flesh.

"Oh, Mair, sweetheart, I love you so. Say this will never end," he whispered hoarsely in an agony of passion.

"Not while we both have breath," she promised, taking his hands and placing them on her breasts.

Needing little encouragement to caress that beloved sweetness, Nico marveled at the firm fullness of her breasts. How sweet would be their passion so long delayed. He wondered why he chose such terrible torture. With every fiber of his being he longed to take her, to end this delicious torment, yet still he kissed and fondled until he was beside himself with desire.

"Now, sweetheart, let me love you now," he whispered at last, unable to hold out any longer.

Patricia Phillips

Murmuring her acquiescence beneath his hot lips, she wondered how either of them could endure a moment longer. Mair spread her legs, anxious to receive his heated love-making. There was no need to direct him, no need to assure him he was doing what she wanted. Nico played her body like a fine instrument. One lesson had been all he needed to master this symphony of love. Sparks shot through her body, and the agonizing frenzy of mutual passion lit a conflagration beyond compare.

In a mixture of impassioned Italian and Welsh, they whispered all manner of love nonsense. Moaning, Mair arched her back, urging him to deeper penetration. How she longed to take him deep inside her, to keep him there, fused as one for all eternity. No other man could ever bring her this ecstacy; no other man could ever love her like Nico.

Suddenly the pleasure escalated to a new level. He fastened his mouth over hers. Mair no longer strove to take him deeper, she merely tried to maintain control over her mounting passion. As he moved faster, more rythmically, so that the heat increased, she knew it was a hopeless task. Mair cried out. She clung to him, digging her fingers in his smooth, hot back, clutching him with her legs, demanding and fulfilling at the same time. Swirling up into light, they plunged together from the pinnacle, arms and legs entwined, lips, hearts and souls as one.

Shuddering, they tried to catch their breath, their breathing shallow and painful, until slowly they returned to the warmth of each other's arms.

"Mair, I love you so much," Nico whispered when at last they lay still, locked close. He held her safe until she returned from that place where passion reigned so strong that it was like dying and where love alone bound their souls.

"Oh, *Cariad*, I don't think I'll ever feel so wonderful again," Mair revealed wonderingly, cherishing him, kissing his hot cheek, his closed lids.

"Oh, yes you will, many, many times. I promise."

She saw him smile, his mouth soft now, the hard grim visage melted in the heat of passion. How much she loved him.

They kissed and held, whispering love words, stroking each other's bodies until the smoldering embers were again fanned into flame. When Nico took her again, this time it was with more control and less speed, so that Mair finally had to admit, with mingled tears and laughter, that she had been wrong. There was no end to this secret garden of delight, to the flowering of his passion, which died only to be reborn the sweeter.

Chapter Thirteen

In the sunlit summer morning, Mair stirred drowsily, stretching in the luxury of the soft feather bed. Sparrows twittered outside the open window from whence drifted the sounds of rumbling cart wheels, horses' hooves and the racous cries of street vendors as the city gradually came to life.

A tap on the door announced breakfast was served.

Mair slid beneath the sheets, pretending to sleep while the maid brought the breakfast trays into the room. Once the woman had left, she tentatively sat up, looking about. To her shock she found Nico had gone!

Her heart slowed its panicking race when she noticed his valise beside the wardrobe. Still plagued by insecurity, she was afraid he had left her. The thought of the silver-framed picture in Anna Castelli's parlor caused her unease, an unpleasant reminder of the proper, convent-reared Italian girl already chosen to be his wife. Even after last night there were still many questions left unanswered.

Last night! The memory of their shared bliss made her smile, and she closed her eyes, shuddering as she relived his kisses, his caresses, the heat of his lovemaking. Surely other women did not feel that same shattering delight, or how could they shun their husband's attentions? But then, their husbands were not Nico Castelli. She would probably join their frigid ranks had she had the misfortune to marry Davy Hughes.

"Still sleeping?" Nico asked, coming out of the dressing room.

Mair opened her eyes, smiling up at him and admiring his maroon wool dressing gown faced with satin.

"You look very nice," she complimented, stroking his quilted lapel as he leaned down to kiss her. "Have you come into a fortune?"

Nico grinned. "Not yet, but I'm working at it. Shall we eat now? Making love to you makes me ravenously hungry. I worked off my Jubilee dinner hours ago."

He carried the heavy tray to the bed. The feast that was revealed when the silver covers were removed included devilled kidneys, sizzling pork sausages, shirred eggs, spiced apple slices, toast and crispy rolls, accompanied by a pot each of tea and chocolate. The dainty china plates and cups were decorated with heartsease and rimmed in gold leaf.

Mair sat up, pulling the sheets up around her chest. Breakfast in bed was an undreamed-of luxury, and this particular breakfast was like a mini banquet presented to her by the most handsome man in the world. She sighed with pleasure as she watched him take charge of serving the meal. Having Nico butter her bread and dish out soft, golden mounds of eggs merely added to her pleasure. Adeptly he speared the sausages as they tried to escape on a lake of tasty drippings. Unable to decide whether to drink the familiar tea, or be adventurous and try a continental chocolate, Mair decided she would have a cup of each.

The meal was heavenly. Nico slid beside her inside the warm covers to eat his own breakfast. Glancing sideways at him, Mair discovered that for the first time since she had known him, he needed a shave. Black stubble prickled his chin and upper lip, roughening his lean features. This small intimacy made her feel even more a part of his life. Mair pretended they were married. Someday, when she was a famous singer, they would stay in posh hotels like this all over the world. Nico would be beside her every day—and most importantly, every night.

"You know, when I'm world famous, we're going to do this every morning," Mair announced as she finished her toast.

Nico was reading the morning paper and he nodded agreement, though she suspected he was not really listening. She supposed she would have to put up with that inattention also, it seemed to be one of the penalties of marriage. But she didn't really mind; today she was too happy to carp over little failings.

"What you reading, *Cariad*?" she asked him, swatting down the paper so she could see his face.

206

"About a meeting held a couple of nights ago. Trying to see if the reporting's unbiased."

"And is it?"

"Yes, surprisingly. That's what happens when you have wealthy friends in high places. You get a little bigger slice of the truth."

"Who are these mysterious wealthy backers I keep hearing about?"

He grinned, laying aside the paper. "No one you'd know."

"Secret, is it?"

"Not really. Gladstone, Parnell and a young Welshman named Lloyd George."

"Go on, you're pulling my leg."

"Well, they're not actually my backers, they're just very interested in my career."

"What with, organising the unions and such?"

"No, not that." He twisted her hair round his finger, smiling indulgently at her questions. "I've gone further than that. I'm going to run for political office. Now, what do you think of that, Mair Parry?"

"Prime Minister, is it?" she asked sarcastically, taking the last of her roll and popping it into her mouth.

"Someday, maybe. First I've got to get a seat in my district. The Castelli and Gambino shipping company owners are behind me, for one. And there's a couple of others, big wigs they are, highly interested in reorganizing the docks. For the time being I'm working with the men agitating for change, but I won't stay with them forever. Somewhere there'll be a dividing point. They'll go one way, and me—I'll go to the House of Commons."

"Always have been ambitious, haven't you."

"Not any less ambitious than you. Always saying you were going to sing in London and now you're doing it and doing it damned well. Don't fault me for ambition, girl."

Mair laughed at his quick retort. Yet, as she digested this latest information about just how high his ambition soared, she felt uneasy. "Did your wealthy backers put you up in this fancy hotel?"

"We met here for dinner a couple of nights ago and Sir Alfred Crawford let me use his suite while he's away from London."

"And the clothes?"

"Oh, they're mine all right. Compliments of Joe Gambino. He fronted me the money to get a real wardrobe made. It's fine for dockers to look like something the cat's dragged in. It's even all right at the workers' rallies. But when you're meeting with rich, influential men, you have to look the part."

Mair's stomach had pitched at his mention of Joe Gambino. Here was another unpleasant reminder of Teresa, the chosen wife-to-be. "Is he Teresa's father?" she asked, trying to sound nonchalent.

Nico glanced quickly at her, and slid from the bed.

"Yes," he replied, taking the tray back to the table.

Had she imagined it, or did this subject make him vastly uncomfortable?

"Thought you worked for your uncle."

"I do. Uncle Sal's the Castelli part of the shipping company. He and Joe Gambino are partners."

"I see."

Mair slid down further in the bed, her heart

thumping uneasily. She was no fool. Joe Gambino would not provide a tailor-made wardrobe out of the goodness of his heart. The gift had been given in consideration that Nico would soon become his son-in-law.

"So her father's investing in you because he expects you'll marry into the family."

Nico paused on his way to the adjoining dressing room. His set expression was hard to interpret.

"I can't deny that probably has something to do with it."

"Then you haven't told Teresa Gambino you don't intend to marry her?"

"Mair, don't let's spoil today with this kind of talk. As I told you before, I haven't seen Teresa Gambino for a long time. Let's leave it at that."

Without waiting for further discussion, he went into the dressing room to shave. When he re-emerged, Nico wore a clean white shirt, tailored dark gray trousers and shiny black demi-boots.

"Come on, get up, lazybones. We've lots to do today," he said cheerfully, making an effort to lighten the mood.

Mair scrambled out of bed. "What are we going to do today that's so important?" she asked, padding across the soft carpet to the flower-decked pitcher and basin on the marble-topped dresser. The oval bar of white soap felt like butter and the delightful fragrance graced her skin like the scent of fresh flowers.

Mair slipped into her gray silk gown. "Well," she prompted, "you haven't answered my question."

He grinned at her. "That's my surprise. First we're going shopping for clothes for you. No more borrowed finery for my Mair. And secondly," here he planted a soft kiss on the nape of her neck, hampering her efforts to fasten up her thick hair. "We're going house hunting!"

His statement made her heart race with excitement.

"House hunting?" she repeated breathlessly. "We're getting a house? For *us*?" This latter she whispered, almost afraid to speak out loud in case the speaking of it destroyed the dream.

Nico gently slipped his hands over her breasts as he stooped to kiss her neck. His touch set the sparks flying and Mair shuddered with pleasure.

"Now, then, we'll not get much house hunting done if you start that," she admonished, leaning back against him. Their reflection was framed in the gilt-edged mirror above the mahogany dresser; they looked perfect together, a medley of dark and light. Tears prickled her eyes, so intense was her emotion for him.

"Will you love me forever?" she whispered, her voice thick with tears as she reached up to stroke his face.

"I swear to love you as long as I live," Nico vowed intensely, his smile fading. "You are my lovely Mair, my sweetheart, my only love."

She closed her eyes, lulled happily by the soft sincerity of his words. "Oh, Nico, I'm so happy to be with you again."

"I promise we'll never be apart—except for the times I have to go away on business, of course." With this last statement, she felt him withdraw emotionally, though he still embraced her.

"What about my singing?"

"You can still sing, you don't have to go away to

210

do that. But you aren't ever going back to Cousin Guido's ramshackle lodgings."

"Because instead I'll be living with you in our house?"

He hesitated a little too long. "Yes. If you like."

"If I like? You know, there's something about all this I don't understand, and I'm not sure I do like it," Mair said, brought back to her senses. "Now you go stand over there and keep your hands to yourself so I can think clearly and we'll get this straight."

Laughing, Nico obliged, retreating several paces to stand beside the bed. "This far enough?"

"It'll do. Now, are we getting a house for us, or not?"

"For you," he corrected carefully. "Of course, I'll be there with you as often as I'm able."

A cold chill spread down her spine. She gasped in indignation. "Like a kept woman!"

"For heaven's sake, you don't have to term it quite like that, Mair. Surely you don't intend to stay in that slum for the rest of your life?"

"No. I expected to be living with you."

He took a step toward her, his impatience mounting.

"And that's what you'll be doing. You'll live in our house every day of the week. I'll be there as often as I can. It'll be a convenient arrangement for both of us."

"And what about marriage? I don't remember you asking me to marry you."

He glanced away at her sharp reminder. Mair had always been too practical, too much to the point.

"In all honesty, love, I can't do that just yet.

Maybe by the end of the year, perhaps sooner. But not now."

"Fair enough," she agreed, swallowing her disappointment.

"Don't be hurt, Mair. Please, try to understand. At the moment I'm too involved in union business and in trying to launch a political career to consider marriage. Besides, I really can't take on such a big expense. I'd thought we'd rent a small, decent house, maybe something in St. John's Wood. That's convenient to the city. You'd be able to have a garden. You've always loved flowers and trees," he added persuasively, warming to his subject. "You'll like it there, Mair, I know you will. So come on, stop being so difficult. We love each other. That's all that really matters, isn't it?"

Though she would have loved to follow him blindly, there were too many strings attached to this gift. "No, that's not all that matters," she contradicted quietly. "I'm a decent woman, though maybe the way I've behaved with you doesn't support that claim. I don't know much about St. John's Wood, but I do know if I live there in your house, it'll be because I'm paying rent. That's the only way to make it proper until we're married."

"Damn it, Mair, can't you forget your infernal chapel background?" he cried, angry that his plans were being thwarted. "You wouldn't be able to afford to pay that much rent anyway."

"I won't always be singing for nothing. I'll pay you from what I earn."

"When we live there you won't be earning anything."

"What?"

"I said you could still sing. But you can't stay on the stage, not if we expect to marry. You'd have to be respectable."

Mair bristled at his remark. "Respectable! Oh, you're a fine one to talk. Here you are proposing to keep me shut away on the sly until it suits you. You say we can't marry because you'll be too busy with your political career. Isn't it more likely that if you tell Joe Gambino you won't be marrying his daughter, there won't be any political career?" Mair shouted, her fists clenched in anger.

Nico blanched at her unflattering summation. And Mair knew she had hit very close to the truth.

"Mair, please, don't start jumping to conclusions."

"And don't you lie to me. Let's have it straight out—have you, or have you not, broken off your arrangement with Teresa Gambino?"

Unwaveringly she met his dark eyes, nearly black now in the passionate intensity of the moment. Nico's mouth was set, his face grim. He need'not answer. She already had the truth.

Gulping, Mair turned away, tears gushing down her cheeks. Outside the window a sparrow warbled in irritating gladness. All her hopes, her joy, at his mention of their house, had been premature. Nothing had changed.

"Please, Mair, just bear with me a little while longer. This way we can be together. You said that's what you wanted."

"It is what I want, but I also want to sing— professionally, on the stage. Going back to singing in the church choir or entertaining guests isn't

enough anymore. Singing's a part of me, just like
your political hopes are part of you. Can't you
understand the thrill I get from singing for an
audience? How wonderful their applause makes
me feel? I'm that good, Nico—how can you ask me
to give it up?"

"Not forever, just for a while. Besides, there's no
comparison between the two. A man's expected to
have a career, whereas you're just a—" he stopped
himself too late.

"A woman who's only expected to scrub dirty
socks and birth babies. Oh, you're not as removed
from Llandare as you like to think, Nico Castelli.
With that outlook you could be any lad just up
from Owen Pit Number Two. Well, let me tell you, I
don't intend to leave Cousin Guido's company and
I don't intend to stop singing. Now, if that spoils
your plans, I'm sorry, but it can't be helped."

Mair's voice cracked on that final word. Appalled
by what she was saying, she swallowed hard. Here
she was, recklessly throwing aside something so
dear to her heart. Yet singing was also dear to her
heart. She had never expected to have to choose
between the two.

"Have sense," Nico cried, seizing her wrist. "You
can't continue to live in that slum and sing at that
fleabag music hall. Instead I'm offering you decency, pleasant surroundings . . ."

"Don't sound much like decency to me," she
snapped, trying to free her hand from his grasp.
"Sounds more like living in sin!"

"And I suppose you're living in proper gentility
at that rat trap of a place."

"No, but I'm not going against what's right. I'm

not sinning. At least I wasn't till you came back into my life, that is," she added contritely.

"Oh, Mair," he groaned in exasperation, "forget all that sin talk. Just remember how much we love each other. Let me put you in decent lodgings somewhere else then, anywhere but with the Agnelli Opera Company."

"In exchange for giving up my freedom, I'll get a nice place to stay? No thanks. I won't always be a nobody. Lots of people in the know have pinpointed me to be as famous as . . . as Adelina Patti!" she cried, choosing the first famous name that came to mind. "I won't give up my chances just to live in sin with you. And however much you try to dress it up, that's what it's still called at home. It's not for lack of love of you, I'm saying this. As I told you, I love you very much, only I always expected to get married before we set up house together. Someday I'm going to be famous, Nico, and then I'll be able to buy my own house. And I won't need to live off a man's generosity then."

"If you choose singing in that rundown flea trap over me, our love can't mean very much to you," he said curtly.

"Oh, is that so! Well, it's just about as valuable to me as it seems to be to you. I don't see you giving up any of your ambitions for me!"

"You silly woman, I've told you that's different," he shouted, trying to control his temper and failing.

Angrily, Mair tossed her head, her hair falling down around her shoulders. "Silly woman, am I? Well, let me tell you, Nico Castelli, I'm not nearly as silly as you think. I saw through your grand plans from the start. Talk about ambition! You've got enough for ten people. At least I'm going to achieve my goals honestly. What you're telling me is that you'll use this Gambino man's help to get you where you're going, and then, when you're all set, you'll tell him you're not going to marry his daughter. Or is that another of those lies men tell their women to keep them quiet? By sleeping with you I've given you the impression that I'm a loose woman, and maybe I deserve to be thought of that way, but let me tell you now, it won't happen again. You can't keep me shut away somewhere like a little doll to play with when the mood suits. When you tell Teresa's father the truth—if it *is* the truth—and when you ask me to marry you, then I'll come to you, and not before."

His dark eyes had narrowed to slits during her tearful outburst. The undisguised anger in his lean face frightened Mair, but she stood her ground. Growing up in Llandare had prepared her well for battle; she wasn't going to give in now. Even though her heart was breaking, she forced her tears to remain unshed, her hands to stop trembling. The shock of what she had just said to him, of how much she had thrown away, made her legs shake. But Nico couldn't see that, thank God.

"Well, girl, if that's the way you want it, that's the way you've got it," he ground out through clenched teeth. "I never dreamed singing in that squalid neighborhood would be so important to you that you'd choose it over me and living somewhere decent. You've changed since I met you and it's not for the better!"

216

His cruel words struck like a physical blow.

"Looks like we've nothing more to say to each other. I'll be going then."

He didn't answer. Mair grabbed the silk roses off the dresser and pushed them through her hair, not caring how out of place she would look at nine in the morning. Though she had no money for a cab, she refused to ask him to lend her any. It would be a long walk back to Duchess Street.

Nico quickly solved that problem for her.

"Go then. I'll get you a cab to speed you on your way. If you ever change your mind, you can locate me through the Castelli and Gambino Shipping Company."

Blindly, Mair reached for the door handle only to find he had already opened it for her. She tried to keep her distance from him, not wanting to touch his body, reluctant to reawaken those memories.

The corridor was empty, a blessing for which she was grateful. Walking stiffly along the carpeted hallway, Mair hoped she was heading in the right direction. Everything wavered through the tears that blurred her vision. The rattle of dishes and the smell of food told her she was headed toward the dining room.

To her surprise, when she finally stepped out on the steps into the bright sunshine, Nico waited at the curb, talking to a hansom cab driver. He must have taken a short cut to get there before her.

Head held high, as if she were playing a theatrical role, Mair carefully descended the flight of marble steps, heading toward the waiting cab. Silently Nico opened the door for her. When he put out his hand to assist her, she disdained his help.

"He knows where to go," he said grimly, his eyes hard.

Mair looked at Nico but could no longer distinguish his features through her gathering haze of tears.

"And you're wrong, Mair Parry, when you say there's nothing more to be said between us. I still love *you*, remember that." And Nico spun on his heel and went back into the hotel.

Mair crumpled against the leather upholstery, her tears bursting forth like water from a breaking dam. Why had he added that final barb? Emphasising the words as if he accused her of not loving him. Not true! She loved him so much, her heart ached. What had gone wrong? How could their wonderful morning be ending like this? She had just thrown away her chance at love with the only man she had ever wanted. Had she not allowed pride to stand in the way, she would have accepted his offer. But Nico would still be betrothed to the other one, said a small voice of reason. By accepting his offer, she would not have altered that fact. When Teresa Gambino no longer overshadowed their relationship, there might be a chance for them. Like a typical man, Nico had concocted a plan whereby he could have his cake and eat it too.

Dismally, Mair reviewed all that she knew about his alliance with Teresa. Always in the past he had spoken about the arrangement as if it could not be broken. The biggest hurdle to her acceptance in Teresa's stead was that she was not Catholic. Had she been asking for the moon to expect him to disregard that fact? His religious background forbade such a union, yet against all odds she had foolishly thought love would prevail. Another factor she could not overlook was his driving ambition. Nico was prepared to sacrifice their love to achieve his lofty goals.

Was marriage really so important to her? she asked herself as they headed through Holborn, back down those dreary, dismal streets where the sunlight failed to penetrate and the few sparrows in sight grubbed for crumbs in the gutters. She could still have Nico without marriage. Though he would provide her with a life of comparative ease, she could not be happy that way. She would always be waiting for his knock, wondering if he would come tonight; then, as her looks faded, she'd be wondering if he would come at all. And she couldn't sing professionally. That edict, even more than his reluctance to marry her, had been the deciding factor. Not to sing would be to die. Maybe not in a physical sense, but in her soul.

Mair stiffened her spine, sitting bolt upright against the hard upholstery. The tawdry billboards outside the Coliseum had come into view. At the top of the bill, right below Agnelli Opera Company, she saw her name. These days she was being billed as the Golden Nightingale. She read, Signorina Maria Parigi, the Golden Nightingale, will perform by special request . . .

All was not lost. A little surge of joy, short-lived to be sure, but real nonetheless, shot through her body. Even though she had lost Nico, she still had the opera, the adulation of the audience. The audience offered her love—safe, distant, but as long as it was not withdrawn, eminently sweet.

Someday soon she would sing on a real opera stage; she could feel it in her bones. Whatever Nico did or did not do, he could not take away her talent.

Mair set her mouth in a false smile as the cab drew to a halt, the horses snorting and tossing their heads. The cabby called out to tell her they were at the Coliseum. Perhaps he thought she was not familiar with the area; that was understandable, considering where he had picked up the fare. On the other hand, he probably assumed she was some fancy woman returning home after a night of sport with a rich gentleman. That idea was not pleasing to her.

"The fare's already paid, mum," the cab driver said, touching his bowler hat as Mair descended the steps.

"Thank you," she said stiffly, not looking back, not anxious to intercept the man's curious stare.

The door to the theater swung open and the familiar smell of food, dust, stale ale and greasepaint met her in a welcoming flood. Dear lord, she never dreamed she would be pleased to be back at the old Coliseum. She was home again. And the realization filled her with mingled pain and joy.

Chapter Fourteen

Mair discovered that living for art alone was lonely and taxing.

She threw herself into her work, practicing scales by the hour, rehearsing with a new intensity that delighted both Guido and Amelia. So delighted was Guido by her new dedication that he readily forgave her for slipping out to see Nico. Mair assured him it would never happen again. And so convincing did she seem, he completely believed her.

Rose had told an involved tale of Mair meeting an old friend from Wales with whom she had gone to supper. When she did not return by locking-up time, the worst was suspected. Much to her dismay, Rose finally had to confess the truth: she had been shielding Mair, not wanting her friend to get in trouble. The angry bellow that greeted Mair's arrival the following morning could be heard clear across Primrose Court. Yet so oblivious to his anger did she appear, Guido rapidly ran out of steam. Mair's unfortunate lapse was not mentioned again.

As his star's fame grew, Guido knew he would have to allow her an interview. After schooling her on what she must and must not say, and making a valiant effort to teach her to use an Italian inflection instead of her native Welsh lilt, Guido finally arranged a brief interview with a newspaper reporter. The poor man was bowled over by Mair's beauty and wrote reams of flattering prose in praise of this newest diva.

With each favorable review, the audience increased—as did the ticket price. Guido was constantly aware of the swiftly approaching summer. Shortly the London opera season would close as high society left the capital to seek cooler pleasures at the seaside, or on some foreign shore. Once high society had vacated the city, he knew his only audience would be the lower classes. Prices would have to be lowered drastically if he was to fill the theater. With this in mind, he pushed Mair and Eddy to more and more performances; Romeo and Juliet as well as Faust and Marguerite had been added to their ever-increasing repertoire of star-crossed lovers.

The late July night was hot. Mair dabbed perspiration from her brow as she sat in the airless dressing room facing Primrose Court. She had been reading about the growing labor unrest in the nation's capital. The dockers were again threatening to strike and cripple the docks. Huge labor rallies in Trafalgar Square were becoming the accepted thing. Now, alongside old-guard radicals

222

like John Burns and Ben Tillet, a new name had begun to appear in the papers. The rising star of these impassioned gatherings was a poor Italian immigrant named Nico Castelli! Though not outright lies, what was frequently written about Nico and his background was not strictly true. Mair assumed these half-truths were part of the campaign launched by his backers to attract the working vote in the district they coveted. In her reading she also learned that the current member of Commons from that district was ailing and not expected to live much longer. Her heart chilled when she pictured Nico, his Uncle Sal and Joe Gambino, waiting like ghouls for the poor old man to die, not to mention influential Sir Alfred whatnot and whoever else had a vested interest in Nico's political career.

Angrily she pitched the newspaper aside. Some of the company members had gone to hear Nico speak at a recent rally. The women came back all ga-ga over his looks and his persuasive tongue. She could have given them a few first hand snippets about his persuasiveness, had she chosen. Fortunately no one was aware Nico Castelli was her mysterious male friend from Wales. Rose, who could have readily identified him and would have been shocked had she done so, had little interest in listening to speeches in support of organized labor.

Because of the heat inside the theater, tonight's performance had been particularly gruelling. Mair had sung to thunderous applause. Eddy Lewis had a touch of laryngitis and was mortified that he could not be heard to advantage, for it was whispered some members of the audience had come from 'foreign parts.' Mair's mouth curled. Probably from Liverpool, or somewhere like that, she thought cynically. She caught sight of her reflection in the mirror and was shocked by what she saw. Where was that joyful girl who lived only to sing? In her place she saw a woman with a set face, mouth already turning down in an embittered smile. The truth was, these days she came alive only when she walked onstage.

"What's this, love, talking to yourself?" asked Eddy Lewis, coming to stand in the doorway where he posed, his profile turned to the most flattering angle.

"How's your throat?"

He grimaced. "Tolerable. Care to come out for some supper?"

Mair shook her head. "No. Cousin Guido's planning a big do here. Had you forgotten?"

"Yes. Too bad. I think maybe you'd have come with me tonight."

Mair smiled. Eddy could think that if it suited him.

"This will probably be our swan song, you know that, don't you, my dear?"

"How's that?"

"After tonight the gentry will be off to the seaside. Why do you think we've been pushed like coolies these past few weeks? Guido wants to pull in every last sixpence while the going's good."

Mair had not realized London would be empty for August. "What will we do then?"

"Oh, we won't be pensioned off, have no fear. We'll go back to what we were doing before. Light opera, music hall turns, the stuff the locals relish.

There'll still be a few toffs around, but it won't be like it has been."

Did Mair imagine it, or was Eddy rather pleased that her time of triumph was nearing its close? Guido could be heard clomping along the corridor, his voice raised in his famous jovial impresario tones. Eddy grimaced, rolling his eyes heavenward; he was not overly fond of their bombastic manager.

"Maria, my love," Guido boomed, "you're still here."

Mair simpered foolishly. Where did he expect her to be? She was rarely allowed out of his sight these days.

"Signorina Parigi, how thrilled I am to meet you."

Mair looked beyond Guido's impressive bulk to see a slight, balding man in impeccable evening dress standing behind him. The man wore a silk-lined opera cloak and carried a gold-headed ebony cane and the obligatory top hat that conveniently collapsed when its owner was seated inside a theater.

"Allow me to introduce myself," he said, stepping forward. "I'm Marc Barbour from the Paris Opera. For some time I've wanted to hear you sing. And I was not disappointed, dear lady. Charming, absolutely charming."

Guido stood behind the little man, beaming like a Cheshire cat, puffing and huffing, overjoyed that so important a man should find favor in his *protégée*.

"Thank you, Mr. Barbour," Mair said, extending her hand for his kiss. The musical rhythm of her

Welsh accent gave her voice a foreign inflection that the casual observer might have mistaken for Italian. At least she hoped so. It would be embarrassing to have to explain her humble origins after all the mystery surrounding her stage persona had been so carefully cultured.

Grasping Eddy by the scruff of the neck, Guido turned him away. "Not you, Eddy, he no want to talk to you," he blundered, doing irreparable damage to his tenor's already flagging ego. "Only to my little Maria."

Mair was left alone with Marc Barbour. Elegantly settling himself on the sagging daybed, the Frenchman carefully laid down his hat, cane, and cloak.

"I can see you have never heard of me."

"No. I'm still very new to the opera world."

Marc Barbour smiled at her candor, his hazel eyes gleaming kindly in his thin, pale face. "Let me tell you first what a magnificent voice you have, Signorina Parigi, quite the most beautiful natural voice I've ever heard. In Paris we are always seeking new voices, new faces. Yours is a very lovely face."

Mair smiled again, thanking him for his compliment. She wondered if Cousin Guido was hovering in the background ready to pounce if this dapper little Frenchman overstepped himself?

"An acquaintance of mine assured me it would be time well spent if I came to hear you sing. But, I can tell you, when first I saw this place, well," here he smiled apologetically, "a less adventurous man might have told the cabbie to drive on."

They exchanged smiles. Mair was beginning to wonder just where this conversation was heading.

Marc Barbour was not a reporter, for he had not asked for an interview; nor did she feel an intimate proposition was imminent. Could he have come to see her in a professional capacity? He had not said what his duties were in Paris and she was alarmingly ignorant of the running of a real opera company.

"Would you consider crossing the Channel to sing for me?"

She swallowed and her ears buzzed. Perhaps she had not heard him correctly. "To sing at the Paris Opera?" Mair gasped. When he nodded, she treated him to her most charming smile as she said, "My dear Mr. Barbour, I'll be delighted." There, she hoped she had given a passable impersonation of a socially adept diva, though beneath her velvet skirts her knees were knocking.

Marc Barbour smiled and, reaching forward, he took her hand and raised it to his lips. "I will contact you soon. Meanwhile, my dear Signorina Parigi, master as many roles as possible to broaden your repertory. It may take me a little time. There are others who must be consulted, of course."

"Of course," Mair agreed, disappointment flooding over her. Here he was, giving with one hand and taking away with the other. Wasn't that the way it always went? She stood up. "I'm tired now, Mr. Barbour. If you'll excuse me."

"Please, Signorina Parigi, do not be offended. I assure you my offer is serious. I'll discuss your capabilities with my colleagues, we'll set a fee, then I'll get in touch with you. Do I negotiate with Signor Agnelli?"

"No. I alone decide where I sing," Mair quickly interjected, remembering Nico's reminder that

Cousin Guido would do anything to hang on to his star attraction. "Please contact me in writing when you've reached a decision. If the terms suit me, I'll agree to your proposal."

"Of course, I'll do that," Marc Barbour agreed, somewhat surprised that no obvious contract existed between the impressario and his brightest star. This would certainly make matters easier.

"Goodnight, Mr. Barbour. I trust this matter will be kept strictly private," Mair said, surprising herself by her calm assurance. Mustering her most genteel tones in an attempt to copy Miss Jenkins's manner, she realized she was giving a superb performance. Fortunately the Frenchman did not know how hard she was working to find just the right words. "Address the letter to me and mark it private, if you please."

Marc Barbour agreed. Bending over her hand, he bid her goodnight.

Mair sat in the empty dressing room listening to his retreating steps. To her relief, a couple of minutes later, she heard the street door close. At least Cousin Guido had not waylaid Mr. Barbour and discovered what he was contemplating. Desperate to keep her here, Guido could have scotched her chances for advancement. She had felt it wiser to negotiate this important move alone. Nico had been right before about Cousin Guido, and though she hated to be taking his high-handed advice, her own good sense had prevailed.

Guido's heavy steps thundered down the corridor.

"Where is he?" he cried, glancing around the empty dressing room. "Is he gone?" Now his expression changed to anger. "Little fool, you should've keep him here. I wanted to talk to him. What he say? Does he want you sing for him?''

"Someday, perhaps," Mair dismissed casually, hugging her secret to her heart. This offer could be just what she had been waiting for—the chance to sing in a real opera house! Yet she had not expected to have to go to Paris to realize her ambitions.

"Someday? Ha! Someday don't pay no bills," Guido growled sourly, disappointed with the outcome.

Mair's conscience pricked her for not revealing more of their conversation. Still, whenever Marc Barbour wrote to her would be soon enough to discuss the whys and wherefores. Until then, all she would have to do was to get to the door first to collect the post before Cousin Guido saw it.

Throughout August with its hot, sultry days and frequent thunderstorms, Mair dilligently watched the post for a letter marked private. It did not come. Through September and October she waited hopefully. A few better class patrons had returned to the city, staying in the finest hotels. Their ticket sales reflected little change, the theater barely filled, and there was no sign of Marc Barbour or his representative. Mair had begun to give up hope of ever receiving the news she had awaited so eagerly. The disappointment was a cruel blow. Secretly she had hugged this knowledge to herself, daily expecting to be whisked away to the Paris stage. At this rate she was never going to leave the Coliseum.

Her emotions were at low ebb. During the summer months the theater bill had gradually returned to its old music hall format, giving Mair only one aria a week. She knew she could have increased her onstage appearances by agreeing to sing the bawdy ditties so beloved by the local audiences, but she had refused to lower herself to that level. She was bored, lonely and disheartened. Secretly she had expected Nico to break down and visit her; she had always fondly imagined his love too deep to allow harsh words to keep them apart. But she had been wrong, and that discovery merely added to her general depression.

More and more Nico's name seemed to appear in the press stories about workers' rallies, or perhaps it was only that because she absorbed every scrap of information that would tell her where Nico was and what he was doing and saying. According to some reports, he appeared to be saying quite a lot these days. And much of it must make sense, for his following was growing. In fact, Nico Castelli had become a folk hero of sorts to several members of their own company who regularly went to hear him speak on Sunday afternoons. Because of their newfound interest in Nico's speeches, Mair found it increasingly difficult to put thoughts of him from her mind. She realized she could have gone with them to Trafalgar Square to hear the speeches without giving herself away, but the ordeal of seeing him and not speaking to him was more than she could face.

Why should she be hungry for news of Nico? she thought angrily. In all this time he had made no effort to contact her. The bitterness of this reality, fueled by her terrible disappointment that the hoped-for Paris engagement had failed to materialize, completed her misery.

November was wet, foggy, dismal and dreary,

the weather mirroring her mood. A knock on the side door and the sound of Fred the postman's cheery Cockney voice sent Mair hastening to answer the door. She went for the post purely out of habit now, for she had given up hope of ever receiving a letter from Marc Barbour. She greeted Fred as she reached around the doorjamb in the pouring rain for the bundle of letters. He brought the letters out from under his voluminous cape.

"'Ere you is, ducks. Coo, somethink special 'ere, all right. Got a foreign stamp on it, it does."

Mair's heart skipped a beat. "Thank you, Fred. Be careful now, don't take your death of cold," Mair called solicitiously as she clutched the half dozen letters.

Her heart thumped erratically as she hurried to the office, attempting to appear casual. In the distance she could hear Cousin Guido still arguing with Amelia in the kitchen. Quickly she spread out the letters on the table in his office, snatching up a buff envelope speckled with raindrops. It was addressed to Signorina Maria Parigi, and marked private. Mair thought her heart would stop beating, so hard did it lurch. This was her ticket to glory—the letter she had been waiting for all these months! How glad she was now that she had established the custom of collecting the company post. No one would be any the wiser to her secret. She could read the letter in private and decide what she must do.

Mair virtually ran to her room. To her relief she found that Rose had already gone downstairs to the sewing room. Though she counted Rose as her best friend, Mair could not share this letter even with her until she had considered its contents and decided what her course of action would be.

When the door was closed on the outside world, with pounding heart Mair went to the window overlooking Duchess Street where the light was better. Her hands shook as she tore open the buff parchment envelope. She had to read the letter several times before its contents sank in. She was being engaged to sing a Gala performance of *Romeo and Juliette* in January of the following year, 1888, to be followed by five more performances of the opera. In February she was to sing six performances of Gounod's *Faust*.

Over and over again she read and reread those glorious words, hardly able to believe this was really happening. She fully expected to wake to discover it had only been a dream after all. No, she knew she was awake, for below she could see Bessie, the neighborhood ragwoman, trundling her handcart, followed by her grandson with his homemade crutch. Rain sluiced down the windowpanes and an army of chimneypots belched smoke into the gray heavens. If this was real, so must be the letter clutched in her shaking hands.

Round and round the room she waltzed, clutching the letter to her heart, laughing, crying, her mind far away in the grand baroque opera house in the heart of Paris.

At last, coming back to earth, she unfolded the crumpled letter to reread the final paragraphs over which she had hurriedly skimmed. Mr. Barbour requested she be in Paris by December 5 to begin rehearsals. December 5 was the beginning of next month! A month from now she would actually be singing in a real opera house! If she were willing, a Madame Duval would meet her at Waterloo Station and accompany her across the Channel, then on to Paris. Accommodations were being prepared for her at a Paris hotel, the Hotel Meurice on the Rue de Rivoli, a suite for Madame and her maid—fancy expecting her to have a maid. Well, she would have to get one, wouldn't she? Mair thought with a grin. On top of these accommodations she was to be paid 5,000 francs a performance providing she sang exclusively for the Paris Opera during her stay in France. 5,000 francs—Mair had no idea how many pounds that would be. They didn't know it, but she would have sung at the Paris Opera for nothing just to have the honor of singing there.

For the next few days Mair weighed how she was going to break this stupendous news to Cousin Guido. Her first inclination was to show him the letter: good sense warned her to be prudent. Nico had probably been right when he said Guido would do anything to keep his star. Mair had no idea what that *anything* included. She would not have put it past him to lock her in her room, imprisoning her until after the arranged departure date, then writing to Paris to tell them she would not be able to appear. Despite her distrust of him, she did not want to leave Cousin Guido in the lurch, for they were gearing up for a full season, which he expected to be even better than last. In his way he had been good to her. True, he paid her no wages and he virtually ruled her life, but he had housed her, fed her, and made sure she came to no harm. Most important of all he had given her the opportunity to sing in public, without which circumstance this wonderful offer would never have been made. She definitely owed him something, but just what that something was, she did not know.

Mair decided she would have to discuss the situation with Nico. He would suggest the best way to handle his mother's cousin. Unfortunately that move would mean swallowing her pride and crawling to him. Her mouth set stubbornly at the very thought. Why should she be the one to patch things up? Nico had not taken time from his political ambitions to enquire even once how she fared. Truth to tell, he maybe never loved her as deeply as she had fondly imagined. He may not have loved her at all . . .

Tears slid from her eyes and splashed on the windowsill where she stood gazing down sightlessly at the street on this cold Sunday morning. The rest of the company had barely crawled from their beds, while she had been awake for hours, wrestling with her dilemma.

"What, sweetest—tears?"

Unfortunately, Eddy had not been one of the sleeping members of the company. Quickly Mair brushed her tears away, swallowing her grief.

"Oh, hullo, Eddy," she greeted him huskily. "You caught me at a bad time. Just homesick, that's all," she lied, hoping he would go away.

"Let me take you to the park this afternoon. It's not raining, that's something to be said for November. Always cooped up here, no wonder you're feeling down in the mouth. Tell that Italian ogre you demand to be let out for one afternoon at least."

"Thanks anyway, but I'll be all right. I've got some studying to do."

"Heavens above, anyone'd think you were about to debut at the grand opera house, always studying and practicing. This is only Duchess Street, my dear. What's the matter with you? Don't you know life is to be lived?"

Mair gulped at his amused statement. If her increased dedication to work was apparent to Eddy, who was not the brightest of people, Cousin Guido must also have noticed. As he frequently berated her for not taking her work seriously enough, perhaps he would merely assume she was taking his words to heart without suspecting any ulterior motive. Fortunately her precious letter from Paris never left her person. Had Cousin Guido got wind of something, Mair would not have put it past him to search her room for some tell-tale clue.

"Singing's my life, Eddy, you know that."

"What say we go with the others to that big do in Trafalgar Square?"

"What do's that?"

"The papers have been full of it! There'll be demonstrations against O'Brien's imprisonment —you know, the M.P. who supports the poor Irish. They're promising lots of fireworks out of this. Could be pretty exciting."

If there were to be any radical demonstrations, whatever the cause, Mair knew Nico would be in the forefront. If she stood near the speakers' box in front of the crowd, he would see her. She could speak to him then without appearing to have deliberately sought him out. That would help salvage some of her pride. The only drawback with her plan was that the others in the company would know she had lied when she said she had never heard of Nico Castelli. But what did that matter? The only one she cared about was Rose, and she would be in Clapham this afternoon attending her brother's wedding. The others really didn't matter. Soon Mair would no longer be part of the Agnelli Opera Company, so their opinion of her was not really important.

"All right, I'll come with you. Maybe I'll enjoy myself. It'll be a change at least," she allowed, trying hard to appear unconcerned, though at the very thought of seeing Nico again her heart had begun to thump erratically.

Encouraged, Eddy moved closer, slipping his hand over hers where it rested on the windowsill. "First we'll go and eat lunch, just the two of us. How about the Albion chophouse? First class food there. We can always join the others later."

"No, let's go straight to the Square. If we waste time going out for lunch, we'll miss the rally. We can always have a sandwich here before we leave."

Eddy scowled. That was exactly why he had suggested the Albion chophouse. A few pints of ale, the warm fire, a good meal, and who knew what he could have persuaded her to. He could not understand this woman; she defied all accepted rules of female behavior.

"You're sure, Mair? You know it would be so much nicer just the two of us, without the others' chit-chat."

"I'm sure. I'll go upstairs now and get ready. Meet me in the kitchen and we'll find out when they're going to leave."

Eddy stared gloomily after her. With the others around there wouldn't be much hope of a seduction. Still, Mair had agreed to go out with him. It was a start.

Chapter Fifteen

During the long omnibus ride to Trafalgar Square, Roland Cheatham, sometime company bass and accomplished carpenter, aired his views of the current sad state of British labor, "Wealth earned on the backs of the poor. Exploited workers. Degrading conditions. A revolution needed . . ."

Long ago Mair had stopped listening to Roland's socialist platform. Anyone would have thought he was running for political office. By now he had the entire bus in thrall as he waxed ever more eloquent in his deep, melodious voice. All Mair really wanted to know was if Nico Castelli would be at this rally. A vast number of unemployed, poor Irish immigrants and London's resident radicals, were to take part in this much-publicized demonstration to demand the release of M.P. O'Brien. The idea of all those hotheads turned loose in the city made her uneasy. Unless she was mistaken, there would be far more trouble than they bargained for. Mair's reckless companions were eagerly awaiting the demonstrators' clash with police, excited by the prospect of a little bloodshed. When the clash came, Mair hoped Nico would not be among the injured.

Nervously she folded and refolded her gloves, pleating her gray wool skirt with shaking fingers. Would they never get to Trafalgar Square? They seemed to have been aboard the swaying omnibus for hours. The other women from the Company were as gaudily dressed as if they were going to a fair. Not wanting to stand out in the crowd, Mair had not followed their example. She wore the serviceable gray braid-trimmed wool costume she had inherited from Olwen, Mr. Williams's former housekeeper; paired with a good white blouse, her cherished Prussian blue hat and a Welsh wool shawl thrown over her shoulders in case it turned cold, Mair looked neat and respectable.

As they jogged and swayed through the gray streets, Mair already regretted coming on this outing. Quite likely they would be too far away to even see Nico. That was a consoling thought, for long before they neared Trafalgar Square, she lost her nerve.

Their high-spirited party finally alighted, and the little band of nine soon blended into the slow-moving crowd. The surrounding streets were thronged with people, which was most unusual for a winter Sunday afternoon. An expectant buzz was already in the air, as if the burgeoning crowd sensed the coming excitement. This morning the Sunday papers had reported that the colorful orator, John Burns, sometimes described as an 'agitator of all work,' would address the assembly. Droves of lower working class Londoners considered it well worth the journey to Trafalgar Square to listen to this well-known advocate of working men's rights.

Dozens of street vendors were servicing the growing crowd. Almost anything could be had to eat or drink: treacle toffee for the children, apples, oranges, roasted chestnuts, meat pies, winkles and pickled whelks for adults, and all washed down with ale or a tin cup of murky tea.

Word that the excitement was already beginning outside Westminster began to filter through the crowd. The rumbling mass abruptly changed direction, moving swiftly back along Parliament Street toward the Palace yard, afraid they were going to miss the spectacle.

The members of the Agnelli company joined hands or linked arms in an effort to stay together as they followed the noisy cavalcade streaming back toward the river.

When they finally came in sight of Westminster Hall, it soon became apparent that no ordinary meeting was about to take place. Hundreds of rough-looking men armed with bottles, sticks and knives were milling about. Many of these wild-eyed marchers were in rags, with their toes sticking out of their worn boots; some were even barefoot. These men came from the worst slums in the city. In anticipation of probable violence, there were scores of police prepared to disperse the demonstrators.

Warned that the situation might turn ugly, many sightseers tried to fall back to safety, not anxious to be involved in a pitched battle. But there was nowhere left to go. Hundreds of people had spilled into the area, blocking the adjoining streets, creating a solid wall of humanity in every direction. Above the general racket made by so many people could be heard a man's voice bellowing encouragement to this ragged army, his rough voice rising and falling with the surging crowd.

Undaunted, the members of the Agnelli Company pushed forward into the thick of the crowd.

Wisely, Eddy grasped Mair's arm, drawing her back to safety, allowing the others to go on without them. He intended to seek refuge in a nearby doorway. To his horror he discovered it was hopeless to try to push their way back through the solid mass of people; they could not even get close to the buildings.

The surging crowd relentlessly pushed them forward until they met the fringe of marchers. Two separate columns of men had now joined ranks to become one fierce sea of shouting, jeering faces. The wall of policemen stood their ground, fearlessly confronting the angry rabble.

In a matter of minutes the protest escalated into a full scale riot.

In an attempt to hold back the rushing demonstrators, the police belabored them with their truncheons. As men crumpled and fell, their furious comrades struck back, battering the enemy with crowbars, clubs, any weapons that came to hand.

Mair was pushed and pulled until she finally lost her grasp on Eddy's hand and was swept along with the surging mob.

The noise became deafening as the police fought

a pitched battle with the demonstrators. Close at hand a second speaker could now be heard, shouting to make himself heard above the din. Mair could see a man balancing on top of a railing, clutching a tree branch for support; he tried to appeal to the angry mob. His message was more of pacification than incensing to riot. Rising and falling, his words were for the most part unintelligible. Though Mair only heard snatches of his speech, she thought the voice sounded like Nico's.

"Fall back . . . don't risk injury . . . not worth dying for, lads." The words drifted to her in the swell of sound.

To her alarm, Mair found herself relentlessly propelled forward, until she crashed into a bearded man who was wielding a stick and yelling at the top of his lungs. He brushed her aside as if she were a fly, thrusting himself back into the thick of the fight.

In desperation Mair flattened herself against the wall of a nearby building. For the moment she was safe, but she discovered her lovely blue hat had been knocked from her head and swiftly trampled underfoot by the mob.

The fighting surged away, leaving a semicircle of calm about this wall. Climbing up, clinging to the railings, she tried to see over the heads of the crowd, searching for a familiar face among the seething mass. To her dismay no member of the Agnelli company was to be seen. Desperately she searched for Eddy's curly blond head, but he was nowhere in sight.

"Thought I was seeing things! It is you! What the hell are you doing down here, Mair?"

A man suddenly loomed before her out of the

crowd, arms raised as if to strike. At first Mair failed to recognize him with his cloth cap pulled down around his ears. Dressed in a worn tweed jacket and corduroy trousers bagging at the knees, he looked like all the rest. When he came closer and raised his head, she suddenly saw beneath the bill of his gray tweed cap.

"Nico!"

"Get the hell out of here!" he shouted to her before stopping to thrust aside a couple of battling rioters who careened into him.

"Who are you ordering about?" Mair yelled back, tears stinging her eyes. Fright and rage combined to rob her of her sense. "I've just as much right to be here as you."

"There's going to be bloodshed, you bloody stupid woman. Now get going," he yelled, trying to pull her down from the railings.

"I don't even know where I am. I can't get going. I've got to wait for my friends," she yelled back, trying to make herself heard above the racket.

Bleeding men and policemen battled in the open expanse before her, their yells of pain and angry shouts becoming deafening. Some men were trampled underfoot. The sound of shattering glass came from the background as the rabble began to invade nearby buildings.

Nico knew the day was already lost. None of the rally's leaders could be seen. Open warfare raged up and down the streets stretching from Westminster Bridge to Birdcage Walk. Making a swift decision, he grasped Mair's arms; then, prying her hands from the wrought iron railings, he dragged her down. Holding her tightly to him,

Nico edged toward a narrow alley that led away from the battleground.

Angrily Mair fought his restraining hands. Afraid of the melee, yet defiant to the last, she struggled to be free of his grasp.

Nico was relentless. "Shut up," he cried fiercely when she screamed in protest. "You're coming with me whether you like it or not. Bloody stupid, it is, coming to a place like this alone."

"I wasn't alone," she shouted in defense, finally giving in. She hoped he knew a route to salvation, for the fighting was beginning to spill into the alley. Now Nico began to run, dragging her along with him.

Shouts of, "Stop! You there, stop!" echoed after them.

Not heeding the policeman's shout, Nico kept on running down the alley, desperate to reach the other end of the twisting escape route. The stench of rotting vegetation and sewage lying stagnant in the gutter nearly felled them as they ran even faster, gulping in great breaths of putrid air, filling their bursting lungs with the abominable stench of poverty.

Then they came out into the light of a wide street that was devoid of police and battling rioters, and suddenly the air was far pleasanter.

Nico seized Mair's arm when she would have slowed down, racing her up a couple of flights of wooden stairs. He rapped on a closed door, which soon opened to reveal a room partially filled with diners. Nico struggled to regulate his breathing sufficiently to order a meal.

Tightly clasping Mair's hand, the expression in

his dark eyes warning her not to protest, Nico led
her to an empty table in the corner. They flopped
down on rickety chairs, trying to still their heaving
chests.

Nico finally pulled off his cloth cap and un-
wound the knitted muffler from about his neck,
thrusting them under the table. After straightening
his collar and adjusting his necktie, he achieved a
passable degree of respectability.

When Mair again opened her mouth to protest,
he silenced her. "You're here for your supper, you
daft girl. Now be quiet."

"Who are you calling a daft girl?" she hissed,
eyes snapping in anger. "Who says I want to eat
supper with you?"

Taking a closer look at her, he suddenly burst
out laughing and she found herself impelled to join
him. Nico took out his handkerchief and wiped big
smuts from her nose and cheeks. Then he pushed
back thick loops of hair that straggled across her
eyes.

"Looks like you've been dragged through a
hedge backwards," he remarked with a grin.

"Not only that, I've lost my hat. And my shawl!"
Mair gasped in dismay as she put her hands to her
shoulders and discovered it was gone.

"At least you're still in one piece. We can always
get more shawls and hats."

Just then the coffee house door opened and two
policemen stood framed in the aperture. Carefully
they looked over the occupants of the room. Nico
signalled to Mair to act as if nothing was wrong
and she hastily lowered her head, pretending to
study the spotted paper menu before her on the

table. After a few minutes' conversation with the landlord, the policemen left without searching the premises.

"Thank God they've gone. That was close. They must be new on this beat."

Wide-eyed, she looked up at him. "You mean they were looking for you, not just for demonstrators?"

"Probably. I'm rather well known in these circles, you know," Nico added with a grin.

The waiter approached their table carrying a loaded tray. There were two steaming deep dish steak and kidney pies, jam pudding with custard and tankards of ale.

"This'll fix yer up, Mr. Castelli, sir," the man said with a wink as he placed the dishes before them.

"You're a lifesaver, Herbert, my lad. I'm eternally grateful."

"You mean the people here know you, yet they didn't turn you in," Mair gasped in surprise when the waiter had gone.

"Friends are invaluable at certain times," Nico replied with a grin.

Mair snorted. "Aye, especially all those fancy friends in high places."

"Friends in low places come in handy, too. Now eat your supper and be quiet."

Surprisingly she found his attitude did not annoy her. Despite the harrowing couple of hours she had spent prior to this supper, Mair discovered she was supremely happy. The man sitting across the table from her was the old Nico Castelli she knew so well, and she felt much better able to deal with him.

Though this appeared to be a poor establishment, the food was excellent; in fact, Mair had never tasted more delicious fare. When her plate was clean she finally laid down her knife and fork with a sigh of satisfaction.

"Running certainly makes you hungry. Had enough?"

"If I eat any more I'll burst my buttons," she confessed honestly.

Nico studied her, his voice terse as he said, "Now perhaps you'll tell me what in God's name you were doing at the rally?"

"I came to hear the speeches with some people from the company."

"I should've known they had something to do with it."

"No need to scowl like that. Seems you were in the thick of it yourself, so it can't be too silly of me to show up, now can it?"

"I was there for a purpose, Mair. People expect me to speak out in defense of the working man's right to a fair wage. Though I'm not Irish, I believe they're entitled to be treated as fairly as the next man. Whereas you—it was so bloody stupid to go to a thing like that! Don't you know these rallies often end in a free-for-all? You're lucky you weren't hurt. Don't ever do it again!"

Mair gripped her hands tight beneath the tablecloth, determined not to be goaded into angry retaliation. Now that she was with him, at least her original purpose could be accomplished, and then she would leave. There was no reason for her to stay and listen to his angry criticism. Carefully smoothing imaginary wrinkles in the tablecloth, she said without looking up, "What would you say if I told you I came to see you?"

Nico's eyes softened and his hand sought hers across the table. Mair wished he had not done that. Now, when she looked up, she saw tenderness in his dark eyes, an expression that never failed to melt her heart. And today she did not want to be softened by his charms. Just like he, she had a mission, only hers could be far more simply accomplished.

"Though I'm pleased to see you—to know you're well—it was only your advice I wanted." There, she had said it. She was not prepared for the hurt in his face.

"Well, no one can say you're not a woman who comes to the point," he said grimly, disengaging her hand. "What do you want to ask me?"

Mair reached to the inside pocket of her jacket and extracted the now softly crumpled parchment envelope. It was difficult to stay businesslike when he was sitting just a couple of feet from her. Reminding herself that her career might hinge upon how she handled this conversation, she said, "Here, I got this letter last week. Read it first."

Impatiently she waited while he silently scanned the sheet, not saying a word while he read those earth shattering sentences.

"Congratulations," he said finally, his voice flat. "So when do you leave?"

Mair swallowed, wondering what to say next. "You don't seem surprised," she ventured, her voice wobbling, "nor really too concerned to think I'll be going away to foreign parts."

"Oh, Mair. You told me you live to sing. This is

the chance you've been waiting for. I'm not so small as to try to deny it to you."

Moisture clouded her eyes and, when he sought her hand on the stained tablecloth, she did not resist. "I intend to be in Paris by December 5th. But I won't be there forever."

"I know." He squeezed her hand, his mouth smiling, but his eyes stayed hard. "Are you traveling with this Madame . . ." he glanced down at the letter, "Duval?"

"Yes. Unless you don't think I should."

"No, if the arrangement was made by Marc Barbour, you can be assured it's respectable."

"You know him!"

He smiled when he saw her amazed expression. "Oh, I've met him a couple of times."

"How?"

"I don't spend all my days screaming from the top of railings," was all he would say on the subject. "Does Cousin Guido know?"

Mair shook her head.

"Then I can guess your next question: how to tell him? Whatever you say you know he's going to explode."

"He'll see what a good chance it is for me."

"Oh, come on. You're yanking the food out of his mouth, surely you realize that? He's not going to say, 'Congratulations, Mair, I'm happy for you. Not bloody likely he isn't, not bloody likely at all."

"I don't want to ruin him. I don't know what to do to be fair."

Nico snorted in derision. "Poor man. Of course, he's never paid you a penny for your performances. He keeps you a virtual prisoner in that slum while he rakes in money off your singing, pocketing it all with a clear conscience. Come on, this isn't your fairy godmother we're talking about, this is Guido Agnelli, of doubtful moral integrity."

"I do owe him something."

"'Thank you for helping me up to this point,' should be sufficient."

"You don't really think I can just say that."

"Look, Mair, whatever you say he's going to be furious. My advice is to say nothing until the day before you leave. Meet this Madame Duval, get the arrangements made, buy your tickets and then, when you tell him, remember to add that you're being met. That'll stop him trying to keep you there. Now, what about this maid?"

Mair laughed. "You know I haven't got a maid."

"No, but the French expect an opera diva to have a maid, so my advice is to get one. What about that little brown-haired girl who does your hair?"

"Rose?"

"Yes, she seems loyal enough. Could you travel with her and live with her abroad for a while, do you think?"

"Oh, yes, Rose would be perfect. But she wouldn't want to leave London."

"Try her. I bet she'll jump at the chance."

"I'll ask her tonight."

"No—not tonight, Mair." He took her hand, turning it palm uppermost. Almost before she realized what he was doing, Nico had pressed his mouth in a burning kiss against her palm.

Sense told her to stop him there, to request a cab to take her home. But today sense seemed to have taken a holiday. Never again without marriage she had told him, had promised herself, now here she was about to yield. "No, I can't stay with you tonight."

"You don't mean that."

"I said it, didn't I?"

"Only with your mouth, not with your heart. Besides, you frequently lie to me about things like that."

His soft coaxing voice, his winning smile, the way his dark eyes softened, growing liquid with tenderness. No, no, a voice inside her screamed. Yet here she was getting up, letting him lead her across the room. They were turning now to go through a side door, after signalling to the waiter who had nodded his agreement.

"Where are you taking me?" she asked at last, finding her voice.

"For a brief glimpse of heaven," he whispered, his mouth hot against her neck. "How do I know how long you'll be away, taking the continent by storm? I want something sweet to remember you by."

"No, Nico. I shouldn't."

"Don't tell me what you should do. Just remember we love each other, that's all that really matters. Please, Mair, don't deny me now."

And she could not.

The room he led her to was at the end of a hallway. Horses were stabled below; she could smell them in the damp foggy air blowing through the open window overlooking the yard. She waited there in the darkness for Nico to unlock the door. He swore beneath his breath as he fumbled with the key in the lock.

The small room was cold. A fire had been laid in the grate and Nico took a match from the mantel and lit the coals. How different this place would be from that magnificent suite at the Coburg Hotel. Hopefully tonight would not end in anger and pain, though Mair realized the pain of parting would be inevitable.

Nico appeared so familiar with the room that she finally asked him, "Is this where you're staying?"

"I've stayed here in the past. Tonight we're just here by chance. The men sometimes hold meetings here. This is a safe place, that's why I brought you here."

He went to the door and shot the bolt. "Now, no one will disturb us."

The fire was struggling into flame as he lit the lamp on a bracket beside the door. The yellow gaslight dimly illuminated the small, clean room. It was the sort of room a working man might rent. The only furnishings here were a bed with a white counterpane, an oak wardrobe, a table and chairs.

Nico turned and held out his arms to her. At first Mair hesitated, knowing she should end this now. If she told him she wanted to leave, being the gentleman he was, she knew he would not force her to stay against her will. Such a statement, however, might end their relationship. She could not bear that. Though he had not offered marriage, she still clung to a thread of hope.

"Mair, darling, I've been so miserable without you."

"Me too," she whispered, nervously licking her lips. "After I got over being angry with you."

He grinned sheepishly. "Sorry I lost my temper. That's what you get for loving such a hothead."

"Who said I love you?"

"You."

"Oh."

She smiled as she reached out to him. A shudder of excitement went through her body as he clasped her cold hands in his warm ones, drawing her closer. Then Mair sighed with pleasure as she felt the weight of his arms go about her, the exciting heat and pressure of his body against hers. She knew she would not leave. Those noble thoughts she had harbored a few minutes before had been merely self-sacrificial nonsense.

"I really intended to leave," she reminded him, needing to strike at least one blow for decency.

"I never stopped you."

Mair nestled her face in the warm safety of his neck.

"I know." She smiled against the warm fragrance of his skin. Leaving the safety of his arms was the furthest thought from her mind.

Their mouths met in a long aching kiss. Mair clung to him, willing everything to the background. At this moment even her singing took a back seat to the driving passion she felt for this man. It was as if they were the only two people in the world, locked away in this small upstairs room while the foggy November darkness swirled outside. The riot and all that had taken place that afternoon belonged to another time. Now there was only Nico, his arms, his mouth, his body . . .

"Did you truly miss me?"

"Yes, so much. Let me show you how much I've

ached for you, little Mair." His hands were in her hair, pulling it free until it streamed loose about her shoulders. Nico lifted a handful of the soft shining mass to his lips. "Have you forgotten, my Mair of the Golden Hair, how I promised to love you forever? You know I'm a man of his word, and forever is a long, long time. So don't always be asking if I love you, if I miss you—you know I do."

"Oh, silly, you don't think I've forgotten that vow." She smiled, recalling that wonderful day on the mountain when she had fondly imagined all her dreams had come true. "Let's pretend we're just like we were then, before all these other things happened."

"That'll be easy with you, sweetheart."

Without haste he moved her with him till they fell across the bed, eliciting loud protestations from the rusty spring. Mair giggled at the unexpected chorus, but her laughter did not break the mood; it merely became a joyous part of their lovemaking.

They stretched out side by side and Nico gently kissed her face, touching her body almost reverently as he had done that first time they made love. At first she had loved it, but now that Mair was more experienced such mild caresses no longer satisfied her. What then had stirred her to bliss, was now merely a preliminary to something far greater.

"You don't have to go quite so slow, Nico," she whispered with a giggle, realizing he intended to recreate that time on the mountain.

"Got a bigger appetite now, do you, girl?"

"You know I do, and it's all your fault."

"And you're glad of that."

"Yes! Yes, I am. Now I've become a real woman."

"That's only because you're with a real man."

Playfully she slapped him, feigning annoyance at his conceit. Laughingly Nico imprisoned her wrists. The fire added a mellow glow to the room and Nico's face was burnished gold in the firelight. Mair shuddered with emotion, struck by his beauty. He was like no other man she had ever seen, mysterious, yet familiar; loving, yet angry. In fact, he managed to turn her life upside down every time she crossed his path, and despite that she still loved him!

Carefully Nico unbuttoned her jacket, then her blouse. Mair shuddered with delight as the heat of his hands engulfed her breasts, cupping and fondling, whispering his pleasure at the sweet discovery. Though she enjoyed his touch through her clothing, such virginal caressing left much to be desired.

Nico felt her quivers of delight and he smiled, slowly tracing her nose and her high cheekbones with his tongue. Like whispers his kisses grazed her brow. Mair ached to have his mouth on hers, to taste the hot fragrance of his kiss. She pulled his head down, fastening her lips on his, sighing in satisfaction as she revelled in the heat of his mouth. No other man could kiss her so passionately, communicating such desire with his mouth.

Soon their clothing was scattered atop the counterpane. The air in the room wafted chill against her bare flesh, and Nico pulled down the bedcovers, drawing Mair inside where they nestled safe in each other's arms. His mounting passion would not be denied, and Mair eagerly sought the pulsing brand that pressed against her thighs. Fondling his velvety-smooth skin, she gently traced her finger about the fiery head of his manhood, shivering in delight at the instant response of his body, thrusting eagerly within her grasp.

Snug beneath the blankets, locked tight in his passionate embrace, Mair never wanted to leave the wonderful haven of his arms.

"I love you, Nico Castelli, fool that I am," she whispered ardently against his hot cheek. "Against all sense, all reason."

"Sense and reason never had much to do with love," he reminded, kissing the top of her head. Nico stared into the shadowy room. Soon Mair would be gone to begin a career that could make her world-famous. Their paths might lead far apart, for both were bent on their own careers. Would that things could be different! A tug of pain wrenched his heart at the reminder. Unknown to Mair, he was instrumental in charting her course to fame. He would never tell her it was he who had asked Marc Barbour to hear her sing. Better that she not know, that she think she was entirely responsible for shaping her own destiny.

"Mair, wherever we are, whatever we do in the future, I'll never change my feelings for you," he promised, his voice husky with emotion. "Don't ever doubt that I love you with all my heart."

"Oh, Nico." Her voice shook with passion as she held him so tight that his muscles dug into her soft flesh, his hip bones grinded against hers, making the embrace almost painful.

"Tonight I'm going to love you till you beg me to stop," he promised, shaking off his gloomy thoughts. Nico kissed her eyelids and tasted the salt of tears. "This may have to last us for a very long time."

Swept up in a rush of passion, Mair never questioned his words. Mouths and bodies joined in heated embrace, she took him deep inside her, desperate to become one with him. At first Nico moved slowly, quickening the pace only when she urged him to more speed. Tonight he was determined to please Mair, to wait until she begged for more.

Their first coming together produced such marvelous heart-stopping passion, their tumultuous climax surprised them both by its intensity. Mair's eyes were moist when she kissed his ear and neck, murmuring her thanks for the wonderful pleasure he had given her. She soon found there was much more to be thankful for as Nico slowly aroused her to even stronger passion. There seemed to be no end to the splendor of their lovemaking. Finally they lay spent in each other's arms, the wonderfully warm, drowsy aftermath of passion transporting them to a place beyond paradise, where they drifted together safe in each other's arms.

Chapter Sixteen

Gray morning light filtered through the thin window curtain, wanly probing the dingy room. Mair opened her eyes and sat up. At first she had to think where she was; then, when she remembered, she was alarmed to discover Nico was not beside her. Once again, as it had done on that morning at the Coburg Hotel when she found him gone: her heart lurched and began a frightened beat.

"Nico," she called, knowing he could not be there, for unlike the suite at the Coburg, this place had no dressing room.

She was debating getting up when the door suddenly opened and Nico pushed into the room, balancing a loaded breakfast tray.

"Breakfast is served, Your Majesty," he announced, placing the tray at the end of the bed. "Sorry they only have tea and coffee in this hotel, but you'll soon be getting plenty of continental chocolate.''

The reminder that she would shortly embark on the adventure of her life made Mair's stomach churn. Though she badly wanted to sing at the Paris opera, the coming ordeal of living in a country where she did not speak the language was rather frightening.

"Toast with butter, porridge, eggs and bacon. Not bad for the Travellers' Arms.''

She smiled her thanks, turning up her face for his kiss. Why, oh, why, did she always go through agonies expecting him to leave her without a word?

"Wouldn't it be wonderful if we could begin every morning this way?'' Nico said as he picked up the tray and balanced it between them. Mair nodded, sighing with happiness and gazing at the black stubble on his chin and upper lip.

When he noticed her curiously studying his appearance, Nico grinned. "This is the real me. As I didn't expect to stay the night, I didn't bring a razor. It's possible, were we to stay here long enough, I'd have a full, luxuriant beard.''

Mair giggled at the thought. "Are we really going to stay that long?''

The smile faded from his face. "No, not really. I have to be in Lancashire today.''

"You're leaving again!''

Mair's heart plunged at the discovery. Foolishly she had allowed herself to imagine them being together for the next few days. It was devastating to learn this was all there was going to be. The impending journey must have been on his mind last night when he said their lovemaking would have to last a long time.

"You knew about it last night," she accused, feeling somewhat betrayed. "Why didn't you tell me?"

"Because I didn't want to spoil last night," he admitted honestly. "I knew you'd find out soon enough."

"Yes, I suppose you're right, it would have made me sad. Will you be in danger this time?"

"Oh, no, no riots, I promise. I'm just going on union business. I've a list of grievances from the dockers. We're trying to write some guidelines that will be acceptable to both dockers and shipowners. Uncle Sal helped me—so, despite what you'll probably hear, not all the shipowners are fiends. Some of them want their dockers to get a fair wage and reasonable working conditions. I'll be back in a couple of weeks—though that won't help us, will it? By then you'll be across the Channel in gay Paree."

"I'll write to you if you tell me where you'll be."

"I have the address in Liverpool." Nico laid aside the tray and came back to sit on the bed. "Mair, I've been doing a lot of thinking about us. Are you sure this is what you really want . . . going away to Paris?"

His face was so intent that Mair's heart missed a beat. Was he going to ask her to stay with him? And if he did, what was she going to say?" "Why? Have you got a better idea?"

"Stay in London. Wait for me to get back. There's a house I've been looking at—yes, I know I said we'd go househunting together," he quickly explained when she let out an indignant protest. "I had the opportunity to see it before the owner left for America. He's going to be away for a couple of years and offered to sublet to me. Tall ceilinged rooms, furnished like a country house . . . there's a rose garden and a summerhouse on the grounds. I swear, Mair, you'd never dream you were in London."

Mair clasped her hands, eyes shining with delight. For a few blissful minutes she indulged herself in dreams of a splendid house set in pretty gardens, which she could share with him. On pleasant summer evenings they could sit in the summer house, or go for strolls in the London parks. Then they'd return to their own home where they'd make love and give no thought to intruders. Once the front door was shut on the world, they'd make their own life inside its walls.

"Oh, Nico," she whispered, her eyes moist. "After all that's gone between us you still didn't give up."

He took her hands in his, turning them over to kiss the palms. "That's because, despite all that's gone between us, I still love you. Mair, darling, will you reconsider? Marc Barbour will understand. You could delay this Paris engagement maybe till next year, or some other time."

"Are you asking me to marry you?"

She knew as soon as she'd asked that question that her dreams were over. Nico's face tightened, and he let go of her hands.

"Mair, we've already gone over that. I told you I can't—not yet."

The lump in her throat was as big as a walnut.

When she spoke, her voice was strangled. She had looked him full in the face and correctly interpreted his guarded expression.

"Well, then, seems as if I'll have to repeat what I said before: no marriage, no house together. Besides, how can you even think of asking me to postpone my debut now, when I have such a wonderful offer? This next year-sometime-never arrangement sounds pretty fishy to me. I haven't forgotten that you asked me to give up singing. Am I right in assuming that's still a requirement, Mr. Castelli?"

Nico got up from the bed and turned away. "Of course. Whether we're married or not, I'd have to ask you to leave the stage temporarily."

"Then my answer's still no!"

"You're sure?"

"Positive. What I told you before hasn't changed. I can't believe you're still asking me to give up singing after me being invited to appear at the Paris Opera."

He turned to her angrily clenching his hands. "I've already told you why. My wife—or fiancee, as you will—has to be respectable."

"I am respectable."

"My constituents don't know that. To them any woman who appears on the stage is suspected of having loose morals. They go to music halls, they know the character of most of the women they see. You know yourself that's true of many of the women in Cousin Guido's company. For the love of God, Mair, why must we debate every issue like this? To put it bluntly, in my district being an actress is the same thing as being a whore!"

"I'm neither an actress nor a whore! I'm a singer who's about to make her debut at the Paris Opera. If they can't accept that, then—"

"Mair, they won't accept it. Believe me."

Tears stung her eyes and she blinked them back. A sneaking suspicion told her that this entire argument was pointless. Nico had not actually asked her to marry him; the issue had been cleverly skirted once more.

"Seeing as you've never officially asked me to marry you, it doesn't make much sense to worry about what your—constituents, is it—what your constituents think, now does it? And seeing as how you haven't told Teresa Gambino's father the arrangement's off, we're simply wasting our time. Or are you going to surprise me by telling me you've already spoken to him about me?"

"It's not nearly as easy as you think, Mair. You don't understand the Italian family."

Nico turned away, and with a sickly, sinking feeling she knew she had been right again. Oh, she would have gladly been proven wrong. Why had she been silly enough to think there would be a change? Nico had not yet run for his political seat. Until he had that in his pocket, he would have been a fool to anger Joe Gambino. Mair was familiar with driving ambition; she knew you couldn't afford to bite the hand that fed you, not until your goal was attained. Unfortunately for her Nico's sights were set extremely high.

"Somehow, after last night, I thought that maybe . . . you'd reconsider," he said softly, weariness overtaking him. Even his shoulders drooped with resignation. "I can see nothing's changed."

"That's because nothing's changed with you," she snapped, trying to maintain her goodwill and failing. "This is just like last time. Because I let you make love to me doesn't mean I'm common and low. I'm a foolish woman in love with you, that's all, someone who hasn't the sense she was born with to expect a man as ambitious as you to throw aside his rich backers just because he has a sweetheart who wants to get married instead of living in sin."

"Are you quite through?" he demanded, his jaw tense. Her voice was rising and he was uncomfortably aware of the thinness of these walls.

"I'm through, Mr. Castelli, quite, quite through."

Mair attempted to get out of bed in a dignified manner, holding the sheet around her to hide her nakedness. After their quarrel it did not seem right to stand before him undressed.

Nico tossed her her clothes.

"I'll be downstairs when you're ready. I'll get you a cab back to your palace, Your Majesty."

Mair hissed after him beneath her breath, suddenly wanting to hit him, to lash out in payment for her own disappointment and pain. How dare he demand she give up her career to satisfy some ignorant workmen's idea of respectability? The irony of it was that while wanting to seem respectable, at the same time he was asking her to set up house without being married! Where she came from that was every bit as shameful as appearing on stage.

Hands shaking, Mair dressed hurriedly, thrusting her hair inside the pins as best she could without a brush or comb. If she had her hat she could have hidden her untidy coiffure; as it was she would just have to hope no one noticed.

Mair opened the door and walked into the cold, dark hallway. This inn was too small for her to get lost. She just followed the corridor, went down several steps and found herself outside the dining room.

Nico was already waiting for her. After bidding the waiter and landlord goodbye, he opened the door and ushered Mair outside. A few people were eating breakfast in the chilly dining room, but they paid little attention to them.

As they strode angrily side by side along the pavement, the murky sky parted to allow wan rays of sunlight to wash the street.

"I want to thank you for not making a scene at the Travellers' Arms," Nico said stiffly.

"Well, despite what your constituents would think, I do know how to behave like a lady. Our differences are our own and I don't want to share them with every Tom, Dick and Harry."

"Mair, please don't."

"I'll not knuckle under and play dead, if that's what you want. You should know me better than that," she snapped back, not looking at him, not trusting herself enough for that.

"When you become a famous singer and I, hopefully, become a member of the House of Commons, perhaps then we can find some middle ground to meet on."

They had stopped beside a hansom cab stand and Nico was already signalling to the first driver.

"If we're to wait for that I suspect we'll have a long wait," she snapped back, her eyes flashing.

He did not retaliate, and his lack of spirit annoyed her afresh. She was angry and she wanted him to be angry in turn. Only by lashing out at each other could she successfully keep those other feelings at bay. When she wasn't angry with him she weakened and began longing for his kiss, his touch, for just a tender smile.

"If I were you I'd meet this Madame Duval as soon as possible. She's staying at the Metropole. Why don't you go over there now?"

"Looking like something the cat's dragged in? No hat, my hair all skewwhiff? You must be mad."

Still seething, Mair climbed inside the cab. Nico gave the cab driver the Duchess Street address.

"Goodbye, Mair, sweetheart," he said, his voice throbbing with emotion. "Hopefully, we'll see each other again soon."

"That depends. You know on what," she insisted stubbornly, not taking the hand he offered in farewell.

"You'll be a great success in Paris," he said softly, a sad smile on his face.

"Goodbye. Have a good time in Liverpool."

Nico stepped back and the driver urged the horses forward. The last Mair saw of him he was standing at the curb, gazing after the disappearing hansom. Her heart plunged. Why did she feel so sad, so hurt? She should have realized things would be no different.

Tears welled in her eyes but she made no effort to blink them back, finding her expression of grief sweetly relieving. Mair cried softly all the way to Duchess Street, knowing her dreams of love lay shattered on the bare board floor at the Travellers' Arms.

Mair did not expect the enthusiastic welcome
she received from the other members of the company on her arrival at the Coliseum. No sooner had
the hansom disgorged its passenger on the pavement than the stage door flew open and Rose raced
outside. She was closely followed by Flo, Janie and
Pie, with a red-faced Eddy Lewis bring up the rear.

Mair dabbed her eyes, surprised and pleased to
discover how much they had all missed her.

"Lord luv us, Mair. We just knew you was taken
away to some dreadful place. The papers was full
of those terrible stories. Bloody Sunday they's
calling the riot. People injured, killed—oh, Mair,"
Rose cried, slipping her arms around Mair's neck
and clinging tearfully to her friend.

"I want you to know it wasn't my fault, Mair. I
did everything I could. I searched for you for
hours," Eddy apologized, his light blue eyes glazed
with emotion. "If anything had happened to you
I'd never have forgiven myself. Where've you been?
Are you sure you're all right?"

"Looks like you've been tousled about a bit,"
remarked Flo, slipping her plump arm about
Mair's shoulders. "Never you mind, you're with
friends now. Come on inside and 'ave a bit of tea,
soon make you feel better."

Mair went willingly with them. Tears still trickled down her cheeks and she was surrounded by a
chorus of sympathizers as she was led down the
corridor to the kitchen.

A welcoming fire blazed in the hearth and an
aproned Amelia manned a battery of pots and pans
on the big cast iron stove. When she saw Mair,
Amelia shouted a joyous greeting and she hugged
and kissed her before leading her to a seat before

the fire. When she was assured Mair was all in one piece, Amelia patted her cheek in farewell and returned to her household tasks.

Rose knelt beside Mair and chafed her ice cold hands while Janey fetched her a steaming mug of tea, "Nicely laced with a dollop of brandy," she confided in a gin-laden whisper.

Clutching the hot mug for warmth, Mair sat before the fire, tears streaming down her face. She didn't even know why she was crying. Perhaps she cried now because she was touched by their concern for her well-being. They had rallied round her, not knowing she would soon be leaving them, betraying them, really, for she still had not told anyone about her upcoming Paris engagement. This treachery made Mair feel guilty in the face of their kindness.

"Now, tell us what happened," Rose insisted, taking away the tea mug and setting it down on a nearby table. "We won't let you 'ave another drop till we finds out, will we?"

The others chorused their agreement, drawing closer, eager to hear about Mair's misadventures.

"There's not that much to tell," Mair began, pushing back her hair, which was falling untidily about her face. In truth, she wondered just how much she should tell them. Wisely she decided to eliminate Nico's part in her story, which left her very little to relate. "When the crowd began to push, Eddy and I were separated. Then, when things got rough, I got knocked about and lost my hat and shawl. That's about all. I looked for you all, but I couldn't see anyone I knew. When things really got violent, I ran down an alley into another street. Then I spent the night at an inn there."

Patricia Phillips

"What didjer use for money?" Pie asked in surprise, knowing Mair was kept as penniless as the rest of them.

Mair's face colored slightly at the unexpected question.

"They took me on trust," she lied.

At this, Janey winked and nudged her suggestively.

"What didja use for money indeed. Where's yer brain, Pie? She didn't need money, not Queenie 'ere. Coo, if I looked like 'er, I'd be livin' in clover."

Still chuckling to herself, Janey sauntered out of the kitchen.

The silence that greeted her departure made Mair uncomfortable. "It wasn't like that," she defended at last, appalled to think they believed she had sold herself for a night's lodging.

"Right, Queenie, don't you let on, let folks think what they wants," added Pie with a conspiratorial wink. Then, realizing there were no further exciting revelations forthcoming, she and Flo followed Janey.

Only Rose and Eddy remained. Amelia had busied herself in the scullery assisting Pearl, the maid, who had shyly peeped around the door to greet Mair before being dragged back to her place at the sink.

"I'm truly sorry for leaving you alone, Mair. The crowd was just so big, I couldn't cope. It wasn't until after dark that I gave up, when people said they were calling in the Lifeguards."

"It's all right, Eddy, it wasn't your fault. We shouldn't have gone there in the first place. I didn't expect there'd be a riot."

268

"Why not let me take you boating as soon as the weather's nice, to make up for this?" Eddy suggested hopefully. As a peace offering he had brought Mair a piece of jam tart, which Amelia had been hoarding for dinner.

"What did Cousin Guido say when I didn't come back?" she asked after a few minutes of contented munching.

"What didn't he say! Coo, he was wanting to rip out Eddy's heart for taking you to such a dangerous place. Fair put him in a pet, it did," Rose grinned at Eddy's discomfort over her disclosure.

Red-faced, Eddy suddenly remembered a pressing task he needed to perform, and, after a speedy apology, he left the women alone.

"Where is Cousin Guido?"

"Out to the police I 'spect, trying to find you. Don't worry, love, 'e'll be back soon enough."

"Rose," Mair whispered, leaning closer to her friend. "Come upstairs for a minute. There's something I want to ask you, something very important."

Looking rather startled, Rose agreed. They slipped quietly from the kitchen so as not to arouse Amelia's suspicions.

Mair's heart was hammering with excitement when at last they reached the safety of their shared room. When the door was closed it was time at last to reveal the secret she had hugged to herself for what seemed like years.

"Sit down, Rose, I've got something to ask you."

Uneasy, Rose perched on the edge of the bed, her sharp-featured face solemn. She had no idea what trouble Mair was in, at least she hoped she had not. There was always the universal trouble that girls got into. She said a silent prayer, hoping that poor Mair was not in the family way.

"Do you think you could live with me, Rose—travel with me?"

Rose gulped, hardly expecting such a question. "Well, I s'pose. We's good friends and all. Why?"

Out came the treasured letter. Mair drew her friend to the window and handed her the letter, forgetting Rose was not a very good reader. Dying with impatience, Mair finally took the letter from Rose while she was still laboring through the opening paragraph. Breathlessly she began to read the letter to her friend.

When Mair had finished reading, Rose was stunned. "Cor, Mair," she gasped at last, "I don't believe it! You sure it's real?" With dark eyes big as saucers, she searched Mair's face, then a disturbing thought struck her. "It's not one of them white slavery rings we keeps hearing about—them that's always luring English girls over for them Froggy's? You'd best be careful of this Madame Duval—sounds awful like a real madam, she does."

Despite herself, Mair had to laugh. Trust Rose to put some melodramatic interpretation on her stupendous news.

"Oh, Rose, it's nothing like that. Remember the little Frenchman who came to hear the show? It was sometime after Jubilee night."

Rose nodded, though she really did not remember him. Her memory was not as sharp as Mair's, but she did not want to disappoint her friend.

"He works with the Paris Opera. Marc Barbour's his name. He's responsible for them making me

270

this offer. It's genuine, Rose, really it is. In January I'm going to sing at the Paris Opera! Just think, I'll be living in Paris! It's a place people only dream about."

"More like a nightmare, if you ask me. All the stuff you hear about them Frenchies. Proper sin city, Paris is. You'd best be careful going there."

"Oh, Rose." Exasperated by Rose's gloomy warnings, Mair swept her friend into her arms. "You silly, there really are legitimate theaters in Paris. You've seen too many of those naughty French postcards they sell down the alley. Besides, I won't be alone, I'll have someone to look after me. Now, to get back to my first question: will you come with me and be my maid? See here—they expect I'll have a maid. I can't think of anyone I'd rather take than you. Will you come?"

Rose frowned as she struggled to read the passage to which Mair was pointing. "You're really asking me to go with you to Paris?" she asked at last, hardly able to believe this was really happening.

"Yes. Oh, please, say you will. I need you to come with me, Rose. We'll see everything together. And I'll buy you one of those French bonnets with the feathers that you've always admired—if you say yes."

"Now then, no need to bribe me. Course I'll come. Wouldn't turn down a lark like that to stay in this miserable hole."

Mair grabbed Rose and they waltzed about the small room laughing and crying in girlish delight. Paris would be more of an adventure when shared with someone she knew. Mair would not mind

France's foreignness nearly as much with Rose at her side.

Finally they sat on the bed poring again over the letter, which Mair reread to Rose, emphasizing their living arrangements at the Hotel Meurice and the departure date, which was three weeks hence.

Caught up in the thrill of the adventure, Rose clasped her hands, eyes shining. "What will you wear? Got to look like a proper singer, you do."

"I'll travel in my gray suit. It's the best thing I've got, but I'll have to buy a hat since I lost mine. A lady doesn't go out without her hat—especially a famous opera singer who has a maid," here they clutched each other, giggling like schoolgirls at the thought of pulling off such a grand performance.

"We could take something out of wardrobe," Rose suggested, having no qualms about requisitioning suitable clothing at Guido's expense.

"No. I won't take anything from him. I'll just have to ask for some money to buy a few things. He surely owes me something for all the hours I've sung for him."

"Try getting it—like trying to get blood from a stone to get sixpence out of old Guido. By the way, what'd he say when you told 'im?"

Mair swallowed, her smile fading. "I haven't told him yet. First I'm going to make arrangements for our passage with Madame Duval. She might lend me some money as an advance on my salary, then I won't have to ask the old skinflint for a penny."

"He's going to raise the roof when he finds out. You should see the programs he's arranging for you this season."

"We have to be in Paris in three weeks. That

means I'll sing two more Saturdays for him, then it's over. I know he's going to be furious at the thought of losing me, but I don't know how else to do it. At least he'll have two more performances out of me before the bubble bursts."

"He'll not just be angry with you—what about me? He'll be losing the two of us," Rose reminded uneasily, twisting her hands together. "He's like to kill me."

"Nothing of the sort, girl. Don't you worry, I'll deal with him. The day we're supposed to leave, I'll send you on ahead before I tell him you're coming too. I'll ask to be met, so's he'll have to let me go or Madame Duval will have the law on him if he tries to lock me in."

"Good idea. Well, you know what you're doing. I trust you to work it out for both of us. You always had a good head on your shoulders—a bit simple about some things, but still clever," Rose added with a cheeky grin as Mair swatted at her for her impudence.

In the weeks ahead Mair wished she shared Rose's confidence in her own ability to organize their departure from Duchess Street. She did manage to slip away one afternoon to keep a prearranged appointment with Madame Duval, to whom she had written at the Metropole.

The middle-aged Frenchwoman appeared kind and was most helpful after Mair explained their difficult situation. Madame Duval assured her she need worry about nothing except being prepared to travel when the carriage arrived for her on the morning of Friday, December 2. That evening they would sail for France.

The more Mair thought about that brief meeting in the lobby of the luxurious Hotel Metropole, the more like a dream it seemed. The reality was the shabby theater where Cousin Guido bellowed orders in two languages as the rattling piano and the raucous music hall tunes echoed through the impoverished streets. Whenever she pictured herself living in Paris and singing on the stage of the Paris Opera, she had to pinch herself to make sure she was not dreaming.

Rose carefully guarded their secret even without Mair asking her to do so.

The next two weeks slid by with painful slowness. Guido had been so relieved to have Mair back safe and sound, he had greeted her like a long-lost relation. He showed her the grand programs he was arranging, wherein she had more exposure time on stage. By now their local patronage had begun to drop off again in favor of the better dressed theatergoers, and he was rubbing his hands in glee as he envisioned packed houses and money rolling in.

In a way Mair wished Cousin Guido would be less pleasant to her, for it made her feel despicable to be deceiving him. Several times she was tempted to reveal what she intended to do, yet always at the last minute she stopped, recalling Nico's warning that Guido would try to detain her. She could not risk losing her chance to sing in a genuine opera house; she had already sacrificed being with Nico for the opportunity to sing in Paris, and she would not let Guido Agnelli ruin it for her now. So she held her tongue, simpering obligingly as he outlined his grand plans, playing the part of the obedient disciple as he waxed eloquent about the spectacles he would someday produce on a scale to rival the famous Astleys.

November dragged to a cold and foggy close.

On Tuesday morning, to Mair's great surprise, an errand boy arrived at the stage door carrying a couple of large boxes addressed to Madame Parigi. Excited by the unexpected delivery, Rose raced to her, carrying the dress and hat box, glad it was she who had answered the door.

"Go on, open it, Mair. Must be from that Madame Whatsit, don't you think?" she surmised, almost in awe of the two beautiful white embossed boxes tied with pink and black raffia.

When Mair opened the lid of the hat box and looked inside, her eyes filled with tears. Nestled inside the box in layers of pink tissue was a beautiful velvet hat. The deep blue toque was swirled with matching blue ostrich feathers and trimmed with ruched satin ribbon. Though not quite the identical blue of her other hat, this creation was far more splendid. When Mair carefully extracted the hat from its wrappings, Rose gasped in admiration.

Mair couldn't see her own reflection in the mirror for the blinding tears in her eyes. Only one person could have sent this hat, because only one person knew how attached she had been to Miss Jenkins's old castoff. Nico had sent her this lovely replacement, which she would always treasure.

Lying in the bottom of the hatbox was an unsigned note.

"May you wear this hat to many glorious events," Rose read with difficulty, finding the message rather strange. "No name on it, Mair. Funny thing for that Madame Whatsit to write, isn't it?"

Rose had already turned her attention to the larger box, sparing Mair the need to answer. She supposed Madame Duval could have sent the hat, yet in her heart she knew it had come from Nico. He must have returned to London. Or perhaps he had ordered the present in Liverpool. The boy who delivered the boxes had already left, and she had not thought to ask where the packages came from.

For a few heady moments Mair contemplated staying in London with Nico. She could leave the Coliseum as planned, but instead of going to France, she could go to the Castelli and Gambino Shipping Company to find out where he was living. Yet in going to the shipping company she would probably meet Teresa's father, to whom she would have to explain her relationship to Nico. Her arrival at the firm would probably be met with hostility. And the Paris opera beckoned most persuasively. The temptation to throw all aside for the man she loved flourished briefly, then died. She could still be a terrible fool where Nico was concerned.

"Coo, look at this wrap, would you."

Blinking back tears, Mair turned to look at the matching blue dolman Rose was holding up. Made of fine dark blue cashmere, it was piped and ruched around the hem and sleeves in blue velvet and lined with gleaming blue satin. Mair gasped with delight, taking the lovely garment and slipping her arms inside the cool satin sleeves. Dressed in this elegant wrap, with the blue velvet hat on her upswept hair, Mair looked like a princess—or an opera diva, she added with a quiver of excitement. Posing before the mirror, she craned for a view of the back of the dolman, which was nipped in at the waist, flaring out again over the hips and reaching to the thigh. In this fashionable garment she would definitely look the part. Worn with her good navy skirt, this new hat and wrap would make her the equal of anyone she met.

One more horror still loomed ahead. Mair knew she would have to tell Cousin Guido today. There was no time left. It was December the first—they were due to leave tomorrow. Already Rose had surreptitiously prepared for departure, packing their valises and hiding them in the wardrobe trunks. Mair felt guilty for having waited this long to tell him, even allowing him to plan next Saturday's performance while knowing full well she would not be here to take part in it. Yet Nico had advised her to wait until the last minute to tell Cousin Guido in case he stalled her plans, and she was sure he had given her sound advice.

The December day was gloomy; thick cloud banked above the rooftops and the north wind was sharp. For the last several days a choking fog had been bottled inside the narrow streets, acrid with the coalsmoke that corroded lungs and blackened clothing. Mair was not sorry to be leaving London. Though it had often rained and it was dingy and grimy, Llandare was paradise compared to this part of Holborn. Mair hated breathing the thick, noxious air. At times she longed for the Welsh mountains with such intensity that tears came to her eyes. How she ached to hear the song of the birds and hear the wind blowing through the trees.

In London, hacking coughs were the perpetual music of winter.

Mair met Guido at the entrance to his office cubbyhole. Her stomach lurched as she anticipated the coming ordeal.

"Well, Mair, December already! We plan a big Christmas program, eh?"

There was nothing for it but to take the plunge. Mair twisted her hands together nervously until the knuckles cracked. "Cousin Guido, there's something I have to talk to you about," she began hesitantly, swallowing the terrible lump in her throat. "Now," she added firmly as he stepped inside his small office, ignoring her request.

"No, I'm busy. Later," he rumbled, his dark eyes hardening. "You get too big for your shoes these days, demanding this and that. Later."

"No. It has to be now," she insisted, planting her foot inside the door to keep him from shutting himself inside his office. "This is very important."

"If it's about money, no money. You the third today ask about money."

"Not about money."

He glared at her, realizing she was not going to be easily dissuaded. "What about then? Come in, be quick. I have appointment soon."

Inwardly, Mair winced. Probably not after you've heard me out, she thought, perching on the edge of the rickety wooden chair reserved for guests. Cousin Guido leaned back in his chair, his large paunch spilling over his stained pinstriped trousers, the frayed cuffs of his tweed coat standing out like frills around his huge fists.

"I've been thinking about this for a long time

278

and I don't know of an easier way to tell you. I've been offered a chance to sing at the Paris Opera."

He stared at her, his dark brown eyes narrowing. "So?"

"So—I've accepted."

"You what!"

"I've accepted it."

"You can't! Only *I* accept for you," he cried, pounding his chest to emphasize his words. "Like I say, you get too big for your shoes these days. Little fool. How you know what to accept and what not? *I* tell you!"

"Just be quiet and listen to me," she said calmly, her tone effectively halting his ranting, which threatened to evolve into a tirade. "I've already accepted in writing. There's nothing you can say to change matters. I sail for France in the morning."

His thick lips moved soundlessly in his darkening face. Finally he gasped, "France? Tomorrow? You crazy! That not possible!"

"I want to thank you for giving me the chance to perform on stage, for helping to groom me and teach me what you know. Now I'm ready to go on to bigger things. Though I didn't expect you to be overjoyed, I'd hoped you'd understand."

"Understand!" he bellowed, leaping up and sending his chair crashing into the wall. "Understand! You ungrateful fool! You can't do this to me! The program's printed—it's too late to change. This is Thursday. You can't leave tomorrow! You sing *here* on Saturday night. You *will* sing here Saturday night if I have to tie you up."

Mair stood and edged to the door. This was every bit as terrible as she had imagined it would be.

Footsteps were thumping along the hallway, and she knew the others were coming to see what all the commotion was about.

"I can't. I'll be in Paris on Saturday night."

"No. You sing here for me. We have agreement."

"In all the time I've sung for you I've never been paid a penny. Everything I've made for you, you've kept. My debt to you has been paid."

Guido's face purpled as he exploded in anger over her calm statement. He could not believe what he was hearing, could not believe this girl's effrontery in calmly telling him two days before the performance that she was leaving. For Paris no less! Preposterous!

"You stupid girl! Who fed you? Who housed you? Who gave you a chance? And now, little bitch, what you do? You throw it all in my face."

By now Amelia was in the hallway taking everything in. Mair quailed inwardly at the growing crowd of spectators.

"What's going on here?" Amelia demanded in English, before lapsing into a torrent of Italian. She and Guido shouted back and forth to each other for a few minutes before she finally grasped what was going on. With an angry exclamation, Amelia grasped Mair's arm. "You go no place," she ordered, her fingers biting bruisingly into Mair's flesh. "Only place you go is up to your room. You wait there till Saturday."

Mair struggled free, glad that Guido did not come to his wife's assistance. "Amelia, you've been kind to me and I thank you for all you've done, but it's a chance for me to move on. I have to take it. You should be pleased that I've been asked to sing in Paris because you helped teach me how to act on stage."

"Pleased!" Guido exploded, suddenly coming back to life. He thumped around his desk and imprisoned Mair's arm. "We have contract! You sing for no one without my permission. Got that, stupid little girl? Now you go stay in your room till Saturday."

"We have no contract. I've signed nothing."

"We don't need signing, we *speak* it—that as good!"

"We agreed to nothing. You told me to sing and I have sung, dozens of performances for you. I've filled this theater night after night, and I sang for nothing beyond my keep. Don't try to keep me here against my will. A carriage is coming for me. They've already been warned that you might try to keep me here. Please, Cousin Guido, give in gracefully and wish me well."

Mair paused for breath, looking from one angry face to the other. The members of the company stood there, not really sure of the cause of this argument. Rose was standing at the back of the crowd, wondering what she should do, but Mair signaled to her to keep quiet.

Wait until they learned Rose was leaving also! Perhaps she should save that brickbat to the absolute last minute; there was enough anger between them for one day.

Mair, Amelia and Cousin Guido stood in the doorway frozen in time, speechless until Guido finally spat, "Get up to your room. We talk about this tomorrow." As he spoke he waved his arms toward the stair.

Mair pushed past them, ignoring the clamoring company members who wanted to know what had sparked their quarrel. She rounded the corner, seeking the safety of her room. She had no idea what the Agnellis would do to keep her there.

"I'll sue you! You'll never get a penny from your big deal," Guido bellowed after her, his voice booming and echoing through the narrow hallways.

When at last Mair reached the safety of her room, she flung herself across the bed, her heart pounding with fear and anger. She could feel the movement leaping inside her bodice; her hands and legs shook. What could Cousin Guido do to keep her here? This wasn't the middle ages. He could hardly keep her prisoner, for if she did not appear on stage, she was no good to him. Hopefully Madame Duval would keep her part of the arrangement and arrive with a carriage at seven thirty in the morning. They were to take a train to the coast and board the night boat for Calais.

The dismal cold room became odious to Mair long before Rose came upstairs with a couple of cold mutton sandwiches and a mug of lukewarm tea.

"All I could get without them seeing, love," Rose apologized when she arrived in the afternoon gloom. "Everyone's buzzing about you going off to Paris. Guido's fit to do murder. He's told everyone to stay away from you. Don't know what he's going to do. We ought to scarper tonight while it's still dark, if you ask me—or at least real early in the morning."

Mair munched on the sandwich, finding the cold

mutton greasy and unpalatable. Perhaps Rose was right. The longer they stayed, the more difficult their situation could become.

Devious Rose had already hatched a plan to put Guido off guard. "Why don't you write him a note saying as how you're sorry," she suggested eagerly. "I could give it to him, and that way maybe he'll think you've changed your mind about leaving. Then we could slip out after things quiet down. The side door'll be open early in the morning for deliveries. Maybe we should wait till then. We could stand in a doorway down the street and watch for your Madam's carriage. How about that?"

Mair hated having to be so furtive, but Rose probably had a wise plan. Who knew what Guido was hatching? Fortunately he didn't know about Madame Duval. "I won't apologize to him; I've done nothing wrong," she insisted stubbornly.

"Course you 'aven't, love. But couldn't you say how you didn't mean to upset him," Rose suggested diplomatically, knowing she had to handle her friend's prickly Welsh pride with care. "That's not admitting to nothin', now is it?"

"Oh, all right, if you think it'll help our chances."

Mair very reluctantly used a sheet of the bond paper she had bought to write letters home. "Sorry for upsetting you both," she wrote. "I want us all to be friends. Mair."

Rose pulled a face at the brief message, but knew it was the best she could hope for.

"Eddy's waiting in the hall to talk to you. Shall I tell him you're asleep?"

"Please. Thank you, Rose."

Mair said goodbye to Rose, who went to slip the note under Guido's door. She had no desire to suffer Eddy Lewis's attempts at seduction today. Sensing she was vulnerable, he probably thought this would be the perfect time to pounce.

Darkness fell early on the December day. Mair lit the lone gaslight and tried to study the score of *Romeo and Juliet*, knowing there was much to learn before she could sing the entire opera.

Sometime in the evening she heard steps outside the door and, thinking it was Rose, waited for her friend to come in. Then Mair heard a key being turned in the lock. In a flash she was at the door, banging on it, shouting for whoever it was to open the door. Her cries went unheeded. So that was what Guido intended to do, to keep her locked up until she had a change of heart. Thank goodness she had not yet revealed Rose's part in her defection. Had it not been for Rose, they would probably not be able to meet the morning carriage. Alternate sleeping arrangements must have been made for Rose, for she normally shared this small room. There was nothing Mair could do but wait until Rose came to let her out.

Mair was dressed and waiting by five, which was when the side door was opened to allow tradesmen to put supplies inside. Wearing her new hat and wrap, Mair sat on the bed, waiting. She had taken her few remaining possessions and placed them in a small carpet bag, along with the score for the opera. She was ready. She waited, listening for a footfall on the stair.

In December it would not be light until after

eight o'clock, so even had they waited till the carriage arrived, they could have slipped out in the dark. But she did not think it wise to wait. Rose was probably right in suggesting they leave as soon as possible. Where was she? Mair waited, wondering what time it was. She strained to hear the neighborhood parish clock strike the half hour, then the quarter. Surely Rose was not going to fail her.

There it was. The slow squeak of the stair, the groan of the boards outside in the hall as someone stealthily crept to the end of the passage.

Mair stood a little to the side of the door, just in case her visitor was not Rose. The key was fitted in the lock, the handle turned, and the door slowly creaked open.

"Mair, are you ready," Rose whispered in a hoarse voice, her hands shaking as she pocketed the key.

"Yes, wondering what was keeping you."

"The old skinflint was down there counting the oranges, arguing somethink terrible with the lad —in Spanish too. Didn't know he knew that lingo, did you?"

"Rose," Mair interrupted, her own nerves taut. "Hush, or he'll be up here next. Are you sure he didn't see you?"

"Positive. Come on then, the door's still unlocked."

Picking up her small bag, Mair followed Rose down the corridor. Rose had a hat and a cape round her shoulders, which Mair had not seen before. She supposed they had come from the wardrobe trunk, but she didn't quibble. All she wanted was to escape from the wrath of the Agnellis as quickly as possible.

They navigated the dark hallways without incident. Rose had already brought out their valises from the wardrobe hampers, and they stood waiting beside the door.

Glancing about to make sure they were not being observed, Rose opened the side door, admitting a gust of cold air. Mair shivered with a mixture of nerves and cold.

They slipped outside into the cold darkness, careful not to trip over the goods stored inside the doorway. Mair was as much afraid of these dark neighborhood streets as she was of being captured by Cousin Guido. Fearfully she looked about, seeing shadows moving close to the buildings: prostitutes on their way home, ragpickers and workers on their way out. The shadows moved through the darkness without seeming to notice the two women standing at the corner.

"We'd better go further along the street. We might be seen out here," Mair suggested, picking up her worldly possessions and staggering under the weight of the valise.

Rose agreed. Hefting her own bag, she started down the street after Mair, who had taken refuge a few doors down in the gloomy entrance to an old clothes shop.

They waited for what seemed like hours in the cold predawn darkness. At every sound of hoofbeats, they peered around the doorway, hoping this was finally the carriage sent to fetch them.

A brewer's dray came rumbling down the street and pulled up on the corner to unload the ale for the Saturday show. Behind the dray came a green-grocer's cart. Both conveyances effectively blocked the street.

When at last the distant sounds of clopping hooves were heard, Mair knew this had to be Madame Duval's carriage. Though the tradesmen's carts blocked the street, they made it necessary for the carriage to stop beside the ragpicker's doorway to await clearance.

Mair hurried across the pavement and asked the driver if he had been sent for Madame Parigi. To her great relief he nodded and clambered down from the box to help them with their baggage. Mair was disappointed that Madame Duval had not come for them in person.

They hastily climbed inside the carriage, feeling safe inside the upholstered cocoon. No one from the Coliseum would suspect they were the carriage's passengers. Yet, for all that, Mair was pleased to see the two tradesmen's carts lumbering away. The carriage driver smartly picked up the pace and they sailed past the shabby Coliseum without incident. Her last glimpse of the wonderful yet terrible place of her operatic debut would stay forever in her mind.

The carriage stopped at the Metropole to collect Madame Duval, and when the Frenchwoman was aboard Mair heaved a sigh of relief. Everything had gone according to plan. Their escape was complete.

PART THREE
THE CONTINENT

Chapter Seventeen

The narrow twisting ribbon of the Seine caught fire from the rising sun. Shafts of light penetrated the silent Tuilleries Gardens, turning the reflecting pool to molten gold. On the Seine's left bank the narrow streets were slowly coming to life. The Sant Germain des Pres district was the haunt of students and poor artists who sometimes used the pavements of the quarter as their canvas.

Mair often watched this slow awakening from her suite high above Paris in the grand Hotel Meurice. During the three months she had lived there, she had explored many of the city's broad boulevards and tree-lined squares. By day Paris was a bustling, exciting city; by night its glittering gaslights made it the 'city of light.' Her life had been so excitingly different these past weeks, it all seemed like a dream. Yet after so long away from all she knew and loved, she was more than ready to go home. It was not for London with its fogs and congestion that she pined, but for Wales. How she longed to see those rolling, sheep-dotted hills, the rugged mountains, to feel the sharp sting of wind-driven rain.

Mair turned from the window. She could hear Rose humming in the dressing room while she prepared her wardrobe for the day. Mair sighed. No use getting tearful, girl, she admonished sharply. She shook her head to rid herself of all those nostalgic pictures, yet still they crept back unbidden. Soon spring would be creeping over the countryside. The mountain ash would come into bud and wildflowers would peep from the grass.

"Want to wear the russet or green costume today, Mum?" Rose asked, holding out a finely tailored russet serge walking costume trimmed with narrow strips of sealskin; the green costume was draped over her other arm. "If you walk you'll need your muff. There's a nip to the air. Or maybe we could take the carriage?"

Mair smiled as she detected Rose's hopeful tone. "No, Rose, we'll walk. You know if I don't get some outdoor exercise I'll go mad, cooped up in the theater all the time, closed in by the city streets. The russet will do for today."

"Well, I thought, seeing as it's still winter," Rose persisted, poised with the garments over her arm, "wouldn't hurt to ride for once, now, would it?"

"Winter? March is the beginning of spring," Mair reminded, reaching for the soft wool garment. "Remember what I told you: exercise is very good for you."

"Yes, Mum."

"And will you stop calling me 'Mum' when we're alone."

Mair's tone sharpened. Rose's habit of referring to her as 'Mum' sometimes grated on her nerves. She understood it was proper in public for Rose was here in Paris as her maid, yet it was not necessary in private. By becoming 'Mum,' it seemed as if she had lost her friend and acquired a servant instead.

Seated at her gilded cream-laquered dressing table, Mair slipped open her wrap; the delicate peach velvet matched her voluminous silk nightgown trimmed with swansdown. The flattering color brought a luminous glow to her complexion and made her hair deep honey gold. This lovely ensemble was some of Mme. Violette's best work. It was new this week. Mme. Violette was a skilled seamstress formerly with the famous Worth salon. She had created this beautiful wardrobe, producing outfits far more glamorous than Mair had ever dreamed of owning. When she dressed in these gowns with their matching hats, gloves or boots, Mair truly felt like the famous opera singer she aspired to be. This new wardrobe was part of the character she assumed for public appearances, inspiring confidence in the often ill-at-ease person who inhabited her body.

Mair glanced at her reflection in the mirror where her face was softly shadowed by a pool of yellow gaslight. Three months ago she had been beside herself with excitement as she stood on the brink of this adventure. Now the dream had become reality. She had sung at the Paris Opera! The marvelous experience had been everything she had hoped for, yet once she stepped off stage she felt hollow. Something was missing from her life. Usually she tried not to analyze what that something was, immersing herself instead in Parisian life. But very soon she discovered the constant round of fetes and galas enjoyed by Parisian society was not for her. The parties quickly became meaningless once she found they consisted of the same guests, all saying the same things, cutting the people who had fallen from favor, embracing those on the ascendance. She was bored by this empty charade, which apparently was designed to fill time. At heart Mair was a simple person who needed something more tangible in her life than endless entertainment.

Mair's triumphant Paris debut had paired her with the famous Polish tenor, Jean de Reszke. Their moving performance as the star-crossed lovers in *Romeo and Juliet* assured them both of a permanent place in romantic Paris hearts. The leading Paris newspapers had lavishly praised Mair's performance, hailing as miraculous the discovery of this newest diva.

As she slowly brushed her long hair, Mair's smile turned cynical. Miraculous discovery indeed. She had thought life at the Coliseum was nothing more than work and performances, but when she entered the hallowed environs of the Paris Opera, an even greater shock awaited her. For that first month she was constantly being coached in every aspect of theatrical performance. She sang scales by the hour and practiced breathing exercises. She hardly noticed that Christmas came and went. By choosing to appear at this famous opera house she had opened herself up to the severest criticism.

Sometimes it seemed she would never be deemed fit to sing Juliette.

Once Mair had made her debut to great acclaim, the pace had slackened slightly. But just around the corner, when she had barely recovered from that ordeal, they began to groom her anew to play Marguerite in *Faust*.

Her singing of that role was also highly acclaimed. As *Faust* was the most popular opera in the current repertoire, her interpretation of Marguerite earned her even more press coverage. The critics hailed her as the new, definitive Marguerite of the decade, praising her youthful beauty, her air of innocence, and most of all her soaring, bell-clear voice which reached the farthest corners of the vast opera house.

At the inevitable moments when everything seemed to go wrong, when she was yelled at by the Maestro, or the director, or upstaged by a jealous colleague, Mair recalled that lavish praise, recounting the comforting words to sustain her through the storm. She had one recital left to perform, then it would all be over. The realization that her dreamlike life was ending brought with it a sense of letdown, almost as if it had never actually taken place. Mair rejoiced to know she would soon be free to go home.

She frowned as she remembered that yesterday Monsieur Gailhard had told her they had a big surprise for her. Not until she arrived at the opera house today would she learn just what that surprise entailed. Perhaps they had decided to add more performances.

Rose hurried into the room to dress her, hand-

ing her the garments, then pulling the clothes out
of Mair's hands when she began to dress herself.

"That's my job, in't it?"

"You've become a tyrant."

"You hired me to be your maid and that's what
I'm going to be."

Mair pulled a face at Rose, who grinned back
cheekily at her. Rose hummed a popular music
hall ditty under her breath as she did up the
fastenings on the back of Mair's lace-trimmed
cream satin blouse.

"You'll be glad to go home, won't you?" Mair
asked curiously, though she already knew the
answer.

"Will I? Just give me a bit of steak pud any day
over all this fancy French food—sauced and
creamed so's a body don't know what the food's
supposed to taste like. Why, won't you?"

Mair shrugged, taking her hat from Rose. Leaning close to the mirror, she firmly placed the russet
felt on her head, tweaking the upturned brim and
settling the mountain of plush fruits and ostrich
feathers. "In a way," she finally allowed, talking
with a hatpin in her mouth. Settling the hat exactly
at the angle she wanted, Mair speared through the
felt and her rolled coiffure, securing the hat with a
long, pearl-headed pin. "Do you suppose we'll be
singing at Covent Garden, or the Lyceum, someday?"

"Not we—*you* will, love. In fact, after all them
reviews, if you doesn't have an army of folks
waiting to sign you up, I'm a Chinaman."

"Wherever we stay in London, it won't be as
grand as the Hotel Meurice."

"Oh, I don't know. What's about the Savoy, or

the Ritz? There's any number of posh places we can be put up in London if they pays you enough. And if not, we don't 'ave to 'ave crystal chandeliers and satin couches, not after living at the old Coliseum with its moth-eaten stuff.''

They both laughed, but a wistful note entered their laughter. This luxurious suite, the splendid theater dressing room with its banks of flowers and bevy of titled admirers who had pursued Mair since her debut, had come with a price attached. No longer was she a lighthearted girl, free to choose what she sang, or when; in exchange for luxury she had sold herself to the Paris Opera and its wealthy patrons.

The sky was still streaked with banners of crimson and gold when they went down the hotel steps and began to walk along the broad Rue de Rivoli. Shivering in the unexpectedly chill air, Mair buried her hands in her soft velvet-lined fur muff. Several early morning strollers doffed their hats and bowed from the waist in tribute to the lovely woman who caught their appreciative eye. She doubted these men knew who she was, for they did not approach her, gushing extravagant praise, forever with an eye to seduction. Mair had to smile when she considered Eddy Lewis's feeble efforts to initiate a love affair. He was no match for these Parisian males. Marquis, comtes, even an obscure prince, had all pledged their undying love in hope of securing her sexual favors. When the heart was not involved, Mair found it easy to laugh, to flirt, then turn them away without completely dashing their hopes. It was also a lonely game, for through it all she remained unmoved. There was only one man able to reach inside to touch her soul.

Mair blinked rapidly. Absurdly, she found herself on the brink of tears. She had no idea why she was so vulnerable to old memories today. It must be because they were on the verge of going home that Nico's memory kept tormenting her. Though she desperately wanted to see him, Mair had little expectation that his position had changed. He may not want Teresa, yet he would not risk cutting her adrift when her father's wealth was still so important to him. Mair knew she could have have him on his terms, but she had indignantly dismissed the idea of living with him without marraige. Now, she was no longer sure. After three months in Paris, observing the way high society lived, she realized she was not cut out for that way of life. Many a time she would have welcomed the anonymity of a quiet villa where she could recoup after gruelling hours of pleasing her public. To have Nico beside her would make her dreams of paradise complete.

Down the broad Avenue de l'Opera they walked, Mair stepping out briskly, glad to feel the chill air sweeping past her cheeks.

Rose, never as fond of walking as she, huffed along half a pace to the rear, her face set mutinously. Rose loved riding in the carriage which had been put at Mair's disposal. Mair's peculiar penchant for walking in the fresh air did not please Rose at all. How much more pleasant and far grander it would have been to have arrived at the opera house in their carriage. Rose's every movement revealed her displeasure.

Dismissing her friend's mood, Mair looked ahead toward the end of the avenue where the magnificent opera house stood. Seven porticoes housing statues depicting the arts decorated its main facade. Though the grand exterior of the building hinted at its interior splendor, nothing prepared one for that burst of red and gold opulence with grand staircases and galleries, all overhung by enormous crystal chandeliers. The opera house was as sumptuous as a palace. The vast stage could easily have held fifty cramped Coliseum stages. Huge productions, complete with horses and chariots, could be presented on the Paris Opera stage, which had room for more than four hundred performers. Or one, Mair thought with a quiver of excitement.

How small and frightened she had felt standing alone under the lights, facing that magnificent jeweled audience in their five tiers of boxes. And, miracle of miracles, she had moved them to tears as she sang Marguerite's beautiful arias. Each new character she portrayed was like the beginning of a new life. At the moment she felt comfortable with Juliet and Marguerite, though Mair understood she could not base an operatic career on the strength of two roles.

"Welcome, Madame Parigi."

On her arrival at the theater, Mair was greeted at the door by a bevy of opera house staff members, finding their effusive greeting somewhat unusual. She was ushered inside the manager's plushly carpeted office where a gilded chair was pulled forward for her use.

Outwardly calm, she was every inch the international diva. But inwardly there still remained a lot of the old Mair Parry from Llandare. When Marc Barbour finally entered the room, Mair relaxed a bit, for he was the man with whom she was the most familiar.

"Madame Parigi," he bowed smartly and took her hand, pressing it to his lips. "We have a most wonderful proposition to make to you."

At his choice of the word proposition, she had to smile. Ah, yes, in recent weeks she had been offered more than her share of those.

"Well, Monsieur Barbour, don't keep me guessing. Tell me what it is," she said clearly, consciously trying to eliminate all traces of Llandare from her speech.

"Signor Bertelli," here Marc Barbour indicated a short balding man sporting a huge hothouse carnation in his lapel, "is here from Milan. He has heard you sing and is enchanted. He wishes to make you a very generous offer. He wants you to delight the Italians as you have the Parisians."

"Madame," Signor Bertelli took her hand and eagerly pressed it to his lips. "We would be honored if you would consent to sing Juliet and Marguerite for us. There has been some sickness, you understand. Our roster has many holes . . . so very fortunate for us."

Mair returned his smile, appearing calm while inwardly her heart almost leaped from her bodice. Italy! Was she to go there now instead of home to England? And, more important, should she accept the offer? She was afraid of saying yes. Yet why not? Paris had been conquered. Why not Milan?

"When do you want me to sing for you, Signor Bertelli?"

At her words, the Italian's beam grew broader. Marc Barbour nodded and smiled at her in appro-

val, assuring Mair she had made the right response. Signor Bertelli clasped her hand in his
sweating palm.

"My dear Madame, we need you to come to
Milan as soon as possible. Now! No need you worry
about accommodations. La Scala is ever generous
to its artists. All will be arranged for you, if you
agree."

Marc Barbour nodded again, and, trusting his
judgment, Mair said, "Very well, Signor Bertelli, as
I've no other engagement at the moment, I'll be
pleased to sing at La Scala."

Later, when she recalled her calmness, her
almost casual approach, her laughter verged on
hysteria. Pleased to sing at La Scala? Who was she
trying to fool? Last year she would have killed for
the privilege of singing at La Scala. Amelia and
Cousin Guido had always promoted the Italian
opera house as being the very pinnacle of operatic
success. Less than a year later, a place was being
made for her on their bill. She doubted sickness
was the cause of these purported 'gaps' as the little
Italian had explained. It was more likely that the
management of La Scala wished to take advantage
of her popularity while she was still the Toast of
Paris, as the local press had so generously named
her. The Toast of Paris—and still not happy!

When Mair saw her reflection in the mirror, she
drew in her breath in surprise. The corners of her
mouth were downturned in repose. Hastily she
forced a cheerful smile to her soft lips. What was
the matter with her? Singing in the famous opera
houses of the world was what she had always
wanted, wasn't it?

Yes, and no. She wanted the satisfaction of singing onstage, of hearing her voice soar into the accoustically splendid theaters. But she had not intended to exchange success for love. Naively she had thought she could have both. Now she knew better. Her heart ached for Nico, for the sweetness of his kiss, the comfort of his arms. Merely the sound of his voice or his tender smile was enough to send her spirits soaring. She could not allow herself to dwell on his lovemaking, for such recklessness caused physical pain, stirring afresh the unassuaged fires of passion burning inside her body. Singing must consume her every waking moment; had she not sacrificed the other for it? Now she must learn to be satisfied with her bargain.

To mollify Rose, Mair had taken the carriage home. And though Rose had rattled on happily about what she would do when she got home to London, Mair had remained silent. She knew she must tell Rose her latest news.

"Rose," she called, getting up from the dressing table.

"Yes, m—Mair." Rose gulped, grinning as she corrected the slip of her tongue. It was difficult being a maid one minute, a friend and equal the next. To put it bluntly, it was becoming a little too taxing for her. Besides, nowadays she no longer felt Mair's equal. All those lovely clothes she wore and the rich, titled men who sent her flowers, even the elegant surroundings of this hotel suite combined to make Mair even more remote. Rose no longer had her friend to herself, for she had become a very minor part of Mair's life.

"Rose, I've something we must discuss. Today I

was made an offer to go to sing at La Scala, then perhaps to other engagements in Italy."

"Italy!" Rose squeaked in dismay. "I thought we was going 'ome. Me brother's got a little one now. I was all set to see her. Daisy's her name."

Mair's face fell. It was as she had suspected, though she had hoped Rose would be pleased with her new plans. Here on the continent, Rose was even more out of her element than Mair herself.

"If you'd rather go back to England, I'll pay your passage home," Mair offered at last, her voice shaking slightly as she anticipated the ordeal of venturing alone into a foreign land.

"Naw, 'ow'l you manage without me? Who'll dress yer, take care of your things?"

"I'm sure the theaters will have dressers to help me. There'll be someone I can get along with. You mustn't go to Italy and be unhappy there if you'd rather go home."

Tears trickled down Rose's cheeks at the thought of abandoning Mair amidst all these foreigners. "Won't I see you again?" she whispered at last, licking tears from her lips.

"Of course, silly, you can work with me again when you're ready. But I know you haven't really been happy here, now have you?"

Reluctantly Rose had to admit she had not. "Things is too different. *You's* too different," she blurted truthfully.

Mair's stomach twisted at the truth. Rose was right. She was not the same girl who had giggled with her friend in their small room over the theater.

"I'm sorry, Rose," was all she could say. There didn't seem anything more to be said about the change in herself, beyond acknowledging it had taken place. "I've put some money in the bank for you so you'll have a nest egg of sorts to tide you over until I come back to London. You can live at your brother's, or we can get a place in the city, somewhere that you'll like too."

Rose's face brightened at the prospect of not being cast off. "P'raps I could take in a bit of sewing, give me something to do. 'Ow long's you going to be gone?"

"A couple of months. Probably not any longer than that."

Rose took Mair's hand in hers and she smiled through her tears. "Awright, Mair love, if you's sure you'll manage. I will be 'appier at 'ome than running about in some eyetie place. Coo, all that garlic in the food. If you're sure you can manage. 'Cause, I'll stay for you if you need me."

"I know you will. I'll be able to manage. I want what's best for you. You helped me when I needed you, now it's time for you to go home. You never bargained for any more than Paris in the beginning. You can wear that new bonnet I bought you to travel in."

"Coo, I'll knock 'em over in that." Rose smiled in anticipation and ran to fetch the straw bonnet heaped with yellow ribbons and silk roses. It was a spring hat, newly created for the approaching season. Mair had indulged her friend with the gift, feeling rather guilty for having virtually ignored Rose during her own hectic schedule.

Posturing like a grand lady, Rose walked about the room, looking at her reflection in the tall mirrors that covered one wall of this elegant eggshell and gold salon. So happy was she over the prospect of going home, she surprised herself by bursting into the opening notes of the 'Jewel Song' from *Faust*.

"Oh, Rose, *Cariad*. I'm going to miss you," Mair whispered when, a week later, she stood on the platform of the Paris station to bid her friend goodbye. The old Mair, unsure of herself in grand surroundings, had come to the forefront today. And Rose wept with her, reminded of all they had shared.

"Now, come on, Mair, buck up," she sniffled, dabbing her eyes. "That new girl's going to be a big help to you, speaking the foreign lingo. A sight better'n me when it comes to shopping too, I daresay."

Mair grinned through her tears as the train whistle blew and she clasped Rose's hand in farewell, finally running along the platform beside the train as it slowly began to pull out of the station.

The last Mair saw of Rose was a small hand waving an embroidered handkerchief, Mair's parting gift along with a flagon of French perfume, until the white scrap of fabric disappeared from view. Dabbing her eyes, Mair turned to Josette, her new maid, who spoke not only French but also English and Italian. She smiled shyly at the solemn-faced girl.

"Shall we go, Josette?" she said, her voice wobbling with tears.

"Of course, Madame, whenever you are ready."

Together they walked toward the station entrance.

Mair understood a new era was beginning for

her. This seemed to be a perpetual time of exciting
new beginnings, yet sometimes she could not help
yearning for all that was old and familiar.

As a kindness to her, Marc Barbour had made all
the necessary arrangements for Mair to sing in
Italy. He studied the contract Signor Bertelli presented, advising her what the legal terms actually
meant. Though she was still not wholly understanding of her duties, Mair was grateful to him for
taking the time to help her.

Several times she was on the verge of asking him
how well he knew Nico and if he had heard
anything about him. Wisely she held her tongue.
Never once had Marc Barbour divulged that he
knew Nico. Perhaps he preferred to keep a distance between personal and business matters.

Mair had not read anything about Nico for some
time. She doubted the French newspapers would
report British labor activities, nor news about their
politicians, and as she did not read French anyway,
it would have been no use if they had. She still had
a London paper Rose found in the hotel lobby
containing an article about the November riot. The
radicals blamed for inciting the workers to violence were listed. Nico's name was not included
with the others. He had the distinction of having
several paragraphs to himself complete with
quotes from his speeches. Reference was made to
his growing affiliation with the ruling Liberal party
and he was named as the foremost candidate for a
seat in a London working class constituency. Mair
had read the piece so often, the paper was tattered.

It was with some sadness Mair took a final look
at the splendid Hotel Meurice. It was raining this

morning and the hedges surrounding the Tuilleries were wreathed in mist. The wide avenue gleamed with moisture and the horses' hooves threw up showers of water as they passed. She was almost glad not to be going home. Distance gave her a little more time to think before she had to make a decision about Nico. Mair knew she was merely delaying the inevitable, but where he was concerned she was a coward at heart.

Chapter Eighteen

It was Paris all over again!

Mair wept for joy as she stood on stage, her arms open wide to embrace this wildly cheering audience. The huge La Scala theater, with its six tiers of private boxes packed with jeweled patrons, seemed friendlier now. When she first saw the vast, horseshoe-shaped auditorium with its sea of seats, she felt faint. How could she hope to please such veteran opera lovers here, in the very cradle of opera? But she had done it. And she had done it handsomely.

"Maria, Maria," they chanted as flowers rained down on her.

After the final curtain Mair walked back to her dressing room in a daze. What made her reception even more amazing was that tonight was not her Milan debut; this was her fourth and final performance of *Faust*. The management had already signed her to a run of ten performances for the following season, the exact dates to be arranged at a later date. The Milan season ran from early December to April. Mair had not known her future plans, and had told Signor Bertelli she would let him know as soon as possible when she would be available.

The truth was that she had few plans. A representative from Covent Garden had approached her, asking her to sing four performances of *Lucia* for them next season. With great delight she had accepted, for London's Covent Garden would be a personal triumph—hadn't she always said one day she would sing at a grand London Opera house? Who knew what she might be offered after that appearance? Venturing away from her current two roles would take work, yet work was what she needed to fill her every waking moment. Mair lived to sing—was that not what she had vowed?

Mair's head drooped until her chin rested on her chest and she allowed her tears to splash the heavenly blue bodice of Marguerite's peasant costume. Yes, singing was all she wanted and needed, she repeated, gritting her teeth in determination. Applause, admiration, satisfaction, were hers for the taking, but they existed only while she was on stage.

"Madame, a note and some flowers." Josette rested her cool hand on Mair's shoulder.

Raising her head, Mair smiled through her tears. "Thank you, Josette. Put them over there."

The girl hesitated, her dark eyes grave as she saw her mistress's tears. Such an emotional ordeal after each performance. At times she wondered how long this woman would last. Sometimes it seemed as if the flame burning so brightly inside her came close to the point of guttering.

"Let me get you some cordial."

Josette poured Mair a glass of soothing cordial made from an old recipe of her *Grandmere's*, designed to restore her mistress's vigor. Mair accepted the glass, sipping the sweet, cherry-flavored drink, as she turned over the note the maid had handed her. The envelope read, "To Madame Parigi from Nicholas Castle." The hand-writing looked vaguely familiar but she did not recall anyone by that name.

"He's most handsome, Madame—English I would say by his dress. Would you like to speak to him?"

Mair shook her head. She admired the lavish bouquet of pink carnations mingled with white lilac and sprays of almond blossom, an unusual combination with such a heady fragrance that it sent her head spinning.

"Put the flowers in water."

Josette did as she was told. Then she came to help her mistress out of her costume. Silently she unbraided Mair's hair. In her role of Marguerite, Mair wore her own hair in two ribbon-wrapped plaits. For the final scene where Marguerite is in prison for the murder of her illegitimate child, one of the plaits was left unbound so that her golden hair spread around her shoulders, hanging almost to her waist.

Tonight Mair could hardly wait to leave the theater. She had already decided not to join the rest of the cast for the traditional after-performance supper at a nearby restaurant. Her head had begun to pound; even Josette's careful brushing accelerated the ache and she gritted her teeth while Josette rolled and pinned her hair into a chignon. She suspected the headache was caused by unshed tears combined with the upheaval of her performance. She gave any number of reasons for her recurring headaches, though she suspected they were really caused by her mounting unhappiness.

Instead of putting on her wrap and making herself available for a few selected well-wishers, Mair decided to return to the hotel. Not home, as she had begun to tell Josette. Home would have to wait. Before she returned to England there were several obligations left to fulfil. She had been booked at Verona's outdoor theater, and at the Teatro dell'Opera in Rome, where she had also been asked to appear at a gala concert. At this rate she might not go back to England till next spring. Her head spun when she thought of all those events to be, of the difficulties still to be conquered. Yet whatever had been offered she accepted, thereby putting time and distance between herself and the inevitable decision about what she would do about Nico. It was quite possible there was nothing 'to do' about Nico. By now he could have cemented his relationship with Teresa, leaving her entirely out of the picture. The very thought gave her a cold sweat.

Mair stooped to pick up the note that had fallen to the floor. Again, as she studied the writing, it seemed to tug at her memory. Curious, she opened the folded paper and read: "My beautiful Maria. Home at last! Won't you join me in celebration? Nicholas Castle."

The letter further intrigued her, though it made little sense.

"Is this gentleman still waiting outside?" she asked Josette, who was helping her to fasten her gown.

"I can see, Madame, if you wish."

Mair hesitated, absently stroking the folds of her pink ribbed silk skirt. On a whim she plucked two carnations from the fragrant bouquet and pinned them to the shoulder of her gown, where they nestled in the fall of creamy lace spilling from a wide bertha collar. Curiosity, loneliness—she did not know what actually made her decision for her.

"Yes, please, Josette, see if he's waiting. Tell him I'll see him."

The maid left and Mair sat before her lighted mirror to remove the last stubborn vestige of heavy stage makeup that clung around her eyes. The whipped white cream in its gray china pot was made especially for her by Josette according to an old family recipe.

Josette had proved to be a helpful, obedient companion, very much the maid and rarely the friend. It was rather a relief. Mair no longer felt guilty when she had no time to say more than a brief hello to this dark-haired French girl. There was none of the old reproach she had felt with Rose. Yet she must admit she missed Rose's cheerful cockney speech and breezy attitude.

"Madame." Josette held open the door and a man's shadow blocked the light shining from the outside. "Mr. Castle was still waiting."

Mair half-turned on her padded stool, her fingers clasping the gray china pot of cold cream. "Mr. Castle," she began lightheartedly, quickly adopting that practised tone she used with her admirers, "your strange note intrigued me. I sense a mystery here. What is it you wish me to celebrate?"

"The end to four months of hell."

She gasped as she heard that husky, intense voice. When he stepped inside the room, so startled was she that the china cream jar fell from her grasp and crashed to the floor. Nicholas Castle! Of course, he had anglicised his name!

"Nico. You!"

"You sound surprised."

"You weren't Nicholas Castle last time I saw you," she explained weakly, apologizing to Josette who was on the floor cleaning up the shattered cream jar. When Mair tried to help her, she could not stop her hands trembling.

"A political expedient. Not too different from the original, when you consider it."

Very carefully Mair stood on weak legs. Tonight's performance had taken more out of her than she thought, or was it his arrival that caused this unaccustomed weakness? Raising her head, Mair forced herself to look him full in the face and her heart lurched. Dear God, he was even more handsome than she remembered, or had time and distance created the illusion?

"You were magnificent. I've never heard you sing better," he said, his dark eyes intense as he searched her face, trying to gauge her degree of pleasure in seeing him again.

"You certainly surprised me. I'd no idea you were in Italy."

"For just a couple of weeks. I'm here to repurchase some family land for my uncle—a villa on the shore of Lake Como. Hence the reference to my being home at last."

"Oh, yes, of course—Italy is your ancestral home."

With fumbling hands, Mair tried to pick up her wrap. Her feet would not fit inside her pink satin shoes as she clumsily struggled to put them on, but swiftly Nico came to her aid. He knelt and took her foot in his hand. Lovingly he eased her slender foot inside the embroidered satin shoe, carefully smoothing her silk stockings back in place, his fingers lingering on her slender ankles. Mair thought she would faint at the tremendous rush of excitement produced by the warm touch of his hands.

"There, Cinderella, now you're ready for the ball. I see you already have plans for this evening," Nico said, indicating her flounced silk evening gown.

He sounded so disappointed, Mair hastened to dismiss his misconception. "Oh, no, no plans. Nothing special," she mumbled uneasily. Was he going to leave her without further ado? He could not. Had she the grandest invitation in Milan, she would cancel it for him—if only he would ask.

They were both so aware of Josette's presence, their conversation had been stilted. As it was, the French girl's brows raised when Nico knelt to put on Mair's shoes, and her mouth had turned down in disapproval.

Making matters worse, Mair hastily explained. "Mr. Castle and I are old friends."

"Of course, Madame," Josette repeated woodenly. Old friends indeed! She had not even known his name a few minutes ago. And she had always thought her Madame was different from these other stage people. The difference had merely been that the right man had not yet appeared. "Will you be needing me further—or are you to leave with your *friend*?"

Mair flushed as Josette meaningly emphasized that word. Not allowing her time to answer, Nico said:

"You aren't needed. Madame Parigi and I are going to supper. We will let you know any further plans when we see fit."

Josette blinked in shock, surprised that he had dared to command her. She turned back to her mistress, expecting her to correct him and was shocked when she said nothing.

"Very well, *monsieur*, I will return to the hotel," she announced stiffly.

"Yes, Josette, that will be all," Mair added, coming to her senses. Her face flamed, for she knew exactly what Josette was thinking.

The maid put away a few final items before drawing her dark cloak about her shoulders. She went to the door, begrudgingly bidding them both goodnight.

Mair felt vastly uncomfortable, aware of Josette's disapproval like a tangible presence in the room.

"Josette disapproves of you. And as for me, I think she'd thought I was different from the others."

"And so you are. To hell with Josette and what she thinks. I don't give a damn whether she

315

approves of me or not. I just wanted her to go away and leave us in peace."

Before she left the dressing room, Mair took the huge bouquet of lilac and carnations. Shaking water from the stems, she retrieved the tissue and wrapped the flowers for carrying.

When they emerged in the passageway outside the dressing room, a crowd of well-wishers awaited. Mair smiled and accepted their praise, working her way toward the exit. After a performance, friends and adoring opera patrons generally crowded the theater, their chatter and laughter ringing through the corridors. Usually the cast, with their selected escorts and parties of friends, went down the street to their favorite restaurant to enjoy a meal and disect the performance. It was hopeless to think she could slip away unnoticed. Then, to her relief, Nico spoke to a couple of theater workers and they obligingly showed the way to a service door through which they made their escape.

Nico quickly handed Mair inside a cab which stood in rank at the curb outside the theater. A light rain was falling and the gaslights were haloed in mist. Mair felt a swift stab of nostalgia for those London nights she had spent with him. Though the Italian spring rain was warmer and the buildings different, she had only to close her eyes to recreate a sense of the past.

The cab ride was over almost as soon as it began. They pulled up outside the Grand Hotel and Nico ushered Mair up the steps and into the brightly lit lobby.

Mair barely noticed the bays of potted palms, the opulent gilded plasterwork and the glittering crystal chandeliers. Nico, speaking rapidly in fluent Italian, was arranging a dinner table for them. A maid took her bouquet of flowers to be put in water.

The maitre'd bowed and scraped before them. The Grand Hotel manager himself ushered Madame Parigi inside the lavish, blue ceilinged dining room. Nico told him Madame Parigi did not wish to be disturbed, and he nodded, assuring him he would guard the prima donna's privacy.

Mair could hardly believe she was actually sitting there with Nico. If the events earlier that evening had seemed like a dream, his unexpected appearance merely heightened the illusion. When she shook her head in bewilderment over the elaborate menu, he ordered for her. Mair's Italian was very sketchy; Josette usually handled the hotel staff and ordered their meals. She had forgotten that Nico also spoke fluent Italian.

The delicious meal appeared quickly. Mair ate breaded veal, cooked in butter and dressed with savory chopped mushrooms. She knew it was veal because Nico told her it was, for she ate without really tasting. Polenta sprinkled with cheese, creamy risotto dotted with green peas and red pepper, marscapone and melon, a three-colored frozen *bombe* full of candied fruits and topped with swirls of whipped cream, all followed. These artfully arranged dishes kept arriving and Mair dutifully sampled each new offering. The food was good, but her appetite could not do it justice. Why did Nico sit there so silently watching her eat, his dark eyes almost black in the candlelight? "You are so lovely," was all he said when she questioned his silence.

At last, when the final dish was cleared away and they were sipping dark, sweet espresso from green-flowered demitasse cups, Nico finally spoke:

"Are you ready to return to your suite, Madame?"

Mair gulped, made increasingly uneasy by his unusual formality. "How did you know I was staying here?"

"Because it's close to La Scala, the staff know you, and I have my methods. You didn't answer my question."

She swallowed the last of her espresso, trying to stifle her pounding heart. "Why do I think you have a better suggestion?"

Nico laughed. "Probably because you know me too well. Would you rather come to Lake Como for a few days? I'll show you the family land and the villa. It's very beautiful there. Please come."

"Am I to stay with you?"

"That's your choice. We can either go by train tomorrow or . . ."

"Or?" she prompted, nervously clasping her hands in her lap.

"We can go by road tonight, take the steamer first thing in the morning, and eat lunch in the grand salon of Villa Castelli."

Mair gasped in pleasure. The latter was much more to her liking. "Tonight," she gasped, her eyes shining with excitement. "Oh, yes, let's not waste another minute."

"As I expected you to choose that option, I've taken the liberty of having the staff pack your bags and alert Josette. Come, Madame, things should be ready by now."

When he stood, Mair stood. The waiter bustled

over, bringing her pink velvet wrap lined with silver. She was surprised because she had brought no wrap with her to the dining room. Mair turned toward the doorway to see Josette waiting, already dressed for travel.

"Why is Josette coming with us?" she asked, her voice faltering.

"We must maintain respectability. After all, we're not married," he replied, turning away before she could see if he smiled.

This was becoming more like a nightmare. What was Nico doing? This attitude was so unlike him. Mair had an unwelcome feeling growing within her that he played some cruel game. Was he making her suffer for her insistance on respectability? No, *he* had wanted respectability . . . she had wanted marriage.

They walked through the silent hotel lobby, a string of porters carrying her trunks and valises out to a waiting carriage.

"Won't they wonder what's happened to me at the theater? I should let them know I'm leaving Milan," she began, grasping Nico's arm to make him stop.

"Why? You sang your last performance—they understand you're tired and need a short rest. What more perfect place than a villa on the lake? Everything's been taken care of, Madame."

Josette listened and watched, still not sure of the propriety of these arrangements. She helped her mistress into the carriage, where they sat opposite each other in the misty darkness.

"I hope you weren't already asleep, Josette. I didn't mean to disturb you."

"Oh, no, Madame, I wasn't asleep. I was pressing

your gowns," Josette replied primly, crossing her hands in her lap.

Mair fell silent. To her dismay, when Nico came, he shut the carriage door without getting inside.

"The driver knows the way. Sleep if you can. The morning will seem all the brighter for it."

Mair's mouth dropped open in shock. Was he not coming with them? "And you?" she questioned, her voice tight.

"I'm traveling with a family friend," he explained, hiding a smile. "We'll meet in the morning at the steamer stage. Goodnight, Madame Parigi. Have a pleasant journey."

Mair was speechless as Nico backed from the carriage and the vehicle lurched into motion.

Within minutes Josette's head lolled and she began to snore gently.

Mair sat in the darkness with only her thoughts for company, her head aching and heart pounding in unison. The more she thought about Nico's absurd behavior, the more she was tempted to have the driver turn around and go back to the hotel. Was Nico deliberately trying to anger her, she wondered? If so, he was succeeding.

Tears trickled down her cold cheeks. Her velvet wrap was not warm enough. After huddling and shivering for some time, Mair noticed several folded traveling rugs on a mesh shelf above Josette's head. Steadying herself as the swaying conveyance rolled at breakneck speed along a twisting road, Mair pulled down the blankets and wrapped herself in their warmth.

As she grew drowsy, all manner of plans swirled through her head. She wanted answers for Nico's odd behavior. She would have her revenge for what he was doing. She even contemplated what manner that revenge should take before she finally fell asleep, her head resting against the velvet upholstery.

When Mair opened her eyes the sky through the carriage windows was pink. She blinked and sat up, then peered out at her surroundings. The road followed the curve of a lake. Dark clouds were visible through the mist hovering over the water. When she looked again, she realized they were not clouds but mountains towering as high as she could see, far higher than any she had seen in Wales. The unbidden reminder of Wales stabbed at her heart. Last night Nico had been so strangely different. She sometimes wished they were back in Wales where they could start again, for surely that time at the dawning of their love had been the happiest.

Leaning back against the seat, Mair shed a few self-pitying tears. Then angrily she wiped them away, determined not to keep bemoaning the past. The future lay ahead. What she made of it was up to her.

The carriage stopped and the driver came down from the box and tapped on the door. Mair undid the inside latch. Unable to speak English, the Italian driver merely gestured toward the lakeside landing stage.

That must be where they were to catch the steamer to take them across the lake. Already a small knot of people had gathered to await the steamer. Most of the women had warm wraps over their dresses, and the men were dressed in top hats and morning coats. Mair felt most conspicuous in her unmistakable evening clothes.

Wrapping her cloak tight about her thin gown, she stepped down from the carriage.

"Madame, your hat," Josette called a few moments later. Magically, Josette had produced a green velvet hat, its sideswept brim trimmed with masses of Palma violets. She had clung to the side of the carriage, straining to reach the luggage and pull down a hatbox. Were her mistress to appear in public without her hat, Josette would never have lived down the shame.

Mair accepted the hat and, looking in the mirrored lid of the hatbox that Josette obligingly held open for her, she set the hat square on her head. After pushing strands of hair back in place beneath the hatbrim and dabbing her eyes and cheeks with a handkerchief, Mair felt more able to face the world.

As she walked over the grass to the landing stage a second carriage pulled up. Nico jumped out.

"*Buon giorno*, Madame," he called as he hurried toward her.

"*Buon giorno*," Mair replied stiffly, freshly annoyed with him for his aggravating behavior. Did he intend to treat her formally for the entire time they spent together? Well, two could play at that game. "Do you know if the steamer will be leaving soon, *Signore*?"

Nico smiled and waved toward a vessel moored alongside the stage. "Within minutes, I expect, my dear lady. Shall we go aboard?"

Very formally she rested her hand on his arm and together they marched stiffly toward the wooden gangplank, following the rest of the passengers who were boarding the *Isola Bella*.

On the deck a small orchestra was preparing to play for the passengers' enjoyment. Many of those boarding immediately went below in search of refreshments. Stubbornly Mair walked to the rail, holding on to her hat with one hand and grasping her velvet cape with the other. The fresh breeze tugged at her garments and she clutched them grimly, determined to stay where she was.

"Those are the Alps behind us," Nico said, coming to stand beside her at the rail.

Simmering anger and disappointment had thus far spoiled the magnificent view for her. Mair turned to look at the mountains towering far into the clouds, lost from sight in heavy blue mist. Surely they must be the tallest mountains in the world. Against the Alps, Pentre Fawr would look like a molehill. The sun slowly rose in the pale sky, making the mountains clearer. The setting was gorgeous. As the sun shone across the lake water it lightened from black to blue.

By now the steamer had pulled far out into the lake and Mair had a panoramic view of the spectacular surroundings. White painted villages nestled at the foot of the mountains, their buildings toylike against the majestic Alps. Lush greenery fringed both banks where villas could be glimpsed amidst thickets of palms, banks of myrtle and round-topped mulberries. Dark groves of cedar on the southern bank of the lake blended with lines of tall poplars, marking the boundaries between pastureland and terraced vinyards.

"Don't you find it beautiful, Mair?"

"Yes. It's very beautiful."

"Not nearly as beautiful as you."

At first she was not sure she had heard his whispered compliment, attuned as she was to expect merely polite formality from him. She turned, her face creased in a puzzled frown.

"What did you say?"

"Exactly what you thought I said. You needn't sound so surprised. God knows, I've said it often enough."

"Not lately."

"What's lately? I haven't seen you for months."

"Lately means these past ten hours to be exact," she hissed, her temper rising. "What game are you playing?"

He grinned. "No game, Mair love, I'm merely treating you as I thought you wanted to be treated. Not pawing you, nor dragging you to bed against your will. In fact, I've been most circumspect. And that's the way I intend to be from now on," he said softly.

Mair glanced about quickly, hoping no one had heard his explanation. Even delivered in an undertone, Nico's voice had a very resonant quality. His words merely irritated her further.

"Circumspect, is that what you call it?" she snapped, moving away from him when he stepped closer. "That's a fancy name all right for playing the fool."

Though she tried to sidestep him, he planted his foot against hers, trapping her beside the rail. When he reached beneath her cape to grasp her arm, she was powerless to stop him, for she still held on to her hat, guarding it from the lake breeze.

"If that's not it, then what do you want, you aggravating woman?" he demanded, a crack appearing in his otherwise formal demeanor.

"To go through all that again would be a pointless discussion," she snapped icily, leaning away from him. Inwardly she reeled, uncomfortably aware of his closeness. Her aching heart cried out silently. *I want you to love me. To tell me how much you've missed me. I want to be kissed, cherished.* The emotional words whirled through her head, but she was determined not to speak them. If he had to be told, then she had no use for him. Resolutely, she set her mouth and stared ahead at the rippling blue water.

"Do you even know what you want?" Nico's fingers bit into her arm as he spoke, gripping tight to emphasize his words. "Now you have your career just the way you always wanted. You're the toast of Paris and Milan, aren't you? Isn't that what you said you wanted? Answer me!"

She bit her lip as his fingers dug into her arm, but stubbornly refused to answer. Then, unexpectedly, he yanked her off balance and she fell heavily against him. Her hands flew to his chest to cushion herself, and instantly the velvet hat was blown off her head and over the rail into the lake. With a cry of distress, Mair tried to grab the hat but she was too late.

Nico pulled her against him, imprisoning her arms.

"I'm going to have an answer from you, woman," he hissed, his voice thick with Welsh accent.

She began to protest, stopped, then looked into his dark eyes and saw again the old Nico she had first grown to love. All the burning emotion was there, the grimly set face, the tension in his jaw where the pulse began to jump in agitation. Her heart pounded as she grew highly aware of the hot strength of his body. Then she tasted the fresh tang of lake air on his hot mouth as he crushed his lips against hers.

The demanding kiss was not tender, but in her current mood of suppressed rage, tenderness would have been lost. This was a battle between them, and as his kiss deepened and his embrace tightened, Mair slowly captitulated. Anger ebbed from her body, to be replaced by awakening passion. The throb of her blood no longer beat in rage, gradually changing to the ache of longing. All these weeks apart, when she had dreamed of Nico, she would have given anything for this moment. To be in his arms, to know he still loved her, was really what she wanted. Those noble high-flung sentiments about marriage and respectability no longer made sense. Two bodies beating as one, two hearts, two souls, were what she craved the most. Too late she had discovered that being the toast of Paris and Milan was not reward enough for losing his love.

"I want us to be together again like we used to be," she whispered against his ear, her face buried in the protective warmth of his neck. At her words she felt his arms tighten around her. "None of the other things we argued about matter anymore. Then I didn't know. It took time and loneliness to find out." Tears choked her voice and she battled not to cry. Lately she seemed incapable of deep emotion without tears.

"Thank God! That's what I've lived to hear,"

Nico whispered, his breath hot against her face. Softly his lips brushed her cheek and he relaxed his grip about her body, making it easier for her to breathe. "But you said . . ."

"I've changed my mind."

"A woman's prerogative," he whispered, moving her into a more comfortable position against his body.

"Loneliness is a very persuasive teacher."

"You've been lonely? With all the adoring press, the audiences—oh, Mair, I didn't dare hope you'd missed me that much. Oh, my sweetheart."

There was a catch of emotion in his voice, which to Mair was more touching than reams of poetic words.

"I thought singing and having money would make up for losing you. I was wrong. We'll take what we can, for as little or as long as we have," she promised softly, feeling her spirit soar at the knowledge he was still hers, just as if nothing had gone between them.

"Just tell me you love me."

"I love you, Nico Castelli—or Nicholas Castle— whoever you are, like no other man ever created."

"More than all those counts and princes I've been reading about who've been falling in love with you?" he asked, an edge to his voice.

He was jealous! Mair marveled at the unexpected discovery. She had thought only she was jealous of other loves. Her heart took a great leap of exultation.

"Definitely more than them," she assured him, her confidence mounting.

Reluctantly they moved further apart, for steps

behind them on the deck announced the arrival of other passengers coming on deck for a view of the approaching land.

How beautiful the shoreline was. Green groves of chestnut and walnut contrasted with gray olive groves surrounding the fairytale villages. The gardens of houses and villas overflowed with brilliant plants and flowers. Most of the steamer's passengers would stay on board to enjoy a leisurely cruise around the lake, admiring more and more spectacular views, their outing punctuated by lunch in the dining room.

Nico told Mair they were to disembark at the small jetty ahead. Several horse-drawn conveyances waited to take passengers to the villages clustering around this slender finger of the lake.

Motioning to Josette, who sat bundled in a blanket in a sheltered corner of the deck, Nico led Mair toward their disembarkation point. "Come on, love, we're to be met, then driven up to the villa."

When they stepped ashore, Mair was glad to have solid ground underfoot. A horse-drawn trap waited to take them along the road winding toward the foothills of the mountains overshadowing Lake Como.

Josette sat up front with the driver while Mair and Nico sat side by side in the passenger seat. Nico clasped Mair's hand in his, conscious of Josette who, though her back was toward them, seemed to impart a certain air of propriety. In a way, he was sorry he had insisted the maid come with them. He would have to set down some rules once they reached their destination. Josette the

Holy certainly put a damper on romantic spontaneity.

"Today we're going to begin a new life," he whispered, his eyes soft as he gazed at Mair. "I can feel it in my bones."

She nodded and smiled. "As none of this can be real, it's got to be one of my better dreams. I'm just going to wait and let it unfold."

Happier than he had been in months, Nico hugged her to his side. As the trap pulled higher and their view of the countryside expanded, Nico marveled at the beauty of his ancestral homeland, though even that paled before the beauty of the woman at his side.

Chapter Nineteen

The old villa stood in secluded gardens that sloped down to the water's edge. On either side along the twisting road were similar villas, each surrounded by its own lushly landscaped garden.

Villa Castelli was a three-storied villa of gray stone with a terracotta tile roof. The narrow windows on the two upper floors opened onto handkerchief-sized balconies edged with wrought iron railings. Off the dining room a broad tiled loggia led into the sloping gardens, affording splendid views of the lake. Beds of fragrant white lilies and climbing pink bougainvillea softened the old villa's austere stonework.

The large tall-ceilinged rooms were sparsely furnished with cupboards and chests of old gilded wood, their painted pictures badly faded with time. The few upholstered pieces covered in tapestry and rose velvet were worn threadbare.

Mair was disappointed to find these rooms so institutionally plain with their buff-painted stucco walls. The only decoration was a large tapestry depicting a biblical scene, which hung on the wall in the main salon; in this room also were the only rugs she saw. For the most part the villa's tiled floors of mosaic marble were bare, as were the tall windows, having nary a curtain among them, even in the bedrooms. She had been expecting an opulence similar to that of the luxury hotels where she had recently stayed.

Very little about this old house was to her taste, yet because Nico was with her and because she likened this unexpected holiday to a brief honeymoon, Mair found the lakeside villa appealing despite its shortcomings.

To Mair's relief, Josette was soon settled in a small room at the far end of the corridor, some way from the main bedchamber, yet connected by a system of bells. It would be easy to summon her when needed.

The villa had a sparse resident staff of cook, maid and gardener, barely sufficient to keep the house and grounds from falling into total disrepair.

When Nico's Uncle Salvatore had learned the property was for sale, he sent Nico to Italy to purchase the house and land, thereby bringing it back into the Castelli family. For years his uncle's goal had been to reclaim the family's ancestral land along the shore of Lake Como. His dream had finally come true.

Mair stood at a window looking out at the very un-English garden. A lot of dreams seemed to be coming true lately. She hoped the trend never stopped.

For their mid-day meal the cook prepared a simple table of crusty fresh-baked bread, local cheeses, fruit and tomatoes, accompanied by a frosty jug of red wine from the nearby vineyard. The meal was eaten off heavy earthenware decorated with rings of jade green and cobalt blue; in contrast to this serviceable peasant ware, the wine-glasses were of delicate blue Venetian glass.

Mair and Nico sat side by side at one corner of the huge walnut dining table, which was long enough to accommodate a banquet. Though the fare was simple, Mair found it very satisfying. Nico laughingly dipped bread into his wine and fed her like a child, his fingers lingering on her lips. Mair bestowed light kisses on his hand in thanks for the offering. She leaned against his shoulder, sighing with happiness. Today they both felt young and lighthearted, a mood neither of them had experienced for some time. Here, beside the sunlit lake, the worries of Paris and London no longer seemed to exist.

After they had finished their meal, they strolled through the open French windows onto the loggia and down the terrace steps.

The sun was hot for spring; in the sheltered garden, the air felt warm as summer. Big beds of scarlet cannas made bright splashes of color against the thickets of shrubbery edging the lawn. Marble statues of gods and goddesses nestled unexpectedly in hedged bowers in what had once been a formal garden but was now sadly neglected. Similar statues stood guard at points on the low stone wall edging the gardens.

A second flight of steep steps led down to the water's edge. The lake virtually lapped against the villa's garden walls. A boathouse stood beside a small jetty jutting out into the lake. Several old boats were stored inside its dusty interior.

Keenly aware of prying eyes, for the villa's three servants and Josette stood watching from the window, Mair and Nico did not embrace as they walked across the garden. Instead, they sauntered hand in hand along the walled walkway. Small boats and steamers plied their way across the blue lake, leaving behind the narrow finger of water as they headed for the open expanse of the lake proper. Though the air was warm and palms and other tropical plants flourished, one had only to look to the north to be reminded of how close to Switzerland they were. The snow-capped Alps stood sentinel on the border.

When Nico was finally satisfied that they were out of sight of the curious servants, he pulled Mair into his arms. They clung together trembling, drawing intense pleasure from each other's bodies. Mair rejoiced in the cutting pressure of Nico's hard muscles against her limbs, almost painful in their insistence. She knew he was aroused, for she could feel that other pressure burning through her clothing. His arms trembled as he held her away from him.

"No, we mustn't—there's not time," he gasped, swallowing as he tried to regain his composure. "Within the hour I'm supposed to be in the village to complete this transaction. Oh, Mair, I've never wanted to love you so much and yet have to turn you away."

She kissed his hot face. "Hush, it's all right. We

have the rest of the day," she soothed, smiling, her breathing ragged. "I'll wait impatiently for you, counting the minutes till you come back."

He pulled her against him. They stood locked in each other's arms, the minutes fleeting. A sudden blast from one of the passing boats shattered their peace and Nico reluctantly put her from him.

"Let's go back. You know the watch committee have already condemned us for what they suppose is taking place."

Mair laughed. "A bit like chapel, isn't it, all the spying and the stories spread by old gossips with nothing better to do? At least they aren't going to drag us before the elders and make us confess our sins."

"Good old Llandare. I'm glad you're here to remind me of where we come from. You know, when you're hobnobbing with the likes of Gladstone and Parnell and rubbing shoulders with the Sir Alfred Crawfords of this world, and they keep telling you what promise you've got, what a leader you could be, you get an elevated opinion of your own worth."

"Aye, and when you become the toast of Paris and Milan, it works the same way. Sometimes I forget just who I am—plain old Mair Parry from Llandare."

"You've got the beginnings of a tongue twister there, girl," he laughed, hugging her to him. "And you've never been plain a day in your life."

A warm sense of camaraderie was growing between them, rekindling something that had been lost along the way. Mair smiled at him in genuine friendship, liking him not just as her lover, but as a friend as well. Yet she felt it wise not to reveal this particular observation just yet, for Nico could still be a bit prickly and she didn't want to spoil their happiness with even the slightest disagreement.

"Will you go home to Wales someday?"

"I might. Might even try to get into local politics. Who knows? Speaking of politics—did you know old spotty-faced Heath Owen is an M.P. nowadays?"

"No—I never! Whoever elected him?" she cried indignantly, picturing the last time she had seen Jasper Owen's unpleasant son and heir.

"Who'd dare not to? You know, if I wasn't so committed to the working men in my district, I'd challenge the bastard's seat. I will someday, when I've enough clout to take it from him. Can you imagine how much more he'll hate me then?"

"Hate you? I'd've thought he'd forgotten all about you by now. No offense, but he does have more important things to do than remember old quarrels."

"That shows you don't know him very well. He never forgets old quarrels. I'm high on his list of grievances to settle because I'm a constant thorn in his side. He'd like to rule the district absolutely, the way his father did in the old days. But having men like me around makes the task difficult. Besides, I jab the knife in him whenever I get the chance. He's shown his nose at a few labor rallies and I've given him hell—to the great amusement of the crowd."

Though Nico laughed about it, this latest revelation made Mair uneasy. Her heart skipped, then thudded in sudden fear. "You'd best be careful of old Spotty Face. There's something about him I don't trust."

"Aye—all five foot nine of him," Nico added with a laugh as they approached the terrace steps. "Ah, there they are, dodging behind the furniture."

Josette's dark gown could be seen fleeting past the window and the cook's and maid's aprons made pale blurrs against the walls. As Mair and Nico stepped inside the room, a flash of disapproval crossed Josette's face before she came to them, a fixed smile on her mouth.

"Will you change now, Madame?"

"Yes, Josette, and you can run a bath for me, if you will," Mair added wickedly, aware of the conclusion Josette would draw from that.

Nico winked at her, knowing she had deliberately led Josette on. He told the gardener, who also drove the trap, to make ready to take him into the village.

With a swift parting kiss and the whispered promise to wait eagerly for him, Mair followed Josette up the broad marble stair. Leaning out over the marble ballusters, she waved goodbye to Nico. As he paused in the doorway to answer her wave, his back to the bright sunlight, she was reminded again of his Italian ancestry. The shadow darkened his skin, and his finely chiseled profile was strong and angular. How misplaced he seemed in modern dress. It was so easy to imagine him stepping from that huge painting of the Adoration hanging in the parlor at Tal-y-Bont. His handsome face was darkly mysterious. And most important of all—he was hers!

Nico strode down the steps and out of sight, and Mair quivered with anticipation as she pictured the square sweep of his shoulders tapering to a slim waist and compact hips. The fitted bottle green coat he wore was well-tailored, hugging his lithe frame without a wrinkle. When she thought about his body, her own responded as she conjured up images of him making love to her. Mair shuddered with pleasure at the reminder, hugging the cherished memories to herself as she turned and went in search of Josette.

An hour later, Mair sat before the bedroom's open French windows, enjoying the cool breeze off the lake. She waited impatiently for Nico's return; she had not expected him to be away this long. Growing drowsy in the warm sunshine, she began to doze.

A woman's laughter from the adjoining villa's garden jerked her awake. When she strained to look over the shrubbery, Mair saw a young black-haired woman rolling a ball for a puppy. The white dog yapped excitedly as the red ball sailed across the sloping lawn, heading ever faster toward the lake. The woman shrieked in dismay and ran after the puppy. As she ran she shouted to someone to come to her aid. Her black hair came loose and tumbled down her back, streaming in the wind as she ran to save the puppy. In the nick of time the ball and the puppy were both scooped safely into her arms.

Mair smiled at the idea of having a puppy. She lay back against the padded cushion of the chaise. She'd have a puppy for her children—her children. The vision of bearing and raising Nico's children was a most satisfying daydream. She had begun to doze again when a strident voice shouting, 'Teresa,' disturbed her.

Sitting up, Mair looked down into the neighboring garden where the black-haired woman was running back to the villa. Teresa? The very name made her heart lurch. Many Italian girls were probably called Teresa. She had better stop reacting like a fool whenever she heard the name.

Though she fought against it, the incident had shattered her peace of mind, revealing how insecure she still was about her relationship with Nico. She could not help wondering if any part of his plans for the future had changed—specifically whether Teresa Gambino was still in the picture. Mair could have asked him—she should ask him— but she would not. Pride stood in her way. She was begging no man to marry her, not even him. Her eyes moistened as she became devastatingly honest. Was her reluctance to broach the subject more because she couldn't face the probable truth? Mair couldn't bear to spoil this idyllic time together. When she'd vowed they would spend however long or short a time this might be, she knew she'd also implied there would be no questions asked. It had been a foolish compromise. Yet so lonely had she been of late that she wanted Nico more than she could face the unpleasant truth. Saddened by these thoughts, she drifted back to sleep.

"Here you are, sleeping beauty? What about this eager anticipation of my return?" Nico whispered in her ear. He slipped his arms around her chest where she lay on the chaise.

Startled, Mair tried to sit up, discovering she was imprisoned by his arms. It was a relief to be wakened from sleep, for she had had a disturbing dream. She had been singing in an opera and her voice had cracked on the high notes. To her great humiliation she had been booed off stage. Worse still, when she had fled to Nico for comfort, she found him lying in Teresa Gambino's arms . . .

"I did wait eagerly. You were gone too long," she defended, her voice quavering with emotion. Oh, how wonderful it was to have him beside her, warmly comforting.

"Tears?" he asked in surprise as he crouched beside the chaise. With his forefinger, Nico caught trickling tears from the outer corner of her eye.

"Just a bad dream," Mair dismissed quickly. "Thank goodness you arrived and woke me up. Did you finish your business?"

He shook his head. "Almost. We'll have to meet again tomorrow. There's some dispute over the wording of the deed."

"Well, now you are here, do you want to eat, or—can that wait?"

They exchanged softly intimate smiles. "It can most definitely wait."

Nico swept Mair from the lounge, shuddering as he felt the vibrant warmth of her flesh through the thin cotton of her white bodice.

They went into the bedroom, shutting the French window and pulling down the blinds to darken the room. Chinks of light crept through the sides of the blind and splashed the walls with gold bars. Mair hugged Nico to her, hardly able to believe he was really here in her arms.

Nico gently laid her across the bed covers and knelt beside her. Mair reached up, pulling his face down to hers. His skin smelled of fresh air mingled with the sharp tang of lemon trees and rosemary. Nuzzling his face, Mair allowed herself to be lulled into a trancelike state of happiness, fighting to hold her passion in check so that this wonderful pleasure would never end.

The tight-fitting bodice of Mair's gown was fastened from waist to neck with small satin-covered buttons. Slowly Nico began to unbutton the fastenings, his hands unsteady with passion as he fumbled with the tiny button loops. "Damn Josette," he muttered under his breath, "I swear she brought this dress just to thwart me."

So fierce did he look that Mair could not help giggling.

"Perhaps she did. She was most insistant that I wear something demurely buttoned to the neck. She must have been afraid that the sight of my voluptuous flesh would drive you mad and you'd be forced to make love to me on the dining room table."

"An excellent idea. I might do that before we leave. Wouldn't want to disappoint your maid, love, now would I?"

The growing heat and pressure of his hands against her breasts was maddening. Touch me now, she wanted to urge, eager for the caresses she had grown to love. Instead she held her tongue, still somewhat inhibited by the mores of her age. Nice girls would never dream of asking a man to do something like that. More fool they, she added mentally, almost sorry she was a nice girl. Bad girls seemed to have much more fun.

"Would you rather I was a bad girl?" she asked him suddenly.

Surprised, he glanced up from his task. "What makes you ask that? I love you just the way you are, saint and sinner rolled into one."

His description made Mair laugh, and when he reached the final button she grasped him, dragging him down on top of her. The glorious heat and pressure of his legs on hers made her strain involuntarily against him, and she was immediately rewarded by the answering surge of his body.

"Oh, Nico, I love you so much," Mair whispered, before his mouth covered hers. Hotly demanding, his hands searched amidst the flimsy dotted fabric, pushing aside bows and frills, until at last he found what he sought. With a groan of pleasure he slid his hands about those pulsing orbs of pink-tipped creamy flesh, cupping and fondling her breasts, sending the blood coursing wildly through her veins. Eagerly Mair pulled aside her bodice, baring herself to him, eager for his arousing touch. Nico bent his head, kissing her breasts, his tongue lapping gently about each nipple as it grew hard and inviting. The heat from his mouth shot like fire through her body until she burned and ached with desire. Pressing harder against him, Mair rubbed that ironhard ridge, molding her body to his, thigh to thigh, feeling the divine pressure of his manhood, longing to have him take her.

"You are a saint, Mair Parry. Nothing you've ever done can be called sin. You're my angel, and I'll always cherish you," he vowed softly, his lips soft against her cheek. Nico traced a passage down her neck and across her chest before ringing her full breasts with kisses until she was beside herself with desire.

"You make a sinner out of me because you make love to me so well," she confided huskily, her hands going up into his crisp black hair. She stroked his neck, still warm from the sun. "You know, there's no virtue in being a saint if I can't have you."

"Oh, Mair, darling, how could I have thought I could manage without you," Nico breathed, his voice shaking with emotion. "Every hour of every day, I thought about you. I wondered if you missed me, or even gave a thought to me."

Mair smiled at his whispered revelation. She stroked his strong back, slipping her hands inside his coat, unfastening the buttons of his shirt. Nico had already removed his cravat. Slowly she peeled aside the thin lawn shirt to expose his heavily furred chest. Eagerly Mair pressed their flesh together, thrilling at the tickling, arousing irritation of his crisp hair against her breasts. Then her hand slid lower until she reached that wonderful leaping furnace of his passion.

"How could I forget you when you always make me feel like this," she answered huskily, tracing the hardness beneath his gabardine trousers, each new discovery heightening her desire.

"There's other men could make you feel like this, girl, I've no monopoly on lovemaking," Nico admitted honestly, though he hated to say it.

"No, no one else could ever make me feel this wonderful. Besides, I don't love any other man but you. That makes all the difference in the world."

"Oh, Mair." He kissed her, his ardor increasing. "You always make me feel so good."

Impatiently she fought the fastening of his

clothes and he chuckled as she grunted in irritation at the barrier.

"And I haven't got twenty-four buttons to unfasten."

"You might as well have. Your tailor ought to be shot," she retorted when at last she had negotiated the final restriction and her hand slipped inside to touch the smooth, silky fullness she had longed to feel.

A few minutes later he moved away from her to strip off his coat, shirt and trousers, pitching them over a chair.

Mair lay watching him undress, her unbuttoned bodice open, her skirts pushed into a mass above her knees. She opened the placket fastening of her skirt, then her petticoats, and pushed them down. Now she was undressed also.

Nico caught her wrists and pulled her up. Standing beside the bed, he put his arms round her smooth back, crushing her against him.

Mair felt the hot insistence of his arousal against her thighs. Then, impatient to feel him inside her, she pulled him down.

They fell together in a heap on the bedcover, laughing, mouths hungrily seeking each other. Impatient now, she caressed his burning, throbbing flesh, breathlessly admiring the treasure he offered. The murky sunlight in the room darkened his flesh, accentuating the illusion of heat until, in her deep arousal, she imagined him to be on fire. The knowledge of his great desire for her only aroused her further.

"Whenever we make love, wherever we are, I'll always remember that first time with the smell of the mountain wind in your hair and on your face," he whispered, lying against her, his mouth gentle against her cheek. "From that day on I've never imagined loving another woman. You're all I'll ever want, my Mair of the Golden Hair."

There it was again, that fanciful name in which he delighted. His extravagance made her smile with pleasure. Only Nico would have thought of something like that to call her.

"I need a special name for you, *Cariad*, but I can't think of one."

"Just call me love, that's more than enough."

"That's easy, because you are my love, my dearest, sweetest love," Mair vowed, her eyes moist with emotion.

The smile left his face, to be replaced by that familiar grimness which quickened her pulses. Eagerly Mair gave herself up to the hot smooth strength of his body, delighting in the pressure of his limbs against hers. She lay back against the pillows, her hair spread in a golden cloud around her, the dim light of the room making her skin appear milk white.

Nico gazed down at her, deeply moved by her beauty. With a groan of desire he moved over her, anxious to possess that joy which could be so fleeting—the perfect union of heart, soul and body.

"My sweetest girl," he whispered, his mouth hot against hers.

Mair clasped him to her, pulling him close, opening her thighs to receive him, helping him, urging him on, desperate to feel the hot throbbing invasion of her body.

They no longer spoke. Passion raged unchecked between them as they soared to new emotional heights. Mair felt as if she was freed from her body, so overwhelming was her inner tumult. Murmuring love words and covering her with heated kisses, Nico enveloped her with his marvelous lovemaking. Mair was swept along in the rhythmic enchantment of surrender. The pressure building inside her body threatened to explode as he moved ever swifter, sweeping her along at ever-increasing speed, until she finally cried out in ecstacy, her voice slowly dying down to a groan as the pinnacle was reached.

Mair sank slowly into the deep sweet aftermath of lovemaking. Feeling warm and cherished, she basked in sheerest pleasure, held safe against his body. Nico's arms kept at bay that sense of loss she sometimes felt as she slowly drifted back to earth.

When Mair finally opened her eyes, he was smiling at her, the grimness gone from his face to leave it softly vulnerable. The hardness she sometimes saw had been erased. His eyes were moist and soft. He looked so boyishly handsome, her heart lurched with love for him.

Softly Nico stroked Mair's arm, her back, his embrace still lightly protective. "Tell me, was that worth waiting for?" he asked with a grin.

"You have to answer first."

"Then I'll say, yes, worth waiting a lifetime for. Does that answer please you, Madame Parigi?"

"More than you know, Mr. Castle—more than you know."

Chapter Twenty

From a secluded arbor overlooking the shimmering blue lake, Mair watched as boats sliced through the placid water. It was so peaceful there in the sunshine, the warm air scented with almond blossoms.

Nico sat at the stone table working on some papers he was preparing to show to Prime Minister Gladstone on his return to London. It was an outline of the proposals agreed on by the dockers' union. He had discussed most of the points with Mair, and she was shocked to learn the terrible conditions under which many of the dockers worked and lived. Theirs was a day-to-day struggle for work with no certainty of being taken on, though they waited for hours in the rain. Poorly fed and clothed, the men were hardly capable of some of the backbreaking jobs they were hired to perform for a starvation wage.

The fervor with which Nico spoke about the exploitation of those men reminded Mair of the fire he had shown while trying to form Welsh miners into a trade union. As always, his fierce commitment to his cause made her uneasy. There were many influential people standing in the way of sweeping reforms, and she feared for his safety. He no longer butted heads with mine owners, but had entered the political arena from which the country was controlled. Nico had the support of Mr. Gladstone, the Prime Minister, who himself was something of a reformer. Parnell and other leading members of the liberal party also supported his ideas, yet those powerful allies would not be there to protect him if the meetings turned violent. Mair had not forgotten Bloody Sunday; she knew the potential for bloodshed still simmered beneath the surface. Mair also understood that a dangerous element in the crowd could easily turn against Nico if he failed to please them. Though he was an articulate, persuasive speaker, sometimes Nico was like a bull in a china shop when it came to getting his point across. She suspected he had already trampled on some very sensitive toes.

Earlier Mair had watched the lake steamer making its morning run back to the far shore, leaving her with a sense of isolation in their holiday villa. Yet she welcomed the idea of being cut off from the rest of the world. She was content to sit there companionably while Nico wrote. It was as if they were already married. That morning, with the sky still soft pink and gold, they had made love inside the trellised arbor. A torrential burst of passion carried them to new heights, and Mair enjoyed every minute of it. Then later, when Nico shared the contents of his papers with her and even allowed her to read private correspondence from the Prime Minister, she felt closer than ever to him.

Mair was awestruck to be reading a letter written by Mr. Gladstone himself. There was also a note of commendation for Nico's efforts on behalf of the workers from Francis, Cardinal Manning, a friend of Mr. Gladstone and an outspoken advocate of fair treatment for the dock workers. A Mr. Brownell from the Labor Electoral Committee, appointed by the Trade Unions to represent the working class in Parliament, had invited Nico to a series of talks, soliciting his cooperation in securing the attention of members of Parliament thought to be sympathetic to their cause.

As she read these letters, one thing became increasingly apparent: Nico was far more important in the labor movement than she had realized. The general congratulatory tone of the correspondence left little doubt he was the choice for liberal representative of the district he sought. Surely there was no further need for secrecy. Could they not now make their feelings public without jeopardizing his career? Unless of course he still had to keep Teresa's father on a string because he needed his financial help.

Mair continued to brood about the situation. They had been at Lake Como for almost a week. As the days passed she grew even more distressed at the thought of ending their bliss. Mair quickly grew accustomed to waking beside him, eating with him, having him there to talk to, and even sharing his ambitious manifestos for the downtrodden dockers.

"Nico?"

He glanced up, his expression serious. "Yes, what is it, love?"

"In his letter that Mr. Brownell mentioned your house—which house is that?"

"Oh, I suppose I might as well tell you, though it was to be a secret." He laid down his pen and reached for her hand across the table. "I'm buying a small house in Highbury. David Lloyd George told me about it—you know, that Welshman who's itching for a seat from Caernarvon. He's getting married and he fancied the house himself, but Margaret, his bride-to-be, didn't like it. He offered the house to me. Even if the worst happens and I don't get the seat, I think I can manage it on my salary from Uncle Sal."

"You're buying a house for yourself?"

"Well, I won't be by myself forever," he countered warily, his smile fading.

"And me? Am I going to be by myself forever?"

"Not if you come to live with me."

Mair said nothing. She was aware of her thundering heart. Here it was, the confrontation she had been dreading. All week she had tried to avoid this unpleasantness. Whenever Nico went into the village in the afternoons, she wrestled with her thoughts, rehearsing ways to broach this subject without entering into a quarrel. Whichever way she looked at it, it boiled down to one crucial question: Did he intend to marry her?

"Is that a proposal?"

"Oh, Mair," Nico groaned, pulling his hand from hers.

Abruptly he walked out of the arbor, stopping at the edge of the gravel walkway facing the lake.

Mair's stomach pitched as she tried to overcome the fear that gripped her. He obviously had no intention of marrying her. Carefully smoothing her blue frilled skirts, allowing herself time to gain composure, she finally trusted herself to follow him.

"Am I safe in assuming nothing's changed?"

"Look, any day now the parliamentary seat could become vacant. There's talk the old man will resign because of ill health. If he does, they'll have to call a by-election. Please, Mair, let's not quarrel now, not when it's so close. Be patient a little longer. This week together's been so wonderful, let's not spoil it. Trust me just a little longer. You know I love you. It's not for lack of love I can't make a commitment right now."

His words were meant to be calming, but on Mair they had the opposite effect. She badly wanted to accept at face value what he told her, yet her sense told her he merely sought to postpone matters. When Nico turned away, she caught his arm, drawing him back to face her.

"How much longer do you expect me to be patient? Teresa must also be getting tired of waiting for you to make up your mind. Do us both a favor and choose . . ."

"Don't start on about Teresa," he warned, his face tightening in anger.

"No, more convenient for you if I keep my mouth shut, isn't it? Don't make trouble, Mair. Let me enjoy the best of both worlds, Mair. Nothing like having your cake and eating it too, Mair, is there?"

"Somehow I knew it would come to this, that you couldn't let it rest even for a week."

"Oh, good, then it didn't come as a complete surprise. 'Spect you've already got answers for me, seeing as how you've had all this time to think them up. Come on, let's hear the latest."

"Stop it," he growled, his voice threatening. "I refuse to argue about it. As you've said before, there's really nothing further to discuss. All I have to say to you is be patient a little longer."

Mair drew in her breath, her chest rising in anger. She could feel her heart racing and her legs beginning to tremble. She wanted to shout at him in frustration, but she suppressed the angry words, biting her lip till it hurt.

"So I'm supposed to stew here all afternoon while you go out, twiddling my thumbs till you decide to come back," she shouted unreasonably, knowing she was being foolish but quite unable to stop.

"You never objected before."

"You never asked me."

"I have business this afternoon—there are some papers . . . Mair, let's not quarrel. Trust me. I promise everything's going to work out for us soon. I just need a little more time. Come on, love, be a good girl," he cajoled, trying to take her arm.

Mair glared at him. "Stop talking to me like I'm a naughty little girl," she cried, pulling away from him.

She marched back to the arbor to collect her hat and parasol, knocking his papers to the floor in the process. She scooped them up none too tidily and slammed them back onto the stone table. A light blue envelope addressed to Signor Joseph Gambino caught her eye. She stared at the name in shock, her eyes blurring. She blinked away hot tears, hoping she had misread the address here at Lake Como. Before she could reread the envelope, Nico stepped behind her and angrily gathered up his papers.

"Look, we've less than two days left, girl. Can't we enjoy it?"

"Is your business this afternoon in the village?" she asked, ignoring his angry question.

"I promise not to be a long time today. I'm only going over to the neighbors. That'll take a bit longer than it did in Maes-y-Groes, but I should be back in a couple of hours at the most."

She watched as he separated several envelopes from the union papers and put them in his inside coat pocket. Mair's heart lurched as she recognized that pale blue bond. Joseph Gambino was his neighbor! But of course, she remembered him telling her they used to have adjoining land in Italy.

As they walked silently back to the villa, Mair fought tears. Slowly the pieces were falling into place. She was sure Nico had said the Gambinos and the Castellis lived next to each other, which meant the dark-haired woman she had seen in the neighboring garden *was* Teresa Gambino!

Nico was striding ahead; he had already reached the loggia. He seemed to be in an unusual hurry to conduct his business today. Usually he went about his afternoon visits in a more leisurely manner. Except for yesterday—he had hurried yesterday also. A dark cloud of suspicion descended on her and Mair had to force her legs up the steps to follow him.

"Now, Mair, forget all those questions. We'll be together in Highbury. I promise."

Nico came to her and lightly kissed her brow.

352

Mair stood woodenly, her mind working overtime as all the painful facts became terribly clear.

"Have a jug of wine waiting when I come back in say . . ." he glanced at his gold watch, "two hours. After this afternoon I'm going to need refreshment. But I'll explain when I get back. Mair, don't look like that!"

"Am I going to live in this house in Highbury as Mrs. Castle?"

"For Christ's sake, Mair! I don't believe this!"

He flung away from her and without a backward glance stalked across the loggia and over the lawn.

Mair walked to the edge of the tiled loggia to watch him. Not even trying to be careful today, are you? that accusing little voice inside her cried. Can't wait to see Teresa, to spill out all your frustration and elicit the warm sympathy of her arms.

As Mair watched Nico stop at the shrubbery and open a small gate, her heart sank like lead in the pit of her stomach. She had never even noticed the gate before. Dear God, how many times had he slipped into the neighboring garden when he had been walking late at night? Sometimes, after they made love, he had worked on his papers, then gone out for a walk. Had he been going next door instead? Surely not even Nico could be seeking further lovemaking after they had already made love so passionately.

What a blind fool she had been! Mair reeled against a pillar, clutching the stonework for support. To have been so blindly trusting after all she knew. How could she not have been forewarned? And all those whispered love words she had cherished. He had told her he would love her forever, would never want another woman. Oh dear God, how could she have swallowed all those sweet lies? To think he had the audacity to invite her to stay next door to Teresa Gambino's villa. She was stunned when she realized how deeply she had been decieved.

The rough stonework grazed her cheek as she rested her burning face on her arms. "No," she groaned. All those sweet vows couldn't have been lies. Surely she was more astute than that. Nico had meant what he said to her. He couldn't have been lying, he couldn't!

She wept, oblivious to the fact one of the servants might come outside and discover her. She felt so betrayed, so heartsick, she no longer cared what they saw. Nico had told her she could use this lakeside villa as a retreat between engagements when she was singing in Italy. As Sal Castelli would not actually be living here, the house would be unoccupied. How lovely it had sounded then, lying in his arms, dreaming of recreating their idyllic interlude!

Raising her head, Mair looked out at the lake where gathering clouds cast a gray pall over the water. She never wanted to see Lake Como again in her life, nor did she ever want to visit this villa. The truth had made every part of the formerly peaceful scene ugly. Knowing what she did, she couldn't bear to spend another day with him.

Mair whirled about, her face tear-streaked. Marching with determination across the tiled loggia, she walked indoors, calling for Luisa, Josette, whomever was in earshot.

A flustered Josette hurried out of the kitchen where she had been chatting to Luisa.

"You called, Madame?"

"Yes, Josette. Pack my trunk; we're leaving. Tell Beppo I'll need him to take us to the stage to catch the steamer. Find out when the next one leaves."

"But the *Monsieur*, what of him?" Josette gasped, her dark eyes wide with shock. "This is all so unexpected, Madame."

"The *Monsieur* can well take care of himself. I have to be in Verona. I've an opera to rehearse. We've wasted enough time here already. Now go on, do as you're told."

Flustered, Josette backed away. Then she scurried away, calling for the maid who was Beppo's wife.

Taking swift action soothed some of Mair's pain and left her little time to dwell on the cheating, the lying, the sheer deception of the man she loved.

Damn him! Damn him to hell! she cursed, stamping upstairs in search of Josette. When he returned from his afternoon rendezvous, she'd be gone, providing the steamer cooperated with her plans. She had no idea when the daily crossings were made.

When Mair reached her room, she found that Josette had dragged out her trunks and bags and was quickly emptying the armoire of her dresses. Though she knew it was not considered proper, Mair ignored Josette's protests and began to help with the packing. When Luisa came to the door, she too was put to work. The maid spoke to Josette in Italian, spurring Josette to even greater haste.

"What did she say?" Mair demanded, catching the word *lago* and guessing she had been speaking about the steamer.

"Beppo says the lake steamer docks and leaves in

355

an hour. We can't be ready in time, Madame. Why not wait till tomorrow?"

"No. We'll take this crossing if I have to leave everything behind. I'm not spending another day here," Mair declared through gritted teeth.

Each dress, each negligee that tumbled into the trunks held sweet memories. Tears streamed down Mair's cheeks as she worked, and she abandoned all effort to check them. The servants would soon learn there had been a misunderstanding. That was putting it mildly. 'Complete break-up of the relationship' was a better description. It really didn't matter whether they knew or not. All that mattered now was that she not stay to be further humiliated. How they must have laughed at her, poor trusting fool, daydreaming while he and his Italian woman made love and drank wine almost within sight of her balcony. Oh, that was a story they would laugh about for some time to come!

Stifling fresh sobs, Mair dragged on a traveling dress of bottle green serge; she snatched the matching plumed hat from its box and jammed it onto her head. When Josette came to assist her, Mair thrust aside the maid's helping arms, telling her to keep packing. She could dress herself.

Beppo came to the door to see if they were ready.

Between them Beppo and Luisa pulled the trunks downstairs. Mair and Josette brought up the rear, loaded down with carpet bags and valises. It would be humorous if Nico were to return now and see this procession streaming downstairs. Mair smiled bitterly at the thought. There was little chance of that. Nico would be too busy with

Teresa. A couple of hours was all he needed—he still had a little time left.

As a final angry gesture, Mair scribbled a note and propped it against the inkwell on the writing table.

"Enjoy your convent-reared virgin. I won't stay here to be humiliated. Mair."

Come to think of it, Teresa Gambino would no longer be a virgin. Still, Mair liked the sound of the phrase and she didn't care if it was no longer accurate.

Grimly Mair walked outside into the cloudy day. She hated this villa surrounded by tall palms and fragrant lemon trees, foreign cedars and myrtles, and those tall slender poplars that predominated in the Lombardy countryside. She washed her hands of the place and the man with whom it was associated. From now on her singing would sustain her. It was all she had left.

Uneasily, because he did this without the master's approval, Beppo loaded her trunks aboard the trap. When Mair urged him to even greater speed, he muttered Italian curses beneath his breath as he complied with her wishes.

Finally they climbed aboard the trap, and Mair took one last look at the tall stone villa beneath the rapidly lowering sky. Never again would she lay eyes upon it. She had a perverse desire to remember exactly how it looked, this place of betrayal. The memory would remind her never to allow herself to be so trusting of a man again.

The trap lurched forward as it began its journey down the dusty road to the lake. Mair turned back, half hoping Nico would come outside, running after the trap to stop her leaving. Would he shout, 'Mair, wait, it's you I love—not Teresa'? But he didn't appear on the road, though she watched until they turned the bend. Of course he wouldn't come after her, she thought bitterly, he was still too busy with Teresa. The odious thought that sometimes he may have come to her fresh from Teresa's bed produced a wave of nausea. She clapped her hands to her mouth.

"Oh, Madam, are you ill?" Josette cried, her arm slipping about her shoulders, for she sat beside Mair on the padded rear seat.

"No, I'm all right. It's just the lurching," Mair mumbled, swallowing the bitterness in her throat.

The journey to the steamer stage seemed to take forever. Mair began to dread arriving only to find the steamer pulling away from shore. They would have to return to the villa. Of course, by then Nico would be home and her hasty grand exit would appear ridiculously childish. How foolish, how humiliated she would feel.

They reached the stage to find the docked steamer already taking on passengers. Mair almost leaped from the trap before it stopped, so eager was she to get aboard. Nico would have to wait for the steamer's return trip before he could pursue her. Sadly she wondered if he would even bother to go after her. By now he must realize she knew the truth. He should guess she had watched him go next door to keep his rendezvous with Teresa. Maybe he would consider her leavetaking one problem less to contend with?

Josette helped Mair aboard the *Isola Bella*. By now it had begun to spit rain and the wind was rising, making the usually placid lake foamflecked and gray. They went below deck and Josette settled her mistress comfortably in the ladies' lounge. The steamer whistle blew, then they slowly began to pull away from the stage. A few minutes later, Josette brought her a tray of tea and a plate of rolls.

Mair thankfully accepted the offering, for she had not eaten lunch. It could be a long time before she ate again. Belatedly, Mair began to wonder if they had enough money to get to Verona. She did not even know if she was expected there yet. By leaving Milan so abruptly, she had not received her usual instructions. What a fool she was to race away in the middle of the night with him. Why, oh why, had she allowed Nico to come back into her life and turn it upside down again?

Fresh tears began to fall, splashing into her teacup, but she made no effort to stop them. Solicitously Josette offered her a lace handkerchief and took away her tray when she was finished. Like the good servant she was, Josette would not question the cause behind their hasty flight. It was likely she would not even mention 'the *Monsieur*' again, if Mair chose not to bring up the subject. Today she had learned to appreciate her servant. She could not have borne the pain of Rose's cross-examination about what had gone wrong between them.

Mair rested her head against the padded wall behind her seat and closed her eyes. A terrible headache had throbbed to life; she felt as if an iron band encircled her temples. If only she could go to sleep and forget about Nico's betrayal.

"Madame, would you like some smelling salts?"

Josette enquired at her elbow as she reached inside her reticule.

"My head aches."

"Ah, then take this, Madame." Prepared for all occasions, the faithful Josette produced a small box of white tablets. The medicine had been prescribed by a leading Parisian doctor for her mistress's headaches.

Thankfully Mair accepted the medicine. These tablets always brought oblivion. Usually she fought against such control of her person; today she gladly sought it.

Chapter Twenty-One

*The Dover train pulled into crowded Victoria Sta-*tion, emitting a huge burst of steam and billows of sulphurous smoke. Impatiently Mair helped Josette take their bags down from the overhead rack. She sent the maid to the goods van to attend to their larger pieces of luggage and hire a porter to carry them to the cab.

Mair stood a moment on the steps of the train to get her bearings, feeling her stomach lurch with excitement at being home in England again. Though she readily admitted it would have been even more thrilling to be truly home, to be able to see a few familiar Welsh place-names on the time-tables. Still, at this point, she would gladly settle for London. She had never realized how emotional the homecoming would make her feel. Self-consciously, she dabbed unexpected tears from her eyes as she went down the steps to the platform, finally achieving that longed-for sensation of setting foot in London again.

So heartily sick of the Continent was she at this moment, Mair would have been happy never to set eyes on it again—though she knew her attitude would probably change after a short respite on English soil. After all, the Continent was where she had enjoyed her biggest triumph. In opera houses from Paris to Rome she had been hailed as a sensation. Her original two Italian engagements in Verona and Rome had soon mushroomed to include stops in Naples, Florence and Venice. Later she had even gone on to sing in Austria and Switzerland, where she performed at a lavish concert in a theater on the banks of Lake Lucerne. At first the sight of the big lake had aroused unpleasant memories, which she had to fight to overcome. There, at Lake Lucerne, and at Salzburg, Austria, Mair had rehearsed for her upcoming debut at Covent Garden Opera House singing the role of Lucia. How strange it was to be rehearsing a London production without ever setting foot in that city. The other principals, the Maestro, even the director, had all been vacationing in various parts of Europe; it seemed perfectly natural that they should meet in a pleasant, fashionable location to conduct their business. And a wonderfully cool location at that, she added with a shudder. It was a nightmare to recall the horrendous heat of the Italian summer: all those suffocating nights, the stuffy theaters and even stuffier dressing rooms. Getting through a performance was an achievement in itself.

As she walked through the station, the autumn

chill struck through her garments. Mair shivered
and rejoiced. This damp, cool, London climate was
a decided change after Italy, and she would have to
adjust to the difference. But she loved every minute. Never again did she want to be so miserably
hot that she didn't care whether she lived or died.

Josette moved along the platform toward her,
followed by a porter bearing a cart piled with their
luggage. Mair told the man they would also need a
cab to take them to their hotel.

As she walked toward the station entrance, Mair
glimpsed her reflection in a large glassed-in time-
table. At first she was stunned by this elegant
stranger who moved so confidently through the
crowd. Her broad-brimmed cream felt hat, edged
round the brim with navy petersham ribbon and
heaped high with navy ostrich plumes, added
several inches to her height. Her high-heeled boots
of soft navy kidskin merely increased the illusion.
A tall proud carriage was a necessity when balancing such a large hat. Her resulting bearing was
queenly. As she walked briskly through the station
her cream wool costume trimmed in navy military
braid peeped from under her navy cashmere cape.
When she passed, people paused to look at her.
Mair had grown used to those curious, admiring
glances, though at first the attention had made her
feel uncomfortably conspicuous.

Men bowed politely and opened doors for her as
she passed. Bestowing a charming smile in acknowledgment of their gallantry, Mair sailed
ahead. Keeping masculine attention at arm's-
length suited her admirably. Never again would
she become a slave to a man's desires, or need his
arms or his mouth. Quickly she dismissed those

treacherous thoughts. Reluctance to confront Nico about his betrayal at Lake Como had kept her a virtual gypsy all summer as she travelled about the Continent to avoid the inevitable. He wrote to her as soon as he found out where she was appearing. Not a difficult task, as Marc Barbour was now her manager; he probably kept Nico informed of her singing schedule. She had destroyed his letters unread. It no longer mattered what he thought of her. She was finished with that phase of her life. It had taken much time and effort but she was finally comfortable as Maria Parigi, international diva. And if Mair Parry sometimes threatened to get the upper hand, she quickly suppressed that facet of her personality before it was too late.

Though Mair was satisfied with her transformation, she admitted it was not wholly complete. Had it been so, she would not have waited until the last minute to leave Lake Lucerne. Now only one week remained for her to meet the rest of the cast, to learn the blocking of the production and get the feel of the theater. The others had been in rehearsal for weeks. Only she would arrive at the last minute.

Mair shrugged slightly at the disquieting thought. One week. Could she really do the part justice in that time? Of course she could. This would not actually be her debut in the role of Lucia, for she had sung the role of Donizetti's ill-starred heroine in both Naples and Florence, gradually easing into the characterization until she closely indentified with Lucia and her pain.

"Madame," Josette placed a detaining hand on her arm.

In surprise, Mair stopped. She had been so deep in thought that she was about to march away down the street, abandoning both maid and baggage. Their cab stood ready at the curb, the horse's nose buried in a canvas bag of oats. Mair nodded in acknowledgment to a well-dressed gentleman who doffed his hat to her as he passed. Even the London male's dress was different from that of the continental man. She had forgotten the subtle differences in the months she had been away.

"Read all about it! Attempt on life of well-known labor activist! Nicholas Castle lies near death! Read all about it . . ."

Mair froze. The newsboy went past, waving a newspaper as he shouted the headlines at the top of his voice. Surely she had misunderstood. She spun about, seeking out the news boards that leaned against the station walls where the newspaper sellers had their stands. There was something about Gladstone . . . the Queen. Oh, God, there it was! 'Attempt on life of labor activist Nicholas Castle.' Blood rushed to her head and Mair thought she was going to faint. Trying to quell the roaring in her ears, Mair waved her gloved hand to stop a passing newsboy.

"Paper, mum? Read the latest about the assasination, thank you, mum."

The paper trembled in Mair's hand as she tried to focus on the spectacular story splashed across the front page. The black headlines stood several inches high. "Labor Activist Shot Leaving Union Meeting. Nicholas Castle was taken to a London hospital last night suffering from gunshot wounds to the . . ."

Mair clutched her throat, her hands shaking. It

had finally happened, the thing she had dreaded since she discovered his importance in the radical labor movement. It no longer mattered that Nico had deceived her, that she had thrown away unread all his letters to her, or even that he intended to marry another woman. All that mattered now was that he was wounded and he needed her.

"Madame, Madame, what is it?" Josette's face went white when she observed her mistress's acute distress. "Are you ill?"

Mair leaned against the cab for support as she tried to organize her thoughts. The cabdriver hovered in the background, concerned for his passenger's apparent illness.

"Come on, mum, get inside. Sit down," he urged, his round cockney face creased with worry. "Feel better in no time, you will."

"Yes, thank you. Driver, don't go to Gerrard's Hotel. Take me to—" She glanced back at the newspaper article. "The Westminster Hospital in Broad Sanctuary."

The cabdriver nodded, and he whistled under his breath at this unexpected request. The lady didn't look bad enough to be needing to go to hospital, but if that's what she wanted, that's where he'd take her.

Mair tried to concentrate on the remainder of the article as they weaved between streams of heavy traffic.

"An unknown assailant shot Mr. Castle as he was leaving a meeting of the Labor Electoral Committee. The assailant later escaped in the crowd."

Mair laid aside the paper and glanced through the window. They were not far from Westminster.

On this bright autumn morning the traffic was so heavy that she wondered if they would even arrive in time. To her relief, when she carefully reread the article, she found no mention of Nico lying near death. That descriptive phrase had been added by the newsboy to dramatize the incident. According to the article, Mr. Castle's condition was unknown.

"Madame, are you ill?" Josette was not able to keep her professional detachment. To have her mistress going to hospital minutes after arriving in London was cause for grave concern.

"Not me. Mr. Castle's been shot. It's he I'm going to visit."

Josette hid her emotions. "Oh, very well, Madame. Do you wish me to go on to the hotel, or wait for you at the hospital?"

"Take the luggage to the hotel, then come back for me."

The gothic magnificence of the large Westminster hospital finally came into view. Mair was already unfastening the cab's door handle when the driver pulled up outside the hospital. To his surprise, his supposedly ill passenger virtually jumped from the cab, leaving both maid and luggage without a backward glance. She hurried up the broad steps and disappeared inside the hospital.

"Driver, take me to Gerrard's Hotel in Covent Garden," Josette commanded, settling herself more comfortably on the empty seat.

Puzzled but ever obedient, the cabdriver climbed back onto his box and they clopped away.

Mair hated the wave of disinfectant that engulfed

her as she entered the large hospital. The entire building reeked of carbolic soap. Her footsteps echoed along the bare floor as she headed toward a desk at the far end of the building.

"Yes, Madam, may I help you?"

Drawing herself to full height, Mair looked the supercillious woman full in the face and said, "Yes, I expect you can. I am Madame Maria Parigi, here to see Mr. Nicholas Castle."

The woman was impressed, but clearly not ready to capitulate. "I'm sorry, Madame Parigi, but Mr. Castle is not allowed visitors. He is resting comfortably. His wounds are minor and he's expected to make a full recovery."

"I've come from the Continent expressly to see him."

"Next week, Madam, come back then."

"Next week I shall be singing at Covent Garden. If you will not allow me to see him, I'm afraid I must speak to your superior. Who is in charge of this floor?"

"I am, Madam," the woman said, drawing herself up stiffly in her chair. "Those are my orders."

"Surely, when I have come all this way to see him, you can bend your rules. I want to speak to the matron."

Mair glanced around to find a semicircle of nurses avidly taking in what was being said, their stiffly starched caps and aprons rustling as they nodded and whispered to each other. Word that a famous opera singer was here in person seemed to have spread like wildfire through the hospital.

She turned toward the smiling nurses and flashed them her practiced, professional smile.

The women stared at her in awe, blushing shyly as they openly admired her fine clothes and spectacular hat.

"I'll see what can be done. Please wait here."

With a faint smile, Mair politely acknowledged the woman's words, waiting impatiently while the supervisor bustled away. On her way past the group of nurses, the woman briskly dispatched them about their duties, threatening strict reprimands if they did not return to work. Several of the young nurses managed to escape her notice and later peered giggling around the doorjamb, gazing at Mair in awe, thrilled that a famous singer was actually here on their hospital floor.

The nurses' unexpected reaction surprised Mair. She could only assume the British press had avidly recounted her continental triumph in detail, thereby turning her into an overnight celebrity at home as well as abroad. The glow of pleasure she felt at the discovery was quickly extinguished when she remembered why she was at Westminster Hospital. If Nico's wounds were only slight, why had the doctors requested no visitors? Then an unpleasant thought crossed her mind. Perhaps the Gambino family had made that request; it was even possible Teresa Gambino was sitting at his bedside. The thought made her shudder.

Gloomier now that that unpleasant idea had surfaced, Mair wondered if this attempt on his life would affect Nico's chance of election to the dockland borough he sought. She twisted her gloves in agitation, considering what the end of his political career would do to a man like Nico. He would never be able to live happily with such an outcome. For sheer audacity his ambitions even exceeded hers.

"Madame Parigi, considering you've come such a distance to see our patient, Matron has given you permission for a brief visit."

Mair thanked the floor supervisor. With thumping heart she followed the woman's rustling, stiffly starched skirts along the corridor, then down a second corridor to a pleasanter, lighter part of the hospital. She was told to wait outside while the supervisor went to notify the nurse that Mr. Castle's visitor was to be allowed no more than ten minutes.

When she came out of the room, Mair exchanged a rather frosty nod with the floor supervisor before the woman hurried away. Nervously Mair walked through the doorway wondering what she would find.

Thin white curtains shrouded the windows, shutting out the sunlight. The room was austerely furnished and, though this wing of the hospital was decidedly less institutional, an overwhelming smell of carbolic soap filled the air. A small vase of flowers stood beside the bed. The sleeping figure under the covers seemed so small and defenseless that Mair was alarmed, for Nico appeared quite unlike the man she remembered.

The nurse nodded to her and went to stand beside the window. So they were not to be allowed a private visit. Mair was disappointed, but knew she had to make the best of it.

She gazed down at his dear face, appearing softer and younger, as if all the fight had gone out of him. Despite all she had tried to convince herself of lately, Mair's heart lurched with love for him and she longed to take Nico in her arms. A bandage was around his temples. His eyes were closed, his thick dark lashes curving against his pale cheek like a child's. She was so touched that she had to blink back tears. A frown creased Mair's brow as she noted the pallor of his skin, almost the same shade as the starched pillowcases and in stark contrast to his black curly hair.

"Nico," she whispered, leaning over him, her hand cool against her brow. "It's me."

He stirred and smiled in his sleep. Did he recognize her voice? Her heart leaped again at the thought that she still brought him pleasure.

Mair leaned over and kissed his smooth mouth, the contact making her heart thud. Now she needed to sit down, for her legs had grown alarmingly weak. Aware she might arouse the nurse's ire if she sat on the patient's bed, Mair pulled up a chair from the corner. Her legs had begun to tremble so badly she virtually fell into the chair.

When she looked back at the bed, she saw Nico's eyes were open and he was looking at her, a smile of disbelief on his pale face. He shut his eyes, then opened them again, a slow smile spreading across his face when he discovered she was still there.

"Mair? It really is you! I thought I must be dreaming. How magnificent you look. Success suits you."

"Oh, Nico, sweetheart," Mair whispered, clasping his hand in hers. She raised his hand to her mouth and kissed his palm. "How badly are you hurt?"

"Not too bad, could have been worse. A minor

flesh wound in the shoulder, no bone involvement, luckily. And a bump on the head and a couple of cracked ribs," he added with a sheepish grin, "though that's all my fault. Must have happened when I fell down the steps." He winced as he tried to move to a more comfortable position.

"I came as soon as I heard. Does it hurt terribly?" she asked, at a loss for words now she was actually at his bedside. The nurse's presence did not encourage confidences.

"I'll live, though I don't like pain, I can honestly say this isn't too bad."

"Who shot you?"

"We don't know. But I have my suspicions."

"Who?"

He motioned for her to lean closer, hoping to speak without the nurse's detection. "I've a good idea Heath Owen could give us his name."

Mair's eyes flashed in anger. "You really think he's at the bottom of this? Have you proof?"

"No, nothing beyond my intuition. I'm not alone in my suspicions, but it's impossible to prove anything. There are thousands of men in London who'd kill for a few pounds."

"We'll find out the truth. He can't get away with this. Oh, I could scratch his eyes out, the rotten creature."

He smiled indulgently at her flashing eyes and angry expression.

"No. Sh, sh, no good will come of it, love. Let it be," he soothed, patting her arm. "We couldn't prove a thing."

"I suppose you're right," she relented, swallowing down her rage. "What good would it do? The

Heath Owens of this world always have been above the law."

"That's exactly why I keep sticking my neck out in the hope of changing things. My ideal is a world where the poorest man stands a chance of being heard."

Mair smiled sweetly at him, freshly reminded that he had a separate mission beyond personal ambition, something she had often lost sight of.

They smiled at each other, a thousand unspoken questions in their eyes. Mair blinked back tears. Absurdly she wanted to weep in relief at finding him not seriously hurt. And to weep even more in relief that he had accepted her emotionally, almost as if nothing had gone wrong between them. She squeezed his hand, not really sure how to begin to ask what she really wanted to know.

"You never replied to my letters," he said after an uncomfortable silence.

How easy it would have been to lie and say she'd never received any letters. That way the transition would be eased. Coming back into his life would be so simple. "I couldn't bear to read them," she admitted truthfully. "It would have been too painful."

"How do you know it would have been painful when you didn't even read them?"

She shrugged uncomfortably and looked away from his penetrating gaze.

"You're always condemning me without cause. If only you'd stayed that day, you'd have learned—"

"Time's up, Madam. You may come back tomorrow."

Appalled, Mair stared in disbelief at the nurse. Nico had been about to reveal something she thought she desperately wanted to hear.

"Surely ten minutes can't be up yet," she protested, holding tighter to his hand.

"It's time to go, Madam," the nurse repeated sternly, her thin mouth forming a determined line. Her steel-rimmed spectacles gripped her sharp nose like talons and she peered at Mair through the round lenses, daring her to argue.

"Yes, come back tomorrow, love. I've got something to tell you. Do you sing tonight?"

"No. At the end of the week . . . *Lucia*," she whispered, leaning over him to kiss him goodbye.

"I wish I could hear you. Never mind, there'll be other times. Goodbye, sweetheart. Thank you for coming."

They kissed lightly, self-conscious beneath the nurse's stern scrutiny. Tear-blinded, Mair turned away and walked out into the corridor.

A young nurse's assistant curtsied to her and indicated she would show her out of the hospital.

On the way out, Mair stopped at the supervisor's desk to make sure she would be admitted tomorrow.

"I don't know about that, Madam. Today was a concession considering how far you'd come to see the patient," the woman replied with a frown.

"Mr. Castle has requested I visit him tomorrow. Surely the patient's requests are taken into consideration."

"We'll have to see, Madam. I can promise nothing."

Mair glared at the woman and turned on her heel.

"I'll be here the same time tomorrow," she said defiantly in parting, not looking at that disapproving face as she walked down the corridor toward the main door.

When she stepped outside into the crisp December air, Mair breathed in great gulps of sweetness. Albeit tainted with the smells of the city, it was undeniably more pleasant than that miasma of carbolic and sickness she had left behind.

The cab, with Josette seated inside, was waiting for her at the curb. Mair descended the hospital steps, carefully composing her face. She did not want Josette to see the deep emotion she had displayed inside the hospital.

"Is everything all right, Madame?" Josette asked, studying her mistress's face for any telltale clues to the state of the patient's health.

"Yes, thank you, Josette. Mr. Castle's recovering nicely. We'll go to the theater first. Driver, take me to Covent Garden, please."

When Mair arrived back at the hospital the following day, she was surprised to find Nico sitting up in bed. Unfortunately their nurse chaperone was still in attendance. Mair had not asked permission for her second visit, but had merely made her way to the room, waiting an opportunity to slip past when the floor supervisor was otherwise engaged.

The bandage had been removed from Nico's head, revealing an angry graze on his right temple. He wore one of his own shirts, his bandaged shoulder strapped across his chest inside the garment. There was life and color in his face and with the exception of his bandaged shoulder, he no longer even looked like a hospital patient.

375

"Oh, you look so much better," Mair gasped, as he glanced up and smiled.

"That's because you came to see me," Nico chuckled, holding out his hands to her. "Come here, you're a sight for sore eyes. Pretty as a picture."

"Now, as I'll probably be allowed only ten minutes today also, let's not waste time. Tell me the important thing you were going to tell me yesterday."

Nico's grip tightened on her hand. He nodded to the nurse who stood beside the window, and, to Mair's amazement, the woman actually smiled as she left the room.

"I finally convinced her if she left us alone we wouldn't get up to any forbidden activity and tear open my shoulder."

Mair blushed slightly at his joking comment, dropping her gaze from his. Strangely it seemed the old intimacy she had shared with him came and went; one minute she felt as if nothing had changed, the next he seemed almost a stranger.

"What is it you want to tell me?"

"Here, sit by me." Nico patted the side of the bed, inviting her to sit closer.

Mair perched there, her russet barathea costume dark against the stiffly starched sheets. The curtains were open and weak rays of December sunshine pierced the room, capturing Mair in a shaft of light that turned her hair to molten gold.

Nico smiled in pleasure at the lovely sight, breathing a contented sigh. Though his wound caused him pain, having her here beside him once more almost made it seem worth it.

"Go on, tell me," Mair urged, nervous in case the secret he kept was not the one she hoped to hear.

"Well, my love, had you stayed at Como that afternoon, you'd have discovered my real intentions. As you already knew, I went to see Teresa and her father."

At the mention of Teresa, Mair drew in a sharp breath, the unpleasant reminder making her uncomfortable. "Why, Nico?" she whispered, not sure she was prepared for his answer.

"Not to make love to her, you jealous woman. I wanted to tell them both that I'd fallen in love with someone else and couldn't keep to our family's plans. When I saw how unhappy you were, I knew I'd let things go far too long. I'm sorry, Mair. I didn't mean to hurt you."

"What about your needing Joe Gambino's financial backing?"

"Sir Alfred Crawford and others have been equally supportive. I decided to risk Joe's displeasure. Mair . . . don't you understand what I'm saying? Teresa's not in the picture anymore."

She smiled at him, allowing a shuddering sigh of relief to escape. And she squeezed his hand, her hopes soaring. Yet pain over his seeming betrayal would not allow her to let him down that easy.

"Why did you take me to the villa next door, knowing she was there? Surely you realized I'd think the worst."

"I'd no idea she was there. Remember when I told you about riding with a family friend? It was Enzo, Teresa's brother. He was the one who told me she was staying at the villa, only by then it was

377

far too late. Oh Mair, it's hard for me to realize you trusted me so little you could believe I was making love to both of you."

"What else could I think when I watched you go over there?" she said sharply, still not ready to let go of the pain she had suffered.

"To the best of my knowledge, the poor woman's still a virgin—a phrase I noticed you're rather partial to," he added with a grin, referring to her angry note.

Mair blushed, made uncomfortable by the reminder. She looked down at her hands. "It seems we both made mistakes, and in the process made complete fools of ourselves."

"I don't blame you for being hurt, yet I was hurt too, thinking you'd condemned me on the flimsiest evidence . . ."

"I'm sorry, Nico," she whispered penitently. "Jealousy makes people do things they're not proud of. Just love me."

"Oh, I do—for all time," he whispered intently.

Mair inclined her head toward his, prepared for his kiss, when a tap came on the door. The nurse walked back into the room, pointedly clearing her throat.

Surely it was not time to leave already, just when they were smoothing over their past misunderstandings. "Surely not," she said aloud.

The nurse smiled faintly and nodded.

"Tomorrow at the same time? I'll wait impatiently for you. By then I might have some more news. Don't be late, sweetheart," Nico said, reaching for her and drawing her face down to his.

"I promise," Mair whispered, self-consciously

kissing him on the mouth, careful not to press against his injuries.

It was only later, while she was sitting alone in the theater dressing room reviewing their conversation, that she realized Nico had still not asked her to marry him. Could it be possible he had no intention of doing so? The very idea gave her a chill. He must choose her now if Teresa no longer stood in the way—unless he hadn't told her the truth.

No! She would not continue being tortured by doubt! Tomorrow they must settle this once and for all. She would pin Nico down to make a commitment and maybe even set the actual date for their wedding.

Chapter Twenty-Two

To Mair's great distress, on the following morning she was unable to leave the theater to keep her rendezvous with Nico. Opening night was near and a problem had arisen with the staging of the opera's first act. The frenzied director had insisted she stay, and Mair, unsure of her position, thought it wiser not to demand her own way.

Consequently, it was almost four in the afternoon when she was finally able to get away. As she rode to Westminster, the hansom cab clattering over the cobblestones, gathering mist wreathed the lamp standards and floated like disembodied wraiths about the buildings. Despite her fur-trimmed coat, Mair shivered in the dank cab.

When she arrived at Westminster Hospital, all the lamps had been lit inside the wards to dispel the gloom of the December afternoon. Again she was able to slip past the supervisor's desk while the woman's back was turned. But when she reached Nico's room, Mair was horrified to find the bed empty and stripped of sheets. There was not a sign of occupancy in the room, and the discovery set her heart pounding in fright. Had Nico taken a turn for the worse?

In rising fear, Mair went into the corridor and stopped two passing orderlies, asking them what had happened to Mr. Castle. They assured her Mr. Castle was in no danger and had in fact gone to a private residence to complete his convalescence.

Anxious to learn where he had been taken, Mair swallowed her pride and returned to the supervisor's desk. There a second shock awaited her. It was a different woman who sat in the wooden swivel chair. She stared down her long nose, looking over steel-rimmed spectacles at Mair when she asked her questions. Without expression, the woman informed Mair she would have to return in the morning to ask the day supervisor where the patient had gone.

Mair suffered through a sleepless night. Frayed nerves over the approaching opening night, coupled with this upsetting development, kept her pacing the hotel floor long into the night.

It was still dark when Mair set out the following morning. Feeble chinks of light peeped from between blinds and curtains as she hurried along the street. She had to walk almost all the way to Covent Garden Market to hail a cab.

When Mair reached the hospital and questioned the day supervisor about Nico's whereabouts, the woman smiled triumphantly before she parroted a brief message, appearing pleased to have put Mair at a disadvantage.

"I'm sorry, Madam, all I can tell you is Mr. Castle intends to complete his convalescence elsewhere."

Mair could hardly believe what she was hearing. That was all, after things were starting to go so well? Surely Nico had left her a letter of explanation, a note—*something*.

"Wasn't there a message for me?"

"Had a message been left for you, Madam, you would have received it," the supervisor replied tartly. "It's obvious the gentleman wishes to keep his whereabouts private."

Stunned by the unexpected discovery, Mair left the hospital, fighting tears. It had been deeply humiliating to have that woman witness her distress, to know she had been spurned, for what reason she could not guess. The floor supervisor had barely concealed her animosity toward her.

Lip curled in scorn, the supervisor watched from a window as the well-dressed woman hailed a cab. She felt a fresh surge of envy for the brown fur-trimmed coat.

As she turned back to her desk, a flush of triumph heightened her cheeks. Reaching into her pocket, the supervisor withdrew an envelope addressed to 'Madame Maria Parigi.' She wanted to read the letter, but she dared not open it. She intended to discover the letter accidentally later in the week, after Madam High and Mighty had suffered a few worried nights thinking her lover had jilted her. It was shameful for women like that to have everything their way. Clothes, fame, money, men—and he was a most attractive man, deserving of far better than she. Stage people were always such a common loose-moraled lot. Served her right for coming in and throwing her weight about and trying to sneak off to his room behind her back.

The supervisor actually smiled as she turned to answer a young nurse's question, finding this small act of retribution immensely satisfying.

For the next few days, right up until opening night, Mair fought recurring headaches, having to resort to the tablets dispensed by Josette. Mair knew it was foolish to be so devastated by Nico's unexpected snub, foolish even to have be surprised by his sudden departure without leaving a message for her. If she had learned anything these past months, it was that she could never rely on Nico Castelli. It had been a bitter truth to swallow—a truth she should have accepted long ago.

Trying to lift her spirits, Mair wrote a letter to Rose asking her to come to the theater to meet with her and discuss the future. Though Josette was an efficient maid, in London Mair had no need of a bilingual girl. When she returned to the Continent she would re-employ Josette, if the girl still wished it. Just as Rose had been unhappy in France, Mair could see Josette's humor growing ever darker beneath London's gloomy skies. Christmas would be here soon and it would be a kind gesture to offer to send Josette home to France for the holiday season.

On opening night Covent Garden was ablaze with lights. The gilded moldings, red velvet seats and lush, gold-edged curtains perfectly echoed the opulence of this special evening.

Finely dressed bejewelled patrons filled the theater boxes, chatting and laughing before curtain time. Staged at a time far from the usual summer season, the experimental December bill would be keenly watched. The special week, with several different operas to be presented, had been arranged as a preview of the coming season. Much of the money to finance the unusual arrangement had been donated by Frederick, Duke of Dorchester, himself an avid operaphile, who through necessity always spent December in the capital and who always deplored the lack of quality entertainment.

Mair had first made the Duke's acquaintance at the Coliseum in Duchess Street; but then she had not known who he was or how influential he was in operatic circles. He had also attended her performances in both Paris and Rome, being instrumental in her securing this Covent Garden booking. Donizetti's *Lucia di Lammermoor* was one of the Duke's special favorites. Knowing he would be in the audience, despite his enthusiasm for her performances, made Mair nervous. To appear in this role before such a knowledgeable critic meant she could not afford even one false step.

Lucia's full-skirted, low-necked sixteenth century gown was of rich gold and black brocade, sumptuous and heavy. For the mad scene, Mair's most vocally taxing piece, she was to wear a diaphanous white nightgown gruesomely splashed with red to simulate the blood of her slain husband. Mair was able to use her own abundant hair for the role, a discovery that had been quite a relief, for she was afraid the added pressure of a wig would make her head ache. She prayed she would not have another of those debilitating headaches tonight, though already she could feel the telltale band of pressure beginning to tighten.

Unfortunately the tension of the moment threatened to be her undoing. Josette offered one of her soothing tablets, but Mair declined, knowing she must stay alert. On this foggy December night, her lifelong dream of singing at Covent Garden was finally coming true.

The finely dressed opera patrons were in a jubilant party mood. Many of them had come in from the country especially to enjoy this unusual week-long event. Old Freddy Dorchester was a permanent fixture in the smart social set, always invited to the best parties and a confidant of the Prince of Wales, so it wouldn't do to snub his little arrangement, however unorthodox it may be. It was also rumored that Freddy had his eye on the new singer, the Golden Nightingale, whom all the Continentals had been raving about.

Mercifully, Mair had not yet heard a particularly juicy snippet of gossip: that the Prince of Wales himself had shown a romantic interest in her. Had she known, she would have been so terrified, she could not have sung a note. As it was, fortified by Josette's herbal drink, well rested, and valiantly trying to overcome her unhappiness over Nico's strange behavior, Mair went onstage to thunderous applause. Her reputation had preceded her.

For the next few hours, Mair was barely conscious of what she did. The powerful, soaring voice took control, floating disembodied through England's grandest opera house. Long ago Mair had ceased to marvel at the phenomenon, merely going along with it and trusting to divine providence to see her through the ordeal.

The last tortured notes of the tenor's death scene died away and the audience's applause was deafening. When the cast took their final curtain calls, Mair was deluged with bouquets of flowers. Her tenor, a passionate, dark-eyed Italian, kissed her hand and drew her to her feet, turning her round to face the audience who were calling her name.

Mair plucked several roses from her bouquet and threaded them inside the fastening of his black velvet doublet. Then she curtsied to Tonio Alberti, graciously acknowledging his fine singing in the role of her lover, Edgardo.

The audience delighted in this bit of stage play, cheering and clapping the two principals through many curtain calls and long after Mair and Tonio had left the stage for the last time.

Exhausted but happy, Mair sat in her dressing room after the performance, trying to draw an even breath, trying to come back to earth after the emotional high of the performance. She kept reminding herself of her achievement, hardly able to believe it had actually happened. She had sung *Lucia* before a packed London house. And, wonder of wonders, this English audience's reaction had been just as enthusiastic as had been the Italian and the French. So much for that sour grapes article she had read, wherein the writer downgraded the continentals as emotional and womanish, easily pleased by second-rate singers. So angry had she been when she read that condescending piece, she could have cheerfully strangled the English reporter. Just let him be here tonight, she prayed, let him hear them and remember.

"Maria."

Mair turned to find a small, dark-haired woman standing in the dressing room doorway. Her beautiful, full-skirted gown was a froth of magenta satin

and lace, her throat dazzling with bands of diamonds and pearls. Mair immediately understood
this was someone of great importance. Without
even seeing her sumptuous clothes she would have
known this admirer was special, for only family or
privileged and important persons were allowed
into the artist's dressing rooms immediately after a
performance.

"Yes." Mair stood, wondering if she should curtsy to this woman who must at least be a duchess.

"I am Adelina Patti."

Mair's eyes opened wide and her throat went
dry. The great opera singer! Surely she had not
been in the audience watching, and listening. But
of course she had; why else would she be here?

"Oh, Madame Patti, what an honor," Mair
gasped, taking her small beringed hand in hers.
Dark haired, vivacious, lively—Mair could think of
any number of apt descriptions for this most
famous diva of her day.

"I liked what I heard, Maria. Oh, you'll be a
famous Lucia someday soon."

"Oh, thank you, Madame. You are most kind."

"A little bird also told me you're from Wales. Am
I right?"

Mair gulped, slightly startled by the diva's unexpected knowledge. Realizing there was no need to
try to hide the truth from Adelina Patti, she nodded. "Yes, from Llandare . . . and my name's really
Mair Parry."

Adelina Patti's tinkling laughter rang out in
delight.

"Ah, what a clever twist of names! The English
are such strange people—always ready to give a
foreigner a chance while turning their back on

387

their own singers. I've never understood that attitude. May I sit down?"

"Oh, of course, forgive me! How rude of me." Flustered, Mair pushed forward her own chair, seating herself on a small folding wooden seat. It was a small, cramped dressing room, but at least she did not have to share it with anyone. As usual Josette worked quietly in the corner, hanging up Mair's gowns and folding up garments, barely noticeable as she tried to blend into the scenery.

"Have you been home to Wales lately?"

"No." Mair shook her head and could not keep the sting of tears from her eyes as she realized just how long it had been since she had been home.

"Did you know I own a castle there? Ah, I can see you didn't. Yes, it's my absolute delight. Craig-y-Nos it's called. Perhaps you can tell me what that Welsh name means."

"Rock of the Night," Mair ventured, surprised and pleased that this world-famous diva should love Wales sufficiently to have bought a home there.

"I've transformed it, you won't believe how comfortable it is. Do come and visit me, Mair. Perhaps we can have the honor of hearing you sing. Someday I'll have a small theater where my friends can perform, but that's still in the future."

"How kind of you! Of course, I'd love to visit Craig-y-Nos," Mair gasped, hardly able to believe she had just been invited to stay at Adelina Patti's estate.

"Are you going home to Wales for Christmas?"

"I don't know. I haven't decided yet," Mair faltered, for in truth she had given little thought to Christmas at all. Only last week, when she had noticed holly and fir trees in the street markets, she had been surprised at how close to Christmas it was.

"Why don't you join my Christmas house party? Oh, you must, Mair, we'd love to have you. Niccolini likes blondes," here she winked and her laughter was infectious. "I won't take no for an answer. You already know one of my guests, dear Tonio, he's such a delight. And there'll be Sir Alfred Crawford and his wife. Oh, and Freddy Dorchester, of course. We might even have the honor of a royal visit for a night or two. His Highness does enjoy visiting the castle. You can travel up from Paddington with Tonio. Don't you worry about a thing, my dear, just bring your prettiest gowns. And of course your lovely voice. Now, I must say goodbye for the time being. I have to get around to see the others. I'll see you at Craig-y-Nos. Come up on Friday. I know you'll enjoy it."

With that, Adelina Patti waved her gloved hand and stepped toward the door.

Josette suddenly came to life and she hurriedly opened the dressing room door for the world-famous diva, her eyes fixed on Madame Patti's enormous jeweled necklace which twinkled and dazzled in the gaslight.

During the remainder of the evening, as Mair accepted congratulations and best wishes from her adoring audience, she had to keep reminding herself she wasn't dreaming. The unbelievable invitation to join Adelina Patti's Christmas house party was most unexpected of all. Never had she thought to be one of those privileged to attend a social event usually reserved for high society.

The invitation had to be the crowning achievement of her return to Britain. Only one other thing could make this time more perfect. Mair forced the thought from her mind. Nico Castelli was not necessary for her well-being, and the sooner she accepted that fact, the happier she would be. She had to live her own life, with or without him—yet if she were completely honest, Mair had to admit that without him the prospects were exceedingly bleak.

The following morning she had a happy and tearful reunion with Rose. True to character, Rose had to tell her about the terrible murders taking place in Whitechapel. Jack the Ripper brutally killed street women, then boastfully wrote to Scotland Yard, taunting them about his clever escape. Women were scared to be out alone for fear they'd become another of the Ripper's victims. After chatting for over an hour, Mair suggested that if Rose would decide to come back to work for her today, they could spend Christmas in a luxuriously appointed castle in Wales.

Rose could hardly believe what she was hearing. The humdrum domesticity of her brother's household had begun to bore her, and she jumped at the chance to venture further afield and 'take a gander at the nobs' as she put it.

The rest of the day they spent packing and preparing a traveling wardrobe for Rose, who had to make several trips across Holborn to her brother's house before her packing was complete.

Mair hugged herself with joy at the thought that when she went the next night, she would be in Wales. There was also pain with the reminder.

Nico was such a large part of her memories of Wales. Their walks on the mountain at the dawning of their love were among her most treasured memories. His very presence seemed to be in the wind and sun; even when she heard the language itself, she thought of him. Tears trickled down Mair's face as she finally allowed herself the luxury of those bittersweet memories. Strange that the very Welshness which set her homeland apart should remind her of Nico Castelli, an Italian. She smiled through her tears, her pain and disillusion softening as she dwelled on what had been so good between them. There must be an explanation for the hospital mixup. Nico simply would not leave without an explanation. Their love had been much too strong for such callous disregard.

Mair dried her tears. After Christmas she would write to Nico's Uncle Sal to learn where he was staying. Unfortunately this simple solution had not occurred to her earlier while she agonized over his desertion, centering on her own pain instead of making a sensible analysis of the situation. Sir Alfred Crawford was also to be a guest at Craig-y-Nos. She would ask him about his political protege's health. There would be nothing unusual about such an enquiry from an old friend, especially after such a traumatic event as an attempted assassination.

Relieved now she was set on a course of action to untangle the mystery, Mair felt the band of pain lifting from her temples as if by magic. She even hummed a Christmas carol as she assembled a few last-minute toilet articles that Rose had forgotten. The omission made her smile. However hard she tried, Rose would never be as efficient as Josette, but Rose would be a good friend to laugh with. Mair needed that simple diversion.

The crisp December morning sparkled with frost as they set off, clattering over the cobbles. As they jogged toward Paddington station in the hansom, they passed windowsills and doorsteps rhimed with white. Poulterer's apprentices were busy hanging strings of geese, turkeys and chickens from hooks outside the shops as they prepared for the Christmas shoppers. The shops and arcades they passed were brightly lit, their garlanded windows crammed with tempting displays of toys and dolls. Haberdashers had shelves of embroidered gloves, fur muffs and tippets, ribbons and laces; every luxury imaginable was available to the wealthy Londoner for Christmas gift-giving.

Rose craned forward to see inside the lighted shop windows, swept up in the excitement of the season. In a way she was disappointed to be leaving all this activity behind. Even in the poor district where her brother lived, the candlelit street markets were bustling every night, their stalls groaning with cheap delights for both children and adults.

"Reckon we'll be stuck in the back of beyond for Christmas," she observed gloomily, uttering a martyred sigh as she settled herself against the seat.

"Now, Rose, no more of that. Remember, you chose to come with me," Mair reminded sternly. She was aware Rose did not share her excitement at the prospect of going to Wales. "You'll enjoy yourself there. It's not everyday we get such a chance. Besides, the staff will have their own

Christmas dance and party. I'll bet it's grander than anything you've ever attended before."

"It'd better be, or you're in for it m'lady," Rose warned mutinously. "The things I do for love."

They exchanged giggles and Mair squeezed Rose's gloved hand in affection. Mair had given Rose one of her old traveling costumes, which Rose had quickly altered to fit herself. The tailored gray serge worn with a white cravat and a feather-trimmed gray hat was perfect for Rose's compact figure and dark curly hair. Mair wore a bottle-green serge costume elaborately decorated with soutache braid and passimenterie clasps. The coat had a black astrakhan collar and cuffs. On her upswept gold hair rode a high black astrakhan toque; a matching muff completed the outfit.

The women were an extremely attractive couple, a fact not overlooked by passing gentlemen. As they walked briskly through the station, many a head turned to admire them. Men bowed politely and swept off their hats as Mair passed; their valets and gentlemen's gentlemen winked cheekily at Rose, who saucily winked back. Her mood had already lightened. She had forgotten the gentlemen's gentlemen would be accompanying their masters to Craig-y-Nos. If they noticed her in the demure traveling outfit, wait until they took a gander at her best dress of silk grenadine with a bustle and pleated cuffs and skirt! Likely she would have her choice of who she wanted to dance with then. And the thought made her smile. Rose threw back her shoulders and marched along confidently. This might be a bit of all right, after all.

The party traveling to Craig-y-Nos gathered on

the platform. Two first class carriages had been especially reserved for Madame Patti's guests. Tonio was already there, and the sight of a familiar face made Mair feel much relieved. She did not know any of the other gentlemen who stood waiting on the platform with their valets and mountains of luggage, currently being wheeled aboard the goods van. Mair had two trunks and a valise; Rose had a small trunk of her own. Though their luggage had seemed so plentiful in the hansom cab, it was virtually unnoticed beside the heaps of boxes and baskets, guns, fishing poles, badminton raquets, tackleboxes and golf clubs. These men looked as if they were going away for years.

Finally the Craig-y-Nos party were aboard and comfortably settled. Mair's stomach pitched with excitement as she heard the hissing of the train and the conductor's whistle. After a lurch of the train the ground began slowly to slip out from beneath her. The platform and the waving people faded into the background as they drew free of the station and the maze of railway tracks. Soon they would be in the country. Oh, how wonderful it would be to smell the fresh air and see the undulating miles of trees and grass, the cows and sheep . . .

"Here, Mair, you're not asleep already," Rose said, nudging her.

Mair stirred herself to find a gentleman in a homburg hat offering her a flask of hot tea. Thankfully she accepted the offering, for they had not taken breakfast earlier; Mair had been too excited to eat. Tea and a plate of plain biscuits and soft cheese were most welcome. Silver, linen napkins, china plates, all came out of the gentleman's well-stocked wicker hamper.

"Allow me to introduce myself. I'm William Corbett, Madame Parigi, so pleased to make your acquaintance. I'm an avid admirer of yours. We'll be fellow guests at Craig-y-Nos. My wife, Beatrice, traveled ahead several days ago with friends."

"Oh, and I thought all you gentlemen were footloose bachelors," Mair remarked roguishly.

Mr. Corbett laughed, his face coloring slightly. Mair got the impression that is exactly what he would have preferred to be. At that point Tonio entered their carriage and took the seat next to Mair, forestalling any further advances by Mr. Corbett, whom he fixed with a fierce gaze, his black mustache fairly bristling with indignation that the gentleman dare make advances to the women under his care.

Rose stayed with Mair in the first class compartment, though several gentlemen informed her the servants had their own carriage. Mair explained that her companion usually traveled with her. The two women exchanged winks as they intercepted many disappointed glances. It was a long ride to Swansea and several of these titled gentlemen had hoped to stake their romantic claim to the Golden Nightingale, expecting to redeem it later at Craig-y-Nos. Country house parties were notorious for amorous adventures.

The train soon left London's urban sprawl behind, heading west toward open country. Mair fancied she could breathe freer even though they were still inside the railroad carriage. If she had her choice she would never live in a city. Perhaps one day she could buy that house high on a mountain that she had always dreamed about. Only now she had refined her plans even further. Now nothing less than Jasper Owen's home on the mountainside, with its Italianate tile and marble, would suit her. Then she would be gentry also. To own the big house on the hill was the ultimate ambition for a poor girl from Maes-y-Groes.

Smiling at the pleasant notion, Mair dozed, feigning sleep to forestall Tonio's amorous attentions. He was attempting to secure her future company for himself. Fortunately Mair was well prepared for Tonio's advances, so she was made not the slightest bit uncomfortable by his ardent, flattering compliments. During rehearsals and the actual performance, she had cleverly brushed aside his advances; the house party would merely be a continuation of the same. With Tonio, love was a game. Perhaps when he found she was not an enthusiastic participant he would shift his attentions to one of these proper gentlemen's wives, thereby releasing them from the boredom of entertaining their wives and leaving them free to hunt, fish and romance the maids.

Eyes closed, Mair leaned against the padded headrest. What a jaded outlook of society as a whole she had developed. Surely there must be some redeeming value to these overdressed, overrefined aristocrats—though from what she had observed, they were extremely good at hiding it.

It was late afternoon by the time they approached Neath, their final stop on the long, tedious journey to the Swansea valley. Out of boredom Mair had finally agreed to play cards with

Rose and Tonio; Mr. Corbett formed a fourth. They played non-stop whist as the misty countryside whisked past the train windows, bringing them ever closer to their destination.

The party finally alighted at Penwyllt Station. Carriages had been sent for the London guests. Mair's face broke into smiles of delight as she heard the musical English of the porters and the station master; she could have hugged them in her delight at being home in Wales again.

The private road constructed especially for Adelina Patti and her guests began just outside the station. Cut into a steep hillside at a gentle gradient, the road led down into the broad Swansea valley where it eventually joined the highway winding up from the village of Ystradgynlais. From the village the road led to the castle, perched on the opposite side of the valley, pale against the autumn bracken ringing the hillsides. The trees were still clothed in a spectacular display of autumn shades, though by now many of them had dropped their leaves, making bare patches on the forested hillsides. Sweeping moorland stretched as far as the eye could see toward Brecon.

Mair's heart sang as she gazed out over this peaceful vista of Welsh countryside. Rose had turned somewhat glum, finding any square mile without paving too primitive for her tastes.

The carriages wended their way toward the castle, which seemed to grow larger by the minute. The light-colored stone was in stark contrast to a dark forest of trees, which were not nearly as impenetrable as they had appeared from across the valley. Acres of landscaped gardens surrounded the castle, which had been converted into what appeared to be a luxurious country house. A new wing had been added to the extensively re-modeled old structure to create a gem set in the peaceful Welsh hills. Mair's heart ached with longing for this lovely place. How she envied Adelina Patti her castle in Wales. Someday, she promised herself, she too would live on a hillside buffeted by the wild Welsh wind and rain, having nothing more unpleasant to breathe than the fresh smell of vegetation.

"Here we are," Rose said, starting to gather up her belongings. "Coo, looks big enough, don't it?"

Mair agreed it did. She got out of the carriage and stood there looking about. The estate was beautiful. No one could ask for anything more lovely than this idyllic setting.

When she turned around she saw Adelina Patti, who had come out to greet her guests. There she stood, smiling, arms open wide to receive Mair. The gesture touched her deeply. It was like coming home.

Chapter Twenty-Three

The following day dawned crisp and frosty.

Mair breakfasted in the large winter dining room, enjoying shirred eggs, devilled kidneys, fresh rolls and crisp smoked bacon. Everything was perfectly cooked and tastefully presented. Although her appetite was excellent, she was no match for some of the guests who seemed to eat a full plate of everything that was offered, from kippers to porridge oats.

Most mornings Madame Patti's husband, the former tenor, Nicolini, took the gentlemen hunting or fishing. The evenings were reserved for feasting and entertainment. In the daytime the ladies chatted and strolled about the grounds, or sat inside the large conservatory filled with exotic plants; here Adelina Patti kept a huge and adored cockatoo, which she called the king of her winter garden.

A large billiard room had been built especially for Nicolini; here he entertained the gentlemen guests. In the evenings everyone gathered to listen to the large Swiss orchestrion, an instrument new to Mair. Nicolini jealously guarded the unusual instrument; only he inserted the rolls for the musical interludes. The marvelous creation had a rich, pipe-organ tone and was operated with electricity, which in that part of Britain was still one of the wonders of the world. In fact, Craig-y-Nos had been one of the first houses in Britain to install electricity.

Today another party of guests would be arriving. Some guests would only stay the night while on route to other destinations; among these was the Prince of Wales, who was breaking his journey to Balmoral. The household was agog in anticipation of the arrival of their honored guest. A special suite was kept solely for His Highness's use, and the castle maids were busily airing out the bed and preparing the rooms for royalty.

This sumptuous, glittering world fascinated Mair, but she felt strangely alien in it.

Though she often moved in such circles of late, Mair did not feel as if she really belonged. This glimpse of the life of the exceedingly rich was exciting, yet it was the country of Wales Mair had come to see. The bracken-ringed hillsides, the moors and the woods comprised the world she had craved to escape to from the splendor of continental hotels and crowded cities. This world beckoned with such persuasiveness that she could hardly wait to leave the breakfast room and race upstairs to get dressed to go outdoors.

More guests had arrived last night and over dinner tonight, and at the informal gathering afterward, Mair would be introduced to them. Adelina Patti had already made Mair promise to sing for their guests. Tonight's evening entertainment would be like a concert. Madame Patti had agreed to sing a few songs for the Prince of Wales's pleasure. One of the house guests was a famous concert pianist; two others were Welsh opera singers. The evening promised to be a spectacular event. Even more reason for Mair to spend some time in the fresh air and revitalize herself in preparation for the evening.

When Mair expressed her longing to be outdoors, Madam Patti jokingly suggested she join the men for the morning shoot, but Mair declined the offer. Although women were not barred from participating, she expected the men would probably take a dim view of her intrusion into their exclusive world. Besides, shooting innocent creatures was not her idea of amusement.

Rose did not object to Mair going for a walk, just as long as she was not expected to accompany her. She already had her eye on one of the valets, a fellow Londoner like herself, and she had offered to assist the other servants in decorating the house with greenery and paper garlands for the festive occasion.

Mair put on a pair of sturdy walking boots and wrapped her warmest cloak around her shoulders. Because the sky looked as though it held rain, she debated putting on her fur hat; instead she chose a furlined hood of crimson wool, which looked brightly seasonal with her loden cape. She had purchased the garment in Austria and found it not only exceedingly warm, but also waterproof.

Taking the footpath through the grounds, Mair soon found herself in the woods. As she climbed higher along the flinty track, with a great lurch of her heart she was poignantly reminded of Pentre Fawr. Only today she knew Nico would not appear on the top road, however hard she wished for it. A few tears trickled over her cheeks and were blown away by the cold wind. Ahead a hawk dropped like a stone into a nearby field to capture some unsuspecting quarry. Mountain ash, heavy with scarlet berries, ringed the track. Mair picked a bunch of berries and slotted them through the buttonhole of her cape. Perhaps she would find holly in the denser thickets; it always grew wild in the woods around Llandare. A sprig of holly in her room would be an appropriate thing at Christmas.

Moisture dripped from the tall horse chestnuts as she walked along a narrow lane. A dog was barking in the distance, and once more she was jolted into the past, to that day when she had rescued poor Efa from Heath Owen's clutches and almost became his victim herself. Now, as she walked, tears trickled down her face. Her heart ached for all she had then. Never had she intended to exchange her wonderful singing career for the other things, yet that was exactly what had happened. Mair wanted a family, a home, a man to love her—and she also wanted to sing. In truth, she wanted it all. And that might be impossible.

She stopped on a knoll to look out over the rolling countryside. It seemed as if all the world was laid out before her. Had the day been clear she could have seen the sea, tucked away beyond those mountains to the north. Mair sat on an outcropping, her chin in her hands, and stared at the landscape. It was Christmas and she wasn't even going home. Maybe they didn't want her at home, for they had never answered her letters. Or was it that she had always moved on before the letters arrived? She had sent a parcel to Maes-y-Groes and hoped it would be received with good grace along with the check she had sent to Roberts the grocers for Aunty Bet to buy whatever she wanted for their Christmas feast. However simple a feast it was, Mair suddenly longed with all her heart to be present. She desperately wanted to be special to someone. All those adoring thousands did not really know her, they loved the person they imagined her to be. No one really loved her for herself this Christmas, possibly not even Nico, she added bitterly. She was envied, adored—and lonely.

Mair leaned her chin on her hand and felt exceedingly sorry for herself. Damn him, this melancholia was really all Nico Castelli's fault.

A voice shouted up from the bottom road. Mair stood, quickly dashing away her tears. How curious it would seem to the other guests if they came closer and found her sniveling in self-pity. She waved back to the figure, but she only pretended to recognize him.

Not anxious to be trapped with a stranger in such a lonely spot, Mair began to walk swiftly in the opposite direction, expecting the road to circle back into the woods surrounding Craig-y-Nos. But to her dismay, she heard the man's footsteps close behind her on the crisp bracken. He must have run to catch up with her. Mair quickened her pace, slightly alarmed by the turn of events. Though the house guests were gentlemen, she was a member of the theatrical profession and, given the usual gentlemen's interpretation of stage women, she did not feel secure in relying on a stranger to behave like a gentleman. He probably thought an opera singer was fair game.

Mair began to run, clumsy in the loamy bracken. A dog barked close at hand. At first she thought it must be one of Nicolini's gun dogs, but she realized it was far too close for that. Suddenly a mixed breed dog darted forward, circling her as it yapped a greeting. She remembered seeing this little dog in the castle yard before breakfast and thought it must belong to one of the staff.

"Are you going to run all day?" a man's voice demanded irritably.

Mair spun about, her face going white with shock.

"No! Not you!" She gasped. His face was partially obscured by a hat and muffler, which almost met above the collar of his overcoat.

"Yes, it's me, Madame Parigi. You've led me a devil of a chase. I am, after all, a convalescent."

Mair didn't know whether to run or stay. She leaned against a nearby tree and tried to catch her breath, for the race she had led him had winded her. That must be why her heart hammered alarmingly and it was painful to draw breath.

"What are you doing here, Nico?" she demanded when at last she caught her breath.

"Chasing after you."

"I meant at Craig-y-Nos."

"I'm a guest of Madame Patti traveling with Sir Alfred Crawford. It wasn't until I got here that I discovered you were also a guest. I couldn't believe it. Things like this don't happen in real life."

"That's right, they don't. So maybe this is only a nightmare," Mair snapped, moving away from the tree. Angrily she grasped her scarf and flung it about her neck. Then she turned and began to hurry away, heedless of the direction she followed. She just had to leave.

"Mair." His voice was harsh as he grasped her arm and wrenched her about. "What silly game are you playing?"

"Game? Oh, no. I'm not the one playing a game. You're the master at that. What's all this hide and seek, first disappearing from the hospital and now popping up here of all unlikely places? What game is that?"

"I left you a letter, which you obviously chose to ignore. Sometimes, Mair Parry, I don't know what gets into you. I can't seem to trust you anymore."

"Me? Trust *me*? What about you? Who's always doing unpredictable things, then expecting me to be a mindreader and know just exactly what you intend without even bothering to tell me?"

"What do you mean? I did tell you—"

"There was no letter given to me. Now, whether it actually existed, or it's just a figment of your imagination . . ."

"That old bitch! I was afraid she wouldn't give it to you. The floor supervisor was supposed to give a letter to you. I couldn't wait any longer. Sir Alfred had sent his carriage for me. He has a house at Richmond and felt I'd be better off there than in the hospital. Why didn't you come when you said you would?''

"Don't you go accusing me. I couldn't get away, that's why. When I did get to the hospital, you weren't there. The bed was stripped! Damn it, Nico, I thought you were dead!"

They were shouting at each other and Mair could no longer control the hot and angry tears that scalded her cold cheeks.

"Stop it!" he cried, grasping her arm, pinning her there. "I wrote to you—surely you didn't think I'd leave without a word, not after all we've meant to each other."

"Oh? And what's that, a convenient woman to sleep with?"

His face went white with anger and he shook her.

"Damn you, Mair, don't ever say that to me again."

"Well, it's true. You don't seem to want to marry me, so I can't be worth much to you, now, can I?"

"I've explained till I'm blue in the face. It won't be long now. We just want to have everything cut and dried first, then it won't matter what you do."

"Oh, still on that old 'got to be respectable' lark, are we? I'm respectable enough for Craig-y-Nos. I hear the Prince of Wales is coming this afternoon, and I'm going to sing for him tonight. Now, if that doesn't make me special, I don't know what does."

"Mair, you're special to me. You always have been. How many times have I told you? Oh, Mair." He stopped speaking and hung his head in defeat. "None of this matters, does it? You're not going to listen to me, whatever I say. Go, then, go back to your audience. I have no right to try to keep you here. It's over between us for good."

Appalled, she stared at him in horror, the woodland scene whirling away. Had their anger brought them to this?

"Over," she repeated meekly, her hands shaking. "Is that what you want?"

"No. But it seems to be what you want."

"I want to have it back the way it was," she whispered, licking tears from her lips. "Dear Lord, it's Christmas, Nico, how can you be so cruel? Couldn't you let me have a few illusions?"

"Look, you daft girl, illusions are what's got you in all this hot water. Listen to me: do you still want me?" he asked bluntly, his voice harsh.

She waited a long time before answering, her inner resolve slowly crumbling to naught. She wanted peace from the emotional upheaval, from the torment of wondering if he wanted her or Teresa. Did he offer marriage? Was that an option? Or did he expect her to live with him?

Mair blinked away tears and she looked at him, searching his lean face for a clue to his real feelings. She could not trust her ears anymore. He said he wanted her, but he had said that many times before. Nothing was revealed on that granite-hard face. He remained darkly mysterious, the healing graze still pinkish on his temple. His tan had turned sallow since his accident; the bulge of his bandage was an unpleasant reminder of what might have been. A few weeks ago it could have been all over. Had the assassin's bullet hit several inches to the left, Nico would be dead. Had that happened, these tormented thoughts about whether they would marry, whether he would even ask her, would all be meaningless. Nico was alive, he was here. She had only to reach out to him. What was she waiting for? Why was she arguing, crying, like this?

A sharp wind blew through the trees and she shuddered. The reaction was like a trigger to her emotions, and she looked at Nico as if for the first time. There were new lines on his face, etched there by worry, pain and stress. Had she been the cause of any of those changes? She knew the answer was yes. But they still had a chance of enjoying this Christmas interlude together. It wouldn't be quite like it had been in the beginning, but they were in Wales. This was a mountain and she was so very lonely.

Mair took a step toward him, the wind whipping the ends of her scarf from her shoulder. Gently she touched his cheek, the flesh cold to her touch.

"I want to start again. I want us to love like we used to, before either of us meant a damn to anyone but each other. We had so few obligations then, yet we thought we carried the burden of the world on our shoulders. Do you remember?"

His mouth quirked to a slight smile and he reached for her hand, tucking it inside his own. "Yes, love, I remember. They always say we live and learn. We've lived, but I wouldn't give much for what we've learned."

"Oh, I don't know, *Cariad*, I've learned life isn't much without you. Ambitions only go so far. There's always a time of reckoning—maybe in the middle of the night, or when it rains, or when the cold wind blows—all those lonely times when heartaches become real and painful. Our souls belong here, not in London."

"Mair. Oh, Mair."

He sobbed deep in his throat as he pulled her into his arms. Here, on this Welsh mountainside, Nico finally felt whole. In all this time he had been searching for something and had not found it. All his ideals, his ruthless ambition, had left him wanting.

"Maybe neither of us will be any good until we're together for keeps."

Mair devoured his lips, reveling in their warmth. Spots of rain pelted against them and Nico drew her closer.

"It's starting to rain," she whispered, nuzzling against his neck, finally giving herself over to him, holding nothing back. It was over, all the posturing, the fighting. She had no fight left in her. "We'll get wet."

"I don't give a damn. I'm so sorry for hurting you, Mair. I never meant to. Everything else seemed so important. There wasn't time to choose my words carefully—I spent all day doing that on behalf of others. When it came to clever speeches for myself, I was a miserable failure. Please, say you forgive me."

"I forgive you," she whispered, leaning against the heat of his body. Nico slipped open the fastening of his wool overcoat and she stepped inside the warm folds, pressing against him. The wonderful closeness made her shudder.

Nico caught his breath, mistaking her shudders for passion. Not that passion was far off. Startled, she looked into his face, seeing the dark intensity in his eyes, finding them almost black in the gloom under the trees. The light rain splashed against her upturned face and she smiled at him, knowing his thoughts. She felt the insistant movement against her body, that unspoken entreaty. Fire swept through her veins, until she thought she could no longer stand.

Never before had he wanted her so quickly, so desperately. Today he felt completely in tune with his surroundings. Like the bracken and the trees here in this Welsh forest, they seemed a part of the land.

Nico caught her to him, his mouth searing against hers. Mair tried not to press against his injured shoulder, aware of the bulky bandage beneath his clothing. Nico brought her close against his body, ignoring her whispered pleas to take care of his shoulder.

His mouth burned against her face as his hands swept beneath her heavy loden cape to capture her breasts, soft, full, eager. With a groan, Nico leaned against a nearby tree; his legs trembled until he scarcely could stand.

"Oh, Mair, sweetheart. Let me make love to you," he whispered in her ear, his breath furnace-hot against her chill flesh.

"Oh yes, yes, please," she replied with a throaty, childish giggle, but her thoughts were far from childlike. When she nodded, he swiftly turned her around so that now she leaned against the broad tree trunk. Eagerly Mair helped him negotiate her heavy woolen skirts and petticoats, trembling in passion. Her desire had grown desperate too, and she gave no thought to discovery; nothing mattered beyond the man in her arms. Fumbling with his clothing, Nico unleashed the pulsing brand she longed to touch. Mair caressed the heated flesh, longing to be one with him, to feel that probing furnace deep inside her.

For a few moments she fondled him until from necessity he urged her on, unable to withstand the pleasure. Swiftly he slid between her legs. Mair helped him, moving to contain him with a delicious shuddering sigh as he slid deep inside her, pulsing fiery and hard. Clinging together, they moaned in ecstasy, passionately devouring each other's mouths, moving faster, desperate for assuasion.

Mair cried out as the sweeping tumult began. Nico moved so perfectly, she thought she could not endure the pleasure. In a violent burst of passion, they reached the pinnacle of desire and plunged together over the top, holding tight, shuddering, whispering love words, barely able to stand against the damp tree trunk.

When her eyes finally opened, Nico was smiling at her. Tears of deepest emotion squeezed from under her closed lids. Great dark circles ringed her eyes as she gazed at him. Her face was ravaged with passion and he loved her so much at that moment, he could think of no words to express his happiness.

Silently Nico laid his head against her, his kiss gentle against her brow.

"How wicked we are," she whispered at last, "we've never done such a shameless thing." Belatedly, she glanced about the deserted wood where the gentle rain pattered against brown leaves and wind-stirred fir branches and larch fronds waved against the overcast sky.

"This has been the most wonderful five minutes of my life," he breathed sincerely. "I never expected this and I wouldn't trade it for anything."

"Not even to be Prime Minister?" she asked wickedly, as she adjusted her clothing.

"Probably not. But you'll have to ask me when I'm completely sane."

With an indignant snort, Mair swatted at him and he laughingly caught her hand and pressed it to his lips. Nico knew she understood, that he could be completely honest with her. And his heart rejoiced for the treasured gift.

"What shall we do now? Go back, or get wetter?" she asked, tucking her arm through his, hugging his arm against her side.

"Let's get wetter."

"Good idea."

Laughing like two children, they turned and followed the track through the trees, winding about the wood until they eventually came out on the open parkland surrounding Craig-y-Nos. By now the rain was coming down hard. The woodland had sheltered them, but out in the open they would soon be drenched.

"Let's make a run for it," Nico suggested, taking her hand and starting forward. With a squeal, Mair ran with him. They pelted across the lawns, arriving at the side door soaking wet.

Clucking and admonishing them for staying out till they both looked like drowned rats, the housekeeper virtually dragged them over the threshold. Within minutes orders were dispatched to the servants and two steaming baths were prepared.

Now that they were back indoors they would have to behave decorously. When Mair looked at Nico he gave her a conspiratorial wink, and she knew everything was going to be all right. Just as she had hoped and prayed, her dreams had finally come true.

Lying in the warm scented bath with Rose punishing her with a loofah, Mair could hardly believe what had just happened. Not only had Sir Alfred Crawford come as a houseguest, he had brought his own guest with him. However could she thank him for this most splendid gift? It had been a miracle—her best Christmas gift ever.

Chapter Twenty-Four

Mair entered the large paneled hall of the old part of the castle. Brightly colored paper garlands festooned the ceiling; red and green honeycomb paper bells and lanterns swung at intervals from the garlands. Great bunches of holly and pine branches had been affixed to the dark paneling. A huge log fire blazed in the immense hearth. Servants were handing around silver wassail cups to the assembled guests who stood chatting and laughing prior to going in to dinner.

Mair glanced about the company self-consciously, firstly looking for Nico, then secondly for His Highness, the Prince of Wales. To her disappointment she did not see Nico; the Prince of Wales was not easy to miss. Queen Victoria's middle-aged son was of medium height and extremely corpulent, hence his nickname 'Tum-

Tum.' His impeccable evening clothes were stretched tight across his large stomach, making him look like an overweight penguin. Various military Orders were pinned to his chest, and he carried a brandy snifter. Mair had only just spotted him when Prince Albert Edward headed directly toward her.

Patting her cranberry flounced skirts into place and carefully smoothing the garlands of cream and cranberry satin roses, Mair nervously prepared for His Highness's assault. She carefully sank to the floor as he approached, aware that her curtsy was flawless, for she had practiced it often for the opera stage.

"My dear, how lovely to meet you at last," said the Prince of Wales as he raised Mair to her feet. "What a lot of good things we've been hearing about you."

In her mid-heeled satin evening shoes, she was the same height as he. Mair looked into his bright blue, somewhat bulbous, eyes, instantly recognizing the gaze of the practiced lecher.

"Good evening, Your Highness. It is a great honor to meet you."

"At parties like this we don't bother too much with boring, formal introductions, my dear. We're all very good friends here." The Prince leaned closer and Mair did not mistake the suggestion he was making. His pudgy, beringed hand was hot and he held on to hers a little too tightly. Raising her hand to his lips, he pressed a hot, damp kiss in her palm. "I understand later you're to honor us with a couple of selections. I hope singing will not leave you too tired to enjoy the other blessings of life," he said in an undertone, his hand moving to her shoulder, his fingers straying toward the corsage of satin roses masking the tops of her breasts.

His gaze was fixed intently on her face as he looked deep into her eyes. Mair gulped. She knew exactly what it was he suggested. She was not that simple. To become the Prince of Wales's *amour* was not what she intended. What had happened to Lily Langtry? Wasn't the actress supposedly his official mistress? As the prince pressed closer, his fingers actually grazing the tops of her breasts, Mair realized, Lily Langtry or no, he had set his sights on her.

"I never sing to the point of exhaustion, Your Highness."

He smiled, his blue eyes twinkling. "Good. A wise woman. I like wise, witty and beautiful women," he confided, his hand sliding about her small waist. "I'm going to stay the night."

"Yes, I saw them preparing your special suite."

He must have thought this was a hint for he shook his head and glanced about in case they were being overheard. "Too crowded, if you know what I mean," he whispered, "not prudent to cause gossip. Put a rose on your door, sweetest, I'll find you."

With that, the Prince of Wales stepped away and began an animated conversation with a couple of his cronies. Never again did he speak to her beyond a polite nod as befitted his rank.

Mair wondered if her face was as pale as she thought it was. She accepted a cup of warm wassail and sipped it, wondering what to do now. Her hostess came over to greet her, and, linking arms with Mair, she took her round the room introducing her to the other guests. No one seemed to have noticed that she had already made the Prince's acquaintance, or if they did, it was ignored. Adelina Patti formally introduced Mair to Albert Edward and he politely kissed her hand. She noticed his twinkling blue eyes appreciatively scanning her low-cut bodice while she knelt before him, but beyond that, he gave no inclination she was anything more than an attractive woman of casual acquaintanceship.

What could she do? Now he expected her to put a rose on her door to show him her room. Could one refuse the Prince of Wales? Mair did not know. Just then she noticed Nico come inside the room, looking especially handsome in evening dress. If she had thought she would get him to herself, she was sadly mistaken. Before he was halfway across the room he was surrounded by a host of guests who besieged him with questions about the recent attempt on his life and his miraculous escape.

Lord Dorchester came across to Mair to inform her he was to be her escort for dinner. A formal parade was forming, the Prince of Wales taking Madame Patti's arm at the head of the line. The glittering procession moved slowly through the morning room to the winter dining room, splendidly decorated for Christmas with boughs of larch and fir, and bunches of tinsel ribbons. Candles and mingled fronds of pine and holly decorated the sideboards, which were loaded with all manner of sumptuous dishes. A beautiful flower arrangement of red and white roses, smilax and silver bows was in the center of the table, the great silver epergnes of flowers virtually hiding from view the diners on the opposite side of the table.

Mair was seated next to Lord Dorchester, who insisted she call him Freddy. In vain she looked for Nico. She finally spotted him at the far end of the table close to Adelina Patti herself, who had the Prince of Wales at her right hand. Nicolini sat at the opposite end of the table closest to Mair. He smiled at her, admiring her beauty, for an Italian, despite age and marriage, never allows a woman's beauty to go unacknowledged.

Mair glanced up, disturbed by a burst of unpleasant laughter to the left of Freddy Dorchester. The man seated there looked familiar, but she could not immediately place him. He was of medium build, sallow faced, with small, hazel eyes; his brown hair was lank and his complexion pock marked. The man caught her looking at him and he smiled, revealing large teeth like fangs.

"Ah, Madame Parigi, how exciting to finally see you in person," he said, leaning forward to speak to her. "I heard you sing in Rome."

"Oh, indeed, Mr. . . ."

"Surely you can't have forgotten me—Heath Owen, M.P. for Mid Wales."

Mair gasped, her face paling. Unconsciously her hand tightened on the stem of her goblet and she wanted to dash the white wine in his face. Heath Owen! She had no idea he would be present at Craig-y-Nos.

"Ah, I see you do remember me," he chuckled, amused by her discomfort before he turned back to his seatmate.

"Nasty, spotty little bounder, that one," Freddy remarked under his breath.

"Exactly so. You couldn't have put it better, Lord

Dorchester," Mair laughed, deciding she must hide her annoyance. It might be unwise for Nico's sake to make an issue of what she had heard concerning Heath Owen's part in the assassination attempt. But she would certainly speak to him in private and find out just what he knew about the affair.

"Freddy, dear one, call me Freddy," whispered Lord Dorchester, his wine-laden breath unpleasant. Beneath the table Mair suddenly became aware of his hand resting against her thigh. Carefully she removed his sweating palm, smiling at him and tapping him playfully on the cheek.

"No, no, Freddy, naughty, naughty."

He grinned, well pleased with himself.

Mair would have liked to give Lord Dorchester a piece of her mind, but she knew that was not how the game was played.

The elegant meal began to arrive, course after rich course. Leek soup and Welsh trout, roast baron of beef and crackling legs of Welsh lamb, chicken pies, braised turnips, roast potatoes, and dishes Mair could not even begin to name. An impressive array of sweets followed, a marvelous queen of puddings with cherries and angelica leaves decorating the peaks of browned meringue. There were silver trays of delicate French pastries and custards floating in bowls of caramel. Plates of biscuits and fruit cakes, even a platter of sugar-crusted mince pies. Mair knew if she ate another morsel she would not be able to sing. Finally, after all were done, the gentlemen remained behind for port and cigars while the ladies withdrew to the drawing room.

Soon it was time for everyone to gather in the vast billiard room. Adelina Patti led the way, splendidly attired in a heavy black satin creation by Worth, a diamond tiara on her black hair. About her neck was a diamond choker, and diamonds sparkled on her wrists and fingers. Her black hair and dark clothing merely emphasized the sparkling gems.

The guests followed their hostess into the billiard room, where the women arranged themselves around Madame Patti, sitting on the leather lounges which skirted three sides of the room. Like a queen with her courtiers, Adelina Patti immediately became the center of the animated conversation.

Coffee was served and some of the men smoked. The guests were ever ready with flattering speech, clucking and cooing in raptures about the splendors of the showplace castle.

When the concert pianist began to play, the chatter died down. Mair caught Nico's eye across the room where he stood with Sir Alfred and his wife. He smiled tenderly at her and her heart pitched with joy for the secret communication that passed between them.

When the pianist was finished with his particularly tedious concerto, Adelina Patti had Nicolini place a favorite roll in the orchestrion. It was the popular 'Espana,' composed by his cousin, Chabrier. Laughing, she called for castanets to accompany the piece, being especially proud of her castanet playing, which was extremely good. Next Mair and Tonio were asked to sing the love duet from *Lucia Di Lammermoor* as a special favor for the Prince of Wales, who had not been able to attend their London performance.

Nervous, but trying to forget the Queen's son listened, Mair walked to the piano. Tonio winked at her before clasping her hand in his. He had such supreme self-confidence. No one, however high ranking, ever made the slightest difference to his performance. Swept up in his confident mood, Mair turned slightly away from 'Tum-Tum,' who nursed his brandy snifter as he sprawled in a leather armchair.

The acoustics in the billiard room were surprisingly good. Mair's voice filled the room. Tonio's tenor blended beautifully with her soprano and they produced a breathtaking rendition of the popular duet. The hearty applause that followed was genuine, the audience somewhat surprised by the caliber of this new singer's voice, for only a handful had heard Mair sing before. They were favorably impressed.

Next Madame Patti sang two songs especially for the prince: Arditi's waltz 'Il Bacio' and the perennial favorite 'Home Sweet Home.' These favorite pieces were greeted by much enthusiastic applause. The two Welsh singers, a soprano and a baritone, sang several requests and finally, when the mini concert was drawing to a close, Adelina Patti asked Mair if she would sing for them 'Land of My Father's', the Welsh national anthem. As the Czech concert pianist was not familiar with the music, Gerald Davies, the Welsh baritone, sat down at the piano and played the anthem.

Mair stood before them, her lovely cranberry flounced skirts belling around her like flower petals. Hands clasped, she gazed outside where she could see little beyond the dark night. In her mind's eye she saw the mist-wreathed mountains, the rainswept hillsides and rolling green pastures of home. With great emotion she sang the old Welsh words, her voice clear and pure as a bell. The old Mair sang this patriotic song, not the polished operatic diva she had become. When the final note died away, there was a deep, reverent silence and Mair did not imagine the sniffles and tears from the women in the company.

"Never have I been so moved by that piece. I know it was sung from the heart," Adelina Patti whispered, slipping her arm about Mair's waist. "I thank you for delighting us." Mair's eyes were moist and she swallowed the lump of emotion in her throat. There was no longer any need for *hiraeth*, longing, that black melancholy so common to the celt. She was home in Wales where she belonged.

Mair glanced up and caught Nico's eye as he moved around the room, eventually coming to stand beside her, trying to appear as if the meeting was a casual one.

"Well done. You'd make any good Welshman cry," he said, handing her a glass of champagne. "May I toast you, Madame Parigi? I've never heard our national anthem sung so well."

Several women twittered around her, interrupting what Mair had hoped would be a few minutes with Nico. The women were clamoring to know how she could sing so fluently in Welsh, for they found the language outlandish and totally incomprehensible.

Mair gulped at their question. So natural had it been for her to sing in her native tongue, she had given little thought to the illusion that had been carefully cultivated concerning her background.

"Thank you. I don't know how proper it was, I did my best," she demurred, smiling sweetly at them. "I have a flair for languages."

"Amazing, my dear, truly amazing."

It was amazing all right, Mair thought, her heart thudding uncomfortably. She would have to be a little more careful. Adelina Patti knew she was Welsh, but these others didn't. Part of the mysterious stage persona she cultivated included being intentionally vague when questioned about her country of origin, yet always adamant when stating it was most certainly not England.

"My dear Madame Parigi, may I congratulate you."

To Mair's dismay it was Heath Owen who took her hand, his clasp clammy and limp. To Mair's great discomfort she discovered they were almost alone at this end of the billiard room. The other guests crowded around the Prince of Wales, who was telling an involved joke preparatory to retiring for the night.

"Thank you," she said, trying to withdraw her hand, but he held fast.

"No, surely you'll allow me to hold your hand for a moment, can't you give me that much pleasure? I've admired you from afar. Frankly, my dear lady, I'm madly in love with you."

Mair detached herself from his detaining hand. "Am I supposed to be flattered by that statement, Mr. Owen?"

"Not necessarily. Any man worth his salt would be in love with you," he replied evenly, his hazel eyes fixed on hers. "Since we last met . . ." He smiled as she gasped at his audacity in reminding her of that unpleasant occasion. "I've come up in the world. I'm a member of Parliament now, a very important man."

"So I've heard."

He moved to trap her against the leather settee, pinning her skirts there with his knee. "Not so fast. I've got a proposition to put to you, Mair Parry," he said this last in an undertone, his hand creeping along her arm, molding about her elbow. "We could be very happy together. I've enough money to keep you in style. What do you say? For a girl from Maes-y-Groes that's coming up in the world—a landowner and an M.P. to boot."

"Because you're probably tipsy, I'll overlook that insult," she said, her face tightening. "How dare you suggest such a thing to me?"

His fingers bruised her arm. "Damn you, how dare you speak to me like that! You forget, I know exactly who you are, and where you come from."

"And I know all about you. Killing dogs and raping women are not the extent of your crimes. These days assassination seems to be on your slate as well."

His eyes snapped in anger. "What are you accusing me of?"

"Depends what you're guilty of, Mr. Owen."

"I don't like your tone."

"That makes us even. There's nothing about you that I like."

He stepped back, his face flushed. "Damn you,

you . . . pit girl. How dare you! I'm offering you the world. That's more than your jumped up rabble rouser can offer. Do you accept my offer, or not? I won't stand here wasting any more time on you. Take it or leave it."

Mair laughed scornfully. "That's what I think of your offer, Mr. Heath Owen."

He stepped toward her, caught his foot on her skirts and stumbled. When he righted himself, his face was livid.

Out of the corner of her eye, Mair noticed Nico striding toward her. A knot of people still stood around the doorway. The Prince of Wales had already retired for the night leaving the other guests free to go to their rooms.

"Wait, everybody, don't go just yet," Heath Owen shouted, "there's something I want to tell you."

Mair chilled, instinctively knowing the revelation had something to do with her. Nico, who had been moving across the room, stopped a few feet from Heath Owen. The two men exchanged looks of sheer hatred.

Laughing good naturedly, the guests ambled back inside the room, some yawning, others downing a final glass of brandy.

"What's that, old chap?" asked Freddy Dorchester, adjusting his monacle the better to see this rather weedy specimen of manhood.

"Do you see this woman?"

"Madame Parigi?"

"Yes—that's what she calls herself."

Freddy Dorchester's face colored in rising anger at the other man's rudeness. Several of the other guests murmured protests, but Heath Owen refused to be hushed. He moved to lean against the billiard table in the center of the room and he waved for silence. Then, drawing himself up to his full height, filled with his own importance, he began.

"Well, I'm going to tell you who, and what, she really is. Her family's known to me. They've worked in our mines for generations. Her father's a drunken ex-miner. And her real name's not nearly so fancy and foreign. She was always called Mair Parry when I knew her. Mair Parry, do you hear? Not Maria Parigi. Just plain Mair Parry. A miner's daughter! Poor as church mice! All that continental nonsense is a pack of lies! She's nothing but a common pit girl . . ."

Adelina Patti stepped forward, her face tight with anger. She seized Heath Owen's arm. "That's enough. You're drunk. You'd better go to your room."

When Heath Owen shook off her detaining arm, Nicolini quickly stepped forward, ever protective of his wife. "Go upstairs, Mr. Owen. You'd better do as she says."

"I'll do as I damned well please! The trouble with you people is you can't stand the truth. Can you? That's what's the matter with you. All of you want to believe the lies. You want to believe she's some noblewoman of continental background. Well she's not, I tell you. She's a common pit girl from Llandare! And he," he turned now, swinging his arms toward Nico, "he's her lover. And he's a scoundrel to boot! My father had him thrown out of town. And his name's not Nicholas Castle. He's—"

Heath Owen never completed his sentence, for Nico grasped him with his good arm, whirling him about. Wildly throwing a punch, Heath Owen swung wide and Nico ducked, avoiding the blow. Angry at being made a fool of, Heath Owen grabbed Nico's wounded shoulder. Gritting his teeth, Nico landed a blow on Heath Owen's jaw, forcing him to fall back with a cry of pain. Heath Owen stood there nursing his bruised jaw, his face livid with rage and hatred.

"Damn you, for that, Castelli. You'll regret it. Just wait till I give my story to the press. You won't have a chance in hell of ever being elected to public office. And you, you pit slut—"

Nico leaped forward, determined to finish Heath Owen once and for all had not the other male guests restrained him. Adelina Patti had already rung for the servants and three menservants now ran inside the room. They seized the errant guest and raced him toward the door, still shouting and struggling.

"Don't just go to your room, Mr. Owen. Pack while you're there. And then leave my house," Adelina Patti ordered sternly.

"Here, here! The bounder," Freddy Dorchester huffed, his face purple.

"Damned bad taste, what?"

"I've never heard such a thing."

"He should be ashamed of himself."

Mair stood weeping quietly, leaning against the billiard table, humiliated by the terrible scene. The other guests' sympathy was with her, she knew that, but it did little to salve the wound. Heath Owen would never be accepted in this household again. His breach of good taste and his abominable behavior would haunt him for a long time to come. But it did not alter the fact that what he said was true. They would all look at her differently now they knew her carefully cultivated stage persona had been a miserable lie. They also knew her sordid background. Those proper ladies need wonder no longer how she managed to sing so convincingly in Welsh.

Adelina Patti came to Mair to comfort her, putting her arm around her heaving shoulders. "There, come now, Mair, don't cry. Nothing is hurt."

A chorus of sympathetic clucks from the background told Mair the others were following their hostess's lead. However, when they looked at her, Mair could already see the guarded look in the women's eyes. She would never again be accepted as an equal in these circles, for everyone knew she was the daughter of a drunken coal miner.

Nico came to her, slipping his arm about her waist. It seemed pointless to keep pretending they were no more than casual acquaintances. The guests had ears; they had heard Heath Owen's condemnation. Damn the bastard! Nico wished he could have got to him before the others stopped him. Bad shoulder or not, he would have made a good account of himself.

"Please, Nico, I want to go to my room," Mair whispered tearfully, too ashamed to look the others in the face.

Several of the women came to her assistance, helping her from the room. Mair was glad the ugly scene had happened after the Prince of Wales's departure. That would have been the final humiliation, to have had the details of her impoverished background dragged out so hatefully in his presence.

Once she reached the sanctity of her room, Mair threw herself across the bed. Rose came to her, wondering at her terrible grief, but she did not press her for details; she just held her and crooned to her as if she were a baby.

There was a tap on the door. When Rose went to answer the knock she found one of the Prince of Wales's equerries delivering a single red rose.

Puzzled, she brought Mair the rose, explaining that a man had just brought it.

Mair buried her head in her hands. Dear God, she had forgotten her supposed assignation with the Prince of Wales! What was she to do? What a foolish game they all played. If the equerry knew which was her room, so must the prince, or at least he could have easily found out. She supposed by putting the rose on her door as a signal, it assured 'Tum-Tum' of a warm welcome. To refuse to play the game would be social suicide; yet, after tonight's revelation, perhaps she no longer had any social standing to be concerned about.

When Nico came into her room some time later, Mair was still lying across the bed, sobbing softly, the red rose lying discarded on the quilt. She had sent Rose to bed some time ago.

"Oh, love, I'm so sorry," he whispered, cradling her in his arms. Although after Owen's mudslinging people would be ready to believe the worst, for propriety's sake Nico had waited until the corridor was empty to come to her room.

"Just hold me. I feel so sad, so terribly hurt and defeated," she whispered tearfully. "Everything we've worked for was undone in just a few minutes."

"Hush, sweetheart, don't cry. It doesn't really matter. When you've slept on it you'll feel better," he soothed. For some time he held her close, rocking her, smoothing back her hair. Everything had been so perfect until this. He would have given anything to be able to turn back the clock. Absently, Nico picked up the rose.

"What's this for?"

"A signal to the Prince of Wales. I'm supposed to put this on my door to show him my room."

Nico frowned, digesting the unsettling news. "He asked you to sleep with him?"

"Not in so many words. Look, Nico, I'm not a child. I know all about men like the Prince of Wales. Lovemaking's a game and you have to play by the rules."

"Are you going to put the rose on your door?"

"What do you think?"

Nico grinned, stroking her back, thinking. "I saw a big display of roses like this on the landing out there. Maybe that's where the fellow got it. It's possible the prince knows nothing about this rose business."

"Good try, but it won't wash. He's the one who told me to put the rose on my door. Can you refuse the Prince of Wales?"

"We'll soon see."

"What are you going to do? Oh, no more scandal, no more scenes," she pleaded tearfully.

"I promise. I'll be back in a few minutes."

Mair lay across the bed, her eyes closed, trying not to cry. She had no idea what Nico was doing; she only hoped he had not gone to the Prince's suite to confront him. Surely even Nico was not that headstrong—yet she was not sure.

"All taken care of," Nico said, coming back inside the room and quietly closing the door.

"What did you do?"

He grinned and beckoned to her. Wondering what she would see, Mair followed him. Nico opened the door a few inches and told her to look out.

Mair stared in disbelief at the long corridor of closed doors. Every bedroom door had a red rose on the handle.

"What does it mean?" she gasped.

"It means that 'Tum-Tum' is in for a lot of confusion," he chuckled, drawing her back inside the room and shutting the door.

"You did it? You put the roses on the door? Did anyone see you?"

Nico shook his head. "Your honor is saved."

"Oh, Nico, what will he say?"

"What can he say? Seeing as it was supposedly a secret code, he can't afford to say much at all. Although you may not be high on his list of favorite women for a while, he'll come round in time. You're too lovely for him not to forgive you."

She smiled and took his hands. "Thank you, dear friend."

Nico held her close, suddenly understanding that tonight she was more in need of a friend than a lover. "Do you want me to go?"

"No, but you'd probably better. We don't want to

give them any more fuel. Hopefully they'll put Heath Owen's ramblings down to drink."

"I hope so."

"Me too. Goodnight, *Cariad*. I'm sorry this happened."

He kissed her and held her for a long embrace, then resolutely went to the door, checking first to make sure the hall was deserted. He quietly left the room.

No one mentioned the scene the next morning. In fact their pointed avoidance of the entire subject made Mair uncomfortable, especially since Heath Owen's place at the breakfast table was conspicuously empty.

After breakfast, Nico stopped Mair in the hallway to show her a telegram that had arrived the night before. It had first been sent to Sir Alfred's Richmond home, and then the message was relayed to Nico via the Craig-y-Nos telephone, which was housed in a small room on the ground floor. Its messages were transmitted to the castle from the closest telegraph office in Ystradgynlais.

"Here, love, read this if you want something to cheer you up."

Mair read, 'Resignation in hand. Merry Christmas, Mr. Castle.' Puzzled by the content of the message, she asked him, "What does it mean?"

"It means, my love, old Buffington has officially resigned his seat due to ill health. All that's left is the by-election and then I'm home free. Isn't it wonderful? I can't believe it. Seems like years I've been waiting for this."

"Oh, how wonderful! I'm so happy for you," Mair cried, chancing a quick kiss on the cheek while they were still alone. "Can we be together later?"

"I don't know. After receiving this, Sir Alfred dropped another bombshell. He has some plans he's had drawn up for a model village for his factory workers. He wants to show them to me and discuss the project. I'm sorry, love, I mightn't be free till this evening."

Christmas Eve was unusually quiet. Mair felt sad. She expected she would soon rally, but the previous night's disclosure had been an enormous blow to her self-confidence. She would have to work hard to rebuild the character she had strived so hard to create. For Mair, all the life had gone out of this Christmas house party. Now it seemed more like a charade she had to endure, almost like playing a despised role on stage. She could hardly wait for the curtain to come down.

Chapter Twenty-Five

Though Mair would have liked to leave immediately after the horrible scene with Heath Owen, she forced herself to stay at Craig-y-Nos for the prearranged time. It was almost a matter of counting the hours. A damper had been placed on the entire Christmas period, and she was vastly relieved when the holidays were at an end.

Most of the house party guests departed the day after Boxing Day.

Mair and Nico took the train back to London, feeling strangely subdued as they both wondered what effect Heath Owen's actions would have on their individual careers. They could only hope his threats to disclose what he knew to the press were empty.

Almost as soon as they alighted at Paddington Station, Nico knew that hope had been in vain. As he walked across the platform, giant headlines met his gaze: NICHOLAS CASTLE SHARES SECRET HIDE-AWAY WITH OPERA DIVA. Whitefaced, Nico bought a paper, his hands shaking as he focused on the spectacular lead story.

Nico looked up at Mair, his pale face drawn. And she knew then it was all over.

"Oh, no! He did what he threatened? Oh, Nico, no!"

Wordlessly he held out the paper to her and they stood shoulder to shoulder to read the worst.

Mair felt the blood drain from her face as she read a decidedly unflattering portrayal of her early life, presented as if she had much to hide and had assumed the continental stage name to cover a squalid past. Nausea swirled through her stomach as she was forced to accept the truth: everyone knew where she came from now. Once she was over her initial shock, she realized it need not necessarily hurt her career. Though they were poor and it was true, Da sometimes drank too much, she had little to be ashamed of. Women barely indistinguishable from prostitutes were cheered on the music hall stage. And all she was accused of being was a drunken miner's daughter from a slum called Maes-y-Groes.

"Slum indeed," she hissed angrily. "There's lots worse than Maes-y-Groes around."

Nico smiled sympathetically and he patted her arm. "That's not the worst of it. Here, read this."

With mounting alarm she skimmed through an article condemning Niccolo Castelli, Italian immigrant stonemason turned coalminer, for deluding his would-be constituents. He was charged with living in luxury, providing a palatial Italian lakeside home for his mistress, opera singer Maria

Parigi, while misrepresenting himself as an ordinary working man to his dockside supporters."

Appalled, she stopped reading, understanding the far-reaching repercussions such an article could have.

"Maybe the dockers won't read this," she offered hopefully.

"Reading the paper is a regular institution with some of them. It'll get around. All you need's a couple to start the story on its rounds. Being Christmas, it's likely they're off work—no, love, they'll have had plenty of time to read the papers. This couldn't have happened at a worse time. My worst enemies couldn't have chosen better. Not now, with the by-election being called today."

"But it's not true!" she cried indignantly.

"We both know that. But the thousands who read it won't."

"You'll have to tell them it's not true then, won't you?"

"Do you think they're going to believe me now? All the secrecy, the hiding, it's all been for nothing."

Mair glanced up in alarm. He was right. All the sneaking about, trying to keep things quiet, not wanting the working men to know his woman was on the stage. Trying to keep a wholesome image, and all for nothing. With one blow this scurrilous newspaper article had destroyed all he had built up. The men not only knew she was on the stage, they also knew they had shared a villa at Lake Como. There was even an especially slanderous bit about her visiting Nico in hospital and creating a scene. Oh, Mair knew who she had to thank for that tidbit, the old bitch! And, here, further down the page, was a catty statement by Eddy Lewis, of all people, saying Mair never knew her friends and was ruled entirely by her own ambition.

In disgust, Mair threw down the paper.

"That's not going to help, Mair," Nico said quietly, slipping his arm through hers. "Come on, we might as well get this over with. It's going to be a long day."

It took a lot of courage for Mair to go to the theater and hold her head up. All around people were poring over the newspaper article, or so it seemed, sensitized to it as she was. She chose not to answer their myriad questions, avidly gleaned from the latest editions. One newspaper story was being carried in serial form, promising even more scandals tomorrow. Mair failed to imagine what they could dredge up for that edition. Yet, if the reporters were stooping so low as to quote Eddy Lewis, they'd go to any lengths for a story.

Finally the horrible day was over. Mair went back to her hotel, wondering how Nico had fared. When he did not contact her, she grew increasingly uneasy.

During the next few days, to her surprise, offers began to come in for her to appear in places as far away as America. Mair found this upsurge of interest in her career hard to believe. And the managers of Covent Garden swiftly committed her to one more opera this season than previously scheduled, in the role of Gilda, in *Rigoletto*!

As she passed a newsagent's on her way back to the hotel, she noticed a large picture of herself in the window. Those scandalous articles had turned her in to an overnight celebrity. Mair stopped to peer inside the dingy shop window, turning up her

Patricia Phillips

fur-lined collar against the cold wind. Strange how scandal had enhanced her appeal. Unwittingly, Heath Owen had done her a great favor. She had become a hot item in operatic circles.

Mair had not long to wait to discover what further scandal could be heaped on the already sordid tale. The continuing saga read, Nicholas Castle Keeps Mistress while Betrothed to Childhood Sweetheart. With sinking heart Mair read all about Teresa Gambino and Nico's subsequent political split with her father once the betrothal was off.

Mair wondered what would become of Nico's rising political star. Everything he had ever worked for threatened to come tumbling down because of one small man's hatred. All the sordid details that could be found had been dredged up from every possible source. This latest article even hinted she had taken rich men for her lovers and that Nicholas Castle was only one of many. That especially spiteful little touch must be compliments of Heath Owen in payment for refusing to become his mistress.

On the fourth day a rebuttal, of sorts, appeared in the papers. A brief story relating how Mr. Heath Owen, M.P. for Mid Wales, had been forcibly ejected from a leading artist's Christmas house party for unacceptable behavior that had scandalized the other guests.

Though Mair was pleased to read this, she knew it was too little, too late. The very people to whom it mattered would probably never see it. Those inch-high headlines had already done their damage.

It snowed the following weekend, though the weather stayed bitterly cold. Mair's heart sank even further. Bad weather would mean no work. The men would be in a foul mood. Bad weather could also mean a slim turnout at the polls. Nico had continued to campaign in the dockside areas, and his supporters had enthusiastically received him, but he knew the damage had been done.

Glumly, on the day of the election, Mair left the theater, going not to her own hotel where Rose was waiting but taking a cab instead to the Coburg where Nico would go after he had finished his final appearance.

The snow was light; hopefully it would not keep too many men from the polls. Nico's leading political rival, a candidate quickly trumped up by the opposition, would also be hurt by the weather. The success of their main slogan, 'A Vote for Jack Mather is a vote against Nicholas Castle,' hinged on the size of the turnout.

Mair waited in the palatial hotel suite that had been put at Nico's disposal by Sir Alfred Crawford. She stood at the window watching the gloomy street. He would walk over from his supporters' offices in a neighboring square. The lamplighter trudged up and down the street lighting the lamps, the hazy light reflected in misty pools over the white-dusted streets. A figure finally walked into view, hunched in a dark overcoat, hat pulled low over his eyes. It was Nico. Mair's heart ached to see him appear so defeated.

As she watched him cross the street and head for the hotel, she tortured herself with recriminations. Had she gone along with Heath Owen's plan, Nico would have been spared this political assassination. Perhaps, had she allowed the Prince of Wales to make her his mistress, his influence could have been used to prevent those scurrilous stories ever going to press. There must have been something she should have done, some way to protect Nico from such terrible failure.

The key turned in the lock and she turned to face him, composing her face in a happy smile. He had no need of gloom; he already had enough of that in his life.

"There you are, love. You're later than I expected," she greeted, coming to him, arms outstretched.

Nico slipped inside the safety of her arms, uttering a deep sigh of relief. They clung together, taking comfort from each other. Mair kissed his cold cheek, tasting the acrid coal smoke on his skin.

"Everything go all right for you, today?" Nico asked at last, sighing heavily as he slipped off his overcoat. He winced as he moved his shoulder too quickly; the wound still gave him pain, though he usually tried to ignore it. It seemed as if this past couple of weeks of stress had increased his discomfort.

"Oh, yes—rather wonderful, in fact. I was offered a contract in America!"

"Are you taking it?"

She shrugged, on the point of saying, 'That's up to you,' but she changed her mind, not wanting to say anything that could be interpreted as hostile.

"How did things go for you today?"

"A large number of the men turned out to vote,

but we won't know who they've voted for until tomorrow. Jack Mather's been handing out buckets of coal and food parcels round the docks."

"He can't do that—he's bribing them!"

"He can do any damned thing he pleases, I'm afraid. Maybe I should have gone out myself and given every docker a chicken and an ounce or two of tobacco . . ." Nico laughed at the suggestion, but there was little humor in the sound. "We're relying solely on our merits, love. There's nothing else left. And, according to some, I've precious little of that to spare. Have you read the latest scandal?"

"Yes. Oh, I could cheerfully murder that rotten creature!" she said, her voice grating as she tried to keep her anger in check. "What has he gained by this? Is this Jack Mather a friend of his?"

Nico shook his head. "Not until he decided to oppose me. Anyone that does that immediately endears himself to Heath Owen. Doubtless he's got a hand in the free food—Jack Mather's not got that much money to throw around."

"What about Sir Alfred and Mr. Gladstone? What do they say?"

"That I should have been more careful. That it can't be helped. I don't know what they're saying. It really doesn't matter, does it? It's all over now."

They sat in the firelight and enjoyed a supper of veal cutlets and baby asparagus from the Continent, followed by poached pears in claret and champagne, compliments of Sir Alfred Crawford. Mair lay back in Nico's arms before the fire, not saying much for he seemed to want to be quiet. After a while she discovered his arms were growing heavy and she realized he had fallen asleep. Carefully she laid him down on the hearth rug and brought a blanket to keep him warm.

Mair did not go to bed; instead she sat by the fire dozing in the wing chair.

Sometime later they heard pounding on the door. It was barely daylight, the cold gray light just beginning to creep between the blinds. Nico jerked awake and jumped up to answer the knock. Bleary-eyed, Mair forced herself awake, trying to listen to what went on at the door, but she couldn't hear what was being said.

When Nico walked back inside the room, Mair's head snapped up. Intently she searched his face for clues. He came soundlessly to her, arms outstretched. Mair was soon folded safely in his arms. When at last she looked up at him, she saw moisture forming in the corners of his eyes. Her heart plunged to the pit of her stomach. It was all over! He had lost!

"Tell me about it," she whispered softly, taking his face in her hands. "Come on, *Cariad*, it can't be that bad."

"I can't believe it. All those wonderful men. They said it made no difference to the way they felt. Can you believe that? They still trusted me."

"Don't be so infuriating," she cried, shaking him. "Did you win, or lose?"

"We won!"

Mair shrieked in joy, hardly able to accept what he was saying.

"We won! You're sure?"

He fished a paper from his pocket. When he opened it, smoothing it out, she saw that it was a telegram.

"Here, read this, you doubting woman."

Mair held the paper toward the light from the dying fire. "Congratulations, Mr. Castle! Wm. Ewart Gladstone, PM."

Eyes shining, Mair gazed up at him in sheer delight. "You really did it! None of this mattered! I didn't hurt your chances, after all. Oh, you terrible man, making me wait, putting me through such misery. I've a good mind never to speak to you again."

Laughing, he swept her into his arms, swinging her about. "No, woman, you didn't hurt my chances. But it's been touch and go. Had I not been such a wonderful fellow, I doubt we'd have overcome the scandal. Working men usually don't take too kindly to their spokesman wanting to marry a woman on the stage."

"Do you still?" she whispered, her eyes clouding.

"Still what?"

"Still want to marry a woman who is on the stage?"

Nico smiled down at her, his expression softening. Mair shivered. When his eyes took on that soft doelike quality, he was so appealing, she was always moved to deepest emotion.

"I love it when you look at me like that," she whispered, taking his hands in hers. "All the hardness, the fierceness is gone. There's just the softness left."

"And the love," he added softly. "Mair Parry, I'm formally asking you to marry me. That's if you'll still have me."

"Still have you? You've got to be daft, after all I've gone through to keep you."

He kissed her then, stopping her voice, taking a

long leisurely time as he devoured her soft lips.
When Nico had thoroughly kissed her, he finally
lifted his head. "Well, I'm still waiting. What's your
answer to be, Mair of the Golden Hair?"

"Yes, yes, yes," she cried, seizing his hands and
waltzing him about. "And please, Mr. Prime
Minister-in-Waiting, can we go to see your house in
Highgate?"

"Soon, love, soon," he promised, drawing her
into his arms. "But first, I'm going to make love to
you."

Mair shuddered in delight at the husky invitation. "I'd like that. I've never been to bed with a
member of parliament before," she added wickedly, slipping her arms about his neck, pulling his
face down to hers.

"Oh, Mair, I love you," he groaned, seizing her
and bearing her to the silk-covered bed. "Promise
always to be mine."

"I will, Nico, for the rest of my life."

Cassie Edwards

When Passion Calls

**"A SENSITIVE STORYTELLER WHO
ALWAYS TOUCHES READERS' HEARTS!"**

— *Romantic Times*

Heartbreakingly lovely, Melanie Stanton had long been promised to Josh Brennan. But marriage was the last thing on her mind until Josh's twin Shane returned to the family's Texas spread. Raised by the Chippewa, Shane was as wild as the untamed frontier, as savagely virile as Josh was weak. Shane's intimate caresses aroused a white-hot desire Melanie had never known in Josh's arms. Their love was forbidden, but Melanie knew that when passion calls, the heart must obey.

__2903-0   **$4.50**